THE DUCHESS HEIST

ART OF LOVE

BOOK ONE

MARISA DILLON

DEDICATION

To Violetta Rand and Linda Koplin
Both romantics, and gone too soon.

THE DUCHESS HEIST

Copyright©2024

MARISA DILLON

Cover Design by Anna-Lena Spies

Published in the United States of America by

Crown & Castle Publishing

1143 Belvoir Ave.

Dayton, Ohio 45409

eISBN: 979-8-9917402-0-3

Print ISBN: 979-8-9917402-3-4

www.marisadillon.com

The publisher does not have any control over and does not assume any responsibility for author or third-party websites or their content.

❀ Created with Vellum

ACKNOWLEDGMENTS

The author thanks:

The professionals: editors Debby Gilbert and Lori Polito; author Terri Valentine, my mentor; author Karin Shah, who lighted the path to publication. Also, author Violetta Rand, my first editor to whom this book is dedicated. She was the one who told me I should write Regency.

My family: sons Jamie and Zach, who are my best creations and who support me in so many ways; my parents Alf and Celia Hansen, who took me all over the world as a young girl, influencing my storytelling today; my brother Eric, writer and author; my supportive sister Carina; my deceased Aunt Linda, who was the ultimate beta-reader; and my husband, Jim, the best surrogate critique partner ever.

My friends: Robin Michaels, who provides the best promotional support; Melissa Johnson, whose counsel is invaluable; Sarah Rhodes, for being a wonderful role model in so many ways; Cairo Mama, the best dance sister ever; Danielle Deramo, my wonderful time-traveling friend; and advisor Jeff Bruce, whose guidance is essential.

Without all of their support, this book would not exist.

CHAPTER 1

ondon, 1817

The model struck her pose on the raised podium at the Royal Academy of Art, exposing her soft curves, illuminous skin, and long legs. The delicate lace mask hid her identity well, but the rest of her was boldly on display. If she was tempting fate, she was also tempting William.

Procuring a proper handkerchief from his vest pocket, William dabbed at his brow, rolling his shoulders back and forth like he did before entering the boxing arena—a place where he was no longer welcome.

Taking this class was the first step in leaving the past where it belonged and building a new legacy, with or without his ducal father's approval.

But if he was to change the *ton's* opinion of himself, he needed to focus. Yet, he could not take his gaze from the model's full breasts.

"Must I repeat myself?"

William snapped out of his daze and turned toward his

easel and his half-sketched artwork. "I'm giving my hand a rest, Professor."

"But not your eyes?"

"Studying the subject is important before putting it to paper. Is that not what you said?" William spun around to give the instructor his full attention.

Beauchamp's temples were punctuated by gray streaks and his discerning gaze studied William through smudgy spectacles. To him, the instructor was as archaic as the books lining the floor-to-ceiling shelves at the R.A.

The professor harrumphed as he turned away, then twisted back to say, "You surprise me, Lord Cavendish. I expected you'd ignore what I say and do what you want. Perhaps you're different."

The learned man peered more closely at him, leaning forward and cocking his head to the side like a bird. "Not like the other privileged Oxford graduates." The professor scratched his chin. "From what I've observed, you have purpose."

William masked his surprise with a neutral smile. How could this learned curmudgeon be this perceptive?

"But I expected you'd be talented," Beauchamp stated, then his gaze drifted to a portrait on the wall. Focusing his attention on one of many revered R.A. artists he muttered, "Considering who your grandfather was."

The curse of a famous relative. Once again William was being compared to another Duke of Devonshire. But he was nothing like his renowned grandfather.

"You are entering the competition?"

William snapped to attention, almost saluting the professor. His training in the British Army had that effect.

The professor eyed him as if he was calculating his worth. "You told me when you enrolled here, you did so to change your future. An award will accelerate your progress. Reverse opinions."

"Am I ready for the grandest of them all?"

"If you question it, then you are not," Beauchamp replied in that tone teachers use when disappointed. Then dismissing him with a tsk, as if he were a delinquent student, the professor walked to the next easel.

Of course he was considering it. William had less than a month to come up with the down payment for the aging mansion in Tower Hill for the boys' school before it went up for auction.

"You certainly must consider it," Nigel said, mimicking the professor's clipped speech to perfection and leaning forward like a toy soldier.

"You could be expelled for such behavior," William warned his friend.

"That wouldn't keep *me* from entering the contest."

"You'd be less favored."

"I am often less favored."

Standing, William came eye to eye with his former Oxford schoolmate to make a point. "My grandfather is a legend. How can I compete with that? He won this contest more than any other peer in London." That was certainly enough reason to question his own ability.

Crunching up his face in a Professor Beauchamp pantomime, Nigel said with a lecturing gesture, "'Our doubts are traitors, and make us lose the good we might win, fearing attempt.'"

Nodding to his friend's empty easel, William laughed. "This is not a thespian pursuit. Quoting Shakespeare will not help you win the five thousand pounds prize money."

"I only joined this class to humor you," Nigel admitted, flashing him a boyish grin and quirk of his brow. "You are the one with the talent. Plus, your purpose is noble." He shrugged his shoulders. "Me, you could say I'm a creative spender."

They each needed the prize money for different reasons. Nigel, to keep the gambling moneylenders at bay. Not that his friend couldn't take care of himself, but they weren't a patient lot.

William had his monthly stipend, nothing more. Earning his title of earl for his military service, not his lineage. That didn't provide for any extravagance, yet alone the kind of funds needed to save an aging mansion in the underbelly of London. Once that was accomplished, he'd need even more financing to turn it into a school that could offer a better life for the young boys who now survived on the streets with nothing but their wits.

He'd expected his ducal father to support his cause. But after making a pragmatic case, he'd been emphatically told there'd be no funding for a boarding school to support London's indigents. And in his father's opinion, poverty was parliament's problem.

The duke's solution? For William to marry a wealthy woman who'd share his philanthropic interests. But that was a ridiculous notion. No one would bet on those odds. Not after William's disastrous courtship with Lady Georgina Farthington. But matrimony could solve Nigel's problem.

"Compton, you could always marry that dowager. What was her name?" William snapped his fingers. "Lady Clara?"

Nigel answered with a hard left jab to William's shoulder.

Biting his lip to stifle a groan, William earned an impudent stare from the student at the next easel.

This wasn't the first time Nigel had caused a disruption in class, but William had only himself to blame. He'd talked Nigel into taking the still-life art class at the R.A. for moral support.

But he couldn't afford to get kicked out. Not now. Not

when moments ago the inspiration he'd need for his entry had struck him almost like Nigel's well landed jab.

Turning, he found the professor glaring at him from a few easels away. William answered with an apologetic shrug while he rubbed out the sting in his arm and Nigel slunk back to his easel.

Sinking slowly into his seat, William pretended to study his work. Observing behind an easel with a pencil in hand was less obvious than gawking at the model. He wondered what she was thinking. No doubt she'd heard everything they'd said.

But at the moment, he was fascinated by her, luxuriating in the liberty of gazing upon a scantily clad woman without consequences.

Who is she? A proper lady of society would never accept such an assignment. *Is she running from something? Or someone?*

His gaze moved to her face again. Pity it was covered. She sat as if her tenure in the classroom was not tentative or unremarkable. She was on display for the sake of art, but he imagined she itched to move and stretch.

Beyond the lure of her voluptuous curves, teasing rather than teaching him about the human form, his attention was drawn to her eyes. Although she kept them closed most of the time, either because she feared licentious ogling from the all-male student class, or she was determined not to be recognized. Would he know her from a Hyde Park promenade?

Framed by overly thick lashes, the model's eyes were an unusual shade. Could he call them violet? She batted them briefly now and he had a glimpse again of their rare color.

Then her cheeks pricked with a rosy shade of pink before she squeezed her dark lashes shut. Did she catch him staring? She'd teased his senses and heated every part of his anatomy.

Just as he believed his admiration was the cause of his internal temperature rise, William smelled the smoke before he saw it. Turning, the hairs on his back rose, confirming his suspicion as the dark smoke rolled across the floor, sneaking through the gothic arched opening like a deadly fog.

Military training gave him cat-like reflexes. He was on his feet and ready, certain if he didn't act quickly and help vacate the room, the ancient books stacked along the walls would act like kindling if the flames reached the classroom.

While the other students scrambled toward the tall windows and pried them open, William rushed to the model. She remained frozen in her seated pose.

"Trust me," he shouted to the mysterious muse, as he scrambled up the platform before her, landing on his knees. When he began to tug on the purple velvet fabric, wanting to wrap it tightly around her, a scent of roses assaulted his senses.

Instead of lifting her up, he stopped and leaned forward, overcome by a bewitching urge to kiss her.

"I trust that you will do no good," she challenged. Then winding up her fist, she smacked him square on his chin, knocking his head to one side. The force, rocking him back on his heels.

He shook his head in disbelief and mumbled, "Love all, trust a few, do wrong to none.'"

"Shakespeare?"

"William," he muttered, still shocked this lady had almost laid him out.

"I know who Shakespeare is," she sputtered and started to protest his second attempt to help her as she stood. Then oddly, she crumbled forward into his arms.

Fainted?

Hoisting her into his arms, he joined the others at the

window. In a calm manner, he began calling out instructions like he he'd done in his battalion. But this was no drill.

The students answered with urgency. Tearing down the long brocade draperies, they threw one out a window while fashioning the other into a knotted ladder.

Nigel volunteered to be the anchor and tied the end of the makeshift rope around his waist. Then, acting like an army sergeant, William lined them up behind each other.

The scrawniest of them jumped up on the windowsill, braced his feet against the outer wall, then disappeared down the escape rope.

As flames licked the door frame, William left his place at the end of the line to peer over the ledge, holding the model tightly.

Good God, must I jump?

"One of us has to jump," Beauchamp shouted, as he rushed toward William. Reaching for the model, the professor's spectacles reflected the flames invading the room behind them.

A shelf crashing to the ground shook the room. Their gazes locked. The professor's expression was a mix of fear and obstinance.

"I'm giving the orders," William yelled above the crackling wood. "Hold her while I get in position."

Beauchamp conceded with a nipped bow and after juggling the model into Beauchamp's arms, William settled himself on the precarious sill. When he was in position, the professor returned the girl, then raced to the other window. Once he had the drape rope in hand, the professor shoved off.

Looking again below his window, William found most of the pedestrians on the Strand had stopped to gawk. But the art students who'd escaped were now holding the second drape taut waiting for him to jump into the makeshift safety net below.

Holding his breath, he finally pushed off the sill. Falling fast, he had a moment of clarity. If his life ended now, at least he'd be remembered for a noble deed. Didn't everyone want to be known for doing something remarkable? Not for killing an innocent man.

Whomp! They hit the taught drape. A cheer rose, and the fabric went slack before they were eased to the ground.

The model sucked in a sharp breath. Chest rising and eyes bulging, she let out an earsplitting scream.

"Was that necessary?" he demanded.

She sputtered and stared at him, chest heaving, as if she'd run a London city block. "Of course it was necessary." She gawked at him. "I'm in the arms of a stranger with almost nothing on."

He grinned at her. "You are quite welcome." He eyed her for a moment, checking for gaps in the Roman-looking wrap he'd created.

"You're covered."

She huffed. "Not properly."

William chuckled. He wanted to point out the obvious, but this was no time to be an ass. "What do they call you?"

She glared at him.

"Your name?"

Her mesmerizing eyes leveled on him. "None of your business."

"You are in my lap, after all?" he said, doing his best to hide his amusement.

She let out a loud tsk and looked around, his gaze following hers. Most of the students had left them and were hailing carriages, but Beauchamp strode briskly to meet them at the edge of the makeshift safety net.

"Lily, let me help you up."

"Lily?" William repeated the name.

The woman gave him a disgusted glance as she accepted the professor's hand.

"Forget that name. Forget me," she said, turning away and walking tentatively on her bare feet, tugging the purple velvet wrap above her ankles.

Forget her? Not a chance. She might be his best shot at winning the five thousand pounds.

CHAPTER 2

*L*illias sat erect on the gaudy, red Egyptian-style chaise. Painted with gold leaf gilding, it was one of her father's recent indulgences for the library at Woodbeck House. The chaise epitomized the pretentious changes in her life since her mother's death.

Although her two younger sisters were under her charge, Lillias needed to hide the real motive for her actions yesterday. Given her position as the eldest, of course, she should lead by example. But her sisters would not relent with their questions, and Lillias couldn't hold back her frustration any longer.

"I barely escaped death and you're more concerned with your social schedule?" Lillias asked her sister Verity.

"Our family name could have been smeared in *The Times*," Verity said with a pout of displeasure. "Imagine this front-page headline, 'Newly appointed duke falls from social grace as his nude daughter falls from burning building.'"

Under different circumstances Lillias might have found Verity's exaggeration witty, but not now when she was unable to defend her actions. "I was not nude and I had my reasons," Lillias mumbled.

But Verity ignored Lillias and continued her tirade, "Not to mention my invitation to the bachelor's ball could have been in jeopardy. Lady Cowper would have cause to scratch my name off the list." Verity glared at her from the safety of their father's oversized desk chair. The middle daughter of the St. Clair family had a flair for the dramatic. "You didn't die, but what if Father finds out?"

True, she didn't die, but Mother's recent death was always a reminder of Lillias's promise to establish marriage alliances with powerful families for her sisters, including Verity's, before the end of this season.

Lillias's sigh was filled with resolution. She had taken a major risk yesterday posing at the Royal Academy of Art, but it was her only way to quickly raise the money she needed. And she was paid well for it. But Verity was right. If the student who claimed he'd saved her life had found her out, much of the work to establish the girls in the *ton* as daughters of the newest duke could have been destroyed.

If only her youngest sister Rebecca hadn't asked her pointedly about why she smelled like smoke, Lillias wouldn't have needed to explain. But she couldn't lie. It made her hiccup uncontrollably. Everyone in the family knew when she was lying.

"Father won't find out," Rebecca promised, breaking Lillias free of her mental chatter. Her youngest sister was often the peacemaker in the girls' squabbles.

Patting Rebecca's head on the way to her father's desk, Lillias walked slowly, like a schoolmarm armed with a ruler.

"What's this?" she asked, plucking what looked like a handwritten note out of Verity's grasp.

The middle sister shot her a perturbed glare and snatched it back. Clutching it to her chest, she shook a finger at Lillias.

"Just because you run this household, you aren't Mother. This is not your affair."

Rebecca leaped from her seat. "Are you having an affair, Verity?"

Lillias gasped. "Rebecca! Watch your innuendoes."

"What's an affair? I thought it was a party. That's my innu-I-don't-know."

Lillias and Verity burst out laughing. When Lillias finally caught her breath, she answered while eyeing Verity, "It can be, but an affair can also mean when two people have a dalliance."

Rebecca's expression brightened, and she blurted out, "Oh, a type of a dance like the minuet, or waltz?" She looked back and forth between her two older sisters for confirmation.

"A dalliance is not a dance," Lillias responded after a short, awkward silence. "It can mean an amorous flirtation. Dalliance can also imply procrastination."

"Well, I'd never call you a harlot," her sister said, turning red.

Lillias doubled over in laughter. "Procrastination is not prostitution, Rebecca."

"Well, you are my governess now too, Lillias," Rebecca answered with a defensive tone. "Apparently I need more schooling."

Rebecca had interrupted her questions to Verity about the correspondence and Lillias chose to ignore Rebecca's slight. She wanted to know more about what was written on the beautiful stationery. "Are you certain that's for you and not Father?" Her eyes narrowed on Verity. The sisters rarely kept secrets from each other.

"Clearly, you don't trust me," Verity said with a huff, tilting her chin up and mimicking a hurtful expression. "It's a private affair."

Rebecca giggled. "Now your party is private, Verity?"

Lillias couldn't hold back a snort, but then she choked on it when Verity said, "It's an invitation to enter the Royal Academy of Art International Competition."

"Give that to me," Lillias demanded and practically climbed over the desk to get the parchment.

"It's not addressed to you," their middle sister ground out.

"Well, it certainly is not addressed to you," Lillias said, trying to respond like a guardian and not an irritated sister.

Rebecca looked back and forth between her sisters. "You are setting a terrible example for me." Then she crossed her arms over her chest.

Her sister's comment stymied Lillias for a moment. "Wait a minute," she said, turning to Rebecca.

"I'm not talking about your posing in the buff," Rebecca snipped.

"Shhh," Lillias hushed. "I was partially covered," she defended.

Rebecca took a seat on the red Egyptian chaise with a huff, turning the same shade as the embroidered pink flowers on her frock.

Verity joined Rebecca on the chaise and nudged the youngest and most reserved of the St. Clair sisters in the ribs.

"Ouch!" Rebecca squawked, then turned to Verity with a wounded glare. "What was that for?"

"Your ignorance." Verity tsked. "You are speaking too loudly and out of turn for your birth order."

But then Verity twisted around and began to shake her finger at Lillias again. "You say you don't give a damn about society but you're a coward about pursuing *your* dreams."

"First, watch your language. And secondly, that's not true," Lillias said, ready to defend herself. "Would a coward sit as a figure model in a room full of entitled rakes to learn how to paint like the great masters?"

She stalked over to the library's fireplace and pointed to the oil painting that hung over it. "Would a coward endure callous comments about her morals—including sophomoric comments about her assets—because she wants to know how to use the techniques of the baroque style in this Rembrandt?"

Lillias paused and took a deep breath. She was anything but a coward. But her real impetus would remain a secret from them for as long as she could keep it.

"If you must-must know," Verity stammered, "I'd planned to rewrite the letter, inviting you to enter, then slip it into the envelope as if it were the original." Verity licked her lips as if she was hesitant about what she'd say next. With eyes downcast, she continued, "I planned to keep it from Father and give it to you." Verity handed over the invitation like a defeated warrior would his sword.

"You know how I feel about honesty," Lillias said. "Lying is deceitful, below your station, and will only bring you misery."

Verity nodded and hung her head. "My intentions were honorable," she said, stubbornness lacing her words.

Lillias scanned the parchment. "The invitation is for any male member of the St. Clair household."

"Does it say that you must be a man?" Rebecca asked with all the innocence of her age.

"There's not much one can do in this lifetime as a woman other than give birth and run a household." When Rebecca gasped, Lillias amended, "Not in that order for a proper lady such as yourself, Rebecca."

"You're not painting a rosy future for our youngest sister," Verity accused. Turning to Rebecca, Verity slid her lips into a starched smile. "There will be handsome men in your future. You will be the envy of the *ton*. A diamond of the first water, when it's your turn to come out," she promised and patted Rebecca's hand.

Lillias swallowed hard. After her father's recent ducal appointment by King George, the debts from his grandiose spending and gambling at the club had put their finances in dire straits. This was why modeling had become a viable option to keep her sisters in the finery expected of their new station.

Managing the household in her mother's place had also given Lillias a taste of what her future looked like if she married a duke. It wasn't all ball gowns and fine wine because society's expectations were weighty. If Lillias found herself on the wrong side of the women of influence, her sisters' matrimonial prospect pool would consist of lowly lords and retired knights.

Brushing her hands back and forth, as if to wipe away her grievances, Lillias stepped away from the fireplace with a shift in perspective. "Verity is right."

"I am?" Her middle sister's face was full of disbelief.

"Well, of course you are," Lillias confirmed, walking to stand before her sisters. "First Verity and then Rebecca, when she is of age. You both are diamonds of the first water, stunning, smart, talented. Any nobleman would fight to win your heart and hand in marriage."

"What about you, Lillias?" Verity asked as Lillias aimed to squeeze herself between her sisters on the chaise.

"Yes, what about you, Lilly?" Rebecca echoed. "You would make a dashing duchess!"

"What about me?" Lillias mumbled.

"What about your hand in marriage. If you want that for us, why not for yourself?" Verity's lips twisted as if Lillias had asked her sister to drink something poisonous.

"You know I promised Mother I'd make sure both of you were married according to society's strict requirements and

Verity this Season." How much she hated those constraints, she couldn't let on.

"You are avoiding answering the question," Verity said bluntly.

Lillias put her arms around her sisters when she replied with the facts. "Charles St. Clair does not have an heir. Even if he fights the tradition of primogeniture and I receive Woodbeck House and its land upon his death, I will forfeit any title. Becoming a duchess is not in my future."

Rebecca wrung her hands. "Can't Father petition King George? He has great influence now that he's a duke."

"Are you plotting my death?"

"Father," they all shrieked in unison.

Lillias turned to find their handsome father leaning in the frame of the library door.

"How long have you been standing there?" she asked, mortified that she hadn't heard it open.

Their father chuckled good-naturedly. "Be at ease, ladies. I didn't spy on you to ferret out your secrets." He strode across the room to his desk as if in a hurry to find something. Tugging on the handle of the top drawer, he continued, "Something about Lillias not wanting to be a duchess."

When Lillias let out a huff, he paused his search to look at the three of them. "It's no secret Lillias detests the whole *haut ton* community." Then he chuckled and went back to examine the contents of the drawer.

Relieved he'd not come upon them sooner and finding no need to defend her father's impression of her, Lillias studied his movements while he scanned the surface of his desk.

"It was here this morning," he muttered, spinning around and looking behind his chair.

Then it dawned on her that the letter from the R.A. must have been addressed to their father, not Lillias, as she'd hoped. Her gaze swung to her middle sister, who was staring at the rug.

Lillias cleared her throat and eyed Verity. "What are you looking for?"

He scratched his chin and answered without looking up, "A letter from the Royal Academy of Art." He rearranged the order of one neat stack of correspondence in his hand. "Most likely they were petitioning for a donation," he added, frowning. "But I don't want to be rebuked at the club for shirking an obligation."

Lillias opened her mouth to speak, but quickly snapped it shut after Verity's heel came down on her toes. Even though they were tucked in her morning slippers, the stomp stung.

"The maid was in here when we came in," Verity replied for the sisters. She gave a knowing look to Lillias. "Departing shortly after with a pile of papers in her hand."

Father's head popped up and he stopped scanning underneath the desk. Frowning again he said, "If it was something important, I'd be remiss not to read it." He started across the room at the same pace he'd entered, briskly. "I must seek her out before her best intentions get tossed in the kitchen hearth."

After he left, Rebecca stood up with a flushed face. "Like I was saying earlier, you both are my role models. If Mother were here, she'd be appalled. One of you sneaks around doing unsavory things and the other lies to those she loves."

Verity shrugged her shoulders and said, "We are turning out to be the sons our father never had."

Lillias would do her best to avoid lying, but she certainly wasn't above sneaking back into the R.A as her alias. For her mother's sake, her sisters' futures still depended on it.

CHAPTER 3

*L*illias settled into a new position, her back to the students, marveling at the smell of smoke still lingering in the room.

All the reference books had been removed, or what was left of them, leaving the singed wooden shelves empty of the once valued tomes.

She was conflicted by her decision to return. Covering some of her father's debts was her first priority, and she made more money in one sitting than painting ten portraits.

But the fire had threatened her anonymity. After she'd fainted, any one of the students could have unmasked her. Even now, Lillias wondered if her mask had been tampered with that day or worse. She shuddered considering the possibilities.

The fire outbreak proved accidents couldn't be prevented, even by those with good intentions. But Professor Beauchamp had promised she'd be safe today, and he'd protect her identity.

As much as she wanted to laugh at her sister Verity's concern for her social reputation, Lillias couldn't afford to ruin her own as the eldest and yet un-betrothed daughter of the newly established St. Clair dukedom. If she fell, they all fell.

Even a simple social stumble could be devastating. In the elite social circles of the *haut ton*, the opinions of the polite world and patronesses of prestige were the only ones that mattered.

Although she'd always been called Lady Lillias from her cradle until now, her father's new appointment had elevated their social status. No one would confuse Charles St. Clair's ascension from baron to duke, as akin to the king. Yet the confirmation gave Lillias more consternation than she'd imagined. And because of the way it had been awarded, as a favor from the king, many of his new peers had rebuked him.

She'd also learned through the rumor mill Prince Regent had tried to reverse it. It was no secret the king was not in his right mind. But he'd refused, and the decree, needing no parliamentary vote, was official. This was all a few months before her mother's death.

Lillias adjusted her mask and struck her pose. This one, with her back to the students, had her lying on her left side with her left arm propped under her head, revealing only her backside.

She snuggled under the provided purple velvet throw. The coverlet gave her some security and comfort, but she wasn't here to take a nap. Even though her bottom was cold, at least this pose was more comfortable than the one she'd struck for last Saturday's class, when the fire had broken out and she was manhandled by that student who took advantage of the situation, and her.

"Lilly?"

The soft whisper startled her. Almost toppling off the platform, she smothered an unladylike oath as she righted herself. *Who would know her by her nickname here?* She craned her neck and looked up, only to find the face of the student who'd fondled her bottom last Saturday.

It was him. *What is his name?*

"Lord Cavendish," he answered as if he heard the words in her head. "Remember me?"

Oh right, Cavendish. "I'm not sure that I do," she said in an icy tone meant to dissuade any further communication.

His cheeks turned crimson. "I saved you from the fire," he told her with pride.

"You carried me in your arms like an unwilling bride to bed."

"You must have me confused with someone else, for you had fainted and couldn't have known by whom or where you were being carried." Then he got down on one knee and looked directly into her eyes as if he had permission. "Can you afford to be an unwilling bride in this line of work?"

What is he doing? Improper behavior will not be tolerated. She took in a huge breath, ready to call out to the instructor when he said, "I'll never forget those eyes."

She was flabbergasted. *What did he say?*

"The other students have taken to, well . . ." He stopped speaking in a flush of embarrassment.

How can he be a rake if he blushes like a schoolboy?

"They talk about wanting to get under that cover with you."

He stopped when Lillias sucked in a sharp breath. *How dare they?*

"Me, I'm curious about you," he said, quickly changing the subject.

Me? Lillias melted a little. How could she be charmed when she should rebuke this rogue?

He studied her face with a genuine curiosity as if he could see beneath the black lace.

She touched it lightly to be certain it was still in place.

When she wore it, the mask made her feel almost invisible, a shield to her identity. But her eyes? They were an unusual shade, like her mother's.

"How do you know Professor Beauchamp?" he asked pointedly when she'd avoided his open curiosity.

That's complicated.

When she stayed silent, he asked a more direct question.

"Why are you here?"

"To learn, like everyone else." She'd blurted out what was honest despite her true motivation, but she'd surprised herself when she meant to keep quiet and evade him. Lillias also couldn't move. While posing for the students, she was required to stay still. She could only hope the professor would come soon to her rescue. But until then, she had to contend with the earl, so she turned the question around. "Why are *you* here?"

"Me?" He glanced away as if he was calculating what to reveal. "This class is a means to an end. I am aiming for something loftier than the other students."

Full of himself?

"Ahem."

The interruption had William on his feet, shuffling backward and leaving Lillias staring at his skintight, dark gold pantaloons.

Heat flashed in her cheeks and traveled through her body. So much so, she worried her exposed cheeks would turn a bashful shade of pink too.

"Fraternizing with the model will not be tolerated."

Help is here.

The instructor tapped the end of a pencil in his palm. "I don't care if you are an earl, back to your seat."

William shuffled his feet but didn't budge from his spot. "Professor, fraternizing is an intended overture." William cleared his throat. "I'm merely checking on the chit's welfare."

Chit? "I am no child, sir," Lillias sputtered from her position. She almost threw off the covering to stand up and defend herself until common sense prevailed. She hadn't a stitch on. But that wouldn't stop her from putting him in his place.

"I'll have you know, I am almost twenty-two, fluent in French, a competitive rider, and can recite complete Shakespeare sonnets."

The classroom exploded in a buzz of private conversations. When William unexpectedly squatted down in front of her again, she gasped as if he'd stung her.

"A complete sonnet by William Shakespeare?" The earl scoffed.

"Pick one," she challenged.

He hesitated for a moment, but then blurted out, "Sonnet one hundred and thirty."

Lillias smiled. "You've chosen a short one." She nodded and took in a deep breath as if she'd need it to recite the words.

"*My mistress' eyes are nothing like the sun; coral is far more red than her lips'red; if snow be white, why then her breasts are—*"

"That's enough," Professor Beauchamp said and somehow yanked the athletic earl to his feet.

Turning and grumbling something under his breath, William shuffled out of her view. Even though the buzzing didn't subside, the sounds of him settling in his seat and the chair scraping the floor, told her what she couldn't see.

Lillias wanted to screech like the chair. How dare he call her a *chit?*

The sound of three loud raps on the music stand next to Lillias almost had her rolling off the stage *again*. The buzzing stopped as she teetered precariously for a moment, until both her hands smacked down on the platform preventing her from losing her covering.

The professor mumbled something apologetic sounding, then cleared his throat. "After many weeks of drawing still life, it's important that we work on figure drawing until the end of the semester."

"I'd rather stare at these peaches than the ones you had in the bowl two weeks ago, Professor."

Ignoring the glib outburst and tittering laughter, the professor continued, "When you draw still life, you are attempting to capture the world as it really is. Studying forms, proportions, perspective, shading, and all the fundamentals that go along with learning to draw."

There was an awkward pause.

"Yes, Lord Cavendish," the professor said, his voice carrying a resentful tone as he stopped the lecture.

"Why not draw our model with her clothes on?"

Maybe he isn't a complete rake.

But William's question was met with groans from the other students and this time, a softer tapping on the music stand.

"Because mastering the figure is more than just shapes and muscles and bones, Lord Cavendish." Beauchamp took a dramatic pause and walked in front of her. "It's about movement, weight, balance, and tension. See how she holds her head up with her hand? Although she's soft, you should note the difference between the forearm that holds up her head, and the one that is resting on her hip."

"Professor, we aren't looking at her arms."

Now that student is a rake! Lillias blinked rapidly. She'd almost said that out loud.

"The next student who speaks disrespectfully of our model will be expelled."

The professor's words silenced the room.

"What you are saying, Professor, is reality never lies."

At least the earl is perceptive.

"Yes, Lord Cavendish, drawing a human clothed makes it difficult to see the full pose. When you study a figure model, you'll discover how to draw minor details. It's only through figure drawing that the mastery of art can begin."

As the professor continued to talk about using the blocking technique to start a blueprint for drawing, Lillias had reason for vindication. Of course, her primary motivation for being in the figure drawing class was to support her sisters, but this was also an act of defiance. Her father had refused to let her attend classes at the academy because in his words it 'would be a waste of his money.'

What else had he said? Oh, yes, it came back. "Darling, I shall provide pianoforte lessons instead. Your husband will appreciate your perfection at entertaining a houseful of guests and the pianoforte will make a wonderful centerpiece for the main hall."

She cared for her father, but he didn't understand. Even if she was now of marrying age, she wasn't in a hurry to find a husband, nor did she worry about what would impress one. And more importantly, she detested the pianoforte.

A husband. Yes, eventually, but never a duke. A modest estate would be ideal. She couldn't stomach the societal necessities of the upper crust.

Duty. Duty. Duty. That would be her marital sentencing if she became a duchess. Her father spoke of her priorities. To learn to be an obedient wife. *Christ,* she had no intention of being obedient. She would marry for love when she was ready. Let her ambitious sister Verity marry a duke.

If not a duke, then at least a marquess. Verity would be able to keep her social standing. Then Rebecca would follow in two or three years. Once the social expectations for her sisters were met, that would free Lillias and her promise to her mother would be fulfilled.

And that's what she must focus on, helping her middle sister find a husband, because it she didn't before the end of the Season, she'd fail her mother. Lillias couldn't let that happen. Her father had already failed them with his irresponsible behavior.

Perhaps he gambled because he missed Mother or was trying to fit in at the club. At least Lillias was an accomplished mathematician and found ways to keep the household running.

But there might come a day when Lillias would be desperate enough to ask her father's sister for help. Aunt Elizabeth, the Dowager Countess of Coventry, had a vast fortune. Although the modeling would displease her father, it might be more forgivable than a loan from the dowager.

Finally, the professor's lecturing seeped into her musings. His voice pushed away her fretting.

"You begin this step-by-step blocking. Get the general shape of the girl's figure on the page."

"That girl has a shapely figure that's too distracting to put on a page," a voice behind her muttered.

"How rude!" *Did I just say that out loud?*

The professor stopped talking.

She had.

"I was just saying," she coughed, "how rude of me to cover my legs when clearly that would help with the exercise." Art education was priceless to her. The last thing she wanted on her conscience was a student's expulsion.

"It's not the model's prerogative to excuse any student of rude behavior. Let this be a warning to you, Lord Fletcher. You are discharged from this class for the rest of the day."

After a strained pause and footsteps echoing down the hall, the professor started again.

"This is called the envelope. When you sketch it, you set the boundaries for the drawing. The blank page doesn't seem so vast when you have a defined space to draw." He paused again, either to check on a student, or because someone was distracting the class.

"Lord Compton . . ."

It was the latter.

There was another long pause.

"Your page is empty," the professor said, sounding displeased.

"I'm still studying the subject's behind, sir."

The comment was followed by a loud thump.

This time, Lillias did fall off the stage.

CHAPTER 4

illiam rushed forward, knocking the music stand over on the way, but he managed to cover the model with his suit coat.

"You again?"

Ungrateful again? "Of course. At your service?" He bent into an efficient bow, wanting to grit his teeth instead of grinning at her like a fool. He would not allow his chivalrous actions to be marred by her ungrateful attitude.

Odd, his heart skipped a beat. *I'll never forget those eyes.* Good God, at least he didn't say it out loud this time.

"Here, here, give me your hand," the professor offered, brushing by William's side, pushing his bookish spectacles back up his aristocratic nose and tossing William an offish expression. "The model is my responsibility. Back to your seat," he ordered and all but shoved William with his hand.

"Everyone take a fifteen-minute break."

When William started back to his chair, most of the other students were edging toward the stage where the professor knelt, helping the model, and repositioning her covering. However, when he found a few students had come too close to the model, he pointed an authoritative finger toward the door and ordered them outside.

William tried to contain his laughter, but it came out as snort. He rushed toward the classroom door with the rest of the men, many snickering as they left.

After he entered the hallway, he walked a short distance to a grouping of clay busts on stands. It appeared the sculpture class had placed their artwork close to the open window to dry and he wandered between them.

"Julius Caesar, I presume?" William said, introducing himself to one of the busts with a bow.

"Who in the hell are you?" asked a voice that seemed to come from the Roman leader.

William almost knocked over the clay creation but righted it before the piece crashed to the marble floor. But his relief turned to frustration when he found Nigel standing behind the collection, grinning from ear to ear. He should have expected at least one prank from him today.

"What the bloody hell?"

His friend's expression changed to mischievous scowl. "You are jumpy," Nigel accused. "Have you lost your boxer reflexes?"

That was the perfect cue for William. He jabbed his friend in the upper arm.

"What was that for?" Nigel asked, backing away, feigning injury and clamping a hand over the spot William had tagged.

"To warn you not to sneak up on me whether ring or hallway."

"Speaking of the ring, let's catch a fight at Crawley Down tonight."

"Are you proposing we go as spectators? You know the rules."

Nigel's expression clouded. He no doubt remembered why William was barred from boxing.

"I know the rules," Nigel assured him. "I just need to settle a few debts."

"'He that dies pays all his debts. '"

"That's a morbid Shakespearian quote, even from you, Cavendish." His friend danced around the busts holding his fists close to his face. "I'm not talking about you stepping into the ring, my friend. I would be taking all the punches. I need you in my corner," Nigel said, then took out a folded paper from his vest pocket and handed it to him.

Scanning the document, William found it to be a promotional flyer for one of those country brawls. "Compton, remember what happened last time we ventured into a boxing saloon?"

"That was different. I picked a fight with a bloke, and you defended me with an upper cut."

"The fact that London's finest had to break it up didn't deter you from throwing the last punch."

"The urchin defamed my mother. I had to defend her."

William's laugh echoed down the long academic corridor. "That's your excuse every time."

"Right," Nigel said, with a resigned expression.

"You look like I sold your favorite stallion to a horse trader," William said. "Chin up. Like Shakespeare would say, 'Insult them before they insult you.'"

That had Nigel laughing, a mischievous gleam in his eyes.

"You, Cavendish, are a social misfit with lowly ambitions and a head made of clay." His friend glanced at the busts between them, grinning. "You couldn't win a beautiful debutante if your life depended on it because your face looks like the rear end of a cow." Nigel crossed his arms over his chest and beamed. "Top that."

His old school mate would not win this fight. William

was just as lethal with insults. "You horsewhipped ninny, how dare you think your verbal prowess is superior to mine when you have the brain the size of a gnat and the intelligence of a sloth, with the wit of a washer woman."

For a moment, William thought his old friend was going to cave to his insult, until the corners of his mouth turned into a smirk.

"Is that the best you can do?" Nigel challenged.

"Are you two finished with your childish game?"

William's head swiveled around like an owl. "Yes, sir, Professor Beauchamp, sir," he answered like a soldier, almost snapping to attention. His army training was overriding his natural reflexes. Without missing a beat, he fell in line behind the professor, who appeared to walk in a cadence much like those of William's old platoon.

Nigel had been an officer too, both in the same regiment, before they'd enrolled at Oxford. William wasn't surprised his friend's footsteps echoed the same pattern. They made sharp turns following the professor into the classroom.

Once inside the formal drawing room, drape-less since last week's fire, William shielded his eyes from the sunlight as the dust of Somerset House floated in and out of the sun beams. When his eyes finally adjusted, he found the platform empty.

She's gone?

William froze mid-step. His eyes darted around the room and Nigel stopped short of plowing into him.

"Looks like our *chit* has flown the coop," William said, taking his seat behind his easel and setting the flyer on the empty chair beside him. A loan would keep Nigel out of trouble.

"If you are finished interrupting the class, Lord Cavendish," the professor started, "you may be interested in why drawing in this class may be worth your while." He turned his back and walked to the center near the platform, then made a gesture toward the empty space. "Beginning tomorrow, this class will start on their R.A. international exhibition contest submissions."

The class participants were still settling into their seats, but Beauchamp's announcement brought everyone's banter to a halt. The room was in total silence as if an audience to Prince Regent had just been commanded.

The professor chuckled to himself. "Finally, I have your full attention."

William perked up. In the past week, he'd considered it. Winning R.A.'s international art contest would bring envious distinction to the man who snagged the prize. Plus, he still needed the down payment for the building on Tower Hill for the boys' school.

"The esteemed judges will be from this elite institution, where our purpose is to cultivate and improve the arts of painting, sculpture, and architecture. We have established the highest cultural standards in the world. Every month of May, since we opened our doors in 1769, the Royal Art Academy has accepted thousands of entries both from students here and across Europe. Only a few hundred will be selected for display and only a handful will win accolades."

William leaned back in his seat and propped his head between his hands. Releasing a slow whistle, he was sure could only be heard by Nigel, he stole a glance his way. "Have you decided to enter?"

"It will settle a few debts."

"Oh, so you are planning to win?"

His friend was grinning. What was hidden behind that strained smile? It had been about two months since they'd finished at Oxford and both had moved back to London for the Season. Nigel with enthusiasm and William with reluctance.

"I can always loan you a few quid," William offered while the professor droned on about the prestigious judges.

Nigel shook his head. "I can settle it all with a good bout in the ring." He gave William's shoulder a light jab. "All I need is a lucky night and a good bloke in my corner to collect my winnings if I'm too stupefied to carry them myself."

William grabbed his arm and feigned injury but conceded with a nod.

"Does fighting really settle the score?" said a voice that almost purred.

Spinning around in his seat, William found the model sitting behind them. Still masked, she was dressed in fashionable attire, a dark blue velvet gown, as if ready for tea. Damn, she was provocative, but he'd answer her, lady or not.

"That depends on what you are fighting for. Justice, liberty, protection, a prize."

"That's quite articulate," she said, sounding amused.

"If you want to hear something articulate, I can quote a complete Shakespeare Sonnet for you," he offered.

"Only one?"

"Name one?"

"One hundred and thirty."

"That's a short one, and you already recited a good portion."

"Fool's choice, then," she said in that velvety voice.

He grinned at her. "Are you calling me a fool?"

"I did not call you Sir Toby."

"From *Twelfth Night?*"

"The one."

"This banter is worthy of the Bard," Nigel interrupted with hint of awe in his voice.

William had an uncanny realization. Had he met his match, wit for wit? A terrifying discovery because this match was a woman. But a strange, uncontrollable urge had him reciting one of his Shakespearean favorites for her.

"'Mine eye hath play'd the painter and halth stell'd
Thy beauty's form in table of my heart;
My body is the frame wherein 'tis held,
And perspective that is the painter's art.
For through the painter must you see his skill,
To find where your true image pictured lies;
Which in my bosom's shop is hanging still,
That hath his windows glazed with thine eyes.
Now see what good turns eyes for eyes have done:
Mine eyes have drawn thy shape, and thine for me
Are windows to my breast, where-through the sun
Delights to peep, to gaze thein on thee;
Yet eyes this cunning want to grace their art;
They draw but what they see, know not the heart.'"

"Twenty-four," she said in a breathless whisper.

William nodded. She knew it. And he'd proven he did, but what else had he proven? That he was an infatuated fool?

CHAPTER 5

*L*illias came reeling around the door into the library, slightly out of breath after sprinting up the grand stairs, only to find her favorite room empty.

The corners of her mouth flattened her smile. *Where can the little minxes be?*

Not to be deterred from her mission to inform her sisters of her lofty plans, she spun on her heel and headed back into the hallway.

"Eek!" Lillias stopped short before colliding with a pile of linens. But the servant lost control of her load and Lillias was soon covered in fresh scented sheets.

Casting aside the pillowcase covering her face, a startled servant revealed herself. It was Jasmine, the upstairs maid.

Lillias laughed, imagining she looked as disheveled as her servant, whose prim and proper white cap now sat askew on her head, making her look like a drunken sailor.

"No harm done," she said to the girl who was giggling too.

"Oh my, let me re-pin your locks, Lady Lillias. I've gone and made such a mess of things."

But Lillias shooed her away and began picking up the sheets.

"No, no," Jasmine sputtered, swatting the air in an unsuccessful attempt to get Lillias to stop.

"Don't fuss, Jasmine," she said, handing over the disorganized pile. "I would offer to help fold but—"

"You're in a hurry," Verity said, joining them and finishing the sentence for Lillias. She had a habit of doing that.

"There you are," Lillias exclaimed as if finding an old friend at church.

Jasmine scooted away shaking her head.

"Come, now, I've news to share, and you have news to share," Lillias promised.

Her sister let out an unladylike grunt. "I do?"

Lillias hooked her arm in Verity's and led them both into the library. "Of course you do," she cooed like a dove.

"What are you about?" her sister demanded, shaking herself free of Lillias's arm and taking a seat on the gold chintz settee by the hearth.

"You to go first," Lillias said, sitting opposite her sister on the gaudy red chaise. "You know, your entrance into the music conservatory."

Verity rolled her eyes. "For your information, that's old news. We settled that a while ago."

Lillias walked to a drum-shaped mahogany table with a drawer below. For years, they'd hidden secrets from their father there. Not serious secrets. But today the drawer held an announcement Lillias had cut from *The Times*.

After a dramatic act of waving her hands over and under the table first, Lillias produced a newspaper clipping from the drawer.

Verity was on her feet in moments, reaching for the clip.

Lillias was faster, snatching it to her heart and spinning out of the way, screeching, "No, you don't."

"Just gossip," Verity hissed. "You can't believe everything you read."

Clearing her throat, and walking a safe distance away from her sister, Lillias began to read aloud. "It was reported today that Verity St. Clair is only the third woman to be admitted to the prestigious London symphony." She paused, raising her eyes above the paper before she started reading again. "She will play third chair violin at this Saturday's concert for Prince Regent." Lillias finished with a low bow before her sister started across the room toward her.

"Let me see that."

Not to be deterred, Lillias began walking backward, toward the door, so she could make an escape if she had to. As she continued to read aloud, her eyes made rapid movements back and forth between the page and Verity. She started to speed up her reading as she sped up her walking.

"And it will be noted here that this author has it upon good authority that Lady Verity recently turned down her admission to the Royal Academy of Music and will instead, dedicate her time to finding a proper suitor for her hand in marriage."

The paper tore in half. Her sister had caught up with her.

"Why did you do that?" Lillias's hands clung to each side of the torn article.

Her sister huffed and yanked the remaining shreds of paper from her grasp. "Because I don't appreciate the *ton's* prejudice against women," she said bitterly. "One of only three women—as if we were mermaids braiding our hair by the River Thames."

Lillias sympathized with her sister, but the bold commentary made her burst out laughing. When Verity's perturbed stare didn't soften, Lillias claimed, "You should be proud of your accomplishments."

"Why? When all Father really cares about is the family's

reputation. To take one of his daughters off the marriage market. That I mustn't miss my Season like you did and become an old maid."

Lillias's enthusiasm went flat. *Old maid?*

Her sister's expression immediately switched from perturbed to sympathetic. "I wasn't implying you were an old maid," she said, sounding apologetic.

Verity took all the fun out of the teasing. She was proud of her sister, and she needed to tell her before she got angry. "Listen, you and I are much alike. We—"

Verity interrupted her with a harrumph.

But Lillias persisted. "Hear me out. Since Mother's death, dealing with daughters has not been Father's strong suit. He wants to protect us."

"And marry us off."

"To protect us."

"Until we have husbands."

"To protect us." This was infuriating. Lillias needed to get to her news. "I'm entering the Royal Academy's International Art Competition," she exclaimed, her enthusiasm returning. "Like Rebecca said a few days ago, we aren't setting a good example for her."

"How?"

"I'll sign the entry, L. St. Clair."

"It's a lie."

"I do not lie. You know that. It's an alias. Everyone will think it's L, for Laurence, or something like that."

"How will you claim your prize? Dressed as a man?"

"It's not your affair."

"Why are you two taking about affairs again?"

Rebecca had entered the room.

Both Lillias and Verity looked at each other as if making a promise.

"We are talking about you," Verity announced.

"That's not fair."

Lillias smirked. "An affair, that's not fair?"

They all giggled.

Lillias crossed the room, then closed the door to the library. "We can't have Father wandering in again or catching bits of our conversation."

"We can't?" Rebecca asked like an innocent.

"Unless you want him to know all our secrets?" Lillias said. Why had Rebecca turned into a toddler?

"We have secrets?"

Lillias looked at Verity and they both said together, "From you!"

"What secrets?" Rebecca shrieked.

"Shhh," Lillias hushed, "if you aren't careful, Father will come looking for us."

"Well, I'm not so certain I don't want him in here when all you talk about is affairs, me, and keeping secrets."

The look of horror on her younger sister's face made Lillias burst out laughing. "All right, we'll share our secrets," she said smoothly. Rebecca was too easy to annoy.

"Actually, Rebecca, we should gang up on Lillias because she's the one who does all the relentless teasing," Verity volunteered.

The two began to walk slowly toward Lillias, rubbing their hands together like trolls, causing her to back up.

"I'm the oldest, it's expected of me." When they were within a few inches of her, Lillias held up her hand. "Wait," she commanded.

It was time to stop hiding the secret of their father's financial woes.

"Sit down," she said with authority. "It's time we had a serious talk. I do have a secret I need to share with you both."

Lillias didn't want to frighten her sisters, but she needed funds to pay for Verity's season. For the gowns. For the carriages. The R.A. modeling had paid Lillias more than when she painted portraits, but she had another idea that could help fill the coffers for the Season's necessities.

"I've had access to the books. Father has taken on a number of indulgences lately." She couldn't tell them about his gambling losses and she wouldn't let them know how bad it was right now. "Mother always took care of the finances and managed to keep the family in good stead. We don't have farmlands or tenants. Most of the family money belongs to Aunt Elizabeth."

Verity's eyes grew round like saucers and Rebecca appeared on the verge of tears.

"Now, it's nothing that can't be fixed. That's why I was posing at the R.A."

"You paint the most beautiful portraits, Lillias," Rebecca said with admiration in her voice. "That could make us a fortune."

"If I was a man," Lillias responded gently, but shot a look at Verity, hoping her sister would not choose this time to start a debate about discrimination. "I can earn a handsome sum modeling in Professor Beauchamp's class, but I'm worried about posing again."

"And you shouldn't have to," Verity said, walking to Lillias and putting an arm around her shoulder in a protective way.

"What can we do?" Rebecca asked, wiping a small tear from the corner of her eye.

Lillias drew out the boxing flyer from a pocket in her skirt. The one she'd found left behind on a seat in the classroom of the R.A. that afternoon. "Go to Crowley Down," Lillias suggested in an even tone, as if she'd recommended a trip to the modiste.

"That's a disgusting place," Verity responded, releasing Lillias and wrinkling her nose.

"Off limits," said Rebecca, the prudent one.

"If we bet carefully—"

"We'll get into trouble," Verity said, cutting Lillias off.

"We'll raise the funds we need to pay the staff and for other necessities," Lillias insisted.

"If we are the sons our father never had, then I'm all for it," Rebecca conceded. "Let's go to Crowley Down."

"I'm sorry, Rebecca, this is an affair you can't attend." Lillias hated excluding her, but it couldn't be risked.

"There you go again with affairs. It's a bloody fight, not an invitation to Almack's," Rebecca snipped, stubbornness lacing her words.

"Your birth order prohibits it as does your language, young lady," Lillias reprimanded her.

"Apparently, my effort to exhibit maturity was unappreciated."

"Immaturity is easy," Lillias snapped back. When Rebecca's cheeks reddened, and her eyes lowered, Lillias offered a caveat. "But you'll play an important role in our scheme. If Father is looking for either Verity or myself, you'll need to cover for us."

"You mean lie?"

"No." Lillias hesitated. "Distract him, and at last resort, offer a half-truth."

"You mean a half-lie?" Rebecca said, challenging Lillias's animosity for false truths.

"If the intention is pure, it's not a half-lie."

"Delude yourself, Lillias," Verity said getting in the middle of the debate.

"I'm the oldest and—"

"The oldest is always right," Verity finished the sentence for her.

* * *

A FEW HOURS LATER, Lillias walked arm-in-arm with Verity into a barn at Crowley Down.

"There must be at least two hundred people here," Lillias estimated, fanning herself vigorously.

Verity grabbed her arm and stopped both their progression and her fanning. "This is dangerous."

"We have Finneas with us," Lillias reminded her sister.

"An old butler waiting at our carriage will save us if one of these men petitions us and we refuse?"

"Like you said, there are at least two hundred people here," Lillias muttered, trying to make herself feel brave.

"Nothing will happen to us."

Hooking Verity's arm, she maneuvered them around the outside of the main crowd, tugging her overtly curious sister along, who seemed to think she was promenading in Hyde Park and not through an illegal gambling establishment.

Sidestepping a couple of unsavory looking men, Lillias finally managed to steer them to the betting counter. Squinting at the two contenders at opposite corners of the boxing arena, Lillias made her decision based on the size of the two men.

"Fifty pounds on the skinny boxer." Lillias pointed toward the ring. The other man in the opposite corner was mammoth, no doubt slow to the punch.

The toothless man hooted before he said, "Sorry, lady." The man didn't look sorry, he looked lecherous. "You can watch, but you canno wager."

Lillias matched the man's scowl. "What do you mean?"

"I mean no," the man said less politely this time.

Lillias tried not to show any fear and countered. "I'll split my winnings with you." Then she bit her lip, hoping the commoner's greed would allow for an exception.

"You'll be throwing your money away betting against the champion," the man said, his resolve softening.

"I'll stick with my choice," Lillias said, as she began stacking her hard-earned coins with her trembling hand.

The man shrugged and scooped her money off the counter and into what sounded like a large bucket next to him. Even this ruffian had figured he'd win either way.

Lillias took the betting voucher and spun away quickly, least the man would change his mind. She glanced at the rough parchment before tucking it in her skirt pocket. He had written out the number fifty with a line through it and a joker's hat next to it.

"Well, that's foreboding," Verity remarked after peering at the scrap of paper.

"You don't have to be contrary," Lillias said to her sister when they started toward the seating area.

"It's difficult to be otherwise, when as the oldest, you always know best."

Lillias ground her teeth together and pinched her lips tight, lest she say something she'd later regret. The promise to her mother would override her want to strangle her sister right now.

"Let's make the best of it," Lillias suggested, turning Verity toward the direction she wanted to take. "I brought my sketch book."

But Verity stopped to gawk at the two shirtless boxers in the roped off fighting arena. "Even though it's brutal, boxing is easy on the eyes," she said, not turning her head to watch where she was going.

Lillias tugged her sister's arm while the announcer introduced the skinny boxer. Now it was her turn to stop and gawk at the man who she'd bet her family's future on.

Nigel? Lillias's stomach sank. She'd bet on Lord Compton, the impudent art student from Beauchamp's class? For a fleeting moment, she entertained the idea of returning to the bookmaker to change her bet. Especially after the local champion, Big Douglas, was announced. He strutted around the arena like a proud rooster.

Finally, it was Verity who yanked on Lillias's arm and led them to a haystack in the back of the barn where they could be high enough to see over the rows of men. They sat down as a cowbell clanged three times and Nigel charged out of his corner toward the center, bouncing side to side, fists clenched in front of his face. Maybe he had a chance?

The champ, on the other hand, strolled out in a nonchalant manner, like a king whose reign was not in jeopardy. He took a stance across from his opponent.

Lillias took out the sketch book from her reticule. It would keep her distracted from the half-nude men trying to best each other in the roped off arena and the fifty pounds she had bet on a fancy lord and art student.

It didn't take long before the champion had Nigel pressed against the ropes. Even with Nigel's quick jabs to Big Douglas's chin and gut, the champion fought as if he wasn't human.

To Lillias's relief though, the bell finally clanged and both fighters retreated to their corners. That was when she saw him. The earl from the R.A. class. The student who'd leaped from the burning building to save her. He was coaching his friend in the corner.

Sinking behind the men in front of her, Lillias wished she could make herself invisible. *Lord Cavendish is here too?*

After giving Nigel what looked like a pep talk, the earl gave him a friendly shove back into the center ring where he began to taunt the champ by waving his fist and inviting him forward.

And the champ came forward in a fury.

Whack!

Nigel took a nasty left hook to his jaw. Then fell. He fell hard. Straight down on his face.

The bell sounded and the fans roared. Big Douglas began a victory lap around the ring while the referee stood over Nigel.

"One, two." The burly judge began his progressive count, pointing his finger toward Nigel with each successive number.

William needs to do something. I can't lose fifty pounds.

"Five. Six."

"Wait!"

Did William just say that?

"Wait?" The would-be victor spun around as if he'd been stung in his ass.

"Wait?" the referee asked.

"Y-Yes," William stammered before he yanked his linen shirt over his head. "I said wait."

Tossing the garment on the ropes, William stepped over his friend into the center, as a boy pulled Nigel by his feet and eased him off to the side.

Big Douglas stared at the earl, the champion's unblemished jaw gapping open. After a long pause, the contender's gaze swung over to the referee. "Can he do that?"

The man nodded solemnly as if he hated to be the one to break the news to the brute.

Not a beat went by before William was ducking from a huge fist aimed for the middle of his nose.

The crowd roared with laughter as Big Douglas nearly swung himself halfway around in a circle with his right arm dangling by his side after the spin.

William began to inch back, drawing the ogre forward. The man was seething, no doubt angry he wasn't celebrating a win with his buddies instead of looking foolish.

Swing and a miss. William ducked under the arm of the boxer and over to the other side of the ring. This time the contender landed on the ropes.

While Big Douglas tried to untangle himself, William nodded to the crowd before he swung around to face his opponent again. Then screaming at the top of his lungs, William rushed forward like a man possessed.

The element of surprise appeared to be in his favor, for the contender stopped dead in his tracks, even staggered backward toward the ropes.

William howled like a rabid dog. With erratic movements, he leveled a left hook that landed on the champion's jaw, sending his head back with a loud snap.

Then the champion released an eerie growl, like a dying wolf. His knees buckled and he fell face down on the dirt floor.

When the referee stepped between the two, William turned and took a victory lap around the ring. Clasping his hands together, he shook them on each side of his head, grinning from ear to ear, as the referee finished off the count.

"Eight, nine, ten."

Then the referee grabbed William's right hand and led him into the center of the ring, raising it above their heads.

"And the winner is—" The man turned to William and waited.

"N-Nigel," William said with a little hesitation.

Lillias couldn't believe it. The R.A. student, the one who'd fondled her derriere and ogled her body in class, had knocked out the local boxing champion. Like it was easy. Like he did it all the time. Like it wasn't dangerous, and he could have been killed. Not that she cared, even if he'd said her eyes were unforgettable.

Lillias closed her sketch book and began to fan herself with it. Maybe it wasn't the heat in the barn that was making her feel flushed but seeing the earl shirtless. The vision alone was enough to overload her senses.

"The winner." Verity started to raise her hand, as if to mimic the referee.

Lillias batted it down before she could bring attention to them in their seats. They were already sticking out like daffodils in a garden of weeds. She scrutinized Verity's expression. It was a mix of child-like stubbornness and outrage.

"Why did you do that?"

"Because I'm the oldest."

"It's more than that. As your sister, I know you better than anyone else. It's that fighter." Verity's voice trailed off as her head swung in his direction. She kept her gaze on William and continued with her accusations. "You know him. How is that?"

How is that? Where do I even begin?

"I know he just saved our fifty pounds." Lillias had to avoid a lie. A breakout of her hideous hiccups would draw attention. Straightening her spine, Lillias adjusted her focus to the task of collecting their winnings.

"Come." She extended a hand to Verity to help her off the haystack. "I don't like the looks these men are giving us," she added, spinning her sister away from the ring and the distraction.

"What did you expect? We left our chaperone in the carriage," her sister huffed.

Lillias ignored her sister's quip and quickened her pace, the rush of men carried them along like a log in rough waters, and finally to the betting counter.

Stepping into a short line, Lillias did her best to tune out the obscenities shouted at the bookmaker. No doubt the disgruntled men who had bet on the champion felt cheated.

When she handed over her betting note, the bookmaker gave her another ugly, toothless grin. Even though he appeared to be ignorant, with his rough exterior and lack of manners, the man had to be competent enough to handle the money. Otherwise, the matchmakers wouldn't have given him the charge. Or would they?

Her skeptical mind began thinking the worst as the man fumbled with the large wooden money box. What if he was a crook who planned to shortchange the winners? Most betting country folk wouldn't be the wiser.

Lillias didn't know anything about betting other than she'd heard odds played a factor in the payout, but to how much that factored into what she would receive, she hadn't a clue.

At least she could count with confidence the coins the bookmaker piled up in front of her. As long as the payout was more than she'd bet, she would take the money and hotfoot it out of Crowley Down.

"Can't you hurry him up?"

Verity's terse question in Lillias's ear was so ridiculous her only response was to ignore it. She wasn't about to risk missing a counted coin to reprimand Verity for her imperti- nence.

It wasn't until the last shilling was added to the stack and the towers of coins pushed toward Lillias, did she let out an inner sign of relief. The sum was triple her original amount. Enough to keep her clothes on for the Season. But there were more coins than would fit into her reticule, even if she removed the sketchbook.

Turning to Verity, Lillias had a solution. "Make haste, open up your reticule."

"Now you are in a hurry?"

Lillias gave her sister the glare she'd saved from the last flippant question. "We need to get out of here with these coins and as soon as possible. Dump out what's in your purse and help me."

"Dump?" Her sister's eyes narrowed. "You mean leave my possessions?"

Snatching Verity's reticule, she emptied the contents on the far end of the betting counter to her sister's consternation.

"You can't possibly be sentimental about a few hair combs, a secondhand fan, and a monogramed handkerchief?"

Her sister let out harrumph. "Your sketchbook is taking up space in your reticule, Sister."

Tucking her sketch book under her arm for safekeeping, Lillias quickly emptied her purse too, then scooped more than half the coins in, while Verity reluctantly filled her own.

Turning toward the moving crowd, Lillias waited for a break in the wave of men filing through the barn doors, none looked happy, some giving the bookmaker an earful.

After finding a gap behind two women who might not meet the definition of lady, Lillias steered Verity into the current as she held tight to her purse.

When they finally made their way through the barn doors, she spied their carriage and said in her best reassuring tone, "We're almost there." But that flash of reassurance vanished when there was no sign of Finneas.

She glanced over at Verity, surprised her sister had remained quiet for so long, but the explanation was clearly written on her face. She was afraid too.

Releasing Verity's arm, she prepared to take charge of the grim situation. "Pick up your skirt. We're going to make a run for the carriage," Lillias said, trying to keep the panic out of her voice.

Just as Lillias bent over, a hand grabbed her derriere.

"Now," she screeched, without looking back, hoping the yell that accompanied her lurch forward, scared the offender.

The distance to the carriage seemed double what it had

been when they arrived as they raced through the tall grass toward it.

"Finneas," she shouted, her eyes frantically searching for the butler, holding on to the hope her amiable servant was on the other side.

Greeted by silence, Lillias slowed, working to squelch her rising panic, holding on to the hope that when she opened the door, Finneas would be on the other side taking a nap.

But when she released the latch and the door swung open, Verity's scream echoed her own.

For a moment, Lillias closed her eyes and shook her head, certain they'd deceived her. But when she popped them open again, the vision was still the same.

Inside the cabin Finneas appeared to be taking a nap, but his hands and feet were tied with thick rope, and across from him sat a wicked-looking man with greasy black hair and beady lifeless eyes. He beckoned them with his hand as he stepped out of their carriage.

"They won't be going for a ride with you if I have anything to do about it," said a commanding voice from behind them.

Without hesitation, the hijacker took off running toward the dense woods a few yards away, and never looked back.

If Lillias hadn't been so terrified, she would have laughed at the comical dash, but instead she exhaled a shaky breath, spinning around, ready to give her gratitude to their savior.

But when her gaze found his, she froze.

"I-I we," she stuttered, not finding her voice or the words.

The shirtless earl bowed with a genuine smile that made her heart melt and asked, "Have we met before?"

CHAPTER 6

"Absolutely not, how could we have?" Lillias's gaze dropped to his boots, her cheeks heating. *He mustn't recognize me.*

"Lord William Cavendish, at your service," he said, seemingly undeterred by her lack of proper etiquette.

When the earl clicked his boot heels together, her eyes traveled up his long athletic legs to his bare chest. It stopped there. *Oh my.*

"Lord William Cavendish, cover yourself or you'll be as frightening as the bloke you chased away," his friend insisted. Then he turned to address Lillias and her sister with a slight bow. "I am Lord Nigel Compton, the—"

"The Baron of Irritation," William interrupted, turning around to tend to his dressing.

Lillias gave Nigel a shaky grin. *The less I say, the less likely they'll recognize me.*

Still in his genuflected position, Nigel released his strained smile and finished his introduction. "The Baron of Good Humor."

William chuckled when he turned around, his shirt now

properly buttoned, his tail tucked in. He was missing a cravat and proper waistcoat. But Lillias couldn't take her eyes off the tuft of black hair peaking between the space where this cravat would have been tied. It matched the thick, but well-groomed hair framing his mischievous expression.

Then it happened. The awkward silence was broken by a loud hiccup. Lillias slapped her hand over her mouth.

"Congratulations on winning the title," Verity intervened cheerfully, no doubt trying to maintain a conversation with the two men and divert the attention from Lillias's bout with the hiccups. Verity had the gift of gab.

"Thank you," both men replied, then they looked at each other oddly. No doubt they shared the honor. If one could call it that.

"We seem to be in a bit of a pickle."

Oh, no, don't ask them.

"Would one of you be kind enough to drive our carriage home?" Her sister gestured to the open cabin. "Our driver is quite indisposed."

Like a soldier executing a command, William peered into the carriage to assess the situation before he answered Verity. "I would be honored to deliver you safely home," he volunteered with a clipped bow.

Lillias tried to hold her breath. The hiccups were unrelenting when she lied. They hadn't formally been introduced but rationalizing never changed things.

Nigel bowed again and said, "I'm also at your service."

William turned to Nigel, his attention off Lillias for a moment. How could she persuade Nigel to do the bidding instead of William and not make it awkward?

"Give us a moment," William asked, placing his hand on his friend's shoulder and steering him around so they could talk privately.

Over their low voices Verity said in her ear, "What happened?"

"You need to ask me?"

"Who else would I be asking?" Verity said loudly, putting her hands on her hips, interrupting the men's discussion.

Turning to face them again, William politely cleared his throat with an "uhm," then put his hand over his heart. "We will both accompany you ladies back to London and see to your safety," he said in a congenial tone, bending over in a slight bow with an arm flourish. "Two is better than one. Nigel will drive the carriage and I'll ride in the cabin."

William's offer was difficult to refuse. But the last person she wanted to spend time with was Lord William Cavendish. The Baron of Good Humor would be a better option.

"We would hate to inconvenience you both." Lillias hiccupped. "After the win, I'm sure there's much for you to celebrate." Hiccup. "How will you get your carriage home?" Lillias swallowed another hiccup and covered her mouth, holding her breath again and hoping it would turn off the wretched retribution.

"They're gentlemen, Lillias. Certainly, they have a driver too," Verity said sweetly but delivering it with a fake smile. "We accept your generous offer." And without consulting Lillias, her sister hiked up her skirts and marched toward the carriage leaving Lillias standing with the two men.

William gestured for Lillias to follow Verity, and after polite exchanges, gallant assistance into the carriage, and untying the unconscious Finneas, Lillias found herself sitting across from the art student and recent boxing champion, also known as Lord William Cavendish.

Yet, after a period of polite interchanges about the weather, the conditions of the road, and the danger of boxing, the lord politely sat back and closed his eyes for a good part of the ride.

Although Crawley Down was in the country, it was not far from their home in Canterbury. With the rocking of the carriage and her companion sitting quietly, appearing to sleep, Lillias was close to nodding off herself when a low, timbered voice startled her with the question she'd been dreading.

"Haven't we met before?"

Lillias's voice cracked when she said, "Excuse me?" And try as she might to form some words, her tongue grew thick and refused.

Out of pity or courtesy, Lord William pressed on. "Perhaps it was at Lady Skevington's event last Saturday?"

But before Lillias could answer, Finneas moaned and shifted his weight, which caused his body to lurch onto William's lap.

Everyone but the unconscious Finneas burst out laughing. But even the mirthful cacophony didn't disturb their butler, nor did he wake when William gently eased him back into the corner again. Adjusting the old man's shoulders, William wedged him in place with a carriage cushion propped behind his back.

The old servant moaned again, but then went silent.

Verity clapped a gloved hand over her mouth to trap a snort.

The three of them held their breath, watching and waiting for an outburst or movement from the butler.

When it finally appeared Finneas was settled and comfortable for the rest of the ride, Lillias discovered her hiccups had stopped. Perhaps they disappeared because Finneas had startled her or because she held her breath. Either way, the debilitating curse had ended. For now.

Lillias let out an exhale of relief when Verity shifted to the edge of her seat. A cue she was going to engage in conversation.

"Our debuts were delayed, and we haven't been to any events this season," Verity blurted out, answering William's earlier question. Appearing to struggle to find the right words, Verity looked to Lillias with pleading eyes.

Lillias swallowed hard. As much as she wanted to disappear she couldn't avoid interacting with William in this proximity. "You see our mother, God rest her soul, was very sick when we came of age." Her voice cracked and she glanced at her sister. "I will be sponsoring Verity this Season." She couldn't say her mother was dead without bursting into tears.

William coughed nervously and wrung his hands. "Compton and I just finished our studies at Oxford and recently returned for the Season." When both girls remained silent, he added, "We've only been to a few balls." He hesitated but then pressed on to fill the silence. "Prior to, we both served a two-year commission in the army."

Verity squealed as if she'd been offered a jeweled box. "A service man, how dangerous," she exclaimed.

"My lady, do not make this out to be more honorable than it was. Most of our duties consisted of making daily rounds at the royal residences like Buckingham House," he explained in an unassuming way.

Verity's eyes went wide. "Really?" she asked in a breathy gasp. "What was that like?"

Their chaperone's cheeks reddened at Verity's reaction. If Lillias had been anywhere but here, she would have scolded her sister for the overt posturing.

When William began to tell them a story about his first time meeting Queen Charlotte, Verity leaned so far forward one extreme bump in the road would set her in his lap.

"Speaking of Oxford," Lillias had to change the subject, "what did you study?"

Verity let out an unladylike harrumph. "We were talking

about our Queen, and you ask about Lord Cavendish's studies?"

Lillias threw Verity a stare full of daggers. "This is quite the appropriate line of questioning," she said through clenched teeth. She was determined to find some details about the man before the carriage ride ended.

"Architecture," William said, then he gave her an accommodating grin. "I'm quite good at portraiture too."

She considered that an exaggeration, due to what she'd witnessed in the R.A. classroom, but Lillias gave him a placid smile. Now it was her turn to lean forward, but she kept a respectable distance, unlike her sister had, who was now pouting in the corner. "Good enough to win the Royal Academy of Art International Competition?"

"That's rude," Verity ground out, becoming animated again.

"A rude question would be, 'Has he ever won any contests?'"

"I don't see how that is different?"

"Clearly, you can't see?"

"Pardon me, ladies. I can see, but I don't know what's going on," their butler said groggily.

"Finneas!" They both screeched.

The poor butler covered his ears. Then he almost did a double take when he glanced to his right and found William sitting next to him. Then he grimaced before he said in his droll, butler-authoritative tone, "Explain yourself, young man."

Lillias let out a huff before she defended him. "Finneas, he saved our lives."

"The earl is the new boxing champion," Verity exclaimed, holding up both her fists.

William coughed nervously before he said, "Co-champion, I had some help. He's driving us to Woodbeck House."

"Us?" the butler said, sounding confused.

Lillias took pity on the longtime family servant. "Do you remember how you ended up in the carriage with your hands and feet tied?"

The butler looked at his hands, which were no longer tied, and shook his head. But then he groaned and gingerly touched a spot on his head. "It's all coming back to me now," he lamented. "I was walking around the carriage when I heard a loud bang and blacked out." He closed his eyes as though it would help him remember. "I believe I was struck with something exceptionally hard."

Poor Finneas. "We'll have Doctor Thomas stop by later tonight and take a look at you," Lillias promised.

Finneas shook his head again like he was ready to protest, but the action had him grabbing his ears as if to still the rattling going on inside.

Verity came to her rescue. "We insist, Finneas."

Their butler slumped back in the bench of the rocking cabin as if giving in was easier than arguing.

With Finneas settled, Lillias wanted to get back the subject of her interest. "You were saying, you might be good enough to win the R.A.'s international art exhibition?"

Verity discreetly stomped on Lillias's toes while she shifted her position on the carriage bench.

Lillias pursed her lips together to hold back a yelp of pain before she amended her question. "What I meant to say was, are you going to enter the R.A.'s summer art contest?"

"Are you?"

"Excuse me?" *How dare he ask me the same question?*

"Are you going to enter the R.A.'s summer art contest?" he asked without rephrasing the question, then he served her a smirk. *A smirk?* And nodded to her sketchbook on the bench next to her.

"I asked you first," Lillias shot back. It wasn't a genteel answer, but it was honest.

Right then the carriage ran over something that caused the cabin to shake severely enough everyone was thrown about. Lillias fell into William's lap.

"We've arrived." Finneas stated the obvious.

Now Lillias had found herself in embarrassing situations before, but never with her bosom in the face of a potential competitor. With as much social decorum as she could muster, she pushed against William's shoulders and eased herself back on the bench across from him. When she did meet his gaze, he looked more out of sorts than she felt. His face was bright red, and he was staring at his feet.

"Can you help our butler up to the house, Lord Cavendish?"

Verity to the rescue. Her sister's request for assistance had William scrambling out of the cabin like a confirmed bachelor from an ambitious debutante's mother.

Once outside the carriage, William stood as if he'd rather hail the next available ride back to Mayfair than dutifully assist Finneas out of the cabin.

But Verity would not let him off easily. "Not only to the house, but with the least amount of disruption." Her sister lowered her voice. "You see we must not alert Father to our arrival."

"What the girl aspires to say," Finneas broke in, taking William's outreached hand and climbing from the carriage in a clumsy manner, no doubt due to his injuries, "the ladies want no one to know about this escapade, particularly, their father, Charles St. Clair, the Duke of Canterbury."

Their benefactor went stiff, almost dropping the arm supporting Finneas.

The butler caught himself on the carriage door handle,

then turned around as quickly as one could, given his age and condition. "Sir?"

William mumbled something under his breath then said, "My apologies, good man. Simply distracted when you mentioned the St. Clair name."

Lillias was next. Placing one foot tentatively on the step, she shot a suspicious glance at William before she extended her hand to him.

"Steady now," he said. Then with no respect for decorum, he placed both hands firmly on her hips, lifting her off the step and in a half circle to the Woodbeck House front walk.

Once her feet were firmly planted, Lillias reacted before thinking and landed a right hook to his nose.

"Ouch," she screeched, her hand stinging. She wriggled her fingers around, hoping to wake them from the numbness.

"Ouch?" William said with disgust, putting a hand gently on the offended area.

Before Lillias had time for a sarcastic reply, Nigel assisted Verity down the steps.

"If you are that serious about the art competition, Lillias, you should have crushed his hand, not his nose," Verity said with a head toss, handing Lillias her forgotten sketch pad.

With a hearty laugh, William turned to her and said, "We have a rivalry going and we've only just met?" The crinkled corners around his dreamy blue eyes appeared to soften.

Dreamy? Isn't he the adversary? But then they shone in a mischievous way and his smile broadened, one side turning up in the most provocative angle, making the dimple in his cheek pop inward.

"What di-did y-you say?" she stuttered.

"Will we be rivals or friends?" he asked, extending his hand to hers. This time she did not recoil but let his lips gently brush the top of her gloved hand.

"More likely, you'll become enemies," Verity snapped as she sashayed past them on Nigel's arm, with Finneas in the lead. "The R.A.'s Art completion is worthy of a war between friends," she said over her shoulder with acid sweetness.

Lillias only shrugged as William released her hand, but not her gaze. Then he shook his head as if waking up. "I thought you looked familiar." He swept into a low bow. "But we've only just met." His smile turned apologetic.

He extended his arm and she accepted it with less trepidation. Although he'd been arrogant in class, he'd been complimentary. What had he said to her?

"Oh." She remembered his words.

He tightened his grip on her arm, "Are you all right?"

She laughed nervously. "I was just trying to figure out how to apologize for punching you."

William laughed too. It sounded genuine. "I was worried you might challenge me to a round at Crowley Down after you landed that right hook square on."

Lillias's cheeks began to heat and for some strange reason, her belly did flips when she remembered William stripped to his waist.

"What do they call you?"

Her eyes flashed and she recalled William asking the same question when he'd cradled her in his arms. Strangely, this time she didn't want to tell him to forget her.

CHAPTER 7

"I know the hour is late, sir, but the girls were in good hands," Finneas explained to their father who stood at the top of the stairs with an expression that could melt butter. Then their servant of more than twenty years bowed and began taking off his white gloves as though nothing more on the matter needed to be discussed.

"If the carriage was also carrying the son of a man I despise, then they couldn't have been in good hands, Finneas."

Lillias hated when their father was angry, which was as rare as snow in April. But the duke didn't say another word. He released his claw-like grip on the balustrade and turned his back on the group, then made his way down the hall.

"That was a close call," Verity said with too much pep in her voice.

Finneas grunted uncharacteristically, and after a short apology and insisting Dr. Thomas needn't be called, bid Lillias and Verity goodnight. As he headed toward the servants' quarters, Lillias steered Verity in the direction of the library.

"Father is rarely home. How are we to know who is— and who is not—in his favor?" Verity asked what Lillias was thinking when the two filed into the cozy room.

Lillias headed to her favorite spot. She loved the enormous, leather wingback chair by the fireplace where Father would sit if he were in the room. For now, she claimed the family throne while Verity sat with a huff on the end of the red Egyptian-styled chaise.

"Why would Father even raise an aristocratic eyebrow over an earl who was accompanying us home?" Verity asked with an air of irritation as if sanctions had been levied against them.

Reluctantly leaving the warmth of her short visit by the coal grate, Lillias headed toward the desk with a purpose. She wanted to get the conversation going in a more positive direction, away from any lingering thoughts about their outing. She was reaching for the invitation when Verity broke the silence and her momentum.

"Tell me more about Lord William Cavendish," her sister asked blithely, veering the conversation back to the carriage ride.

Lillias turned after snatching up the envelope and shrugged her shoulders. "There's nothing to tell."

Verity smacked the chaise with a gloved hand. "You punched him in the nose." She gave Lillias the look. One an Irish setter would when tracking down prey. "Clearly, you two have met before." Verity knew how to dog Lillias for what she wanted.

Lillias thought back to Finneas's rendition of where they'd been and how they'd arrived home with the earl. Their servant was as honest as the day was long, but he was also the most convincing liar when covering for her and her sisters' escapades. Lillias was indebted to him for letting him handle the explanation. Her father would have been the first to know she was lying if she'd relayed the tale. Who knew mentioning the Earl of Devonshire would rattle the new Duke of Canterbury?

Ignoring Verity's innuendo, she slid the elegant stationery from the envelope and began to read instead. "Ladies voucher for Almack's. Deliver to Lady Lillias St. Clair for the balls on Wednesdays, April 1817. Hosted by the Duchess Dowager of Leeds, the Marchioness of Stafford, and the Countess of Cholmondeley."

But when she glanced up from the invitation to gauge Verity's reaction, she found her sister in a fainting position on the chaise lounge with the back of her hand to her forehead. Verity was always overly dramatic.

Lillias pressed on. "This ticket, issued by the patronesses, is not transferable. The ballroom will be appropriated for waltzing and the adjoining rooms for French and English country dancing. Signed, Lady Sefton."

Lillias's announcement was greeted by silence. Not to be deterred, Lillias produced a second invitation from the envelope. She cleared her throat before she read. "Ladies Voucher for Almack's. Deliver to Verity St. Cl—" But before she could finish reading their surname, Verity let out a gleeful howl and was at her side peering over her shoulder.

"Let me see, let me see," her middle sister begged.

Lillias was relieved she hadn't tried to take it from her like the newspaper article the other day and quickly acquiesced.

Verity scanned the invitation for legitimacy, as if expecting Lillias of a prank. Which would have been a good one if she'd have thought of it.

"The London Season is beginning," Verity gushed with enthusiasm, spinning in a circle with her invitation clutched to her chest. When she stopped, breathless, her gleeful countenance turned into a concerned frown. "But whatever will I wear?" Then Verity took her seat back on the chaise, still clutching her invitation to her heart and said dreamily, staring out the window, "Maybe Lord Compton will be there."

"Lord Compton?"

"Or someone as handsome as he is."

"You saw him with his shirt off and you can't get it out of your mind."

Lillias was just as guilty when it came to William.

Enemy? Rival? Son of her father's nemesis?

When her head hit the pillow later that night, Lillias wasn't sure how she'd get to sleep without thinking of a man named William who could recite Shakespeare almost as well as she.

* * *

AFTER NIGEL JOINED him in his carriage and they were on their way to White's Gentleman's club, William closed his eyes and made a confession. "Boxing is exhausting."

"You are out of shape."

William's eyes shot open. "I beg your pardon. Who's out of shape?"

"Well, I thank you for stepping in for me when I needed a break," Nigel said, without sounding thankful.

"When were you napping in the boxing arena's dirt?" William drew up to the edge of the bench and waited for a response. Stepping in for Nigel was dangerous for so many reasons and yet, he did it to save his friend.

"What happened at the St. Clair's?"

"I didn't see that punch coming." Leave it to Nigel to take the heat off himself and put it on William. "It's difficult to explain," he added, hoping Nigel would ignore his awkward reaction to the family name and move on to talking about the winnings.

"Difficult isn't the right word," Nigel persisted. "You almost let the butler fall flat on his face," he accused. William eyed his friend, considering how much should he reveal. "Why do you think it was an unusual reaction?"

"Because you have the reflexes of a boxing champion. You let go of him on purpose."

"Are you suggesting that after the poor servant was hogtied and beaten, I would have let him fall, and if not for ladies present, have finished him off?"

"When you put it that way, it does sound ridiculous," his friend admitted, turning to stare out the carriage window.

Nigel's curiosity could be curbed.

"You must have met that woman before."

But it might take some cleverness to deter him. "You mean the pretty one?"

"They were both pretty." Nigel leveled his gaze. "The beautiful one who hit you."

"'Beauty is but a vain and doubtful good; a shining gloss, a glass, a flower, lost, faded, broken, dead within an hour.'"

"Really, William. Shakespeare is your answer?"

"Her father's title is a joke." He paused, still trying to decide how much to share. "And to make matters worse, our fathers are enemies." There. That should suffice.

"Your father is a snob," Nigel said, straight-faced serious.

"I take offense to that."

"Are you saying he isn't?"

"No, I'm saying he isn't that snobby."

Nigel doubled over with laughter until he choked out, "There are degrees of snobbery? Enlighten me."

William would never ignore a challenge. He stuck out his chin and peered down his nose at his college friend. "There's the 'I know you are there, but you are beneath me' form of snobbery." Then he crossed his arms and looked out the window. "You may be familiar with the 'How dare you breathe the same rarified air I do' snub. And finally"—He held out his hand for deference, then turned his head toward the window again—"the last of the degrees, the 'kiss my rings, kiss my ass, and get the hell away from me' reaction."

When William turned to Nigel again, his friend's nose was turned up, his gaze out the window, and his arms were crossed. "It's only because I still consider you a college associate that I'm not asking you to kiss my ass."

Now it was William's turn to laugh. "Because with a worldly friend like me, you are more enlightened than ever."

"And I assume your father falls into the 'kiss, kiss' category?"

"Precisely," William said, looking down his nose again at Nigel.

"That's still no reason to snub the butler and that beautiful brunette with the violet eyes."

William's head snapped up from the tufted carriage seat. He had met her before. "I'd never forget those eyes."

"Why I'm so flattered." Nigel batted his lashes like a socialite and took the punch to his left arm in stride too.

William shook his hand out. "You're pretty solid."

"You shouldn't be messing with the champion," Nigel teased.

"Co-Champion," William shot back.

"Not when you hit like a wet nurse."

"When you take a swing, you wind up like a three-year old."

"That's better than acting like one."

"It takes one to know one."

"Now who's acting like a three-year-old?" Nigel asked, leaning forward with a comical expression, eyes bulging and tongue sticking out.

"You are," William declared, then pointed to the prize-winning money bag sitting next to his friend. "What was the purse?"

Nigel twisted toward the pouch and scooted away from it with a short hop on the seat as if it was a squirrel that had snuggled up to him.

"Did you count the money?"

"I'm afraid to," Nigel said in a genuine way, but with an aversion to the satchel, as though it was jinxed.

"*Christ*, man, for whatever reason would you not want to know?"

"If it's not enough, I don't know what I'll do," his friend bit out and then dropped his head in his hands.

William was taken aback. Nigel had always been a stand-up kind of man. Perhaps he had underestimated the gambling debt. "How much should it be?" he asked, hoping Nigel would get off his sorry pout and figure it out.

His former army chum snatched the pouch from the seat and tossed it William's way.

Catching the bag before it landed on the carriage floor, William bounced it up and down in his right hand as if he had the ability to weigh the coin inside. "Seems substantial."

Nigel grunted. "Count it."

William began to untie the leather cords. "What a pushy woman you are." He looked up from his work. "Are you going to watch me or close your eyes and wait for the answer."

Nigel twisted his face into an unbecoming expression.

"Don't hold your breath like a three-year-old until it's counted," William warned. "I'm not that fast."

Nigel exhaled with a sputtering chuckle. "You got me. Stop the carriage and I'll get out and pace until you're finished." To show he was serious, Nigel tapped the ceiling of the conveyance with the top of his walking stick.

The carriage came to an abrupt halt.

"This stop wasn't on the driver's schedule," William said to his friend, amused that it was Nigel who had to grab onto the side door handle to keep from tumbling forward like a three-year-old.

"Life is like that, Cavendish." He tipped his hat and got out. "Sometimes you must make unplanned stops." Once he was outside the carriage, his friend spun around and poked his head back in. "I need five hundred pounds, more or less. I'll tell the driver to wait." Then he closed the door, leaving William to the task.

Shaking his head at his friend's sophomoric behavior, William dumped the coins on the carriage bench and began to sort them into matching piles. Pence, shillings, crowns.

Once that was complete, he started to tally, but before he was halfway through the stacks of smaller coins, his frustration stopped him cold. The bounty was a sizable one. This was his money, not Nigel's. If it was five hundred pounds of coin, that sum could easily cover the down payment for the Tower Hill property and buy him some time to raise the rest.

William clenched his right fist and took a swing in front of his face at the adversary that was loyalty. The money lost by Nigel, lost in games of chance born of irresponsibility, was now being rewarded with money won by gambling.

He'd taken a risk fighting in public, and won, but now had to forfeit the reward to bail his friend out one more time. And what assurances did he have that Nigel wouldn't end up in the same situation again?

William's boiling resentment was interrupted by a tapping on the glass. He looked up to find Nigel holding his pocket watch against the window. The behavior wasn't endearing and further fueled his growing resentment toward the situation. He ignored the faces his friend was making at the window and quickly finished the task. After scooping the winnings back into the pouch, he reached for the carriage handle.

When the door swung open, a thud sounded, followed by a few oaths before Nigel's head popped back into the carriage with an anxious expression.

William returned the pouch to his friend after he'd settled onto the bench. "You have enough to get out of debt."

Nigel combed his hands through his thick, blond hair, not looking any too settled. "With one bloke." Then he turned to the window and mumbled, "Maybe I'll be lucky at White's." Then he turned to William. "Can you lend me a few pounds?"

CHAPTER 8

$\mathcal{L}$illias gestured toward the steps leading up to *Boutique de Belle* the next afternoon. "It will be all right, Verity," she promised, tugging the petite, gloved hand of her sister and hauling her up the steps.

Verity walked like her shoes were heavy with lead. It had been almost two years since the she and her sister had entered the elite French dressmaker's shop. It was the last public place they'd visited with their mother before she died.

"Come on," Lillias urged, pushing gently on the small of her sister's back, while the valet held the door and tipped his hat as they came through. Now that they had their first formal invitation of the Season, there was much to be done in the next few days.

"*Bonjour, ntrez s'il vous plaît*" the modiste screeched, rushing to greet them.

A powerful concoction assaulted Lillias senses when the robust woman hugged her. Madam Pompadour smelled of expensive perfume and wig powder.

"And you." She released Lillias and grabbed Verity's chin like a fine piece of china, turning her face gently side to side as if looking for imperfections. "You, *ma petite*, have grown into a gem any gentleman would treasure." The woman's French accent was noticeable, but her English was good as British born.

Verity beamed and glanced at Lillias. All the trepidation had drained from her sister's face.

Stepping back from the strong perfume, Lillias said, "Madame Pompadour, you must know why we are here." Clasping her hands together, the proprietor let out another squeal. "You are coming out?"

Lillias couldn't help but get caught up in her enthusiasm and grasped her sister's hand. "Verity is coming out," she announced with pride in her voice.

The modiste's eyes went back and forth between Lillias and Verity, then finally an expression of understanding crossed her features. "Well of course you aren't coming out together."

"I promised Mother I'd look after my sisters," Lillias offered after the awkward silence lasted too long. Of course, the obligation of having Verity married by the end of the Season weighed heavy on her. What did she know of matchmaking? All of this was foreign to her.

"Of course you are," the dressmaker said smoothly. "*Suis moi*, we have all the colors of the rainbow. Let's get you matched."

No doubt getting the color match would be easier than the marriage match. Lillias sighed, her gaze moving past their hostess to the bolts of silk fabric and lace lining the wall behind her. She marveled at all the finery.

Just as she was about to ask about recommendations, Verity let out a squeal and strode toward a lemon-yellow silk bolt in the middle of the wall.

"This one," Verity said as if picking out a rose from a prized garden. Then she turned her head and grinned.

Lillias's heart filled with joy at seeing the glow of excitement in her sister's beautiful eyes. The St. Clair girls were blessed with fair skin, but each had her own unique combination of their parents' attributes. Verity had their father's dark hair and eyes. The yellow her sister had selected would look stunning on her.

"Lady Verity, you have wonderful taste in fabric. Although I love this color, few women can pull it off."

At that comment, Verity's generous smile dropped.

"Oh, *non, non, non,*" Madame Pompadour sputtered, rushing to Verity's side. "I didn't mean you, *chéri.*"

Grabbing the edge of the cloth, their hostess drew the shiny, sunshine-colored fabric across her sister's chest, then turned to Lillias for approval.

"She's right," Lillias agreed, not to make her sister feel better, but because it was true.

Madame Pompadour waved her two assistants over and, in a few moments, Verity was standing in front of one of the store's full length oval mirrors admiring the fabric as it was wrapped around her shoulders.

"This color is you, *la demoiselle,*" Madame Pompadour exclaimed with excitement. "No one has been able to wear that color near their face, only in the skirt." The proprietor stepped back and cocked her head side to side. With the plume of feathers jutting out the side of her powered wig, she looked like a peacock studying herself in the mirror behind Verity.

Her sister spun around, tugging most of the fabric with her. "What do you think, Lilly?" her sister asked with a voice that sought approval. "Will I look like lemon meringue pie?" Her sister's shoulders drooped and her expression turned sour.

"Absolutely not," Lillias said, indigently. "I was thinking you remind me of a delicate daffodil."

Verity smiled broadly and appeared relieved. "I know you'd be honest with me and tell me if I looked ridiculous."

Brutally honest, was more like it. Yes, her sisters could count on Lillias to tell them the truth whether they liked it or not. And in this instance, here at the dress shop, even though Lillias assumed Verity was still thinking about their mother and strained by the memories, she was certain her sister was moving past grief and looking toward a future as bright as the fabric.

No matter how much they argued or wanted to kill each other at times, Lillias would never let her sister look foolish. Verity might act foolish on her own accord. But over that, Lillias had less control.

"Your turn," Verity said with child-like glee.

Lillias's gaze drifted back to the wall of fabrics. The French shop owner had them set in groups by color, with the darkest on the far right and the palest on the opposite end. She was tempted by the lush fabrics. Now that Lillias had some money to cover the Season's expenses, she could splurge, but it was more important that Verity be the belle of the ball.

While the assistants began measuring Verity for her dress, Lillias headed to a black-and-white striped chaise lounge by the window. It matched all the curtains in the shop. Taking a seat, she stopped for a moment of reflection while she peered at her own in the window.

Delayed by almost two years, Lillias wasn't sure what eligible men might catch her fancy if she ever had a coming out. She wanted a love match, that was for certain, but she'd taken herself out of the social circles to provide emotional support to Verity and Rebecca. They'd been only fourteen and sixteen when their mother had passed, and the girls had been broken by the loss. The only thing that had kept Lillias going was her caring for them. Her dreams put on hold, her emotions numb.

It was her art that had saved her from wallowing in grief. And although stepping into the role of figure model at R.A. had been a risk, it helped her come alive inside again. To the outside world, she portrayed the proper role. But her rebellious streak loved that she could buck the social norms anonymously. Although she had no talent for the stage, she envied the freedom from obligation those artisans enjoyed.

"No, Lord Cavendish, it would be best if you waited outside," a high-pitched argumentative voice announced, breaking into Lillias's thoughts.

Turning toward the commotion, her eyes locked with Lord William's. *That William.* But he didn't acknowledge her. Instead, his attention swung back to the woman leading the way, a gorgeous creature who was making a fuss about his entrance.

"You'll need help carrying all the parcels," he insisted, continuing into the shop, looking like a thorn among roses.

The woman tsked loudly, ignoring him, as if her indignation would be enough to stymie his insistence. The proprietor dropped what she was doing to greet the brusque woman dressed in a maroon-colored velvet cape and matching skirt.

"*Bonjour,* Lady Sarah," the shop owner said in her enthusiastic breathlessness, rushing to take the woman's elbow and walking her to the counter as though she couldn't do it herself. "I wasn't expecting you until tomorrow."

"Well, my escort is indisposed tomorrow, so I came today," Lady Sarah said in a disgruntled tone, tossing a disgusted look over her shoulder at William.

"We," William said to the woman at his elbow.

Lady Sarah's back stiffened. "You don't need to speak French, the dressmaker understands English." And after mistakenly putting William in his place, she put her focus on Madame Pompadour. "I trust you'd have my gown ready." She paused, looking expectant. When there was an awkward silence, she put her hands on the hips and said, "Or I'll wait."

"*We* will wait," William said over her shoulder as if he loved irritating her.

Lady Sarah bristled again.

But Madame Pompadour patted her patron's cream, satin gloved hand. "Not to worry, my lady, I believe it's ready." Then her eyes darted around to find one of her assistants. "You'll want it fitted."

"Of course," Lady Sarah agreed with reticence in her voice.

Lillias was certain the fitting would allow whatever hadn't been finished to be completed now.

William glanced about the shop looking out of place. Even if he'd never been in a dress shop before, he'd be smart enough to understand this wouldn't be a quick errand.

When his eyes found hers again, Lillias dropped her gaze to the floor. She was sitting on the only reasonable piece of furniture in the entire shop. She hopped to her feet, not raising her eyes. But that was a mistake because she walked directly into him as she started away from the chaise.

"We have an uncanny way of running into each other," William said, grabbing her shoulders to keep her from toppling over.

Even if she meant to utter an apology, his pointed gaze took her breath away. Mind scrambling, Lillias attempted to register his meaning, R.A. classroom or the boxing match? Neither was the proper place for a lady.

Though she did remember his words to her days before. *Those eyes, I'll never forget them.* She wanted to be forgotten right now as she finally exhaled only to allow for a sharp inhale.

"I was just leaving," she mumbled under her breath without making eye contact, petrified that her face would be as red in color as it felt. Without consideration for manners, she made a beeline for the counter where Verity and Lady Sarah stood. The undertones in the conversation didn't sound congenial.

"I selected the yellow first," Lady Sarah declared as if she was a five-year-old fighting with a sibling, not an elegant socialite.

But Verity did not cower. No, she was pitched slightly forward, hands on her hips, with her proud chin leading the orchestration. "I don't care if you selected the yellow, one cannot lay claim on a color."

Lillias almost laughed out loud because of the look of terror on Madame Pompadour's face. The modiste stood between the two women like a referee in a boxing match, her feather plume making her look like a rooster cocking his head side to side.

"I will lay claim and I will demand exclusivity," Lady Sarah replied when the storekeeper did not intercede.

"Excuse me," a baritone sounding voice interjected.

Perhaps a voice of reason?

All heads swiveled to find William had joined the group of women at the counter. He took the elbow of Lady Sarah and dipped forward in an apologetic bow. "*We* will be back tomorrow."

"*We* will not be back tomorrow," Lady Sarah said through gritted teeth as William looked at her with an expressionless face.

"*We* will not be back tomorrow," William confirmed in his stoic stance. Then he gently, but firmly, took the shoulders of Lady Sarah and turned her to face the door.

When she stomped one foot, he put a hand to the small of

her back and gave her a little push, and he pulled her elbow at the same time.

"Well, I never," huffed Lady Sarah at his persistence as she was guided toward the door.

"I never should have come," was William's last words walking out as the valet held the door with a tip of his hat.

"Who was that?" Verity asked after the heavy door made a thud.

"That, my dear, is a force of nature you do not want to get on the wrong side of," the proprietor said, as if that explanation was enough.

CHAPTER 9

William shoved the Almack's invitation card into his front coat pocket. Strolling into the private studio at the R.A., he pondered his options. Could he skip the Season this year? The major reason for his return to London was to stave off the predators who were after the Tower Hill property. That was more than enough to keep him busy if he could raise the money.

But the building would be torn down next month by the *new* duke if he didn't have the funds, regardless of William's argument for the preservation of its architecture.

No doubt the man wanted to build a gambling establishment because he was a lousy gambler. That was according to William's father, who said the new Duke of Canterbury's weekly debts at White's were rumored to be the amount of all the club's total weekly winning payouts.

Gambling, however, would not be a solution for William. He'd witnessed the addiction and wanted no part of it. The R.A. contest awards would take place the week before the preservation of historic buildings exemptions ran out. Unless he came up with another way to fund the purchase of the building, winning the R.A. project was his only solution.

But then there was Nigel. From what he had recently learned of his friend's gambling habits, a large marriage dowry would help him get out of serious debt. It was a common solution among his peers. Nigel needed responsibility and accountability. Both would come in the form of matrimony. Better that than being knocked out at Crowley Down every week or getting in deeper trouble at White's.

For himself, William wasn't in a hurry to find a wife. Relationships were complicated.

Considering William was the second in line to the dukedom, his father gave him a ticket to procrastinate about his future. Residing in the shadow of his eldest brother, Alexander, the prodigal son, William received no pressure from his widowed father to marry. The last thing William needed right now was an engagement.

Taking the invitation out of his pocket and pressing it smooth in his hands, he read it again. 'Gentleman's voucher for Almack's. Deliver to Lord William Cavendish. Tickets for the balls on Wednesdays, April 1817. Hosted by the Duchess Dowager of Leeds, the Marchioness of Stafford, and the Countess of Cholmondeley. This ticket, issued by the patronesses, is not transferable. The ballroom will be appropriated for waltzing and the adjoining rooms for French and English country dancing. Signed, Lady Sefton.'

A cold chill raced up his spine and he shuddered imagining the ambitious mothers chasing him around a parquet floor while he did his best to hide in the shadows from them and their overly prim, debutante daughters.

"Ready?"

A voice from behind William snapped him out of his thoughts and he crammed the invitation back in his pocket. "I'm always ready," he said, turning to face his friend.

"To compete?" Nigel asked, rolling up his sleeves as if they'd bareknuckle it out to decide.

"Fists?" William feigned horror. "What happened to the gentlemanly way of fighting with words?"

"Oh, you'd rather battle wits than fists?" Nigel scoffed. "There's no money to be made in that." He paused and stuck his chin out. "You'll only set yourself up to be knocked down in a battle of wits."

"Is that a threat?"

"A challenge."

"For Shakespeare made a shilling or two from his wit and words."

"Taken a beating for them as well," Nigel offered, balling up his hands.

William batted them down when he said, "'I'll beat thee, but I would infect my hands.'" Then he dusted them back and forth with vigor. "*Timon of Athens*, Act Four, Scene Three."

Nigel puffed out his chest when he said, "'Me think'st thou art a general offence and every man should be thee.'" Following a salute off the brow, he said, "*All's Well that Ends Well*, Act Two, Scene Three."

"'More of your conversation would infect my brain.' *Coriolanus*, Act Two, Scene One."

With a snort, Nigel replied in a rather placating voice, "'Thou art unfit for any place but hell.' *Richard III*, Act One, Scene Two."

"Hell, yes, you two know your William Shakespeare, I'm impressed."

William spun around to find one of the R.A.'s student professors standing in the doorway to the studio, leaning on the jamb, looking amused.

The man started toward the two of them. "Hell could be subject matter for the contest," the instructor offered, rubbing his well-trimmed goatee with an absentminded gesture.

"There's no way in Hell I'm entering the contest," Nigel said, waking past the professor and through the doorway.

"'Thou artless, Hell-hating canker-blossom,'" William said to his back.

His friend froze mid-step and let loose a laugh that sounded like the Devil's. But that was all. He continued his way down the hall, the remnants of his laugh echoing into the studio.

The student instructor shivered. "That was a friend of yours?"

"It depends on the situation," William said, smiling. "You must be Devon?"

The R.A. student was lean and a few inches taller than William. And that was getting into some rarified air, for William was over six feet.

"*Oui*," the student answered back, taking William's hand and shaking it vigorously.

"French?" William whistled. "I didn't pick that up until now."

"My mother is." Devon laughed. "*Parlez-vous francais?*"

"*Nein, ich spreche Deutsch.*"

"Spent time in the army, I assume?"

"You too?"

Devon nodded. "French is helpful when we have guests from the Louvre visiting." Devon stroked his beard again. "Art is the life blood of the Parisian," the instructor said with absolute certainty, holding his fingers gently pinched together in the air as if smelling an imaginary rose.

"*Je ne sais quoi?*"

"*Oui*," Devon said, laughing, "and here I thought you said you didn't speak French."

William grinned, but then a rustle of skirts outside the hall had him dodging to the left to look past the student instructor into the hallway.

"Who was that?" William rushed past Devon to the door. Grabbing the sides of the frame, he leaned out into the hallway, scanning the corridor in both directions, like a conductor at the train station as the train pulls away. He cursed, then turned around and reentered the studio.

"Was it the Devil?" Devon asked.

"A she-Devil, perhaps," William replied, shaking his head. "I had a sense that we were being watched," he said. "But why would a woman be lurking in the R.A. corridors?"

"Spying on your entry for the contest?"

William shook his head and the rest of his body followed like a dog shaking off water. He had an eerie sensation that someone had been peering around the corner before he looked up. By then, all he caught was the sound of rustling fabric and the confirmation in the flash of purple taffeta.

The student professor had been in the way, blocking most of the view of the hallway, so by the time he'd made his way around the student instructor, any sign of the woman or sounds of her retreating had vanished. Poof, like a magic trick.

Devon laughed at William. "You look like you saw a ghost." The student professor moved toward the easel covered with an oil-resistant cloth, hiding and protecting the canvas underneath. "The competition is a few weeks away and you are as skittish as a feral cat."

"Wouldn't you be?" William wondered if the professor had ever entered.

Devon chuckled and began drawing back the canvas covering as he said, "It's safe to say there is a level of paranoia that runs rampant among the contestants, why in my—"

And then Devon stopped talking as the portrait William planned to enter was revealed. After a few beats, the professor finished with, "—my wildest imagination, I would never have expected this." Devon took a few steps backward, cornered his thumb and forefingers into a mock frame, then whistled.

While William waited for the professor to provide specific feedback, the silence was interrupted by a gasp. Pivoting around on his heel, William expected to find Nigel lurking in the doorway and demanding he drop his paint brush for another Crowley Down bout, but there was no one there.

William strode quickly into the hall, expecting to find someone spying, but it was empty. Again. Cursing softly under his breath, he walked back into the studio, sorting through possible candidates in his mind. The only option that made sense was a student competitor.

But it was Sunday. Classes weren't being held today. A student would need to have an appointment with a professor to be in the facility. Stymied, he walked toward Devon to ask his opinion. The professor was looking at William's work with a glass spectacle in one eye.

"Worthy enough to garner serious consideration," the professor mumbled as if he was alone in the room.

When William cleared his throat, Devon slowly spun around from studying the canvas, as if reluctant to turn away. After the professor rose to his full height, he peered at William through the thick glass monocle. The magnification must have been awkward because Devon immediately rocked back on his heels and dropped the tool, letting the chain around his neck catch the instrument.

"Yes?" The instructor stood waiting as if he expected a significant reason for the interruption.

William cleared his throat again. "Err," he hemmed. "I—Did you hear that gasp a few moments ago?" He needed confirmation that he wasn't imagining things.

"A gasp?" Devon's eyelids closed and opened methodically as if he could not believe he'd been interrupted for this kind of questioning.

"A sound like a woman breathing in quickly because she was surprised."

"I know what a gasp sounds like," Devon answered, as if he'd been insulted.

"Of course you do," William said, stalling. What could he say? Maybe he imagined the sound because he was paranoid?

The professor's eyelids closed and opened again as if he was using all his effort to keep from saying something derogatory. But instead of saying anything further, the student professor walked past him and shut the door. "There," he said and returned to the canvas. "This will keep us from distractions in the hallway."

Or imagining them. Why hadn't William shut the door after the purple taffeta had flashed by earlier? Maybe he half expected Nigel to return.

"This nude is exquisite."

"She is, isn't she?" William answered, gazing at his work as if the nude was in the room.

After a long period of silence, William's attention shifted back to the assistant professor, who had his monocle to his right eye again and was studying William's brush strokes. It wasn't finished. The model hadn't shown up yesterday, and Beauchamp had them painting peaches in a basket again.

William needed one more hour with her at least. One more look at those luscious curves. What Beauchamp would call her anatomy of form. He'd only used the sketch from class for the base of his composition. The pose the nude struck on his canvas was never one she sat for in class. No, this one was crafted from pure imagination. His.

And because the spy had seen it, he was certain the model would never return. Both women had to be one in the same, with a love for the color purple.

Outrage and shock. The two emotions whirled inside Lillias as she walked briskly down the corridor of Somerset House on her way to the gallery to meet Professor Beauchamp.

Gulping in mouthfuls of air, she couldn't get enough, as if she'd risen to the surface of the water after being held under too long.

She had only a quick glimpse of William's work. Then she'd heard voices and had recognized his. Without thinking, she had walked to the doorway expecting— What had she expected? To say hello? To apologize for punching him in the nose? To ask who Lady Sarah was to him? Although she shouldn't care.

When she did discover it was William in the student studio, she'd rushed off, not wanting to be caught spying. But she'd been intrigued by his entry, so she'd circled back, hoping to find it uncovered on the second pass.

And that was when he may have seen her. And she had seen herself. She was his entry. Irony and the calamity all wrapped into one.

Tears were pooling in the corners of her eyes, threatening to cascade down her cheeks. She hadn't cried since Mother had died. She had to lead by example and show her sisters she was mature enough to provide guidance and emotional support.

But now she was facing failure. A man who was dashing, dreamy, and not a duke, had no reason to keep her from ruin.

She'd gathered enough from her own father's reaction. A Cavendish would have no reason to protect her identity. Not that her name would be on the entry, but any woman worthy of social standing would recognize her from the rendering.

He'd captured her unique eye color.

And Lillias's social standing could not be tainted.

Not yet. Not before Verity and Rebecca were married off. Lillias's reputation only mattered when it impacted those she loved.

If only her mother were alive. She would know what to do. What would she suggest?

Steal it?

After Lillias turned down the last corridor leading to the gallery, she began to consider it. Her lips twitched. The Royal Academy had guards. Around the clock. But she had access and she was a desperate woman. Desperation could lead the way.

Yet, as she strode toward the gallery a wave of reason washed over her. How could she add thief to a resume that included figure modeling and expect not to be ruined by either?

"There you are."

Startled, Lillias froze as if she'd been caught stealing. It took her a moment to grasp it was Professor Beauchamp and not the guard who had spoken to her.

When she faced the instructor, his expression was filled with concern.

"Are you all right, Lilly? You look like you did when you fainted in the classroom." The professor straightened the thick-lensed glasses on his nose and peered at her keenly.

"Of course, I'm fine, Professor. Winded. That's all. From the walk to the gallery."

"From the front door?" The instructor squinted and scrunched up his nose when he stared past Lillias to the entry behind her, which was clearly visible from where they were standing.

Lillias couldn't lie but offered a truthful and reasonable explanation. "I arrived early and took myself on a short tour but lost track of the time until one of the student professors provided me with the particulars, and then I had to rush." She forced a pleasant smile and glanced briefly at the unmoving guard by the entrance before she asked, "Have you been waiting long?"

"No, I'd been conferring with another student of mine who left about twenty minutes ago to work on his contest entry. Perhaps you remember him, Lord William Cavendish?"

When Lillias didn't respond the professor added to the description as if she needed her memory jogged, "You know, the student who saved you from the burning classroom?"

She feigned delayed recognition when all she really needed was an extra moment to regain her composure before she asked her next question. "Did you see his work?"

"No, I'm leaving the actual critiquing to one of my student professors," he told her, but he said it in such a way as if he'd find the task beneath him.

Lillias forced another smile but was relieved at the moment. Until she could figure out how to steal the painting, she needed to keep anyone else from seeing it.

"If you aren't tutoring any students, how is it that you've set an appointment with me today?"

"Technically, you are not one of my students. You are not enrolled in the school."

"Why are you willing to help me?"

"Your mother."

"My mother?" There was an awkward pause until Lillias said plainly, "You know my mother is dead."

The professor's cheeks reddened. "I apologize if I'm making a mess of this." He took out a handkerchief and wiped his brow as if the entire meeting was uncomfortable for him. But he had been a friend of the family for years and had called her Lilly even after she was too old to be called that.

He held out an envelope. It was sealed with a wax stamp she recognized. She hesitated to take it.

"Your mother," he blurted out, "asked me to look after your artistic interests, and to give you this when the time was right."

Lillias took the envelope. A message from her mother, like a gift from the other side?

After another awkward stretch of silence, she looked up to find Professor Beauchamp waiting patiently.

He nodded to the guard. "He's our chaperone, but if you'd like a few moments to yourself to read the missive, I can step out." He started to turn toward the doorway as if she'd already given him permission.

She blinked a few times. The envelope almost tingled in her trembling fingers. Of course, she wanted privacy, but she also didn't want to wait for her family friend to leave the gallery before she could read her mother's message.

"I'm sure she'd like for you to hear it," Lillias offered, then motioned to the professor to follow her. She walked them in the other direction, away from the guard. When they were out of earshot she nodded to the envelope. "She entrusted this to you."

Lillias carefully tucked a fingernail under the bottom of the wax to preserve the seal and her mother's correspondence. After slipping out the stationery, she unfolded it and took in a deep breath. She glanced at the professor before she began to read.

Dear Lilly,

You've been in charge of the girls for a while now and I'm certain you've taken good care of them, but there's something else you must do for me.

With my days running short, I reached out to Professor Beauchamp, insisting he find a way for you to enter the R.A.'s international contest.

I know it's not easy for women to be taken seriously in the arts, but times need to change, and you are strong enough to lead that change.

Don't give up, no matter how difficult the competition. I'm rooting for you.

Love always,

Mother

Lillias still wasn't going to cry. She'd held the tears back this long and was determined to make it through the appointment with Professor Beauchamp without letting the dam break. If she was going to have the backbone her mother expected her to have to compete, then sentimentality needed to be set aside. It was time for courage, cunning, and perhaps cheating, if necessary.

She looked up from the letter to find the professor's gaze searching her face, the corners of his eyes crinkling sympathetically. He appeared moved by her mother's letter and no doubt felt a sense of responsibility in carrying out her wishes, even if they were out of the ordinary. He'd already been kind enough to arrange for the modeling to help her, without asking any questions, and was supportive of her decision when she backed out of the commitment.

"Are you ready?"

She nodded, filled with renewed purpose and a sense of obligation, as if this were her mother's last request of her, beyond helping her sisters. The letter hadn't been about her wishes for Lillias to find a husband or become a duchess, but about encouragement, urging Lillias to follow her artistic passion. And her mother had given her an ally in Professor Beauchamp.

"Let's begin," he said softly, and pointed toward the back of the exhibition room.

The sky-lit gallery was flooded with light. The sun shone through a ring of lead-lined windows which formed a halo at the top of the ceiling. But the democracy of the sun's attention was not equal. One side of the gallery was draped in shadows, while the opposite wall was showered by the sun's natural golden glow.

The far center wall entertained splashes of both light and shadow. But all three walls, regardless of the light, were covered with grand framed creations from floor to ceiling.

"This is the winners' gallery," Beauchamp said with a tinge of pride in his voice. The professor pointed to the sunny side of the room. "These masterpieces on this wall are winners from 1811 to 1816. They don't always reside here. Many belong to the British Museum or are displayed in private collections. But every year the R.A. commissions the winning entries return for the summer exhibition and most find their way back on these walls."

Lillias was humbled by the grandeur before her as she walked over to the wall bathed in soft streaks of light. The beams cut across the canvases, caressing the masterpieces and bathing them in a honey-colored glow.

Most of the winning entries were landscapes, popular in the day. As her eye traveled left to right, then down, one row to the next, like reading an extravagant picture book, she found an occasional hunting dog or lovely portrait, but not one nude. The masterful strokes were evident and unique for each piece. Not one was like another, yet there was a quality to each that unified the group. *Excellence.*

Lillias strolled to the middle wall with her hands behind her back, as if she didn't trust herself, fearing she might reach out to touch one of the masterpieces unconsciously. She was aware of Professor Beauchamp trailing behind her, but he kept silent as if he wanted her to absorb the artwork without editorial input.

The more she studied the winners, the more doubtful she became about her own abilities. "They are all so marvelous," she muttered. "Oh, Professor, how can I compete with this?" she asked, turning to face him and extending her arms out as if to encompass all that hung in the winners' gallery.

"You will because you won't let your mother down," Beauchamp said pointedly.

"But how can I enter when I'm a woman?"

"Let me worry about that for now. We've had women enter before."

Lillias gasped, then covered her mouth with a gloved hand, hiding the little smile that began to form.

"It was never in the papers or common knowledge. The art world is a secretive one, Lillias. You must be willing to buck restrictions, and never apologize for what you do for the sake of art."

Whether it was the challenge of rebellion or the intoxication of Beauchamp's invitation, Lillias was certain her mother's invitation from the grave and her desperation to save herself and family from potential ruin, would be enough to let her consider it. Now what she needed was a cup of hot tea and a co-conspirator.

"What time is it, Professor?"

"Hmmm," the instructor murmured as if he'd awakened

from a deep sleep, but at the same time studying one of the winning masterpieces in front of them. "What did you say?"

"The time." Lillias didn't want to appear impatient, but she was expecting Finneas with the carriage at half past two.

The professor's eyes regained focus and he peered at his now open pocket watch. "A few minutes before half past two," he said in his professorial tone, like a lecture was about to end. "Yes, I have another meeting," he added, snapping his timepiece shut. "Let me escort you to the front entry." He peered at Lillias through his thick, smudged glasses. "Shall I call a carriage?"

Lillias shook her head. "My butler should be waiting but thank you." She hesitated, then gestured with her arm in a sweeping arc at the grandeur before them in the gallery. "Where do I begin?"

"With a blank canvas and a spark. Reach into your heart for an image or a person who moves you. It can be helpful if it's someone or something you know well."

As the professor guided her to the front entrance, he chatted about some of the guiding principles of portraiture, much of what he had covered in the two lectures when she'd posed for his class. Helpful, but not exactly what she'd hoped for.

She had much to consider. Winning the R.A. contest would aid the family's finances and perhaps set her up for a life on her own once her sisters were married, a small house in the country and an art studio.

Now she'd need a plan to keep her biggest rival from displaying his artwork and thwarting her efforts. For that, she'd need an accomplice. She knew just the person to ask.

CHAPTER 11

*V*erity was in the carriage when Finneas arrived to collect Lillias, a perfect coincidence. So instead of heading straight home, because she had a potential ally in her middle sister, Lillias insisted Finneas take them to her favorite tearoom, Gunter's on Berkley Square.

While Verity chatted about the first Wednesday Almack's ball where she'd make her debut, Lillias tried to tamp down her rising animosity for a talented aristocrat who was taking more risks than his social station should allow.

After the two of them were seated at the last open table in the tearoom, and had been served, Lillias did her best to listen to Verity's discourse on the appropriate way to approach the dance floor with a suitor, courtesy of the dowager countess who'd come to visit yesterday.

Lillias's stomach was growling, making it easy for her to let Verity lead the conversation while she focused on a second scone already covered in blackberry jam. After she added the sweet cream, she took a bite of the satisfying treat to keep from muttering sarcastic commentary.

But after she finished the second scone and had topped it

off with her favorite tea, she sat her cup down with consternation. It was her turn to lean in. "The Earl of Devonshire has a painting of me."

Verity didn't appear shocked, nor did she miss a beat when she replied, "You consented to sit for his art class."

"I don't have any clothes on."

"You are nude?" Verity asked loudly enough for a few heads to turn their direction.

"Keep your voice down, please," she hissed, heating up like the air over her teacup. Then glancing over her shoulder, Lillias met the gaze of Lady Remington, who waved at them with enthusiasm, a friend of their Aunt Elizabeth's. But she needed to avoid socializing, so she nodded obligingly, then turned to face her sister again, holding her temper the best she could.

Verity looked up from studying her teacup and asked, "Do you feel violated?"

That was it. *Violated.* The Earl of Devonshire had taken liberties. He had filled in the gaps with his imagination. She nodded at her sister and bit her lip to stop the tears that threatened to invade. A feeble sounding, "Yes," finally escaped her lips. "I didn't have time to tell you in the short carriage ride here. It wasn't the type of thing you chat about, like the weather." Lillias sniffed and took the tearoom linen napkin to her nose. When her attention settled back on her sister, Verity was looking at her with a grave expression.

"Oh, I'm not crying," she defended her action. "The tea is making my nose run." It was the truth and if her eyes did leak any in the minutes before they were on their way back to Woodbeck House, she'd use the excuse again.

When one of the servants made a stop at their table and offered to refresh their pots, Lillias nodded, rotating the handle of hers toward the girl so she could grab it.

"Chamomile for me and orange ginger for Lady Verity."

Once the servant was out of earshot, Lillias started up again. "Verity, I'm serious. He did take liberties." She took in a shaky breath. It was better to have a conversation about the artwork here. Even though there were others nearby, they were far enough away not to be heard if they kept their voices low. It would be worse if Rebecca, her father, or one of the servants overheard them.

Verity was like any other sibling, competitive and suspicious. But in times like these, she could also be a best friend.

Before Lillias began again, she glanced around the tearoom. When they'd entered around three o'clock, it had been the peak hour. But as it was a Sunday, most of the ladies had scurried off to run their households, giving her a better opportunity to share some of the sordid details.

"I only had a brief look at the portrait when I inadvertently passed the earl's student studio." She sighed but willed herself to get on with it. "The glimpse of the canvas was brief, but it was enough for me to gather he'd used my body to paint a woman lying on a grand bed"—She took in a sharp breath before she finished her description—"totally nude with her legs apart."

"With her legs apart?" Verity asked loudly.

Before she thought better of it, she kicked Verity's calf under the table.

"Ouch," her sister ground out, reaching under the table to rub the injured area. "You didn't have to do that."

"Sorry," Lillias said quietly. "When you don't keep your voice down, I need to give you a reminder. Gossip can be worse than the truth."

"You always find a way to remind me to stop a bad habit when you are offended by one," Verity said. "My shin or my toes take the brunt of your displeasures."

"One way to impart the importance of a good memory."

"As if you owe me any favors," Verity bit out.

"Now that we are totally off the subject, let's get back to it," Lillias said, growing serious again.

Verity looked around her, apparently earnest about being more discreet. "How exactly were you posed?" Verity asked, her voice lower this time.

Lillias considered the question for a moment. She'd been so shocked at seeing the portrait of her naked body, she had to think about it before answering.

"It was as if I was in the thralls of ecstasy with an imaginary partner," Lillias finally said. "I was raised on my elbows, head thrown back, hair loose and cascading around my shoulders, with my body perpendicular to the top and bottom of the frame."

"And you perpendicular to your imaginary partner" — Verity paused and looked around once more before she finished—"who was on top of you?"

Lillias let out a little gasp. "Young lady, how would you have any idea?"

Verity's cheeks reddened before she said, "Servant's gossip. I certainly didn't read about it in Austen's latest novel."

Lillias let her penchant to reprimand pass and pinched her lips into a straight line before she spoke. "I hate to admit it, but it does seem you are spot on. I was so shocked—" She stopped when she noticed the servant on her way back to their table with the two pots of tea. When her gaze shifted back to Verity, she caught her sister snatching the last scone from the serving tray.

Thief. "You already had three of the six," Lillias said sourly. "They were supposed to be divided equally." She crossed her arms and pouted for a moment.

Then the servant swept up to the table and carefully set one of the pots down while she posed with the other.

"Chamomile?"

Lillias nodded and held up her empty cup. "Yes, I'm calm like this tea," she said to the servant.

The young girl smiled politely, before she switched pots and started pouring the other tea into Verity's cup.

"Yes, and I'm sweet and fiery like my brew," Verity said after the liquid was to the brim and the servant quietly left.

Verity held her cup in a toasting motion. "To calm and fiery, may they always balance each other out," her sister said triumphantly, then blew across the top of the hot tea before she took a tentative sip, looking across the rim at Lillias.

"The pose of the nude in the painting is scandalous to be sure," her sister said in a soft voice.

Lillias blinked rapidly. Talking this out with Verity wasn't as cathartic as she'd hoped.

"You can't see your ah, well, unmentionables, right, because you are facing toward your imaginary partner?"

"The artist depiction of me," Lillias said, correcting her sister. She'd never imagined herself in that position. She hated to admit it, but the image thrilled and frightened her at the same time. Taking a sip of her tea, Lillias allowed her eyes to focus on something else, as her imagination made her as boiling hot as the liquid in the cup.

"Your face is turning red."

"Yours did too when you took your first sip from the fresh pot."

Her sister set down her cup. "You are on your fourth sip."

"Are you counting my sips?"

"Sisters are known to do odd things," Verity said and quirked a brow at her.

Lillias retaliated. "Perhaps it's because you are an odd sister?"

Verity laughed at Lillias comment, her outburst so infectious she couldn't help but join in.

When they finally settled down, Verity's expression drew

serious again. "Let make sure I understand," she said, sitting up taller in her seat, as if that would help. The art student, who appears infatuated with you, plans to enter the R.A's contest with a nude painting of your likeness in the throes of having sex with an imaginary partner?" She stopped and waited for a response with both eyebrows raised high.

Lillias sighed and nodded before she said, "That about sums it up."

"How did he know what your face looked like when you were wearing a mask?"

That's the same question she'd been asking herself, but she imagined the man was as smart as he was educated. "I suppose my eyes gave me away," Lillias admitted. "If I hadn't met Lord Cavendish at the fights or spoken to him at Madame Pompadour's boutique, perhaps he wouldn't have —" A horrible realization took over Lillias. "He must know who I am."

Verity pondered that for a moment, but since Lillias had said it out loud, it appeared to be the only logical explanation.

"Was the face of the nude in the painting a strong resemblance to you?"

Lillias nodded solemnly. "As if I'd posed for him at his private quarters with no mask."

"There's only one thing we can do then." Verity paused until she could lean in over her edge of the table, her eyes as big as teacup saucers. "Steal it."

Lillias slapped her hand over her mouth to keep her from laughing out loud. Her sister, God bless her partner-in-crime, had come to the same conclusion.

CHAPTER 12

"The modiste's shop is on the way," Lillias informed her sister once they were settled into the carriage. "Finneas will return us to Woodbeck House in plenty of time for dinner with our aunts."

"Your detour to the teahouse was not in my plans," Verity said. "It's too late to stop by the modiste's."

Lillias pulled out the timepiece she kept attached to her chatelaine. "What do you mean? Madame Pompadour's shop will be open for another hour."

Verity scrunched up her nose as if she'd tasted something foul before she said, "This is precisely the time we could run into that woman I want to avoid."

Lillias tuned out the rest of what her sister said because her mind was formulating a plan to steal William's contest entry. It would be easier to destroy it, but she could never damage another artist's creation. Instead, she'd need to find a way into the earl's student studio. No doubt Professor Beauchamp would have a master key. Perhaps she could find a way to insist she pick up the supplies he'd promised and . . .

The carriage ground to a halt before her mind cleared

and she found the doorman reaching for her hand while she was remembering why they were stopping.

"My lady, are you coming in?"

"Of course we are coming in," Verity all but shouted in her ear. Her sister hopped on the side of the bench next to Lillias, almost shoving her out of the carriage, scooting across it and nearly into her lap.

"I can't climb over you," Verity huffed, her periwinkle blue skirts bunched up in her fisted hands. "Get out of the way or get out," she ordered.

"We're not hunters chasing a fox. What's your hurry now?" Lillias held up a black-gloved hand in Verity's face and extended the other to the doorman. "Thank you," she cooed to the servant, who was too handsome for his position. If the man hadn't been standing right at the carriage door to assist, she was sure her sister would have set a boot to her ass to hurry her up.

Once they reached the steps of *Boutique de Belle*, Verity turned and glared at Lillias. "I told you I was in a hurry because I do not want another encounter with Lady Sarah," her sister hissed. "I will not defend the purchase of my ball-gown again." Then she took a half turn toward the door but hesitated.

Standing behind Verity, Lillias tamped down the wrinkles in her sister's overskirt with a good shake, while the doorman grasped the shiny brass lever and opened the entrance to *Boutique de Belle*.

Lillias was ready to give her sister a good shaking too if she didn't stop her demanding attitude, but Verity finally crossed the threshold into the shop with Lillias shooing her in like an overdressed shepherd.

"*Bonjour, mademoiselles.* You both look ready for the marriage market today," Madame Pompadour gushed. Her plume of feathers in rusts, browns, and gold bobbled about on her fashionable hat, making her look like a strutting pheasant.

Smothering a giggle with her gloved hand, Lillias turned her head as if hiding a cough, not wanting her amusement to offend.

"Is it ready?" Verity asked Madame Pompadour before she gave her an appropriate greeting.

But Lillias bobbed a quick nod before she said, "Translation, did Lady Sarah come in yet?"

The modiste tried to hide her consternation but didn't dally. She quickly strode through the black-and-white striped curtains to the sewing room before answering over her shoulder. "I told Lady Sarah her dress would not be ready until six o'clock, closing time. You are not the only ladies in the *ton* who rearrange their schedules to avoid Lady Sarah."

When Verity released her scrunched up shoulders, Lillias wanted to tease her sister about her impatience. But she thought better of it when the door opened and Lady Sarah strode through it like a queen, pausing at the entry as though she needed a royal trumpeter to announce her arrival.

Verity swore under her breath and her spine went erect, the air around them thrumming with dread.

"You again?" Lady Sarah ground out with a sneer directed at Verity.

This could get ugly. Lillias put her protective nature on high alert. "Where is your chaperone?" she asked Lady Sarah, creating a distraction to give Verity a moment to gather her wits.

"I beg your pardon. You are not my social monitor."

"Even if you begged, I wouldn't give you my pardon," Lillias scoffed, crossing her arms and stepping up to the pretty but verbally lethal Lady Sarah.

The pompous noblewoman gasped and took a step back. "Well, I never stop—" the blonde sputtered.

"Stop assuming you are more important than other people?" Lillias finished the sentence for the stammering blonde.

Lady Sarah gave Lillias an aghast look and her lips flapped open and closed like those of a fish out of water. Then the socialite turned to the modiste looking for retaliation.

Before Madam Pompadour could respond or Lillias had time to lob another verbal strike at Lady Sarah, the front door burst open. All eyes turned to find Lord William, *that William*, casually strolling in.

The modiste appeared relieved and rushed to greet him, the feathers atop her head moving in a comical fashion. "Lord Cavendish, I was going to say to Lady Sarah that she's an hour early for her fitting." Madame Pompadour pulled out her pocket watch and tapped on it. "We are just a few minutes past five."

"Good woman, I do not doubt your timepiece. Rest assured its measurements are still accurate." William grinned and bowed, his hat almost magically rolling down his arm.

Madame Pompadour tittered with nervousness. The proprietor's laugh was so infectious it had Lillias, Verity, and even Lady Sarah smiling for a moment.

Before the mood shifted back to confrontational, however, William was at Lady Sarah's elbow. "It's my fault this time, Madame. I have an engagement with my friend Nigel, and I must be there by six o'clock."

Lady Sarah let out a loud huff, as if she was put out by her escort's priorities. But William's admission appeared to have smoothed the initial sting of Lady Sarah's abrasive actions.

"We aim to please and I do have your dress ready, my lady," she said to the noble woman with an exaggerated bow.

Lillias tsked under her breath. This irritating lady was not Queen Charlotte.

Then Madame Pompadour gestured to one of her assistants, and in moments, the blonde bully had morphed into an amiable aristocrat. No less snobby, but no longer confrontational.

Once Lady Sarah had been ushered to the back, Verity was directed to the other side of the salon to a separate fitting area. Lillias was certain Madame Pompadour knew her client's idiosyncrasies inside and out. Where else did the well-heeled *ton* get to share their gossip but inside *Boutique de Belle?*

With all the fuss over fabric, and egos slightly bruised from the verbal battle, Lillias had almost forgotten about William until she turned from the counter and barely avoided a collision. Her gaze shot upward. "My, you're tall."

"Is that your excuse for running into me twice in the same place?" He rubbed his nose purposely. "But I know not to cross you." He gave a snort before he said, "You have a deadly right hook."

His reminder of her faux pas made Lillias blush. It wasn't any average blush. No, this rushed through her veins, burning her insides along the way. She was without words. At least any that would be coherent. Instead of forming neat and orderly in her mind so they could be presented, they spun in a vortex inside. She had so many questions.

"Look, this is embarrassing," he admitted, shuffling his feet the way he had when Professor Beauchamp had berated him over fraternizing with her in class. "But I must have a word with you." His eyebrows drew into a serious line and he pointed toward the striped chaise lounge where they'd sat a few days ago.

After the short, silent walk there, Lillias settled herself at the far end of the furniture, expecting him to sit on the other end, but instead, he stood looking down at her as she gazed up at him in anticipation.

"Perhaps we'll both be in attendance at the Almack's Ball this Wednesday?" he asked tentatively, as if he didn't know how to start the conversation.

"Do you have an invitation?"

"Do you always ask a question instead of answering one?" She blinked rapidly.

"My apologies, I must be out of practice," Lord William said, staring at his feet.

"In being charming?"

His gaze shot up immediately and instead of displaying a shocked expression, he appeared amused with her impertinent comment. "Small talk." He paused and wrung his hands. "I seemed to have lost my grasp of it." He looked out the window behind the chaise, seeming to search for words outside. In the awkward silence her attention was drawn to a pin he wore on his lapel.

He's a Freemason?

"You see, I'd like to spend time with you."

Immediately forgetting about her discovery, it was Lillias's turn to be to be flustered. "What about Lady Sarah?"

"Forget about her. I don't care what she thinks."

Lillias put her hand up to her throat and held back a gasp.

"That came out wrong," William admitted, his face turning red. "What I wanted to tell you . . ." He paused as if it was difficult to articulate. "I remember how we met. I'll never forget those eyes."

Lillias's heart began to pound. She breathed in short gasps, as if the air couldn't get in quickly enough.

What could she say? *I'm ruined.*

* * *

LILLIAS WAS STARING up at William with those unforgettable dark—damn, they were purple—eyes. Lady Lillias St. Clair turned lily white before she turned rose red. Then her mouth clamped shut, mind whirling, no doubt at his words.

The query had the desired effect and, depending on her reply, what his next move would be. His sister would be tied up for a while in her corset, literally, giving him time with this so-called lady.

As he watched her struggle, like a fighter with the wind knocked out of her, she finally took in a big gasp and said, "Why thank you." Then she promptly snatched a fan from her reticule and began beating it furiously in front of her face adding, "That is quite a bold compliment from a gentleman such as yourself."

Not missing a beat, William replied with some panache, "I'm sure you've heard it before. As remarkable in color as they are." *Touché.*

She paused, then lowered her lashes, and replied in a sticky, sweet tone, "You took me off guard. We are not that well acquainted and it rung with familiarity."

Ring the bell. One round won by Lady Lilly. But William was ready for round two. "You remind me of a girl who posed for a figure class." Then he moved slowly like a fox stalking its prey to join her on the chaise. "You asked me about the R.A. competition when we met." He put his hand over his heart and closed his eyes for a moment, as if to give an apologetic pause before he opened them. "Forgive me if I thought you, she."

Lillias was either totally confused by his insinuation or a great actress. He'd put money on the latter, as she continued to fan herself as if it gave her more oxygen.

"I will forgive you." She took in another deep breath before continuing, "More for assuming a lady like me would find it permissible to pose for a class at the R.A."

Aha! I have her now. "I did not say anything about where the class was held."

He could have heard the proverbial seamstress pin drop in the shop. Once again, Lilly's face turned from white, to pink, to finally red. All the colors of a lily. But like a fighter, she stood up and put her hands on her hips, apparently not ready to lose this round.

"Well, I know enough about figure drawing that it must have been Professor Beauchamp's class."

"How would you know?"

Lillias stumbled back a step. But he would not ease up and was ready with punch number two. He stood and said in an accusing tone, "It must have been you. The instructor was Beauchamp."

Lillias stared at him before she snapped her fan closed, and her eyes began to tear. He expected her to cry but instead she wound her arm back like a champ getting ready to land a blow. And sure enough, like a boxer, she smacked the fan right into his gut. Then to add insult to injury, she stomped on his foot.

"I'll have you know Professor Beauchamp is a close family friend and he's been schooling me privately at home for years," she told him with a fury.

What?

"And furthermore, this conversation has made me extremely uncomfortable. It sounds like you are accusing me of indecent exposure."

When she spun away from him, his head began to spin.

Could I be wrong about her?

"Wait," he called out.

Lillias's back stiffened.

He took a step toward her but shook off the attempt to touch her shoulder lest she'd turn and give him a solid punch in the nose, which he was now thinking he deserved.

"Please accept my apology for the erroneous mistake." He held his breath. The last thing he wanted to do was ruin a relationship with a woman who he must woo to get her cooperation. He was not conceited, but conceded his good looks and accessible charm, although rusty today, could put most debutantes on notice. It was time to make Lady Lilly swoon.

"If we shadows have offended,
Think but this, and all is mended,
That you have but slumber'd here
While these visions did appear.
And this weak and idle theme,
No more yielding but a dream.
Gentles, do not reprehend:
if you pardon, we will mend:
And, as I am an honest Puck.'"

Lady Lillias turned slowly, every ounce of her appeared to be wrapped in the effort. The once clenched fists at her side were now relaxed. It was the only Shakespearean apology he knew by heart.

Once Lillias had fully turned, William found her expression soft, like the one he wanted to capture to finish his portrait. He struggled with his breath, now a bit erratic, stunned by the beauty in her expression and then she spoke.

"If we have unearned luck,
Now to 'scape the serpent's tongue,
We will make amends ere long;
Else the Puck a liar call;
So good night unto you all.'"

As if pulled by some unknown force toward her, he wanted to finish it and reached for her.

"'Give me your hands, if we be friends, And Robin shall restore amends.'"

They stood in silence, holding hands, for what seemed an

eternity until the moment was shattered by Lady Sarah's squawking voice. "Lord Cavendish? Where are you?"

Lillias glanced down at their jointed hands and pulled back immediately.

"It appears the woman who you said I should forget needs you." She began to walk away, but turned to add, "Regardless of my momentary lapse in judgment, do not confuse my actions with an acceptance of friendship."

Then Lillias turned on her heel, taking William's integrity with her.

Reeling from her icy farewell, he rubbed his stomach to alleviate the sting, but it was his character that had taken the beating. He hadn't counted on Lillias being a stubborn opponent with a lethal wit. This would be the last time he'd underestimate her.

CHAPTER 13

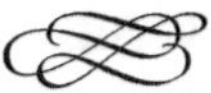

The house was full of frantic activity when Verity and Lillias finally returned to Woodbeck House. Finneas seemed flustered by their questions but had hastily informed them the Dowager Countess Elizabeth and Lady Emma would be expected at half past six for dinner.

Glancing at the grandfather clock in the hall, after receiving a quick bow from the butler for his leave, briskly for Finneas, Lillias spun in an about face and started toward the stairs instead of taking her usual tour to the library.

"Where are you going?" Verity called after her as if she really didn't have a clue.

Turning halfway around on the stairs, with one hand on the banister, Lillias pinched her face up and scowled at her sister.

When Verity shrugged her shoulders, Lillias huffed. *If only mother were here.* "Don't you remember the last time we dined with our aunts?"

"Oh!" Verity exclaimed. Apparently, that was all the prompting her sister needed for she rocked forward and ran up the stairs ahead of her.

Lillias chuckled when she spun back around and proceeded to her room. Although their aunts had arrived yesterday, it had been at least six months since the dowager and her sister had joined them for a formal dinner. Lillias shivered at the memory. But no matter how much the two had peppered their father with questions and insisted she give the girls up to their oversight, Lillias would be indebted to him for not giving in.

Shoving the day dresses out of the way, Lillias dug to the back of her closet, searching for the one that was waiting for such an occasion. But releasing it from the wardrobe quickly became a tug of war between tulle and taffeta.

While she was struggling with the dresses, her thoughts returned to her conversation with Verity on the way home from the dress shop, when she'd told her about the exchange with Lord William at the modiste's. They both had agreed something had to be done to remove the portrait from contest consideration. To Lillias's horror, Verity had suggested burning it. But even in her desperation, Lillias still couldn't destroy it. She needed to get her hands on the portrait and hide it from everyone. Perhaps she could find a spot for it deep in their attic behind all the forgotten and outdated furnishings.

Yet, as much as the interlude with William had disturbed her, something strange had taken place when he was quoting Shakespeare's *Midsummer Night's Dream*, one of her favorites. Even though she'd rebuked him after Lady Sarah had interrupted their private interlude, for a brief moment, Lord William Cavendish had become William Shakespeare.

In that moment, she'd been drawn to the aristocrat in the most unladylike way. Was she really a harlot posing as a lady? No doubt she had a penchant for parading around nude in her room. But shouldn't she be embarrassed for being comfortable exposing some of her figure in a public classroom? It was for the money. Or was it? Her cheeks burned with embarrassment. Without a mother providing a moral compass, perhaps she had broken hers?

Of course, her sisters teased her relentlessly about her infatuation with Shakespeare. But she considered his writings brilliant, beyond reproach. Not only was he a playwright, but a poet too. She'd read his sonnets with her governess, Lady Catherine, over several years of tutoring. And she'd convinced her if memorization was a skill that must be won over, Lillias would accomplish the task with something she loved rather than loathed.

Who wanted to know about Britain's wars with Scotland? Maybe the Highlanders? Although she'd never condone what the British did to them after the Battle of Culloden, she wouldn't find it useful to remember it all.

Lillias was solemn for a moment. Her mother had been unconventional when it came to the girls' education. She wanted them to be as smart as the men they married. Lady Catherine used to tell them she would make sure they were smarter. But neither Lillias nor Verity had tested that hypothesis, yet.

"Whatever are you up to, my lady?" Lillias let out a shriek.

"Oh, I didn't mean to frighten you," her maid, Irina, said in a meek voice.

Lillias let out a sympathetic chuckle. "I didn't hear you come in. Trying to fend for myself," she replied a little sheepishly without turning around, still expecting to triumph over the warring fabric.

"Then I would be out of a job," the woman said softly.

Lillias spun around quickly, ready with an apology, but the tangled dresses would not acquiesce and she was whipped back around toward the wardrobe.

Irina burst out laughing when Lillias let go of the tangled fabric and stepped out of the way.

"As you can see, Irina, your job is secure." Lillias let out a big sigh. "I don't know how I would put my clothes on if I couldn't get them out of the wardrobe to begin with."

Lillias busied herself shedding her day dress and slipping into a fresh chemise while her maid easily parted the dresses and eased out the dark green, lace frock. It didn't take long for her servant to turn Lillias out in a manner that would make her aunts proud. And in short order, she was downstairs entering the dining room, giving her father a peck on the cheek because no one else was in the room.

"My dear, you remind me of your mother. If I were no longer here, I know I could count on you to carry on."

Although the words were meant to be thoughtful, they also reminded Lillias of her mother's absence.

He was a handsome man, her father, and she'd asked him many times to sit for her. She wished to paint his portrait. But he'd said she shouldn't waste his time. As the eldest daughter of their new dukedom, he'd told Lillias she should be building their social alliances, not dallying with paints.

"I'm not ready for you to leave us, Father," she said, her throat tightening with the words.

He touched Lillias's cheek affectionately with the back of his hand and his usually aristocratic stance softened. He gave her shoulders a quick squeeze and tugged her into a fatherly hug. Then he released her before she could take in the full benefit, but he held on to her shoulders as he stepped back to assess her. "You should pass the test."

She knew what he meant. His dowager sister was known as the fashion authority of the upper set and no accessory was worn without notice or ensemble without commentary.

Lillias peeked around her father at the mirror behind him and her action prompted him to spin them around, tucking her under his shoulder with his arm around her waist. Lillias touched the emerald necklace at her throat that had been her mother's.

"You look beautiful, Lillias. It's time you find a man almost has handsome as me to take your hand."

"To take me off your hands," she joked, happy to have a playful moment with the Duke of Canterbury, who was most often too busy for her.

He chuckled too and spun her out of his embrace again. "Do you wonder why your aunts are coming tonight?"

"We come to visit even when we've been forgotten."

They both twisted around to find the dowager and her sister standing in the dining room entry, with Finneas behind them looking unsettled.

"They would not allow me to announce them, sir."

Lady Emma waved off the flustered butler. "We are family, Finneas. It's all right."

"We need no introduction," said the dowager countess, walking to the spot where she normally sat when she called. She waited for Finneas to stop fussing and pull out the chair for her.

It didn't take long for her father's good humor to fade as he made his way around the table to give his elder sister a peck on the cheek. She grumbled something under her breath Lillias could not make out, but it made her father do a double take. Then he worked his way over to Lady Emma, sitting at the countess's left, and he gave her homage as well.

"You are early," her father said, after he finally took his rightful seat at the head of the table.

Lillias took her cue to sit next to him, across from the dowager.

"You know better, Charles." She'd always called her father by his first name. The only person to do so. "If one is not availing oneself for dinner at least a quarter to the hour, then one is considered insolent and rude to their host and hostess," she bit out. Taking the duck-shaped napkin on the charging plate before her by the bill, the countess shook it out violently, then calmly spread the yellow linen cloth on her lap.

Lillias conquered a giggle before it escaped. She shuddered to think of the ramifications of her aunt catching her in anything less than a respectful countenance.

Before anyone else spoke, however, Verity came roaring around the door frame, screeching to a halt when it was clear company had arrived.

Unfortunately, Rebecca had entered at the same speed and ran into her sister, causing both to cry out. No oaths were uttered, but when the countess, in her stuffed, partridge topped hat turned to see what the fuss was all about, both girls were limping toward her.

Before she received them, she shot a perturbed glance at her father and said, "I distinctly see regimentation has fallen by the wayside here at Woodbeck House since my last visit." Then she accepted a kiss on each cheek from the girls and finished saying, with one raised gray brow, "I really thought they no longer needed a governess."

Rebecca wore an indignant expression as she took her seat next to Verity on the same side of the table as Lillias and said, "Aunt Elizabeth, we are too old for a governess. I can assure you our manners are quite refined."

The dowager countess harrumphed and glanced at Lady Emma. "We shall see."

Lillias's youngest sister's cheeks colored as she peered at the duck-shaped napkin before her, a cue to Lillias it was time to lead and prove to their father's sisters there was no need for a governess.

Reaching for the bill as the dowager had done, Lillias snapped it out, then gently laid it on her lap. Shortly after Rebecca followed suit, appearing relieved. Then after a gentle sideways kick to Verity under the table, her daydreaming sister also complied.

"Well," the countess said, with a nod to her father, "at least we are off to a good start."

Barely a beat went by before the first course was brought into the dining room and set on the serving board. Lillias's father had a capable staff and a fine French cook, purportedly trained by one of Prince Regent's own chefs.

While the dowager watched the head waiter ladle soup into her bowl, Lillias pointed to the spoon on the left making sure both Verity and Rebecca took note. It was difficult getting Verity's attention. She was always distracted, but Lillias had suggested they both keep an eye on her for cues.

It wasn't that the girls hadn't learned the finer points of dining, it was that they rarely practiced them. At the formal table there were two sets of everything—forks, knives, spoons, and glasses, even two for wine. If the girls didn't remember to work from the outside in, her aunts might insist on a governess. It would be difficult to finance ball-gowns and new hired help. As far as the *ton* was concerned, the ink of her father's dukedom was barely dry, and Lillias had the challenge of keeping up appearances or risk Verity's future.

Once they all had the proper spoon in hand, her sisters waited for the countess to scoop up the turtle soup and take the first taste.

Blowing over the top, the dowager happened to glance up to find them all eying her. A stern expression crossed her features before she leaned back and said, "You do not need to stand on ceremony for me, go ahead and eat."

After a few moments of silence, followed by incessant slurping sounds, it was her father that finally started the conversation again.

"Elizabeth, you are looking well this evening. I must say the country air agrees with you."

The dowager countess uncharacteristically blushed. The old bird could be flattered.

"Charles, the country is good for most ailments, but I must say I never wish to miss a Season." She announced it to the room as if that was the great reveal of the evening.

Her father turned to Lillias. "As I was saying when your aunts arrived, my sisters are here to help plan for the Almack's Balls."

The Almack's Balls? Lillias's heart sank. She hadn't asked, but she'd assumed her father would escort them to the Wednesday balls, at least at Almack's. No matter the good intentions, her aunts would be interfering.

"Girls, I must tell you. It's important you have my assistance at these balls." Lady Elizabeth glanced over to her sister. "Emma will agree with me. We'll each have one of you in our charge."

They will spoil this.

Without taking a breath after swallowing the last of her soup, the dowager countess expounded. "Every last detail is important, girls," she told them in a superior voice, nodding vigorously, making the stuffed bird on her hat appear to be pecking.

Lillias held her breath to keep from laughing as her aunt continued, "From the order of how you are announced when entering, to the side of the ballroom where you take your reprieve between dances, to whether or not you drink lemonade or punch."

All unimportant to Lillias. She looked to her father in the hope that he might insist he escort them, but he'd taken up a conversation with the wine steward about which variety would complement the ragout of beef now being served.

The grand dame set down her spoon. "Appearances are

everything, girls," she said with conviction. "You aren't attending an Almack's ball only to impress future suitors, you are also there to impress the women: the dowagers, mothers, aunts, and sisters." The countess twisted toward Lady Emma and gave her wide-eyed conspirator look, as if wanting to recruit her confirmation.

"I must agree with Elizabeth," her Aunt Emma said immediately, and nodded, but her eyes sparkled with mischief. "But when I was your age, it was a lot simpler. We were promised off while we were in the cradle and swaddling." She grinned and tried not to make eye contact with her sister again. "Saved everyone a lot of pomp and circumstance," she said, finishing with a giggle.

The dowager countess let out a huff and turned away from her sister as if she hadn't said a word. "As I was saying, appearances are everything." Then she eyed her sister and said emphatically, "Today."

The dowager turned to their father, piercing her meat, saying, "A duke must be visible in the *ton*, he has more important matters than attending balls."

Verity blurted out, "But who will approve of my suiters?"

The dowager gave a low, throaty laugh, almost manly, but the register of her voice was always close to masculine. "Don't worry about the suitors," the dowager said, puffing up her chest and sitting taller in her seat, "we've already made our approved list."

Verity almost choked on her food and covered the slip with a cough, then glanced at her father with an expression of alarm.

Lillias was trying to manage her emotions as she always did when her aunts were present, but her blood pulsed through her veins and her neck stiffened. Swallowing hard, she bit back the concern in her voice as she attempted to sound lively. "I can't wait to hear more."

Lillias didn't expect her remark to produce immediate results, but as the main course was being cleared, the dowager was quick as a magician with sleight of hand and produced what appeared to be the list. Shaking the paper, as if it would stiffen the parchment into a sturdier document, the dowager looked over the top of the list.

With a slight adjustment to her spectacles, the countess began, "For you, Lillias, the Duke of Beaufort, the Earl of Darlington, soon-to-be duke. His father is in failing—"

"Aunt Elizabeth, please stop." Lillias hated to interrupt, as it was rude, but she had to set her aunt's course straight. "You must have misunderstood. This is not my Season." She glanced at her sister to reassure her. "It's Verity's."

"Nonsense. It's a matter of birth order. You must both come out."

CHAPTER 14

Wednesday finally came, filling Lillias with hope and dread. It had been three days since her aunts had arrived and it was three days too long. Never mind that she loved them. Even with their best intentions, they meddled too much. The drilling of etiquette and formalities had given her three sleepless nights.

A good part of her restlessness stemmed from counting the eligible bachelors instead of counting sheep. Her Aunt Elizabeth was relentless with her quizzing too. She expected both she and Verity to know the names of all the socialites that mattered. At last Lillias invented a rhyming game to help. Countess Felicity loves publicity. Duchess Veronica plays the harmonica. Countess Adel was always pell-mell and the Marchioness of Pleases hates green beans. Well, the last one wasn't much of a rhyme, but it made her smile and remember the name.

The final test had been at breakfast this morn, and although Verity didn't get all the answers correct, Lillias had. When the dowager had threatened more drilling, Lillias had come to the rescue, promising her aunt she would handle any formal introductions if the sisters were separated from their aunts.

Succumbing to their pleas, the dowager finally acquiesced.

Now the time had come to dress. Lillias let out a little sigh when she considered what was ahead for the preparation.

But at least the witching hour had begun.

Lillias gazed at the violet gown hanging on the outside of her changing screen. Her reasons for avoiding a social ball had expired. No doubt her aunts' social connections would eliminate bumbling introductions. If she could focus on helping Verity find a suitable husband, she was sure her anxiety about the social obligation would subside.

The knocking must have been going on for a while before Lillias noticed and she finally gave permission for Irina to enter. The servant tried to conceal her frustration when she presented Lillias with a square envelope.

"For you, my lady," the maid offered politely with a dip in her knees.

"Up from your curtsy, Irina," Lillias insisted, then let out an unladylike snort, taking the envelope and studying the handwritten message addressed to her. "Why the formalities?"

Irina blushed and almost curtsied again until she caught Lillias's stern expression. "My lady, it's your aunts." Irina looked down and wrung her hands. "They insist."

"Yet, I do not insist."

The girl raised her eyes and nodded to the unopened envelope in Lillias's hand. "Do you recognize the handwriting?"

After giving Irina's free hand a squeeze, she released it and gave the missive a closer look.

The stationery was fine, but none she'd seen before. The

front held her address, Lady Lillias St. Clair of Woodbeck House in a beautiful scrolling script, most likely written by a skilled hand. Although she was impressed, most letter writers rarely addressed their own correspondence. Usually that was left to the secretary of the house or a business officiant.

Turning the envelope over, she found it sealed in red wax, but with no identifying stamp. She ran her finger over the wax. It was sticky. Her eyes darted up to meet Irina's. "Did you receive the missive at the door or did Finneas?"

Irina cocked her head to one side. "If it matters, my lady, it was me. Is there something amiss?" Her faithful servant's expression was full of concern.

Lillias shook her head. "The wax is tacky, as if the sender rushed through the errand and dropped it off themselves." It was her turn to blush. "I guess it surprised me. I should just get this open and solve the mystery."

"Wait, my lady." It was Irina's turn to grab her hand. "It may not mean much, and you will have solved the puzzle when you open it, but the man who delivered the message asked me not to describe himself to you."

Lillias was even more perplexed and curious than before. A man had delivered the missive, one who wanted to remain anonymous? "This is quite baffling," she murmured, hurrying to the table by the window and fishing for her letter opener in the drawer. Taking the blade to the top corner of the delicate stationery, she sliced through the fold like a loaf of soft bread. After withdrawing a matching stationery parchment, Lillias unfolded the paper and began to read it to herself.

Lady Lillias,

Our chance meetings have disturbed my once orderly life. I have a habit of getting what I want, and my current path of persuasion has apparently not been convincing enough.

I must dance with you tonight.

Sincerely,

Yours in waiting

Lillias's heart began to pound. She didn't like the demanding tone of the letter. It was enough to make her want to cancel her appearance at Almack's. Breathing in sharply and digging deep to muster her courage, she reread the note, only too aware that her servant was waiting on her response. After the second pass, she was just as disturbed, but she had a possible candidate for the missive. Her gaze moved up to meet the patient but anxious gaze of her maid. "What say you?"

"I serve my lady first."

The bold allegiance of her servant made her smile, but she didn't want to take advantage of the woman's devotion. "I will not make you break your word, no matter how loyal you are to me."

When the girl was about to protest, Lillias placed a hand on her shoulder. "But I can phrase the questions for yes or no answers." When Irina hesitated, she pointed to the bench at the end of her bed. "Sit for a moment so I may know more about the delivery."

Irina glanced behind her as if a small animal had startled her. "Sit, my lady?"

"Well, it's not uncommon." Lillias tsked. "You've done it before."

"Only when you were sick in bed, my lady, and you needed tending to," Irina insisted as if the action of sitting would be worse than describing the visitor.

"Very well," Lillias agreed and smiled. "You may stand if it makes you more comfortable."

The girl looked back at the tapestried covered bench in rich shades of burgundy and gold as if she'd dreamed of sitting on it. "If you insist," she uttered softly and daintily took a seat on the edge. Then her eyes filled with dread. "But you must get ready for the ball."

Lillias waved off Irina's concern while taking a seat in her favorite burgundy, jacquard wingback chair that was positioned at a comfortable angle from the bench. "We have time. I am not dressing myself."

They both laughed at that.

"Now, then," Lillias started, "was he a servant?"

Irina shook her head.

"Nobleman, then?"

"Yes," Irina confirmed softly, as if the mysterious man was waiting outside the door listening.

But when Lillias clapped her hands together spontaneously it made Irina almost topple off the bench.

"I didn't mean to startle you," Lillias apologized. "I enjoy solving a mystery."

The girl blushed, no doubt wanting to know what was in the note, but the details of which Lillias was not willing to reveal. Even good servants were prone to gossip.

"Was the man tall and athletic and handsome?"

When the servant blushed, Lillias laughed before she said, "See, you did not even have to answer that one."

The girl shrugged and smothered a giggle with her hand.

Then Lillias drew her brows together and grew serious. The confirmed description of the mysterious messenger, tall, handsome, and athletic, could apply to several gentlemen in the *ton*. Not that Lillias imagined she had secret admirers, but she wanted to prove Lord William Cavendish was the man behind the missive. The innuendo in the communication pointed to the priggish earl. What was his true intention beyond the polite social invitation? To threaten her with suspicions of her modeling again? To blackmail her?

Lillias's attention went back to the servant sitting tentatively on her bedroom bench. "My final question, Irina. Was he wearing a lapel pin that looked like two overlapping V shapes—one face up, one down—with a letter in the middle?" Lillias used her thumb and index fingers on each hand, overlapping them because Irina couldn't read and wouldn't recognize specific letters.

Her servant stared across the room, as if reimagining a handsome aristocrat in their outer alcove smiling at Irina as he handed her the envelope. It would surprise Lillias if her maid noticed anything at all, as disarming as the earl was when she'd been in his presence. Let alone, a Free Mason lapel pin.

Finally, the girl shook her head. "I can't be certain that he did, or he didn't, my lady. I can't recall. I'm sorry." Her maid's disappointment was evident when her eyes misted, and her gaze dropped to her hands.

Lillias sprang from her seat and grasped Irina's hands. "You did true to me and your promise. There's no reason for you to apologize." Then she pulled her servant to her feet. "Come, you must ready me to meet my mystery man."

But when she spun around to allow Irina to tug her day dress over her head, Lillias promised herself to be leery of the Earl of Devonshire and to be suspicious of his every move.

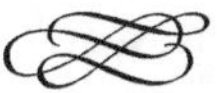

William looked at his pocket watch again. The time was half past nine and it appeared the ball was well underway, but where was she?

"You're looking quite sour-faced tonight."

William snapped his watch shut to reply with an appropriate Shakespearean snub, "'Away, you three-inch fool.'"

"'I am sick when I do look at thee,'" his friend Nigel replied, then put a friendly hand on his shoulder and turned William toward the ballroom floor. Sweeping his arms forward in a grand gesture Nigel added, "All this beauty before you and you stare at your watch as if you want time to stand still?"

"'I scorn you, scurvy companion.'"

"And I you."

"Now that we've updated our opinions of each other in proper Shakespearean style, let's see if we can get a strong drink to make this process more palatable," Nigel said, pushing William's shoulder in another direction with friendly insistence.

"The process of getting you engaged to the wealthiest woman in the room?"

"Am I that transparent?"

"Like glass," William said over his shoulder.

"Maybe that's a good thing. I have expensive habits and need to marry above my title," his friend said, walking in front of William. "Here, follow me through this maze."

As William passed the elder ladies on his way to the refreshments table, glowing, hopeful eyes followed him like lighthouse beacons. He'd been approached by the aggressive mothers of several debutantes already, but he'd promised a dance to someone else. And he was determined it would be his only dance.

William tried not to stare as they approached the table where a young debutante sat nearby with her head buried in her hands, her shoulders heaving up and down.

"What you'll have, sirs?"

"Definitely not what she's having," William said with an empathetic grin. The poor chit was howling like a lost hound and there seemed no one in the group gathered around her that could provide solace.

The servant nodded toward the girl. "That's what happens when your glass is filled with virgin lemonade."

Nigel spoke in William's ear and said, "I would assume the girls are virgins."

"Clean the wax from those cauliflower ears of yours," William chastised and pretended to swat Nigel's head. "You have the hearing of a dowager. No doubt from too many punches to your ears in the boxing arena."

"Well, at least I don't act like a dowager."

"Are you two brothers?"

The servant's question prompted William to pause for a moment and recall how his older brother, Alexander, heir to the Dukedom of Devonshire, had recently threatened to tell their father about William's public boxing. Yes, he had broken an oath, but to save a friend. But Nigel was more a brother to him than his own. Alexander was the type of man he'd never want to be. Prejudiced and entitled.

Shaking off his brooding thoughts, William hooked an arm around Nigel's neck and asked, "Can you tell because of the affection between us?"

"I'm offended you'd even think I am in the same class as this man," Nigel claimed, shrugging off William's arm. "Anything with alcohol in it."

The servant turned to a sideboard and filled two crystal glasses efficiently, while the wailing woman filled the silence. Nigel whisked his from the table and was off, while William gave the girl one last fastidious glance before he turned his back, promising himself to steer clear of that kind of drama.

Although he'd thought to avoid these soirees, the only way now to complete his agenda was to lure his rival onto the dance floor and turn up the charm.

Scanning the scene for Nigel, he found his friend already halfway across the room. Although William had attended a fair number of balls at Almack's, he'd not been in *ton* for the Season in two years. And as much as he considered Nigel a grown man capable of fending for himself, he knew otherwise. It was time to rescue Nigel. Again. But not with his fists.

Heading toward the group Nigel had joined, William's gaze swept over the guests, searching for a glimmer of the familiar. One woman stood out. It wasn't until her companion began to move away from the cluster that William's heart leapt in his chest. Those violet eyes. The ones he'd studied for hours at a time.

"Wait!"

Did I just yell across the ballroom floor to a woman too far away to hear me?

Dozens of curious revelers turned to stare at him.

Mortified, William spun around, pretending to look for the person who'd called out. Good Lord, he'd need to keep his emotions under control. But he had expected to hear the ladies of St. Clair announced. That way he could have made his way toward the entrance and started working his plan.

Trusting it would settle his nerves, William took the drink in his hand and knocked it back quickly, then strolled toward the refreshment table for another. He was going to need all the courage he could muster.

* * *

Breathless, Lillias skirted around the corner and out onto the balcony at Almack's, a rush of relief washing over her. She'd made a dash for the alcove when he'd called out. What folly. Did he expect her to wait for him?

As she made her way to the balustrade to hold on to something solid, her lungs began to fill with the cool air the late April evening offered. How did that man bring out the wild range of feelings she was warring with right now?

Fury. Intrigue. Passion. Why couldn't she control her emotions? How could she even consider anything but contempt when the man had taken liberties?

Lillias held on to the thick and trusty stone railing with both hands, gazing over the impeccable Almack's lawn, wishing she was seated in the rose garden below rather than trying to escape a prickly thorn named Lord William.

"There you are."

Lillias heart stopped right then. She recognized his voice. She would anywhere after the lessons at the R.A., when she couldn't see most of the class from holding her head still while he ogled the bare parts of her.

"You are as still as a stone statue."

Yes, I'm a statue. Go away.

When the footsteps started up again, her heart seemed to as well, though now it was picking up the pace because he was making his way toward her.

"But a statue would never look as lovely as you do in violet, I might add."

Flattery will not get you a response. Only an apology will.

"I am sorry if each time we've met it's been, well, I can't put my finger on it."

The start of an apology. She turned to face him. "Awkward."

His expression lit up at the word, as if she'd gotten the answer right to a guessing game. "That's it. Awkward."

They stood on the balcony together with the sounds of the ball drifting in behind them. Lillias was less sturdy now that she wasn't holding on to the railing and the awkwardness returned.

"There you are."

William's face showed a trace of surprise before he turned around with Lillias.

The dowager countess stood in the doorway looking none too pleased to find Lillias unchaperoned. Even if it was just on the balcony.

But beating the old bitty to an outraged reaction, Lord William swept into a deep bow. "Your Grace, may I introduce myself. I'm Lord William Cavendish, at your service."

Lillias had to give her aunt credit for her good breeding and composure, for the dowager smoothed the stray hairs around her face and her cheeks colored slightly, but she did not reprimand. Not immediately.

"If I may rise, Your Grace, I will be happy to explain my purpose," Lord William said, his voice sounding muffled, his words bouncing off the stone balcony floor.

"Rise, Lord William Cavendish. Please explain yourself."

With a flourish of his arm upon standing he said, "You

found us at an inopportune moment, my lady. We had both acknowledged the absence of a chaperone just before you arrived. I was about to invite Lady St. Clair back into the ballroom for refreshments."

"Indeed, Aunt Elizabeth, what Lord Cavendish says is true," Lillias piped up. She couldn't afford having her aunt form a bad opinion of him because she needed to know more about his plans for his painting. For now, she felt safe with the dowager in their company, and she had to find out if he'd penned the anonymous letter.

The dowager smiled at William and snapped open her fan, batting it and her lashes for a few moments before she spoke.

"It appears I've come at a propitious time, for my greatest gift is easing the awkwardness of others."

Lillias ground her teeth together to stop from saying something off-putting. It would be best to let the dowager take control, which was her greatest gift. Lillias would liken it more to commanding an army than gentle persuasion, but William had been a military man, so perhaps it would be best if he fell in line and obeyed her orders.

The grand dame turned on her heel and walked back into the ballroom from the balcony entrance, the laughter and bits of conversation enveloping her as if she'd stepped through an invisible curtain which allowed in only those of social privilege.

Yet as Lillias willed herself forward to follow the dowager, her feet remained anchored. Was it William's overly handsome face with its patient expression that had her stone still again and as he'd described, 'like a statue'? She broke her gaze from him to glance down at her feet as if doing so would make them magically move.

"Lady Lillias?" William's call was hesitant. "Are you not well?"

She did a quick assessment, and although her stomach was behaving, her mind was whirling and her heart was still pounding, but her head could not seem to make her feet move.

"Here." William gestured for her to take his elbow.

When Lillias's gaze met his sophomoric grin, she couldn't help but smile back before she said somewhat boastfully, "It must be from all those hours of sitting still that I control my movements so well."

William's thick right brow rose, and his head cocked to one side. "Many hours sitting at the R.A.?"

She swallowed hard. "From painting portraits," she said in a clipped voice. Then ignoring William's outstretched arm, Lillias bolted from the balcony as if her skirts were on fire.

In moments, she was winded, but standing politely next to her Aunt Elizabeth, cooling her overheated cheeks with her lace fan, just as the dowager had taught her. Only her eyes could be seen as she hid her face in the lace of her fan, and she wished to become invisible behind the voluminous skirt of her aunt's dress.

"Lillias, darling, what are you doing hanging on to my skirt as if you were a toddler?"

She wanted to tell her aunt that this wasn't a good idea. This was Verity's Season and she blurted out the first excuse that came to her mind. "This isn't my cup of tea."

"This isn't a teahouse," her aunt drawled. Then the dowager made a little 'ah-um' noise in her throat and nodded in the space behind Lillias. "Turn around, my dear."

She spun around to find William behind her.

"You promised me a dance."

"I don't recall you asking."

"I don't recall you refusing my written request."

"If you'd hadn't been secretive about your identity, I could have put you straight when we were on the balcony."

Before she could flatly deny William, her aunt tugged on her arm and pulled her close. "You are embarrassing me," she whispered harshly. "All eyes are on us. Turn and curtsy, then let Lord William Cavendish take the lead."

"He's not on the list," Lillias protested. But her aunt turned to greet another dowager and ignored Lillias's last hope for refusing a dance with Lord William Cavendish.

Begrudgingly, with no other options, Lillias let William lead her toward the dance floor, all the while she prayed the musicians would set down their instruments and take a break. She was certain the party would last for hours, but if the music wasn't playing, she might find a way to back out and convince Finneas to take her home early.

With a flourish, William moved to her left side and with his right hand, led her onto the parquet floor while the quintet finished their interlude. The couples on the floor clapped politely, but much of the sound was muted by their gloves. A few of those bowed to each other, then walked cordially off to the side for either a new partner or refreshments. There was an awkward moment when the musicians flipped pages on their music stands. How apropos, as it appeared all their time together had been filled with awkward moments.

"You look beautiful this evening." The baritone level of his voice was smooth, and his compliment appeared genuine, putting Lillias more at ease, although she couldn't recall being called beautiful by anyone but her father.

As much as she wanted to say thank you, her aunts had told her with specific instructions not to thank any man for a compliment. That aloofness was a sought-after quality. But before she thought better of it, she murmured, "Thank you."

The exchange had bought them time, but the music still hadn't started yet. She glanced in the direction of the musicians and her whole body went rigid with anticipation when she found the violist's bow raised, waiting for the conductor's cue.

William must have followed her gaze because his right hand tightened on hers. Once the music finally began, his left hand settled gently at her waist, startling her.

The waltz? It was a controversial dance for the times.

"Here we go," he whispered with a slight twinkle in his eye.

Barely a beat went by before Lillias found herself spun around the floor. The one, two, three had a distinct up and down movement to it like a gentle horse's gallop. Up, down, up. Lillias was lifted on her toes to the point they were almost floating off the floor. With William's strength, along with the momentum of the turns on the third count, she found her silver slippers skimming the surface instead of sashaying across the ballroom's parquet floor.

How could it be that she'd wanted to run from the room only moments before? Now, she felt lighter than air and the belle of the ball. Her dancing partner had called her beautiful, and she was enjoying the music and the movement.

But beyond the immediate pleasure, her mind was working hard to figure out how to cover up the gaffe she'd made on the balcony when William caught her off guard.

"I'm not on *the* list?"

For some reason she hadn't expected him to converse while they were dancing. She'd have to crane her neck to look up at him so instead she stared at his cravat. "What list?" she asked, sounding as confused as she felt.

"The one your aunt spoke of. I'm wondering what kind of list."

She wanted to say he's only on the list of men her father wished her to avoid, but that was even too rude for her to say. But at least she could tie it to Aunt Elizabeth.

"You must have a dowager in your family," Lillias began,

assuming all landed gentry had an elder woman at the helm. Most women outlasted their husbands. Not because they took better care of their health, but because they weren't likely to accept the challenge of a duel or any other kind of chivalrous folly.

William remained silent, making Lillias stop staring at his cravat and adjust her head to gaze up to see if he was listening. His pained expression wasn't what she expected.

"My aunt passed about three months ago," he said flatly. His Adam's apple bobbled up and down before he said, "She was like a mother to me."

All the angst she was holding squeezed right out of her. "Oh, I'm so sorry," she blabbered, mortified at bringing up the subject. "I only asked because they are usually the political patriarchs of the family." Then she paused and gave him a slight grin. "Men who are marked as agreeable."

"And I'm *not* on the list of agreeable men?" William paused as if deciding if he wanted to take an easy path or a difficult one. Then his eyes warmed from a dark brown spice color to deep amber, glowing, as if a flame had been lit behind them when he asked, "Do you find me agreeable?"

The question left her speechless. Empathy for William's dead aunt was still caught like a lump in her throat and a different kind of awkwardness had taken over. Her eyes didn't blink. "Of course, you are agreeable," she said with as much conviction as she could, clearly thrown from the defensive saddle she'd sat on proudly moments before.

A look of gratitude swept over his handsome face. She was surprised that it would matter to someone like him. And as much as she wanted to hate him, hate wasn't on her mind. It was a foreign feeling.

"There's something I must tell you," he said in a rush and not in an elegant sort of way, but more like school gossip.

Lillias let out an audible gasp. Her curiosity peaked. What secrets would he divulge on the dance floor?

"Our painting has been stolen," he said outright, without blinking.

Lillias's nostrils flared. His admission had her reeling as if she'd taken a whiff of something foul. Her feet missed a beat and her knees buckled.

Whether it was instinctual or because she'd almost swooned, William grasped her more tightly around the waist to keep her mobile.

Turning to look over the ballroom floor, Lillias said indignantly, "I don't understand what you are implying." She hoped her lack of an outright lie would abate a bout with hiccups. If she had an attack, at least she'd have an excuse to go home.

Apparently, her answer made William stumble, but he righted them both without incident and continued to lead her into the middle of the ballroom floor as if he wanted to insulate their conversation.

"You cannot deny that you are not the beautiful form model who posed for Professor Beauchamp's class." William spoke over her head softly. "We'll be better off if we work together to retrieve it."

Retrieve it? He spoke as if a hunting dog could find it. Lillias resolve was wavering. The closeness of him was making her senses spin out of a control. He smelled of newly tanned leather, black currant, and what was that other scent? Whiskey? And he'd used that word beautiful again.

He made a low humming noise before he finally said, "I suspect it's still in the R.A."

"What makes you so sure?" she asked hotly, not able to be casual about her self-interest.

"The process. All the paintings in the R.A. are registered, even the students' work. An artifact, whether completed or in progress, is not allowed in or out of the R.A. without the detailed paperwork. All exits require an on-duty archivist day and night." He took in a huge breath as if he knew she wouldn't like what he had to say next. "It's registered for the exhibition."

Lillias let out a little puff of air. Her suspicions were confirmed. *He plans to show my nude body to all of London.* She had to think quickly. "Listen, Lord Cavendish," she said with the sting of a woman who should not be interrupted, "I know Professor Beauchamp. As I told you before, he has tutored me privately. Why would a woman like me pose for a student class?"

He looked down at her and his eyes swept over her face as if checking to see if he'd made a mistake.

Good. He doubts his accusation.

"When the fire broke out in the classroom and I carried you to the window"—he breathed in deeply, as if in a garden with his eyes half closed. His lids flickered for a moment— "you smelled as you do now." He hesitated. "Like a summer's morning, roses and fresh linen."

Gazing up at him, she remembered what the dowager had said about why William wasn't on the list for herself or Verity. It wasn't just that her father hated the Duke of Devonshire. The Cavendish family had a dislike for the St. Clairs. The dowager couldn't remember how it all began.

"What are the next steps?"

She looked at him quizzically. "Do you not remember this dance?"

"To court you?"

Just then the quintet finished the song and the two came to an abrupt stop. Somehow butterflies had taken residence in her belly and were now beating to get out.

"You can't be serious," she said, turning toward the outer ring of the dance floor, ready to make her way to safety.

Still holding her hand, he gently tugged on it while musicians thumbed through their pages. The simple motion and momentum brought her spinning back to him. She bumped into his taut midsection with a light thump and settled into his arms as if she belonged there.

Her eyes met his and his expression was fierce when he said, "I've never been more serious."

As much as she wanted to argue, she burst out laughing instead. "I'm not sure if I should be honored or afraid," she taunted. "You look more like you're ready for battle than looking for love."

His face relaxed and the corners of his sensuous mouth turned up. "Love is a battle worth fighting," he said with a lift of one brow. He was staring at her mouth as if he'd kiss her or was thinking about it. "Do you believe in love at first sight?"

Lillias wasn't sure she'd heard the question correctly. She was flummoxed over the fact that she'd not only danced once with William, but she was about to start her second. That would have consequences.

But she stepped back from his embrace as other couples began to gather in a new formation. From what the dowager had told Lillias, most of the ballroom dances were line dances, cotillion or quadrille, and didn't allow couples to stay in one place for long, but he continued to hold her left hand in his right.

"I do," he confessed, as if he answered the question himself it might prompt her to do the same.

"Are you saying you are in love with me?" she asked, not realizing how bold that sounded until the words slipped from her lips.

A couple walking past them on the dance floor turned their heads to stare but kept walking until they stood across from each other.

William's face turned red, as though he'd said the most inappropriate thing. "You are lovely, but no, that's not what I'm saying."

"Well, that's a relief," she said with a light giggle, "because I do not believe in love at first sight." She paused, working to take her time to think of what she wanted to say instead of blurting it out. "Curiosity at first sight, more likely," she said more to herself than to him.

"You are a curiosity," William said with a sweep of his gaze up and down. "But in the most auspicious way," he amended, looking a little sheepish as if he'd offended her.

Lillias tilted her head back and laughed as he spun her around. "I'd rather be a curio than an idol," she admitted, surprised she was enjoying this witty banter.

"Either would qualify as an object of desire."

She gave him a dubious look and pursed her lips. "Are we speaking of a museum description?"

"As a student of art and architecture, my references are purely academic," he said to her with a wink as if she would have to wonder.

With a lingering smile on her lips, Lillias turned to follow William's gaze as he glanced over her shoulder only to find all eyes along the dance floor staring at them.

"We should assemble," William said in a hushed voice, releasing her hand so they could line up with the others.

Now across from each other, there were four couples in a square set. The dance proceeded as the dowager had taught her, and Lillias changed partners several times throughout the number. Each time she was paired again with William, their eyes locked. Was he lying about the painting's disappearance? He had acted as if it was her responsibility to help 'retrieve' it. What appeared as gossip to him, sounded like a social death sentence for her.

The scenarios of possibilities whirled around in her mind

like her partners on the dance floor, winding in and out, spinning round and round.

Why did William insist on a dance? Then a second? How had the painting gone missing? Could Verity have stolen it for her? And Verity, how was her sister faring with possible suitors? Lillias had been torn from her duty by the frivolous attentions of an aristocrat whose intentions baffled her.

"There you are," William said softly, jolting her out of her manic musings.

She was promenading with him again. The breath almost sucked out of her. Where was the kindly gentleman who'd kept her pulse from racing? She looked behind her. He was now with another. And here was William's handsome face grinning at her again as if they were what? He wanted to court her?

Then he surprised her by moving away from the formation. He set a direction of their dancing to the far side of the ballroom toward the balcony where the awkward evening had begun. That part of the room was almost vacant except for the dowager, who was walking out through the broad, open French doors.

Spinning and spinning, the cotillion steps now forgotten, they must have looked like an ocean wave heading for the shore. He only slowed a little as they moved from parquet floor to carpet and finally over the tiny ledge to the balcony.

"My word," the dowager said in a shrill voice.

They came to a bumpy stop on the balcony a few feet away from her. It took a few moments for her aunt to recover from the initial shock.

"That was impressive, Lord Cavendish," Lillias said with awe.

Stepping away from her and with a low elegant bow, his arm wrapping under his waist, William uttered, "The pleasure was all mine."

She popped her fan from her reticule and hid her flushed cheeks. Blushing had become as regular as breathing around William this evening.

"The air out here is not as cool as I'd expected and the ballroom has been more than stuffy," William said, seemingly covering for her as she had done for him earlier.

"Two dances, Lillias," the dowager said in her entitled air, "you know what that means?"

Frantically searching her memory for the ballroom protocols, Lillias steadied herself as her knees almost buckled again for the second time that evening. William had been watching her closely and reached for her hand and pulled her to his side.

"Of course she does, grand dame," he said smoothly in that low voice that sounded like a sweet cello.

"Half past ten?"

"That would be a fine time to come calling," William said to the dowager.

"Calling for what?"

The dowager gave her a look of disbelief. "He's now on the list," her aunt hissed low from behind her fluttering fan.

Lillias's eyes darted to William.

"I'm on the list," he mouthed, a little quirk to his lips to suggest it had been part of his plan all along.

CHAPTER 16

The morning after the ball at Almack's Lillias paced the library like a caged animal, willing her hand to stop trembling. Instead of sorting through her feelings about William, which ran from suspicion to infatuation, a sinister disruption was now holding her hostage.

She folded the parchment in half, then stuffed it into the secret drawer. The black words on plain cream paper were forever burned into her mind's eye. 'Your painting is safe with me. But are you safe from the painting?'

Blackmail? A bad joke?

This was all William's fault. Not only had he charmed her into accepting a ridiculous faux courtship, he had hood-winked the most callous and discerning of all chaperones, Lady Elizabeth, the Dowager Countess of Coventry.

The twisted fate now required her to play ally to William when all she wanted was to protect herself from ruin by stealing his nude portrait of her.

And after only two dances, the dowager appeared posed to support a proposal from Lord William, which would be the one thing that might put her father in an early grave.

Aunt Elizabeth's enthusiastic addition of William to the approved list was counter to her earlier stance the day before, when the older woman had implicitly explained to her the St. Clair and the Cavendish families had a long-running feud. Why would the dowager meddle in the affairs of two dukes who wanted nothing more than to one up each other?

But then Lillias recalled her aunt did have a penchant for scheming, even though she could be rigid about protocols.

The more she considered the circumstances, the more she wanted to gain control over them, and her sister's welfare began to override the precedence of the threatening note.

The sooner her sister was married, the sooner Lillias could be free of the burden she was carrying. It was Verity's suitors who needed vetting. Somehow, she would manage William and the rest.

"My lady, we have a contingent in the vestibule."

"Oh, my, Finneas, you startled me." Spinning around to greet their butler, Lillias almost doubled over with laughter when she found him adjusting his vest. It wasn't often the mature man of sixty plus years was ruffled. A quick once over found his cravat askew and one glove missing.

"Finneas?"

"I had to break up a fight, my lady."

Lillias covered her mouth, but before she had a chance to respond, Verity waltzed into the library.

"What is all the noise, Finneas?"

The butler's face reddened. "Lady Verity, your suitors are here, but there have been a few disagreements."

Now it was Verity's turn to hide her amusement, giving Lillias time to set priorities. As the eldest and the one ultimately responsible for Verity's match, it didn't matter what her dowager aunt wanted to believe, Lillias would weed out the undesirables at once.

"Finneas, we will not entertain a rowdy group of ruffians. Tell the offenders they are dismissed. If the rest are not dukes, or future dukes, send them home."

Their butler nodded but didn't appear too pleased. Never mind his preferences, however, Lillias needed his help eliminating the undesirables up front. With William calling at the same time, she'd have to trust her aunts would ferret out the best suitors from the lot that remained.

And with a turn toward her sister, Lillias held up a finger.

"And those orders are final."

"What about Lord Compton?"

"The Baron of Good Humor?"

"He's good looking."

"Not a good match."

"You promised I could have a say in the matter and find a love match."

"We are looking for a good match first."

Verity took a dramatic dive onto the chaise. "Is this how it's going to be? Where is Aunt Elizabeth?"

"She can sense a gentleman suitor like a bloodhound hunting a rabbit." Lillias glanced toward the open door. "I expect she will be here in short order. As you can see, I have not begun to entertain."

"*You* have a caller?"

"You make me sound like an old maid."

"Well, you've made your wishes clear. You will remain unmarried as long as you can, but—" Verity interrupted herself, which was unusual, and her jaw dropped open. Even more unusual. "Lord William Cav—end—ish?" she sputtered.

"At your service."

With her back to the open parlor door, Lillias spun around to find him outside the doorway in a complete bow.

Her cheeks heated immediately. That was not the reaction she needed right now, so she turned her back on his gentlemanly gesture to speak to her sister again. "I was just getting ready to tell you, Lord William Cavendish is coming to call."

Her sister's expression turned from surprise to envy.

"For you?"

"Yes, I'm here for Lady Lillias." William swept into the room and rescued Lillias from having to form an explanation. Of course, she had told Verity even though Aunt Elizabeth had insisted she come out this Season too, Lillias had promised her sister she would only go through the motions.

Although Verity was the prettier of the two, Lillias vowed there'd be no competition. Her sister couldn't be interested in William after all she'd told her about him, could she?

But when William took Lillias's hand, he took her breath with it. Giving her gloved knuckles a quick brush with his lips, he charmed her with his brilliant smile.

And there was that alluring scent again. It had stripped away her defenses yesterday evening when they'd spun and spun and spun on the dance floor in a trance-like state.

"Lord Cavendish. There you are."

Lillias sucked in a sharp breath. The dowager countess had broken the spell.

Clapping her hands together with a look of delight, Lady Elizabeth strode into the room and headed directly toward William.

He eased into an elegant bow again, as if it was his profession, gently taking the dowager's gloved hand in his and placing a small peck of a kiss on her knuckles before saying, "At your service."

The dowager giggled like a schoolgirl.

He stood and took a few quick steps to Aunt Emma before repeating the same. When William finished, he moved next to Lillias.

She wasn't surprised to find both aunts snapping open their fans and batting them like debutantes.

Everyone but Verity was staring at William.

He shifted his weight back and forth. "The weather is very agreeable," he said, breaking the silence. "May I suggest a stroll in your garden?" Then he glanced over at Verity's dramatic posturing on the chaise. "I understand your sister has visitors in the vestibule."

Chaperones would be required for a visit even on the grounds and the dowager made the first move toward the door.

"Lord Cavendish, I understand you have an entry for the R.A.'s international competition," the dowager said, offering her arm.

And so, the division was decided. Lillias took one glance at Verity and was not surprised to find her sister's eyes still closed and her hand over her brow. Lillias shrugged her shoulders, then she turned to give Aunt Emma a sympathetic nod toward her sister and mouthed, "she's acting."

A wink was her aunt's reply, as Lillias walked past her and followed the dowager and William down a short corridor, then out to the patio that faced the rising sun. They descended the steps a few paces ahead of Lillias and began a stroll along the smooth stone walk that led into the garden.

"The tea roses are a difficult variety to grow," William told her aunt as Lillias hurried her steps to catch up.

After what seemed a gasp of wonder, the dowager stopped and stared at him. "You know the tea rose, bred by Joseph Pernet-Ducher?"

William released his hold on the dowager and bent down to cup one of the delicate buds in his hands before he took a deep sniff. Lillias stepped next to her aunt, and when he turned his head to speak to them, he'd dropped his formal posturing. Instead, he looked like a young boy ready to dig in the dirt.

"You must promise to keep my secret." He chuckled, as if at a private joke. "I wouldn't want to ruin my reputation as a rake."

The dowager gasped and clutched her chest. But William's mischievousness was evident when he continued to grin at her until she smiled too and batted at the air in front of her.

When he stood to his full height, he linked his arm in Lillias's, then without a word, turned her on to the path. The movement reminded her of when they'd first approached the dance floor at Almack's last night.

Heaven help me, she pleaded to the clouds hanging over William when she gazed up at him. His motives were unclear, unsettling at best, but somehow, he'd bewitched her, for she hung on to his words now as if they were nourishment for her soul.

It didn't matter exactly which variety of rose he was discussing, it was the passionate way he referred to their hues, graceful stems, and velvety petals. If he'd offered her to eat one right now, she wouldn't have resisted, because he described the world around him in delectable detail. Like a fine artist.

Artist? Thief? Blackmailer? Maybe he was a rake, a charlatan, who wanted to charm her so he could start over on his R.A. project and replace the missing painting? *If it is missing.*

As she battled between infatuation and loathing, Lillias knew one thing was certain. She would have to protect her heart. Either she'd been too sheltered, or she was uneducated in the ways of men because her mother had left them too soon.

William was chatting about the roses in his own garden when they reached the turnaround and he set her on one of the stone benches strategically placed there. Then he guided the dowager next to her.

"There now. Two beautiful, rare roses have been added to the garden."

The dowager let out a little sigh, only audible to Lillias. She took her aunt's hand and gave it a squeeze.

"Lillias, this would be the perfect spot for my portrait," her aunt said as if it were only the two of them together.

William had just gotten settled on the bench directly across from them. "Who will be your artist?"

"Lillias, of course," the dowager said as if she'd been offended he'd asked the question.

"Of course," he echoed the dowager, then his gaze fixed on Lillias as if expecting details.

"You must know how accomplished she is," her aunt told William. Then she looked back and forth between them. "I may assume you both share a natural talent for drawing."

William nodded. "Lady Lillias tells me she's been schooled at Woodbeck House by one of my professors." She narrowed her eyes. *He's calling my bluff.*

"Are you referring to Professor Beauchamp?"

When her aunt asked the question, William's gaze remained on Lillias.

"Precisely," he answered, still staring at her. "He's a bit melodramatic." Then he blinked a few times as if calculating his words carefully and shifting his attention to the dowager. "Many artists are." His cheeks reddened before he added, "But not your niece."

"Not this niece, but I trust you have met Verity?"

William dropped his head to smother a chuckle. "Is she an artist too?"

The dowager smiled brightly. "She is a talented musician. And my youngest niece has not come into her own yet," she said, before glancing wistfully toward Woodbeck House.

"All in good time," William offered.

"That's what my deceased husband would say."

William gave the dowager a nod of respect before he said, "I'd love to see some of Lillias's work."

Before Lillias could speak for herself, the dowager said, "I'm sure she'd love to see some of yours."

William perked up on the bench. "Our next call should be at the R.A. If you patronesses of the arts would be so kind to join me tomorrow, it would please me to show you some of my work."

"My aunt is no stranger to the R.A., as she is in a most noble position as one of—"

"We'd be delighted," replied her aunt in a low sweet voice.

And just like that, Lillias found her future was once again determined by someone else.

CHAPTER 17

The time had arrived and William regretted his invitation, even more so because he had no way to back out. Through proper training, he'd learned to gain control over his emotions when he was trapped. After all, a boxer fought until he was out of a corner. And he had to remind himself that he was pursuing Lady Lillias, not the other way around.

But Nigel's antics dispelled his inner demons when he held up William's oil painting of 'Doves on a Windowsill.'

"You want me to lose, don't you?"

Nigel shook his head but contradicted himself with an evil grin.

"Take it out of my sight," William demanded, mocking dramatic flair with a wave of his hand.

"'I must tell you friendly in your ear. Sell when you can. You are not for all markets.'"

"Compton, I do not need Shakespeare now. I need your help."

His friend served him a twisted grin before he began to rummage through the canvases stacked against the wall in the R.A. studio. After a few mutterings of "hmm," "oh," "that will not do," Nigel drew out one from the back of a stack as if it was a treasure. Turning it to face William he said, "Now this could win the coveted prize."

William burst out laughing. Although he was within minutes of entertaining guests, he had hoped to find a worthy substitute for the now missing nude. But this was the farthest offering of a winning entry his friend could have suggested.

"That is so awful the only place it belongs is in the trash." William snatched the canvas from Nigel's grasp. The painting was his first, a black and white Dalmatian lying next to the hunting boots of his master. One boot was larger than the other and the dog's right ear looked like it belonged on a corgi, straight and pointy. William had forgotten about this poor example of his work and was intent on destroying it.

"'There is nothing either good, or bad, but thinking makes it so.'"

"The bard would not agree with you," William said, shaking the canvas at Nigel before setting it in the large rubbish bin outside his studio.

"Are sure you want to throw that away?" Nigel questioned, then bit his knuckle before adding, "'What's done cannot be undone.'"

"Shakespeare?" a voice asked from behind him.

William turned to find Lady Lillias, Lady Verity, and their aunts in the hall.

"We have an affinity for his writings," William said to the women, not sure where to begin explaining the exchanges between himself and Nigel.

"'I like this place and could willingly waste my time on it,'" Lillias replied.

Ah, beautiful and well read. "From *As You Like It*," William murmured.

"Now, you are both talking in riddles," Lady Elizabeth said with a huff.

Lillias hooked her arm in the dowager's. "Come, let's take a look at Lord Cavendish's work." She peeked into the dumpster as she started to lead her aunt into the studio.

"Don't look in there. It's dangerous," warned William with a mocking smile.

"'He thinks too much. Such men are dangerous,'" Nigel suggested.

William shook his head. "Such men as Lord Compton should stop quoting Shakespeare now that there are noble ladies present."

Nigel's face reddened as he glanced sheepishly at Verity who looked smitten and not a bit judgmental.

"Although I'm not as familiar with Shakespeare's plays, I have read his sonnets," admitted the dowager as she walked into William's studio and the others followed. She stood by his easel and closed her eyes before she said, "'Thy sweet love remembered such wealth brings, that then I scorn to change my state with kings.'"

William started clapping, and everyone joined in. "Lord Compton, I recommend you memorize the sonnets rather than the insults. You could win more hearts that way."

"At least one heart," Verity said, then she followed that with a giddy grin.

But that reaction was not lost on Lillias. He imagined she would marshal her sister out the door and to a convent before she'd let her linger here with Nigel.

Leave it to the dowager, however, to take control when she clasped her hands together and said, "As lovely as that was, we are not here for a literary lesson when we are in the finest art school in the world."

And after a brisk glance about the studio the dowager looked directly at William and said, "Show us your contest entry." It was as if she was a demanding judge who'd been kept waiting too long.

But William wished he'd had more time to come up with a suitable substitute. Now was the moment he'd dreaded. With all the finished work available, he hadn't been able to find one worthy to display for Lillias. For some reason her opinion mattered, and now he had to provide an excuse.

"There is an issue with the entry," William finally volunteered.

"An issue?" the dowager asked, reminding William of the time he was assigned to guard the armory and ammunition went missing.

"I'm proud of my—my work," William stammered. "The best I've ever produced, but the painting is—"

"Missing," Nigel blurted out.

"Missing?" The dowager looked skeptical.

"Missing," William concurred.

The dowager tilted her head and eyed him up and down like a constable. "As in stolen or lost?"

No doubt the dowager will pepper me with questions until she's satisfied with my answers. He shrugged. "I believe stolen, as it was here two days ago and then it wasn't."

"Well then, certainly it wasn't misplaced," Lady Elizabeth suggested, looking at him suspiciously.

"Not likely." William pointed to the empty easel in front of them. "It sat here in this spot, quite large and heavy."

The dowager's mouth pursed into a most unbecoming shape, like a dried-up prune as she contemplated the circumstances and muttered something under her breath. Then she looked up at William as if she'd made up her mind to do something about it.

"Have you reported this to the authorities?"

Standing next to William, Lillias gasped then said, "Why would you contact the authorities, Aunt Elizabeth?"

"Why not?"

"Well, William said he doesn't know if it was stolen." Lillias's defense sounded reasonable.

The dowager gave a wary look about the studio. He had several paintings he'd gathered for consideration along the far wall. She walked over to one of his favorites featuring water lilies on a sunlit pond. "This is lovely," she suggested, pointing to the work.

Nodding, William walked to the piece and picked it up, then carried it to the easel. "I was thinking this one could be a substitute," he agreed, standing back and scratching his chin absentmindedly.

"Problem solved," Lillias said, sounding relieved.

"Only the missing portrait was better," he admitted with a heavy heart. "This one would do but won't win."

"The missing painting was better," Nigel agreed. "It would have won the show," he said with the confidence that made William decide right then he'd do whatever he could to find it.

"You could offer a reward," Lady Emma piped in.

The dowager brightened. "Yes, put a notice in the papers."

William hadn't considered that option, but he doubted a thief would read the papers and shot down the suggestion with facts. "Most criminals are illiterate and don't have the means to buy much, let alone a newspaper or two."

After an awkward pause he half muttered to himself, "If only I could recreate it."

"Can you?" everyone but Lillias asked at once.

William had considered it but doubted without a model it could be done. He'd created the Dalmatian without a model, and it had been a disaster. No, he was the kind of artist that had to see the object to draw it.

As if the dowager was reading his thoughts she said, "Why doesn't Lillias pose for you?"

William looked to Lillias as did everyone in the room.

Her face lost all its color, and a sincere sense of remorse rushed through him for the first time, realizing how violating it must have been for her to see his painting. If she had indeed been the one spying on him.

"Because I don't pose for portraits," Lillias replied, turning to her aunt.

"Because?" the dowager asked.

"I'm an artist."

"Wouldn't you gain some perspective from being the subject?"

"She'd have to be nude," Nigel blurted out. Then his face turned a ruddy shade.

All the women gasped except Lillias.

"Nudity is encouraged here at the R.A," said a voice from the hall.

The older women twittered at the remark and William turned to find Professor Beauchamp standing outside the studio.

"From prehistory to the earliest civilization, to today's Prince Regent's reign, nude female figures have symbolized fertility and well-being," the professor said as if he was lecturing in class.

"I appreciate nudity for the sake of my well-being," Nigel blurted out.

The ladies all gasped again.

Nigel shrugged and added, "For my art."

"For the sake of art, you mean." The bespeckled instructor walked into the crowed student studio. Then he gestured to William's easel. "Speaking of nudes, are you finished with yours?" The instructor's eyebrows arched high above his circular wire rimmed glasses in an almost comical expression.

But the situation was grim, and William couldn't laugh. It

was better he answer the professor's questions than have the dowager try to explain the situation. He shook his head.

"It's missing."

"What do you mean missing?" the professor asked, stepping up to the easel and looking behind it briefly as if the art entry had been misplaced.

"We suspect someone stole it," Nigel volunteered.

"Stole it? From the guarded R.A? Impossible!" The professor blinked rapidly. His mouth opened, but it hung gaping.

"It was here two days ago and gone today," William explained.

The dowager cleared her throat.

"Where are my manners?" William gave a curt bow to the ladies. "Professor Beauchamp, as distressed as I am about the painting, my good breeding reminds me to introduce you to the four beautiful ladies who grace my studio."

With a grand sweeping gesture, he took the appropriate formalities, giving titles and a fitting appraisal of each of the women, finishing with Lillias.

The professor bowed and gave honorable remarks to each but bowed more deeply to the last. "My goodness, Lady Lillias, it's been ages," the professor remarked.

Ages? As in not recently? William believed until this very moment that Lillias was the model from his class. But now Beauchamp's comments had him wavering.

Lillias's curtsy was accompanied by a coy smile, as if she guarded a secret between them. But when she offered no reply, the professor filled the awkward silence. "I'm a friend of the St. Clair family and one of Lillias's art tutors."

The dowager's gaze narrowed on the professor. "If it's impossible for a piece of art to disappear from the R.A., according to you, Professor, what do you recommend?"

William was anxious to hear Beauchamp's suggestions.

Even better now that the dowager's hawk-like evaluation of potential options rested on someone else's shoulders.

The professor steepled his fingers. "First, I'll alert our head security officer. He'll want to interview the guards who were on duty at the time and record their observations."

"What about the Bow Street Runners? Should they be contacted?" the dowager asked. When the professor shook his head, she didn't stop there. "What about the Thief Takers? The papers at least?" She finished with an exasperated sigh.

"We must keep to our own," Beauchamp insisted. "The worst thing that could happen is word gets out to our esteemed artists and those who deem this a great institution. We cannot let fear incite panic or infer precious artifacts aren't safe here," he warned.

The dowager put her hand to her throat. When she'd entered the room she'd taken charge, but now she appeared unsettled, as if she was playing Beauchamp's scenario in her mind. The patrician had a vested interest in the R.A.'s reputation. No doubt she'd use all her resources to protect it and find a solution. When it seemed she'd decided, her razor-sharp focus settled on William.

But because of his training in the ring, he'd learned how to fool anyone with a confident expression even when he didn't feel that way. "I'll cooperate with the R.A. authorities," William volunteered.

The dowager gave him a short nod, then swung her attention to Nigel.

He squirmed in his suit coat as if she'd caught his coattails and wouldn't let go. But he put his hands together in supplication before he announced, "'Seal up your lips and give no words but mum.'"

A deep chuckle rumbled in the dowager's throat after Nigel's Shakespearean quip. Her infectious laugh drew them all in. After she caught her breath, she whispered to no one in particular, "The word is mum."

Turning toward the door, the dowager took the arm of the professor. "Come, Beauchamp, we'll take Nigel and Verity to the grand gallery, and you can send your head guard to interview Lord Cavendish. But until then, my sister will stay here to chaperone as he sketches a portrait of Lady Lillias."

When no one objected, as if anyone dared, the dowager waltzed out of his studio followed by Nigel arm and arm with Lady Verity.

But Lillias looked anything but agreeable.

CHAPTER 18

*D*id the dowager understand what she was asking of Lillias? Hadn't Nigel's 'nudity for the sake of art' made an impression on her? Certainly, Aunt Elizabeth wasn't suggesting Lillias pose nude.

While William stood in front of her with an expectant but doubtful expression, Aunt Emma began humming and walking around the studio.

"The painting could still be found." William's suggestion snapped Lillias out of her distraction. "Considering Beauchamp's arguments," he added.

The painting was not missing. Lillias was certain of that. She couldn't fathom who the perpetrator was behind the threatening note. Perhaps it was still in the building but hidden? Another student of Beauchamp's who had recognized her and was jealous of William's work?

There were more questions than answers. And the most troubling, could she tell him about yesterday's threatening message?

"Constable White at your service."

Lillias shrieked and spun around to find a tall guard

standing in the middle of the studio. The gold buttons of his jacket, too numerous to count, gleamed in the soft glow of the studio lantern. The standup collar, shiny knee-high boots, tall stovepipe hat, were black and regimental.

Yet, his size alone was imposing enough. Lillias imagined a thief would be deterred by the mere thought of the officer in pursuit. Although he had the Royal Art Academy logo embroidered on his jacket's right breast, he appeared as regal as the officers working for Prince Regent.

"No need to be alarmed, my lady," the officer said, tipping his hat. "I'm here to investigate the alleged missing painting. Let's have a look round and tell me what happened," the guard said to William, sounding cordial but commanding. With his billy club attached securely to his waist, he appeared ready for action.

As William began to tell the officer what had transpired, Lady Emma excused herself to get some air with the promise to be back soon. No doubt the small studio felt cramped with the addition of the imposing officer.

With the two men engaged deep in conversation, Lillias took the opportunity to stroll over to a large stack of canvases. Half listening to their dialog, she picked up bits of conversation as the constable nodded and made grunts of understanding. Without William's direct attention, she had the freedom to sort through his artwork.

In her imagination of best-case scenarios, she would find the nude in one of these stacks, purposely hidden away, and then prove William was playing a cruel but effective game with her.

She began her casual search by leaning the first painting toward her shin and let it rest there. Continuing in that fashion, tilting the canvases forward, resting on the back of the one before, she worked rapidly but cautiously. At each new piece of work, Lillias was less intent on proving William a rogue and more intrigued by his talent.

When the stack leaning against her leg grew heavy and the voices closer, she quickly reversed her efforts and as neatly as possible returned the canvases back to their original positions.

"Did you say nude?" the constable asked, his voice booming in the small studio.

She smothered a giggle. Hadn't the guard seen his fair share of naked portraits while making his daily rounds?

"Are you claiming your studio was locked when you weren't here working?" The officer sounded skeptical. "You understand what you are implying?"

"I'm not implying anything, Officer." William's reply was clipped. "I am simply giving you the facts," he added, walking behind the easel, and finding Lillias there as if he was looking for her and not the painting.

"This is the woman," William said as the officer joined him in the small space behind the easel.

Swearing under her breath, Lillias was angry at herself for not paying closer attention to William's conversation. Could William have implied the painting was of her?

The officer tipped his hat and gestured for her to come out.

"Well, of course, Constable, how may I be of assistance?" She batted her lashes. It wasn't as if she'd been hiding, but she didn't want to appear she was avoiding him either.

"Well—I—you see," he stammered.

"What the officer is trying to say is he wonders if you observed anything out of the ordinary when you were here last?"

Lillias's heart jumped to her throat. She didn't want to lie. "You mean as in today?" She cocked her head to one side and waited.

The officer looked at William and then back at Lillias as if confused. "Didn't you tell me she was here Sunday?"

Now William looked as if he wasn't sure what would be the best answer. But he wouldn't have to contend with a bout of hiccups if he were lying.

"I thought Professor Beauchamp said you had visited the R.A. this past Sunday." When she raised a brow, William amended his statement. "Perhaps I'm mistaken."

"Perhaps you are," she said, wanting to glare at him for trying to trick her. Beauchamp had already mentioned it had 'been ages' since he'd seen her.

But the constable didn't appear satisfied and gave Lillias his full attention. "Were you or were you not at the R.A. Sunday?" he asked as if ready to interrogate her.

Her smug smile dropped. She hadn't lied yet, but this question was another matter.

"Well, I did meet with Professor Beauchamp on a matter, but he instructs me at Woodbeck House." *Still not lying as the two facts independently are true.*

The officer appeared appeased by her answer when he nodded and turned back to William. "You must understand we have never reported a piece of artwork missing from the R.A," the constable said, his neck skin flapping above his taut collar. "Our reputation is sterling."

"Does that mean you've never had a painting missing, stolen—or otherwise?" William slowed his question to a stop as the face of the officer had turned quite red.

"We have never reported a piece of artwork missing from the R.A," the officer repeated without flinching.

William nodded and raked his hand through his dark hair, unaware it was now quite disheveled and Lillias let out a sigh. The last thing she wanted to see were newspaper stories about a missing nude contest entry from the Royal Academy of Art.

Yet, as much as she didn't want this piece to be shown, she was more terrified of what the anonymous letter had implied. Someone had taken it and that someone suspected she was the nude in the painting. She shuddered and pulled her wrap more tightly around her shoulders, not because she was cold. She was afraid.

Still, her instincts were telling her not to share the note with William. Although he continued to be charming since calling on her yesterday, Lillias had to assume his motives were self-serving.

At the moment she was baffled, remembering that Verity had suggested they steal it, but even she wouldn't be that conniving. Her sister might have attempted to bribe her with it, but not threaten her. Regardless, she wanted the painting to stay missing until after the competition. That way William would have to come up with a substitute. Just not another portrait of her, no matter what her aunt ordered.

She plastered a smile on her face and squared her shoulders. It would be better to appear interested in solving the case. "Did you and Lord Compton search through every one of these stacks of canvases?"

"Did you?" William started to laugh. "Forgive my manners, but the evidence appears to be incriminating," he suggested, pointing at the bottom half of her skirt.

To her dismay, she glanced down to find a large smear of oil paint on it near her knee. Not that she was worried she'd ruined the garment, but she was embarrassed by what the stain implied.

With another forced smile she turned to the constable, wanting to avoid any further questioning. "I was admiring William's work. As a portrait artist myself, I had yet to view any of his paintings until today." She took in a quick breath, ready to defend herself further, but then it happened.

Hiccup. She slapped her hand over her mouth and heat

filled her cheeks. *Hiccup.* She had to get some air. "Excuse me," she said breathlessly before the next hiccup escaped.

Spinning on her heel, she headed toward the door. She *had* seen one of William's paintings before today. *Hiccup.* The nude.

She strode out of the student studio and walked briskly down the hall toward an open window. With every step, her shoes echoed in the long hall. Each clack of her heel was accompanied by a hiccup.

Reaching the ledge of the sill, she stuck her head out the window. She breathed in the crisp air and she let her shoulders relax. *Hiccup.* She swore under her breath. The fresh air felt good, but it hadn't chased away her dreaded curse.

"Does that happen often?"

Lillias didn't have time to suck in a big breath before she screamed.

CHAPTER 19

After the shrieking subsided, so did the hiccups. William uncovered his ears. She was as jumpy as a rookie boxer in a ring.

"I didn't mean to scare you."

She gave him a weak smile, as if the embarrassment over the hiccups and the constable's questioning had taken the wind out of her. Yet, her steady gaze was soft, eyes full of varied flecks of purple, sending waves of heat through his body instead of regret.

"I didn't hear your steps behind me," she offered, her grin widening.

"It appears I've brought the antidote on accidentally."

Lillias's eyes brightened while she looked up to one corner of the R.A.'s arched ceiling and then the other, as if she'd find her answer there. Placing her gloved hand over the rise and fall of her overly luscious bosom, she breathed shallowly, no doubt worried about setting the hiccups off again. Parting her rose-colored lips ever so slightly, she let out a sigh and a small puff of breath, audible to William, as he waited for her claim to be cured of the offense.

"I do think you've done it, Lord Cavendish," she exclaimed in a breathy voice. "Although it's normally a choice of last resort, frightening someone with the hiccups often is the absolute cure." She looked at him with relief.

He returned the wide grin. "Do these come on often?"

"Typically when I'm startled," she admitted with chagrin. "It makes sense that fear would reverse them. But most often a little honey or raw sugar chases them away."

Lillias was beautiful in the frame of the R.A. window, gardens over her shoulder, and the breeze ringing the curly tendrils around her face like little bells.

Stepping closer than he would normally if her aunts were present, he asked, "Are you afraid of me?"

Lillias sucked in a sharp breath. She couldn't move back as she was pinned against the window. Her eyes widened as he stood close. Not as close as he wanted to, but as close as he dared.

"I—you—we . . ." she mumbled.

Before he let his lips rule over his rioting emotions, he took a large step backward. Chuckling nervously to break the intimate tension he'd created, he offered his arm, tamping down his infatuation. He needed her cooperation and could not risk scaring her away.

Lillias stepped boldly forward and hooked her arm in his. "Why would I be afraid of you?" she said smoothly. "It was that constable who'd rattled me," she admitted, looking straight ahead as he walked them away from his studio. "Where did he go off to?"

"Promised to interview the other guards and then check the registry."

"The registry?"

"You may have missed his description of how artwork comes and goes from the R.A.?" William didn't want to call her out. No doubt she hadn't been listening while she was snooping through his paintings.

"Yes, I was distracted by his presence and frankly quite startled by his size."

"Thus, the hiccups?"

Lillias's cheeks flushed with color. "Eventually."

Not wanting to linger on her embarrassment, he explained the process. "It's very rigorous," he said, guiding her through the entrance to the grand gallery. "The constable confirmed each piece coming or going from the R.A. is cataloged at the security office. From what he said, only the R.A. staff has access to the book, but works of art are allowed travel to and fro at the sentry's gate."

"Do you know where this office is?" Lillias asked as he steered her toward the far wall.

He shook his head. "I'm assuming it's a well-kept secret, but the constable said there's a carriage path that goes only one direction circling the back of the building." He turned to the painting in front of them as if they were speaking of the work. "With that information, it can't be hard to find the entrance."

"At least it would be kept from common knowledge."

"The problem with thieves is they make that kind of knowledge their business."

Lillias mumbled an "umm" sound to his statement, then went silent as he began to wonder who, and more importantly, why someone would steal his work. The questions from the constable didn't give the situation any more clarity. The circumstances still puzzled him. Someone didn't want the portrait to be finished or to enter the contest. Maybe both?

He took a sideways glance at Lillias, who appeared to be enraptured by the work to her right and she'd moved to stand in front of it.

"Did you know you're looking at last year's R.A. winner?" He moved to join her by the portrait of an English pointer proudly holding a red fox between its jaws as the dog gazed up at its unseen master.

"Are these in order from the most recent to the oldest?" she asked, turning to her right, and pointing around the room to the entrance behind them.

"Yes, and eye level is the most prestigious position," he said as she began to walk to the right and stand in front of the previous year's winner, a portrait of a young girl in a pink gown clutching a rag doll to her breast and staring out of the frame as if she hadn't anyone to love or care for her.

Lillias frowned as she viewed the work. "She appears abandoned," she said softly, "either emotionally or physically." Lillias tilted her head to one side and then the other, studying it carefully. "It conveys so much emotion, but the beholder has to make up their own story."

"The best works are such," he said, agreeing with her. "That's what I was aiming for in my work." He let out a sigh.

"The highest emotion."

Lillias seemed to search for the word before she uttered, "Ecstasy?"

"You ask as if you'd seen it?"

Immediately Lillias averted her eyes, gazing down first before she busied herself with examining the next work more closely, a middle-aged woman playing a pianoforte.

"This one is full of emotion too," she said as if she hadn't uttered the word, 'ecstasy.' But William wouldn't let her slip away from the reference so easily.

"You could say the woman in this painting is emoting ecstasy," William said softly. By now a few more visitors had filed into the gallery, and he was mindful of their presence.

Lillias kept her eyes on the portrait when she replied,

"I've seen a similar expression on my sister's face when she plays."

Upon closer observation, it did remind him of his own attempt at capturing raw emotion. Although advancing in years, with wisps of gray hair framing her face, and crinkles at the outer edges of her eyes, the woman appeared orgasmic in her position on the bench. With her back arched and her lips slightly parted, the performer maintained her hands on the keys with a light touch as if stroking a lover.

"The piece is breathtaking," Lillias murmured.

"Her breath is taken away . . ."

"With an overwhelming feeling of happiness and joy," Lillias said, completing his sentence. "That is the definition of the work no matter the context," she said, blushing pink, but not looking at him.

"My thoughts exactly," he agreed. "And I don't have a piece worthy of this competition."

Lillias's eyes lighted on him as she spun quickly to respond. "That's not so," she exclaimed as if affronted. Then she blushed a hotter shade of pink this time after she glanced down at the evidence on her skirt again.

But he was smart enough to invite her to collaborate and ask her opinion. "What work would you recommend for the entry?"

Pursing her lips together tightly, she lifted her gaze to the ceiling again as if all the answers she needed were stored neatly up there for her to retrieve.

After a long pause it was clear none of his works stood out.

"You see," he said, catching her elbow and walking her around the corner of the gallery to the next display of R.A. competition winners and farther from the other guests. "I must find the missing work."

"Is there a place where we could talk more privately?"

Lillias asked, glancing over her shoulder. When she looked back at him, she reddened slightly before she added, "properly chaperoned, of course."

He was about to offer a suggestion when she tugged at his arm, leading them into the adjacent gallery.

But it needn't be with one of my aunts," she amended.

"I can't promise we won't run into your aunts, but there's a lovely patio two galleries over on the west side of the building where an outdoor café offers refreshments this time of year."

Lillias nodded. "That sounds perfect. A spot of tea would be wonderful right now."

Without further delay, they walked briskly through the two smaller galleries until he led her out to a secluded but public patio with six iron tables hosting two chairs a piece.

There were two older women seated at one of the tables next to the R.A.s outer wall, making the obvious choice for him to select the table farthest away by the flower garden.

"Here we are," he said, moving one of the chairs out for Lillias. Once she was seated, he helped scoot her chair into place. By the time he'd rounded the small table and had taken a spot across from her, the waiter was at his elbow.

"Tea and cakes," he told the man.

The servant bowed and was off as if he'd interrupt a tete-a-tete. William returned his attention to Lillias.

Her eyes were studying him. He imagined as closely as she'd studied the portraits in the galleries, with an artistic eye. She was a portrait artist after all. Perhaps if he spoke to her as a peer, he'd get the answers he sought, or at least explore a relationship that appeared to be budding like the roses behind her seat.

"You're staring."

He blinked hard and rapidly. "Oh, I had no idea," he muttered apologetically. But how could he not help himself.

She was like a living portrait. Now that he'd had more time to study her face, it was just as fascinating as the rest of her. *If she is the figure model she claims not to be.*

"After viewing the finest the R.A. has to offer in portraiture, my mind is full of images swimming about in a sea of colors and I was thinking you looked to me like a living portrait." Often the truth was best when caught ogling.

Lillias's gaze lowered to her hands and a bashfulness came over her. It appeared the slightest compliment would set color to her cheeks, this time it tied her tongue as well.

William seized the opportunity. "If only you would sit for me," he said rushing, wanting to get all the words out before she could refuse him. "You told me you would not sit for a portrait. How could you deny future St. Clair generations? Perhaps that's why your aunt suggested it?"

While he was talking, he'd watched her closely. Lillias's lips were ripe like a red apple, full and luscious. She had a habit of pursing and twisting them before she spoke as if her spinning thoughts pulled at the corners creating a menagerie of shapes until she was ready to form her words.

Every punctuated twist made him yearn for a chance to nip at their luscious edges and taste the sweetness he hungered for.

"When you put it that way, it gives me pause," she finally answered without looking at him.

She'd given him an inch. He was hungry for more. "Your mother must have insisted you sit for a portrait as a child?"

When she shook her head, he persisted, "With your sisters?"

Again, she wagged her head back and forth, the golden-brown tendrils around her face bouncing with the movement.

"Then you have done the world a disservice," he said with indignation.

Her head shot up and she leaned slightly forward, her eyes keen and full of concern. "Do you think so?"

"'Shall I compare thee to a summer's day?'" He started to recite the one Shakespeare sonnet he knew by heart. "'Thou art more lovely and more temperate. Rough winds do shake the darling buds of May, and summer's lease hath all too short a date.'"

Lillias let out a sigh. "When you put it that way, how could I refuse?"

* * *

AT THAT MOMENT the waiter returned with the tea and cakes, but William nearly knocked over the servant as he leapt from his chair and clapped his hands together, then went to Lillias on bended knee.

Somehow the comedy of his response helped cover up her own surprise. How had she just agreed to pose for William? When what she had planned was to finally share the anonymous note she'd received yesterday. That was why she wanted a quiet spot to talk.

"Are you celebrating an engagement, mi lord?" The startled servant stood at attention gripping the teapot in one hand and a tray of cakes in the other, as if they could be wielded as shield and sword if necessary.

But Lillias sobered when she spied the look of horror on William's face and asked, "It couldn't be that intolerable to be engaged to me, could it?"

"Oh, my dear Lillias?" bubbled a voice from behind her. "I leave you both of your own devices and you are engaged?"

The dowager.

"'Tis customary to gain permission from the father before proposing, but as you have already done the asking, I will accept on behalf of the duke."

Now it was Lillias's turn to hold her mouth agape. Speechless. The dowager looked like she'd signed a peace treaty between England and Scotland. How could either of them argue with her?

"You are just as surprised as Lillias was," William said to the dowager.

On his way up from bended knee he winked at Lillias, giving her a moment's reprieve from the shock of what appeared to be a misunderstanding.

"No doubt you have much conspiring to do," the dowager announced, waving the servant forward.

The poor man glanced at William sheepishly. No doubt he wondered what part he'd played in the misunderstanding that for now, no one was brave enough to undo.

"Would you join us, Lady Elizabeth?" William scrambled to his feet and pulled out his chair.

Looking satisfied with herself, the dowager waved him off.

"Goodness, no. I wouldn't want to spoil this moment and overstay my welcome. Your flushed complexions tell me you want to be alone."

Coward. When did the dowager ever worry about overstaying her welcome?

When William hesitated to take his seat again, the dowager turned to the servant. "Come along now, serve the tea before it gets cold." Then she tapped William on the arm with her fan. "Lady Emma will ride home with your fiancée and I'm off for Woodbeck House to tell the duke the news."

Lillias didn't know what to say. She was still in shock over the whole innuendo. But William was playing along, and she couldn't possibly embarrass the dowager. Despite her meddling and overbearing personality, she loved her aunt. As the dowager turned to leave the beautiful courtyard, the servant quickly filled their cups and set down the tray of cakes, then he disappeared as quickly as a rabbit running for its life.

Now the two of them were alone, except for the older couple at the far end of the patio. Her aunt's retreating footsteps echoed through the R.A. doorway, and she disappeared.

With some reluctance, Lillias turned back toward William, meeting his gaze, not knowing what to expect.

"Well, that's one way to get your permission to paint your portrait." He gave her a seductive grin. "Your engagement portrait."

"You aren't serious, are you?"

"About the portrait?"

Lillias wanted to throttle him. *Men.* "About the proposal?"

"That you sit for my R.A. entry?"

"Did you not hear what my aunt implied?"

He waved his hand in front of his face as if batting away a pesky fly. "Engagements can be casual." He paused, and then to her utter surprise, got down on bended knee again. "Or they can be formal." After a bit of fumbling in his breast pocket, William produced a tiny ring and slipped it on her right ring finger.

She gasped and covered her mouth as she stared at the petite, crowned silver heart clasped between hands on either side.

Lillias's eyes shot up to meet William's. "A *Claddagh*, Lord Cavendish?"

Leaning forward as if to share a secret he said, "When we are alone, please call me William."

When she began to object at the impropriety, he elegantly cut her off with a warm smile and squeezed the hand wearing the ring. "We are engaged in friendship. Let's start there."

"But what about—" She hesitated, cutting off her own question. A *Claddagh* ring was a *fede* symbol, meaning joined in faith. Engagement rings and wedding rings were made like these three hundred years ago and farther back still. *Why did William have one ready to offer her?*

"The dowager?" He smiled again.

She wasn't certain if she'd call William's intentions devious or delightful. And she'd need to be daring to accept such a proposal of *friendship*.

William gave the ring a peck on the top of her glove. "It suits you."

Gaze affixed on the ring, which glinted in the sun's rays, she turned it from side to side. She wanted to ask him questions at once, just as she did her siblings when she needed information, but she reached for her cup and took a slow sip to allow her mind to put her queries in a reasonable order before she began and before she could tell him about the note.

"Whose ring is this?"

"Yours," he said all too quickly.

Cocking her head to one side, she narrowed her gaze on him. "Before me?"

"Mine," he said smartly.

Two could play this game. "Before you?"

"Someone other than you or me," he said, crossing his arms over his chest and leaning back in the patio chair most pleased with his ability to make her questioning a game.

"Did you steal it?"

"I'm not a thief," he snapped, affronted. "I won it."

"From whom?"

"From the loser."

She eyed William over her cup as she slowly raised it to her lips and blew across the hot water before she took a sip. He flinched, then leaned forward on his elbows as if mesmerized by her mouth.

She didn't think she was beautiful, but she understood

enough about men to know they could be led by what lay between their legs. She was ready to change the game.

Taking her lips to the brim, she lowered her lashes to gaze into her cup as if the tea was more fascinating than her companion. She began to sigh with satisfaction after each sip. Her nostrils flared with each deep inhale of the tea's lovely aroma and after a few delicate sniffs, she was tipping her head backward and arching against the chair akin to the woman in the pianoforte portrait.

Finally, for the piece de resistance, she dramatically set the teacup down and clutched the top of her lacey neckline, tugging it away from her breasts as she fanned herself with her free hand.

"Are you feeling all right?" William asked in a shaky voice.

She stole a quick glance under her lashes, raising her lids about halfway. "What makes you ask?" she said breathlessly.

"You appear overheated, even though there's a light breeze." Then he paused and moistened his lips as if getting them ready for resuscitation.

"I do feel a bit lightheaded," she whispered. "All the excitement." Although she was not the actress Verity was, she'd observed her sister's phony fainting spells and could mimic one without fail.

William quickly pulled his chair to her side. "Let me come closer and make sure you are all right."

She gave him her best dreamy look. When she started to sway toward him, he quickly caught her in his arms as she spilled halfway out of the chair.

"Oh, my," she exclaimed on her way down into his lap. "We shouldn't be this familiar already." She closed her eyes, fluttering her lashes with drama before she let all her muscles relax and she slumped, falling fully onto William's lap. As much as she wanted to peek at his expression, she didn't want to spoil the ruse. He deserved it for all his evasiveness.

"What's wrong with Lillias?"

Nigel.

William coughed nervously, adjusting her in his lap. "I— She— I think she's fainted."

A roar of laughter spilled over her. No doubt it was Nigel.

"Is this how you encouraged your beloved to accept your proposal? When she refuses you?"

"You can't be serious," William said with a disgusted tone.

Lillias imagined William would have swatted his friend if his hands weren't full of holding her.

"'The course of true love never did run smooth.'"

"Don't be a fool. This is no time for Shakespeare."

"Better a witty fool than a foolish wit," William's friend argued.

The rumble started under her back, then it traveled up to her shoulders and in moments she was shaking with William's laughter. Now was the best time for her to come around.

"Am I surrounded by fools?" she asked sleepily, rubbing her eyes like a child waking up.

"According to William Shakespeare, 'I'm not bound to please thee with my answer,'" Nigel said.

"Is William here?" she asked in a wobbly voice.

There was silence.

"I am a fan of your sonnets, William," she added in a breathless whisper.

Before there was an answer from either of the men, William's face peered over hers. Staring into her eyes rather than at her face, he appeared to do his best to assess her well-being. Picking up her hand wearing the *Claddagh* ring, he lightly pressed three fingers against her wrist above the edge of her glove.

"Do you know my name?" he asked with concern in his voice.

"William Shakespeare?"

He shook his head. "Lord William Cavendish," he told her, grinning weakly, "at your service."

"William?" she teased. Then twisting her head slowly toward Nigel, she asked, "Is that William Shakespeare?"

Nigel bowed. "Some days I believed I am, my lady, but the Bard lived over two hundred years ago."

When she returned her attention to William, she tried to give him a blank stare.

"We enjoy his words and celebrate his spirit as if he were still with us today," William said, trying his best to explain their behavior. He studied her again as if trying to make up his mind what to do.

"We should get you home," Nigel said sharply, as if he was the one in charge.

"She should see a physician at once," William contradicted.

"A physician?" She tried not to sound alarmed, but she'd had her fun. "Why, Lord William Cavendish, would I need a doctor?" Glancing down at her inclined position in his arms she added, "And why in heaven's name am I lounging in your lap?"

William tucked his chin back as if he were affronted. "What's your name?"

"That's a ridiculous question when you already know the answer," she said indignantly.

Nigel chuckled as she squirmed in William's lap trying to right herself. William gently guided her back to sitting, then gave her a light boost into her chair.

Brushing her loose curls from her forehead first, she righted her bodice with a quick tug. "I think we were discussing the former owner of this ring," she said tartly, holding up the professed artifact on her finger.

"It belonged to me," Nigel said, walking over to her and gently taking her gloved hand. He then looked up at William.

"Are we no longer friends?"

"Were we ever?" William shot back.

Nigel grabbed his chest near his heart and staggered backward as if wounded. "You give my ring to another? Have you forsaken me?"

Nigel and Verity would make quite the theatrical pair if they became a couple.

"It was my ring to give," William argued.

"The ring was stolen."

"You stole it and I won it fairly."

"I'm wearing stolen property?" Lillias asked as she began to slip the *Claddagh* ring off her finger.

"No," both men yelled at once.

"It's mine to give," William said, glaring at his so-called friend.

Nigel shrugged his shoulders and nodded.

She wasn't sure who to believe as she swung her gaze back and forth between the two men. Then she let out a polite cough.

"I do receive this in the spirit it was given, as a token of your friendship, as it appears Nigel has denied all current claims to it and agrees it's yours to give. Considering our family's histories, it's a monumental step."

William cleared his throat in a way one would before saying something grand. "Most squabbles between families and the subsequent animosity are carried generation to generation without recollection, or reckoning."

Not to be outdone, she responded with her own grandiose statement. "On those grounds alone, I agree the St. Clairs and the Cavendishes should make amends and bury the prejudices of their ancestors. I can only hope our friendship will start with a new bond of trust and collaboration," she offered. But judging by William's expression, she may have assumed too much.

"It may be too early to presume our agreement will change the past, but perhaps we can start with the portrait sitting," William said with a boyish grin.

She opened her mouth to say something and then couldn't put to words anything that could contradict what she had said. She sputtered, letting out the air she would have used to argue. And now that Nigel had made it a threesome, she'd have to wait until she was alone again with William to talk about the threatening note.

"Congratulations, Cavendish, you have won the round," Nigel said, taking his friend's hand and holding it up like a referee.

Certain the bout wasn't over, Lillias held her tongue.

CHAPTER 20

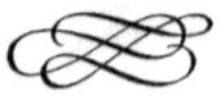

I'm engaged again?

William stared at his blank canvas in the empty R.A. classroom the following day, recounting the actions that lead to his comical proposal to Lady Lillias St. Clair. The memories of a previous betrothal flooding his thoughts.

At the time his father referred to it as 'the incident at Oxford.' Then, he was unhappily engaged to Lady Georgina Farthington, an alliance designed to further the Cavendish legacy.

After his boxing opponent was killed—by his hands— the Farthington family had immediately rescinded their blessings for the nuptials and the banns were taken down.

Not a day had gone by since then that he didn't regret what happened when he took on Byron Donavan in the ring for a student competition.

Both Oxford seniors, he and Byron were considered equally matched. It wasn't until after the 'incident,' William was aware he had a condition doctors described as amnesia stemming from a concussion. Initially, a list of maladies too long to remember had been reviewed, and a number of ones related to head injuries. The one that clinched the diagnosis was his having no memory of what had happened in the ring.

Perhaps it was because his father had influence with every magistrate and most representatives in his parliament party that William hadn't been tried for murder, but the ending was the same. One innocent life had been taken while he was in the ring. And that was why his stepping in for Nigel had been such an enormous risk.

Two years had passed, but the shame and angst hadn't. William thanked God daily he'd had no further incidents, but he'd often wondered if the stress of an engagement was the trigger and not the boxing. And that was another reason for his ongoing engagement avoidance.

But this flirtation with Lady Lillias St. Clair was no formal engagement. It was more a means to his end. He continued to stare at the blank canvas, his memory now retracing the outline of the contest entry portrait he'd started weeks ago in Professor Beauchamp's class.

Even if Lillias continued to deny she was the student model in his still-life class, there were too many coincidences for him to stop persisting.

After the constable's inquiries with the R.A. staff led to dead ends and no suspects, he decided to abandon the hunt for the painting and start over. Even if he offered a reward in the papers, he was certain it would only cause distress and possible ruin for Lillias if the painting was found.

What began as a whimsical, and somewhat perverted distortion of an unknown model posing for an art class, could turn out to be an ostracizing and an inheritance-ending event if the portrait was displayed in public.

Now, he had become more than overly fond of the self-proclaimed old maid of the of St. Clair daughters. Instead of painting the provocative portrait of Lillias, he'd paint the professional one.

He pulled out his pocket watch and pressed his thumb against the clasp until it sprang open. She was five minutes late, and so was Professor Beauchamp, who'd agreed to chaperone the sitting.

William suggested the R.A. as neutral territory and to avoid the scrutiny of the St. Clair family. Even though he and Lillias had called a truce to the feud, that didn't mean her father had. William had learned more than a few life lessons from the military. One of the most important, a man could only fight one battle effectively at a time and his chances of winning were better on his own turf.

"This is going to challenge me," he said out loud, turning his head side to side, studying the outline.

"This is going to challenge me too."

He lifted his head to find his subject framed in the doorway. Dressed in a golden gown that glittered in the light like a faceted diamond, Lillias took his breath away. The fabric hugged all her curves, and she reminded him of a bubbly glass of Champagne.

"Everything worth doing should be a challenge or why do it?" he said, walking toward her.

"Yet, a challenge should be accepted with caution," she replied, moving into the room and standing in the center where the figure model had posed weeks before.

"But being cautious can activate avoidance," he countered, meeting her in the center of the room.

"Which leads to keeping away from something."

"Or someone," he added, taking her hand and giving the *Claddagh* ring a quick peck.

"Or rendering void an agreement."

He rose only far enough from his bent position to look directly into Lillias's eyes, glittering in their own right from the reflection of the golden fabric about her neck. "But when challenge is used correctly, it inspires growth."

"It defines a contest," she insisted, raising an eyebrow.

"Disputes a belief," he pressed.

"Demands proof."

"Don't tell me you've never stood in this spot before."

The gleam in Lillias's eyes dimmed at his affront. He didn't want to anger her, but he didn't want to be lied to.

"What do you mean?" Her cheeks tweaked with color, and she took her hand from his.

"If you weren't the model in Professor Beauchamp's still life class, then you have a twin."

Lillias's head bent back, and her beautiful long neck was exposed as if she were offering it to him. While she let out a polite giggle, his left hand stopped his right from doing what he was thinking.

"You've met my sisters," she murmured with her eyes closed and her graceful neck stretched long like a swan's.

Then she struck a pose.

"That's it, hold that."

"You're not serious," she mumbled, moving only her lips through clenched teeth, but remained still.

"Every artist is serious about their work," said a voice from behind Lillias.

He didn't need to look up from his rapid sketching to recognize the voice of Professor Beauchamp. He was expected. Even though there was a loosely bound engagement with Lillias, protocol dictated decorum, even in artistic pursuits.

"Every serious artist is obsessed with their objects," he murmured to himself, caught in the moment of putting pencil to paper and filling in the larger details of Lillias's pose.

The sun filtering in from the tall R.A. windows, where he'd carried the model only weeks before, allowed just enough light to cascade over her and fill the space around her with flecks of refracted colors. She appeared to reside inside a globe of sparkling fairy dust.

Oblivious to time, he worked with a fever of intention. If the professor was still in the room, he was unaware, as he studied Lillias's curves and duplicated their generous rounding. She was the perfect model with one hand behind her head as if using it as a pillow, and the other wrapped under her bosom.

How was it that one woman could be perfect in face and form?

After making a few quick strokes to fill in the loose tendrils of golden-brown hair around her face, he held his pencil aloft and took in his first full breath since he started sketching.

A shift of energy was evident in that moment as Lillias relaxed her pose and let her arms drop.

"How did you know I'd finished."

"Because I am," Lillias said with a sigh, stretching her arms over her head. "I'd expected I'd be sitting for a portrait, not standing." She sounded more observant than contrite.

Perhaps she had experience. He wouldn't let go of that assumption just yet.

The rest of the room came into focus. He too stretched his arms over his head and glanced about the room looking for the professor. "Where did Beauchamp go?"

Lillias peered about the room as if she'd awakened from a nap, with dewy eyes, arching her waist to each side, then twisting back and forth. "Although my eyes were closed, I recall hearing his voice at the beginning and having a sense he was in the room, but then everything fell away, as if I was transported somewhere else in time."

Oddly, William had felt the same. "That's not unlike Beauchamp," he volunteered. "He's chaperoning today and not teaching. Perhaps he was bored." He shrugged his shoulders.

"Are we finished?" Lillias raised her eyebrows, then her shoulders, before both fell back into place after she gave him a pleading look.

His experience with live subjects was rare, so he'd become accustomed to long periods of active work. "For now," he abated.

Lillias's posture relaxed. He was still keenly attuned to her figure having studied it for . . . how long? He pulled out his pocket watch and flipped it open.

"It's high time," she said with a little exasperation in her voice. "Do I get paid in compliments or cups of tea?"

"Come," he offered, taking her hand, "you deserve both."

* * *

Lillias found herself at the same table where William had fumbled through a mock proposal the day before. The memory of the events still as fresh as her trepidation. When she'd returned home late yesterday afternoon, she'd found the house abuzz with the news and Verity pouting. Lillias had promised her sister's engagement before her own, and it was expected she'd be disappointed. But unfortunately, Verity had retired to her room before dinner and refused to come out.

Pushing aside her concern for her sister, Lillias decided she must focus on her current companion at the center of her drama. Another threatening note had been delivered this morning and she was close to tears thinking about it again. Yet as much as she wanted to finally make a confession, there wasn't much privacy. No doubt if she had mentioned it to William sooner, she might have been able to avoid another incident. Not that he could solve the mystery, but perhaps he had a way to circumvent the threats.

Although she'd donned the light cloak and was more appropriately dressed for the patio, it appeared most of the patrons were gawking or whispering about her. William must have sensed her uneasiness.

"You still look dazzling even with your cover-up on," he promised. "Please tell me you've posed before." His earnest expression and their budding relationship made the appeal more critical to her answer than ever before.

Instead of answering his question though, she snapped open her reticule and dug out the offensive note. Handing it to him she said, "Read this."

A wave of concern flittered over his features as he reached for the note. Surprisingly, he gently took both her hands in his and the folded paper fluttered down to rest on the tablecloth.

"Your hands are shaking." His eyes searched hers.

She squeezed his hands. "Read the note," she insisted.

But William set his chin in a stubborn jut.

She managed to slip one hand out to retrieve the message that had her head swimming. "Read it," she said again.

After finally unfolding the parchment, he began to read what had caused her such distress. As his eyes scanned the words, she remembered them as if they were seared into her eyelids.

When he was finished, he looked at her in alarm. "Do you have any idea who sent this to you?"

Lillias bit her lip and shook her head.

"We must go to the authorities now. This is serious."

"I have the money. I have plenty of money."

William's face reddened. "Of course you do, but that's not the point."

"It's true," she said, dropping her head into her hands.

"What's true?" William asked as she started to hiccup. She hadn't been honest. She didn't have the money. And she had to tell him the truth about the modeling.

Hiccup. "I- It— Was—" *Hiccup.*

"You."

Hiccup. She nodded. They came fast now, and her shoulders shook. She couldn't control them. Lillias closed her eyes, afraid to look about and find the other patrons staring at her again.

Before she started to panic, he sprinted around to her chair. At first, she thought he aimed to scare her out of them as he had at his studio, but he began to rub her shoulders instead.

"It's all right. I'll handle this," William promised in a soothing voice.

"The patrons," she mumbled between hiccups.

"Need to mind their own business." There was a pause, then he added, "There's only one old gent sitting by himself with his back to us. The others left a while ago."

Whether it was true or not, William's reassurance helped. Lillias stopped gasping for air between hiccups, which only could have exasperated the problem. After taking in one deep inhale and pushing it out after counting to five, they slowed. And after two more of the same, in a few moments they were gone.

"There," he said as if to a baby. "Better now?"

Lillias nodded, slowly opening her lids halfway and stealing a look at the open patio. He was telling the truth. The space was almost abandoned except for the old gent in the corner.

His strong but gentle touch left her shoulders, and the action immediately left a void. Before she had time to mourn the loss, he'd taken a seat in front of her and smiled.

"I guess there's not much of me left to your imagination," she admitted, her cheeks heating.

"My hands are craving what my mind can only touch." William's tone was smooth. When his pupils narrowed, the blackness of them deepened.

Thinking herself more noble than desirable, Lillias was without words.

"Embarrassing you is not my goal, only finding you." William's words rang with sincerity. "Your form is perfection." He paused and looked around.

The old gentleman was still there, but far enough away.

"Even though I was devastated when my painting of you vanished, *not* finding you would have been more the tragedy." He reached for her hand with the *Claddagh* ring.

Lillias was distracted by someone over William's shoulder. It was the server from yesterday. But after recognizing her, the man bolted back through the kitchen entrance. She laughed, then covered her mouth before her focus returned to William. His confused gaze meant he'd misunderstood her reaction.

"I'm not laughing at what you said." She pointed behind him. "It was the steward who sparked the engagement."

William brushed away the miscommunication with a wave. "I meant what I said." He leaned forward. "Those eyes." He gazed more intently at her. "Do you remember when I said I'd never forget them?"

Lillias had been told by her closest relatives, people who loved her unconditionally, that her eyes were beautiful, especially her mother. But with the passing months, caring for her sisters and rarely going anywhere but their family library to reread her favorite Shakespearean treasures, she was certain those compliments were meant to placate her.

But now was her turn to compliment William. "You were so brave, taking me to the window when the fire broke out."

She fanned the air when she spoke, as if the flames were there again and the thick smoke. "I fainted. I don't remember much," she admitted.

"I do remember you wanted me to forget you." William stared at her with anticipation, as if he was waiting for an apology.

She'd give it to him.

"I'm sorry, but I was frightened," she confessed. "I'd never done anything so risky"—she swallowed hard— "or risqué. Without a mother to keep me in check, I went about my own devices to get what I wanted."

"I see what I want, and I go after it," William said in an understanding tone. "Like you."

The heat in her cheeks had long found its way through other parts of her body. By now, she imagined she'd look like she'd taken a bath in cherry juice. Everything from her neck to her toes must have turned rosy red. She glanced down at her arms. At least they appeared normal in color.

When she looked up at William again his brows were knotted together.

"I hope I don't sound too forward," he said apologetically.

"Said to a woman who posed for a figure-drawing class?" she joked, melting his stern frown into a generous smile.

"Did you see my portrait of you?"

The anxious expression on his face made her wonder if that was how he'd looked as a young boy asking for approval. She'd already had a nasty bout with her hiccups and would have trouble explaining them away a second time. It was time to let honesty rule.

"You took creative license with the pose."

The guilt in his eyes conveyed more than any words he would have spoken, as if he'd stolen the painting himself to keep it from overexposing either of them. His head bowed.

"I'm not upset," Lillias started, "now."

His head shot up and his gaze locked with hers. "When I started the project, I didn't know you." William rubbed his regal chin as if it would help him articulate his words. "Professor Beauchamp called you, Lilly." Then his mouth turned down into a slight, but noticeable frown again. "You said to forget your name and you."

He reached for her hands again. "At first, I thought that was possible. No one believes in love at first sight." He paused and eyes clouded as if a storm was brewing inside. "But no one falls out of love with something of beauty, either." William sighed, meeting her gaze again. "Perhaps it was infatuation, or just loving an object, like you love a piece of art, but when you came back a second time and you put me in my place, well, that's when it hit me hard."

It was her turn to squeeze his hands when he seemed uncertain of what to say next.

"After that, I was devastated when Professor Beauchamp told me you'd quit the role."

"I couldn't go on," she said in a small voice that she didn't recognize. "It was too dangerous."

"Of course, the professor explained to me that your father was ailing, and you needed to be by his side," he said.

She shook her head. "Beauchamp was protecting me." Then she took in a big inhale as if ready to ward off another bout with the hiccups. "You can see what happens when I don't tell the truth." She paused as a new servant approached the table.

"More tea, my lady?"

After Lillias nodded, William added, "And some of those delightful finger sandwiches."

The girl took a gentle bob and was off.

They both looked up from their joined hands at the same time and started to speak on top of each other.

"You go first," William said, smothering a chuckle.

Lillias gazed down at their hands again. "Have you ever wanted something so badly it clouded all your judgement?"

"Yes, it's happening now," William answered and squeezed her hands.

Startled by his answer, she breathed in sharply and her heart picked up speed like a runaway horse, galloping faster and faster. Afraid to meet his gaze or answer, she struggled to get her emotions under control.

"Lillias, I must set aside my personal needs and find out a way to protect you," he said with genuine concern, giving her a moment to collect herself.

Puffing up, she eked out the question, "Protect me?" Only her father had ever offered to protect her.

"This is my fault," he said indignantly. "I will defend your honor and worry about the consequences of a missing nude portrait of—"

"Shhh," she hushed him and nodded to the servant a few feet from the table with the sandwiches waiting to be waved over. Behind her stood the steward who'd served them yesterday, holding a tray of two tea pots and two cups.

"Let's refer to it as the object of obsession," Lillias whispered before William chuckled and gestured to the servants.

Once the sandwiches and plates were placed, the young woman plucked the cups off the tray, followed quickly by the hot tea. Then after a short nod and a bob again, she was gone.

Lillias couldn't help giggling after the male servant gave a backward glance as he followed the girl through the doorway and into the service kitchen.

"If you wanted the man fired, you have the power," William suggested.

She would do no such thing. "Why would I want to have the man fired when he's the one responsible for your proposal?"

"It would have come eventually."

"And how long, pray tell, is eventually?" she asked before blowing air across the hot tea.

William's gaze immediately went to her lips. As much as she'd enjoyed yesterday's mischief, the matter at hand was more serious.

"Until you eventually said, yes."

"Before long you'll have me quoting Shakespeare again," she threatened with a conspirator smile.

"You will make for a better companion than Nigel. I can promise you that."

Nigel was an anxious and complex fellow and Verity seemed to be infatuated with him. No doubt the shirtless exposure had something to do with it. Still, Lillias wasn't convinced he was the match she sought for her sister. But before she delved into William's personal friendships, she needed to make a plan for the threats she'd been receiving.

"Then as my protector, what do you recommend?" she asked. No games today, she promised herself.

"Did you say your man Finneas told you both deliveries were made by young boys?"

His question came just as she'd taken her first bite of her sandwich, so all she could do was nod. William had already devoured one of them, somehow, but there were still another four on the plate.

"Was it the same boy or different ones?"

She hurried and swallowed her bite. "I asked the same of Finneas, but he couldn't recall." She blotted her lips with the napkin from her lap, then she added, "But he said either way, the lad or lads must have been from the East End."

"Because of how they were dressed?"

"Not so much that," she said, wrinkling up her nose. "He said it was the smell of them."

William leaned back in his chair uttering a sound of agreement, as if he could recall that smell. "A runner."

"A what?"

"The gaming hells pay the homeless lads a wage for running money, property, food, or dice between establishments for their employers."

She shook her head.

"It's true," he persisted, "lads as young as six or seven are in the employee of unsavory business owners."

"I'm not disagreeing with you. I'm bemoaning the atrocity of it."

"It's a hard life and it doesn't get any easier when they start with petty theft and advance to more criminal activities," William said, clearly agitated with the situation as well. "That's why I want to build a school for them. Keep them off the streets and teach them a trade."

So, he wasn't lying to impress her when he said he had loftier goals than his peers. Save the souls of those who society had cast aside was honorable. She'd expected rakish aspirations. Even if she'd begun to admire his work as an artist, now there was reason to admire his heart.

Then as if William woke up from his deeper musings while she was having some of her own, he snapped his fingers and said, "We'll need to set a trap."

"A trap?" At least he wasn't asking her to report the instance to the authorities, but she was worried about trying to trick a criminal. "And how, pray tell, will you do that?"

"The criminal world is a small one. I have an idea already of how we'll catch the culprit."

We? Now that wasn't the answer she was expecting.

CHAPTER 21

A gathering storm outside the library window mirrored Lillias's mood. She'd put her easel away for the day, finding her inspiration for the R.A. contest entry squelched by her building anxiety.

When she had surrendered to the truth of what had now become more daunting than matching Verity with a proper husband, she'd somehow gotten herself into a discussion with her father about William's intentions.

Although vetted and approved by the dowager countess, apparently her father was not of the same opinion.

Yet, she'd later convinced herself the Earl of Devonshire's proposal was solely a ploy for her salvation. In a world where women were merely chess pieces, being moved around by the players, what else could she do but follow the wills of others in the scheme of it all?

Now she had to answer to the engagement.

"Lillias?"

Now? "Father," she replied in as strong a voice as she could muster.

He strode into the room as if intimidation was a creature

riding on his shoulders. Walking past her like she was a part of the ridiculous looking Egyptian chaise, he stopped at his desk and stared at her. "I'll need you to leave."

"Leave?"

"There will be a duel."

"Here?" Her stomach lurched.

He cast her a disconcerting glare.

"Duel?" Repeating the word, she couldn't help choking back a sob. "There must be another way."

"The Cavendishes have had it out for this family and now the duke's son threatens to take everything that I have built."

Lillias dropped to her knees. "We are merely friends, Father." Her hands snapped into prayer. "Don't do it," she pleaded. "I will break off the so-called engagement."

"That is not the point," he said, reaching for her supplicated hands. "Come, off your knees."

"What is the point?" she asked as she started to rise, but she caught her foot in her hem.

Rescuing her from a fall, her father set her right before he turned away, as if he didn't want her facing his fury.

"Revenge." He paused, fists clenched. "I had a chance once. But I let the blueblood live."

"That was gracious and generous." She would say anything to placate him right now.

"It was idiotic and immature," he shot back. "I wasn't a duke then."

She wrung her hands. This was her fault. She was determined to stop him from walking into danger.

"Listen," she said softly, taking his hand and tugging on it gently until his head turned to look at her. "It's a silly flirtation. That's all," she promised.

"Not according to the dowager." He bristled, noticing something beyond her shoulder.

"What's not to my according?"

Aunt Elizabeth, turning up at the most inopportune time. She made a career of it.

"The future husband of your eldest niece," her father said tonelessly.

Lillias turned to give the dowager a polite curtsy.

"It's time the decades-long disagreement between you and the Devonshire family ends now," the older woman said. "Especially given the circumstances."

"I couldn't agree more," her father said, grinding the words with his teeth as if they were gristle.

The dowager smiled at her, stepping close enough to brush a few whips of hair off her brow.

Lillias shook her head, putting them out of place again. The action spoke to the futility she was feeling. "Do you agree with a duel to the death?" she asked the dowager, using all her practiced reserve to keep her emotions in check, trying not to fly into hysterics.

The dowager's smile slid into a look of horror. "Charles?" She spun back around to face him.

He shrugged. "It's what must be done."

The dowager tsked. "What must be done is a meeting of the families to put the old wounds behind us."

"Again, I couldn't agree with you more," Lillias's father said stoically, placing his hands on his massive, mahogany desk. Every serviceable object had its place there, quill and ink, wax and seal, parchment, and paperweight.

Her father drew a key from his breast pocket and after jiggling it in the lock, triggered a soft click. Lillias didn't need to peer into the box to know what was inside when he set it on the top of the pristine surface. It was the right size to house a pistol.

The dowager stifled her gasp but would have deduced the same as Lillias. The duke of St. Clair was preparing for a duel. But instead of mincing words with her brother, the dowager rested her hand on Lillias's shoulder and with a slight press against it, steered her toward the entrance. "Come dear, we have some strategizing to do of our own."

Lillias started forward but dragged her feet. Although it wasn't her place to argue with her elders, she paused to peer back at her father.

Finding him staring down at the open box, she swallowed her gasp like a bitter pill. Laying in a bed of red velvet that hugged its profile, the pistol gleamed from the window's filtered sunlight.

As her aunt silently led her out of the library, Lillias prayed. *Please Lord, stop my father from killing in his effort to protect his misguided pride.*

The dowager may have been praying too as she guided Lillias down the steps of Woodbeck House and into its well-appointed garden. As long as the weather was fair, the women used the outdoor refuge like the men used the parlor.

After taking up her favorite bench, her aunt patted the seat beside her. "It's difficult letting men be stupid creatures and even more when you can't do anything about it," the dowager said with a sigh, staring ahead as if she was talking to the adjacent rose bush and not Lillias.

"With all due respect, can't you do something about this?"

The dowager continued to look straight ahead. "I already tried." The dowager sounded defeated.

"What do you mean?" Lillias tugged on her aunt's sleeve. She wanted to have a conversation, not talk to her neck.

When the dowager turned toward Lillias, she found her eyes filled with tears. "My husband died in a duel," she volunteered, choking back emotion. "Same war. From a bullet shot by a Cavendish."

Lillias's gaze dropped to her lap where her gloved hands fought with each other to stay still. What she wouldn't give for a carefree afternoon with brush in hand right now, rather than twisting her fingers in agitation. "Was it a war?"

"A war between families."

"Why did you welcome an engagement with the blood between us so poisoned?"

"I wanted a treaty. And me, to be the peacemaker."

Lillias shuddered. Her gaze lifted to study her aunt. "Are we just pawns to you?"

"This is more than a game of chess, Lillias," her aunt snapped, not absorbing the innuendo, and deflecting the hurt Lillias could not hide. "Unrequited love."

"This is about love?"

Her aunt turned to Lillias, looking through her rather than at her. "Your Uncle Richard, and Lord William's Uncle Nash, were both in love with me," the dowager whispered as if speaking only to herself, her eyes misting over again.

"What happened?" Battling for love was more important than arguing over trivial disagreements. "Did Lord Nash Cavendish kill Uncle Richard?"

Her aunt nodded gravely. "Your father was Uncle Richard's second. And William's father, Thomas, was Nash's second."

"His second?"

The dowager patted Lillias's wringing hands, forcing her to let them drop into her lap. "The second is usually a servant, friend, or family member who helps with the particulars."

When Lillias shook her head, the dowager went on. "The second is responsible for coordinating the location of the duel, inspecting the opponent's weapon, and when necessary, stepping in for the dueler."

"Isn't dueling illegal?" Lillias asked, standing, then she started to pace.

"Dueling certainly isn't legal," the dowager said blithely,

holding her spine erect as if she was sitting in the first pew at church with all eyes on her back.

"Then we must go to the authorities and end this before it begins," Lillias declared, stopping in front of her aunt with fisted hands. She wanted to punch something.

"Just like we notified the authorities of Lord William's missing painting?"

Lillias bit her lip, stymieing the rest of what she wanted to say.

"This is a family affair, not a community infringement," the dowager said in her remote tone. "Your father feels he allowed an injustice to take place when my husband was killed in the duel."

Lillias's pleading look must have conveyed her need to know more and after a deep sigh, her aunt stood and began to pace, and Lillias took a seat to give her the space to roam.

"In a pistol duel, there's only one bullet for each participant." She spun and looked at Lillias. "But I told you each man has a second, a family member or friend who attends to make sure the rules are followed. The second can step in and finish the job."

Turning toward the setting sun, the dowager began to pace again. "They met at dawn, at Battersea Fields." The dowager took a long pause before she said, "The location is always a secret, but there aren't too many places outside London for dueling."

Crossing her arms over her chest, as if to protect her heart from an imaginary bullet, the dowager turned to face Lillias. "Your father never gave me the details, I had to read about it in the papers."

"Do they ever get it right?"

"There were no disputes in our house after the publication, so I'll assume what I'm about to tell you is true."

Lillias scooted to the edge of the hard, stone bench. As

mortified about the whole business of dueling, even though it was illegal, this was about her family's honor.

"My husband shot Lord Nash Cavendish in the leg, no doubt with the intention to scare him. But when Lord Nash fired at my husband, he shot him in the chest. Dead."

Lillias covered her mouth in horror.

"According to the story, there were words exchanged that were not fit to print, but the duel ended there. However, under the code of honor and the rules of dueling, your father had just cause to retaliate."

"This illegal activity has rules?"

The dowager sighed and looked at Lillias as if she'd asked how babies were made. With an expression of unraveling patience, her aunt began to explain. "At the beginning of a duel the weapon is chosen, pistols or swords. Then, it's decided if they will fight to first blood, until no one can stand, or to the death."

Lillias nodded, still shocked by the whole idea of dueling and its rules. "I don't understand. They decided to the death?"

"That's the dishonorable part of this story. The duelers had chosen pistols and first blood. When Lord Nash shot my husband dead, he broke the rules."

Lillias nodded. "That's why Father said he had a chance to kill a Cavendish but didn't." *Now he does because of me.* She shot up from the bench and rushed to the dowager's side. "We cannot let this happen," she said, tugging on her aunt's sleeve until she turned to face her. "If you let Father go, it will be two men warring over a woman again."

A loud cackle was the dowager's answer to Lillias's plea. Her aunt did nothing to hide her morbid amusement, clasping her hands together and laughing even more. "Men will always war over women."

Shaking her head in dismay, Lillias was more confused than ever. "What do you mean?"

Her aunt turned a grayish sort of pink. "No matter how smart a man is, or wealthy, or prudent, a woman can derail his reason."

Lillias was not amused. Perhaps she was too young to appreciate her aunt's acerbic wit or understand how men could be idiots, because it appeared most were. But now she had a clue to why hadn't her aunt remarried.

"What happened to Lord Nash? Did you hate him for killing your husband?"

After wistful look at her ringless left hand, her aunt spoke in a hushed voice, "Lord Nash died a few weeks later. Some say of a broken heart. But even if he'd lived beyond my year of mourning, I couldn't have married him." She glanced up at Lillias with a hardened expression and lifeless eyes. "The duel changed everything."

"Aunt Elizabeth, then how can you let Father go through with this duel?"

Her aunt sighed deeply. "My dear, have you not listened to anything I've said?"

"Men are idiots."

"Good," the dowager said after a snort. "You have.

There's nothing we can do. You'll have to let it play out."

"Then I must be Father's second," she blurted out.

The dowager let out an oath, then clamped a gloved hand over her mouth.

Lillias ignored the uncharacteristic slip and asked the obvious. "Who will do it then?" In a family with only daughters and aging sisters, where would her father find his second?

"Finneas will do."

"Finneas?" Lillias shrieked. She didn't mean to yell and no doubt her aunt wouldn't have known about the mishap at the boxing match in the country. "I can't imagine him with a sword."

"Your father is cleaning his pistol," the dowager said calmly. "Most likely the gentlemen will fire their one shot into the air and be done with it."

"Who challenged whom?"

"Lord William's father challenged yours."

"And we are back to the beginning again," Lillias said, heaving a sigh as she plopped down, hitting her ass hard. She'd forgotten it was a stone bench, she'd been so distracted.

Her aunt sat softly down next to her. "We have an understanding."

Lillias nodded yes when she really meant no.

$\mathcal{B}$ack at Chatsworth House after spending the morning at the old Byward Street mansion, drawing up plans as if he owned the place already, William headed down the long corridor toward the parlor in a good mood. He'd found when he worked for the good of others, he could keep the demons out of his head and his anger at bay. Since that incident at Oxford, doctors had described his lack of memory as brain commotion brought on by an extreme hit to his head.

After he was banned from boxing by his father, the only time his uncontrollable anger had come to fists outside the boxing arena was when he had a raging argument with Alex last summer. If only his father had ordered him to avoid both the boxing ring and Alex, William might be cured. But today, he couldn't evade his brother when he walked into the parlor.

"Must you invade the room?" Alex asked, not even looking up from his billiard practice.

William would have done an about-face if he didn't need the information his brother would be privy to. A rumor was brewing among the staff about Father, and Alex would be able to settle it.

"I left my weapons locked up. I'm not here to start a war. I need a drink." Best to make his purpose for the invasion a diversion and not an inquisition.

Alexander grunted.

"Who at the club got Father's ire up?"

"You mean who didn't?"

Alex is making a joke? That's out of character. But it wasn't unusual for the duke to have a falling out with one of the members at White's. It was a gambling establishment after all. And although the Cavendish offspring had a credit limit, their father didn't.

"Tell me you really don't know," his brother challenged, dusting the billiard stick with new chalk.

"Why should I keep up with the duke's social schedule?"

"You are clueless." Alex snorted. "Read about it in the papers tomorrow."

William had made his way to the sideboard and after pouring a short glass of the golden-brown liquor, knocked it back while his brother knocked a red ball into one of the corner pockets. William was curious, but he wouldn't grovel. One of the servants would tell him what he wanted to know.

With that assurance, he stepped out of the parlor without another word and headed straight for the stables. If a duel was in the making, his father's groomsman would be aware of it.

After a quick walk through the gardens, and swinging through the front entrance of the stables, he headed straight for the stallion's stall. No doubt George would be within shouting distance of his father's favorite horse.

"There you are, Champ," William said soothingly, reaching out to rub the nose of his father's white Arabian.

"Where are you going Thursday morning with the duke? Not a promenade, I hear."

"A promenade?" A burst of laughter followed. "That's the farthest from a good guess, Lord Cavendish."

Favoring his good leg, his father's groomsman walked with a limp to meet William at the stall. The fall from a horse a year ago had done permanent damage, but his father had kept George in his position.

"I take it the duke will be venturing out to Putney Heath?"

"You must have heard the rumors," the groomsman said matter-of-factly, leaning against the stall wall for support.

"Isn't this the duke's second duel this month?" William asked in a casual tone.

The most oft-serious servant cracked one corner of his mouth into an amused half-smile. "You've been keeping count?"

"He counts my monthly quid. I count his indiscretions. Perhaps there will be a day when one influences the other."

George snorted like one of the horses. "May you be on the correct balance of that equation."

William couldn't help but laugh aloud at the servant's astuteness, then sobered. "No doubt a duke's honor is checked more often than a commoner. He's a target for solicitors and criminals."

George nodded from experience, having a hand in readying his father's horse for any occasion, particularly the challenges of honor. "This time it's different I presume. His Grace said it's war."

"A war?" The simple question didn't roll easily off William's tongue. "Not a petty argument? It's serious this time, George?"

The loyal servant nodded gravely. "Your father said it was time for retribution and a long overdue chance to seek revenge on the St. Clair family."

"A duel to the death with the Duke of Canterbury? He must be mad."

Champ reared back and snorted. Either the horse didn't like William's words or their volume.

"Mad, angry, justified, no matter how you describe it, this is no ordinary duel," George promised, reaching out to place a steady hand on the horse's withers.

William stepped away from Champ's stall and put the groomsmen between them. The last thing he wanted was his father's horse to injure himself reacting to his tone or movements.

"You are a reasonable man, George. What do you think of this duel?"

The servant looked at his highly polished boots before he met William's eyes, but the servant's gaze slid past him.

"The duel is necessary," a voice he recognized said soberly.

William turned to face his father and the groomsman hobbled forward and dipped his head.

"You may be excused, George."

The servant nodded and shot forward toward the main house leaving William to address the duke directly.

Straightening his shoulders and standing tall as if at attention in an army rank and file, William asked the obvious question. "Why?"

"Your actions have disgraced this house and brought ridicule to my tenure in the House of Lords."

At least his father was direct. "You must be speaking of my engagement to Lady Lillias St. Clair."

"I'd rather you speak to it. I cannot fathom any reason save for profiteering."

A slow burn began in William's gut as if he'd been punched.

"You must have known it would come to this," his father said with a deep sigh.

Christ. He hadn't been quick enough and now his father was ready for an argument.

"Father, I—"

"You are the second son."

William nodded and clapped his mouth shut, looking down.

"You've been given dispensation for that position."

I can't argue with him over that.

"My hatred of the Duke of Canterbury has never been a secret."

William nodded again. Physical affirmations seemed most prudent at this hour.

His father began to pace in front of Champ's stall and the horse let out a loud whinny as if encouraging him. "I expected St. Clair to object to your engagement to his daughter," his father bit out, as if grinding the words with his teeth first.

Resisting the urge to say something about the dowager, William gnawed on his upper lip to keep from defending Lillias's family and the casual engagement. *Weren't they just friends?*

"When Lord Charles St. Clair bet at the club that you wouldn't go through with a marriage, being only an Earl and his daughter duchess material, I decided it would be the last time I'd be the brunt of his disingenuousness."

"This is about defending me?"

His father stopped pacing and turned to William. "Haven't you heard anything I've said?"

William blanched and coughed. *It's about his father's pride.* "It's about family honor."

"My honor," his father corrected him.

"*The duel.* You've used that declarative, but never explained it."

"A father never needs to explain himself to his son."

William sighed. "We're in a circular conversation."

"Consider the circle broken, because I'm ending it." William's father huffed and strode off in the direction of the house.

Champ whinnied after him.

William hadn't planned on confronting his father. He'd suspected Alexander had sent him out to the stables. It's the kind of thing his brother did. But he didn't want his father to have the last word on this, so he took to a quick jog and fell in step with him as he reached the stable's entry.

"I'll call it off," William promised, a bit winded. "I understand how significant this feud is."

His father stopped and turned. "You still don't understand. It's not about you." Then he stormed off again.

Left to sort through his options, William trailed behind his father, who was heading back to the house. Scratching his head, as it seemed to be the appropriate action to suit his confusion, he was aware of his family's hatred toward the St. Clairs but had never understood why. Until recently, he hadn't cared.

As William walked slowly back toward Chatsworth House, he considered the societal norms of the day. First, nobles were not bred to get along. There were alliances to be sure. Not that they were long standing. But no one could survive the *ton*'s scrutiny alone.

Next, although illegal, duels were the polite elite court of the day, most often met with a repenting statement from the one who was challenged. This would mean Lillias's father would need to make amends.

Lastly, he considered as he crossed the threshold into the

foyer, love was not required in a marriage, but convenience and ranking advantage were.

"Sir, a message has arrived."

William blinked quickly and turned to the servant who'd interrupted his analysis. He picked up the envelope from the silver platter. "Did you see the messenger, Walter?"

"I did, my lord." Their butler genuflected with a quick bend at the waist.

William slid his finger through the envelope's folded edge, breaking the unmarked wax seal. Anxious to read its contents, he slid out the message. "And?" he asked, without looking up.

Walter cleared his throat. "The runner said you owe him five pounds."

William chuckled. "Then I do not need you to describe the messenger after all." He'd found an accomplice on his visit to the gaming hells. A different kind of win he'd had. Not money, but information. The ransom messages originally marked for Lillias, were now diverted right into his hands.

William's head shot up and gave the servant an appreciative nod. "Thank you, Walter, that is all."

"Sir," the servant said with reverence, then turned and walked away.

Once alone, William devoured the message.

The day draws near. The one your fear. Time flies when evil deeds are beguiled. Six hundred pounds and the painting may be returned.

Whilst that be enough though to keep it from sight?

Security can be yours when you follow the rules. If you don't have the quid, then bring me jewels.

Almack's the place where all the gentry go. Bring the bounty, but don't tell your beau.

No one will expect it. Leave it to me. Drop the goods inside their old oak tree.

More educated than he expected. The message was almost prose. Not likely written by a laborer or petty thief. But he was worldly enough to understand that those of noble blood, if desperate enough, could still be thieves.

"Sir."

It was Walter. *Again?*

"Pardon me, sir, but this just arrived from Woodbeck House."

William tore his gaze from the parchment to find a lady's fan on the silver platter his servant bore. He looked up at Walter with amused confusion. "Who delivered this?"

Walter appeared petulant. "Sir, I did not ask his name, nor did he offer one, but said it was imperative and urgent that you receive this fan from Lady Lillias St. Clair."

William chuckled, taking the delicate object from the platter. It appeared to be made of fine rose-colored silk and spines of ivory.

"Am I not the one to deliver the tokens?" William asked himself.

The servant quit the foyer without another word, leaving William to stare at the fan in one hand and the parchment in the other, his mind bouncing between what to do about the threat to Lillias and the looming duel between their fathers.

When he made a quarter turn in the foyer like a regimental soldier, with the plan to head to his personal study, a folded paper dropped from the closed fan.

After tucking Lillias fan into his coat's front breast pocket, he bent to picked up the accordion shaped parchment. With keen interest on this new discovery, he shoved the first missive into his breeches' pocket.

Taking a few steps backward, he stretched out the accordion-shaped parchment to its full length. Staring down at artistic penmanship in thick black ink, he read the secreted note from Lillias.

Dearest William,

It's with regret that I must break our friendship engagement. You may now be aware that our fathers plan to duel this Thursday at dawn. As oft is with bruised pride, I had assumed it was over a trifle, but I have found that not to be the case. As much as I hoped my pleading would allow for some reconsideration, it has not. It appears my casual engagement to you, although sanctioned by the dowager, has opened old wounds.

I have resigned to take the noble course and withdraw my agreement with you. Of course, I will return the Claddagh ring as soon as it can be done.

Meanwhile, I trust you have what you need to complete your new R.A. contest entry. The only unfinished business is the missing painting. I shall wait your word on that account.

Sincerely,

Lillias

William's head jerked up. A flood of conflicting emotions washed over him and he balled his fists. How had it become more than a mere fancy, his casual engagement? Ever since the day he'd placed the *Claddagh* ring on Lillias's finger, he could think of nothing but her.

Although he was certain his father was steadfast on dueling, would the Duke of Canterbury recant now that Lillias had broken off their engagement? It would be the noble thing to do at this hour.

Pushing aside his own frustrations and desires, he rushed out to the drive, hailing one of the duke's waiting carriages.

"Compton's townhouse, my good man," he said to the driver before the door shut. It was high time to bring in an accomplice to help him catch a thief.

"It's done, Father. I've broken my engagement with the Earl of Devonshire. You may call off the duel."

Lillias did her best to hold back the unshed tears. She'd refrained from crying since the day her mother died.

The duke was going over a thick ledger in his study, the deadly weapon within reach if he needed it.

Glancing at the weathered but fine leather case first, his eyes met hers. They were hard and unyielding. "I told you before, this is a score to be settled. You just ripped off the bandages. You cannot heal it by putting on fresh dressings."

"You profess the wound is so deep I cannot mend it, but this does not sound like the father I know."

"Then you do not know me well, Child."

Lillias gathered herself up like she'd seen the dowager do when taken offense, backbone stiffening, chin high in the air. Her aunt could stare down any offender. "Yet, you do not know me now, Father. For the last eighteen months I have tended to my sisters and given them moral support, taught them proper etiquette, and counseled them through their fears. What I've learned in this short time, doing right by your family, is the most honorable thing you can do."

"I could not agree with you more."

Lillias let out an exasperated sigh. "Then your proposed actions confuse me."

"Come here." Her father waved her over. "Some differences between men and women are impossible to overcome. This is one of those. I do not expect you to understand. When men go to war, it's not with the thought that they will die, but that they will triumph. War is not called off."

"What of peace treaties? Did not Napoleon withdraw from England?"

"Only until he could invade again, Daughter."

Lillias's shoulders sagged. She did not want to admit defeat in this war of reason with her father. Perhaps gender differences were not as great as her father suggested. It was time to test that.

"To settle this war would you apologize to the Duke of Devonshire and call off the duel, then you'd have no war with me, and it wouldn't matter if I marry Lord William or not?"

"Daughter, there are at least three questions in your one. Let me address them separately." He motioned her over, patting the ottoman next to the desk.

As she took her seat warily, he studied her with those hard eyes.

"First, I've already told you, the war has been waging for years with no ammunition fired, but that does not mean a treaty can be made by anyone's actions.

"Next, I hope to never be at war with any of my daughters. Take no action to change that course."

Lillias cracked a weak smile. As much as she loved her father, she feared him too.

"If the Duke of Devonshire is dead, I have no quarrel with his son, but he may have quarrel with me."

No doubt William will have a quarrel with him.

"Finally, if the Earl of Devonshire still wants to marry you after I've killed his father, then he is a bigger man than I, and you have my permission."

What man would marry her after her father killed her proposed father-in-law? Perhaps that would end all future proposals for her hand?

Her father touched her cheek, startling her out of her musings. "I know you miss your mother."

What would Mother do?

"And living with me isn't easy. I can make arrangements with a friend of mine if you want a husband?"

Lillias vehemently shook her head.

"Well, then, you've resolved to take your mother's place, helping your sisters come out into society. You know I don't place that burden on you." His gaze softened, and it was the only the second time since the dowager had appeared for the Season he'd given her a fair glance.

"I could never take Mother's place." Lillias bowed her head, although she wanted to refute his claim, she said what an obedient daughter should. "I can only hope to help my sisters find their ideal matches. Mine can wait."

The back of his hand brushed down the side of her face again and she sighed.

"You have the makings of a fine duchess," he said. "Why would you want to be a countess?"

If she could be honest, she'd tell her father the burden of her mother's death was crushing her spirit. Although she wouldn't mind remaining unmarried and pursue her love of art once her sisters where married. The promise of such a simple life appealed to her. Societal life terrified her.

"Pardon me, Your Grace, but there is a caller for Lady

Lillias." Finneas's gaze settled on her. "He's in the library, Miss."

"I'll have a word with him first," her father said sharply, standing.

"Lord Compton said it was unusual for him to call on Lady Lillias, but he needed to seek her advice. That I was not to alert Lady Verity."

Her father harrumphed. No doubt unsure if he preferred any callers for either girl today. "Very well." He patted Lillias's hands. "Be off. If you are playing the marriage mart for your sister, be sure to get my permission first."

She nodded numbly and followed Finneas to the library, her head filled with questions.

Once inside, a nervous looking Nigel leapt to his feet from her father's favored leather chair. "Lady Lillias, thank you for receiving me without notice," Nigel said in a rushed breath after Finneas took a seat in the corner of the room and eyed their guest suspiciously. "Does this fan belong to you?"

My fan. She glanced at the butler before she rushed forward. Finneas began flipping through the daily newspaper and appeared engrossed.

"Thank you," she gushed, keeping her back to Finneas, and purposely blocking the servant by standing directly in front of Nigel. She took the item in her hand and gave a curtsy. "I must have left this at Almack's. Thank you for retrieving it."

Nigel's gaze went to Finneas as he bowed with his head up. No doubt satisfied with the servant's preoccupation with the paper, his gaze settled on Lillias, and he mouthed, "William sent me," before he spoke aloud. "The gentleman who found it wanted it returned right away so you wouldn't worry about its absence."

"That is most kind of you both. Although it's returning won't change what will happen next."

Nigel nodded. "No doubt you wouldn't want to be seen with the same fan tomorrow."

Lillias laughed the way Verity would, with a burst and then a twitter. "You are so astute, Lord Compton. There is much uncertainty in my plans."

"Rest assured, every day begins with uncertainty. We are rarely makers of our own fate."

"Shakespeare?"

"My own words, my lady." He took a short bow, tucking his right arm at his waistcoat.

Her cheeks warmed, triggered by embarrassment as well as admiration for the depth of his prose. William's friend was quite the flirt. Noted. He and Verity were much alike.

"Perhaps studying Shakespeare's words has given me a deeper understanding of the human condition," he added after an awkward silence.

"Shakespeare is worth quoting on many occasions," Lillias agreed, her opinion of the baron much higher than before.

"Lord Compton?" The voice was shrill, but Verity's.

A look of impish embarrassment washed over Nigel's face, tinting his skin with a touch of rosy color. "My lady," he said with reverence and bowed.

"You were not announced?" Her sister looked back and forth in confusion between Lillias and Nigel. Smoothing down a few loose locks behind her ear absentmindedly, Verity popped a tiny curtsy. "If I'd known you were coming, I would have dressed."

Finneas coughed from behind the newspaper and Lillias tittered.

It was Verity's turn to blush. Reddish streaks moved up her sister's neck as if they were wayward vines of embarrassment moving to her cheeks and filling them with vivid color.

Lillias let out a surprise shriek when Verity yanked the fan from her grasp and snapped it open. Immediately her sister began fanning her face to hide her reaction.

In the scuffle, a folded piece of paper fluttered out. Snatching it in midair, Lillias quicky shoved the paper under the top lip of her glove while Nigel looked at Verity like a trapped mouse whose tail had been stepped on by a cat.

"I was merely a messenger today, not a caller," Nigel explained politely.

"You can understand my confusion," her sister said, batting her long lashes as she always did when flirting.

"Do you have something in your eye, Verity?" Lillias couldn't help but be a bit meanspirited. After all, her sister had practically shoved her aside upon entering the library, no doubt surprised to find Nigel with Lillias. She wasn't going to let her sister get off with the offense lightly. Now she wouldn't have a chance to query William's friend as she'd hoped.

"Here, let me have a look," Nigel offered, walking right up to Verity, and staring down at her, his lips moistening as if he'd kiss her right then and there.

"Back away, sir."

All heads turned toward Finneas. His face was still shielded by the newspaper, but it was as if he could see through it to the goings on in the room.

Nigel cleared his throat and took a large step backward. His head bowed as he did so like a child who'd been lectured.

"Here," Verity gestured to the Egyptian-styled chaise by the window. "You must stay awhile even if your intended errand was short."

Finneas let out a not-so-subtle grunt from behind the paper but said nothing more. Clearly, Verity wasn't going to let Nigel complete his errand and be on his way. And Nigel appeared in no hurry to leave.

But Nigel had served his immediate purpose and with a parting thanks, Lillias quietly slipped from the room. Turning in the direction of the garden, she was out in the sunshine in a few quick and efficient strides, choosing to bask in the sun outside the porch door.

Running her hand over the top of her glove, she touched the bump. Itching to read William's note, she hurried down the steps, taking quick strides to her favorite secluded bench not far from the garden's entrance and out of view from any of the Woodbeck windows.

Releasing her pent-up anxiety with a deep sigh, she slipped out the pleated note and unfolded the paper with shaky hands. Her future hung in the balance. She wanted to know, and she didn't want to know.

My Dearest Lillias,

When you are already married to my heart, how can I possibly concede to your request? I thought at first my flirtation with you was merely that. You did not give me signs of encouragement, and may I gently remind you, I've received a punch in the nose to prove that the interest was not returned. Not until our dance at Almack's.

I hope you do not think this too bold, but I believe your heart is married to mine as well. When I can't sleep, or eat, nor make coherent sentences when thinking of a life without you, I know I am affected by more than mere fancy.

Although you've asked me to release you from our engagement, I cannot. Not yet. After proposing the same option to my father, I found it made no difference to him. His war with your father is an old offense made new by the challenge of the duel. My father explains that it's not about me. And if you would marry me after he's killed your father, we fools deserve each other.

Perhaps I'm a fool to think you would consider my plea, but I hope you will look within your heart for the answer.

A fool in love,

William

Lillias folded the note, sighing with relief. She considered what William had said and found her heart indeed held the answer locked tightly inside. She might be in love with William, she decided, but not in love with the responsibility of it.

Later that night, when she tried a rhyming game to help settle her whirling thoughts, she wondered what William was doing in his chambers. Was he thinking of her? Was she keeping him awake as he was her?

If so, that made two fools in love.

CHAPTER 24

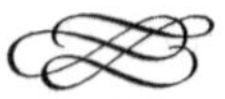

$\mathcal{A}$ persistent banging woke Lillias up. She rolled over and swore at the door, her eyes still filled with sleep. She wished the noise would stop. Before she had a chance to tell the offender to go away, Verity burst through the entrance. In her wake, two maids filed in. Trailing behind was Rebecca, looking like Lillias's room was the last place she wanted to be.

"Have you forgotten what day it is?"

Lillias's stomach lurched. Was it Thursday? Had the duel been fought? How could she have slept through it?

"Our second Almack's Ball is tonight," her sister Verity said with too much perk in her voice. "Irina, Julia, and even Rebecca, have come to help us prepare."

Lillias groaned while Verity began directing the maids like they were part of a regiment. Rebecca took a seat at the end of Lillias's four-poster bed and frowned.

As much as Lillias wanted to throw the covers over her head and hide, she was worried about her youngest sister. "You looked like your cat died. Thank goodness we don't have a cat."

Rebecca's frown quivered as if she didn't want to relinquish it. Lillias could relate to her irritation. When Verity set her mind to something, it was fruitless to go against the tide of her will.

Lillias beckoned Rebecca to join her under the covers. "If it's any consolation, I don't want to get up until lunchtime. You have my permission to sleep until then with me."

Rebecca giggled and climbed in.

"Are you excited for the ball tonight?" Rebecca asked Lillias once she'd hidden herself under the soft coverlet, which let in some filtered light through the delicate lace appliques.

Lillias nodded. "And scared," she admitted.

"Scared? I've never seen you afraid," her sister objected.

I must hide it well. "We are all afraid sometimes," Lillias confessed. "Perhaps some of us are better at hiding it than others."

"Do you think Father is afraid?"

"You know about the duel?" Lillias was surprised, but servants talk.

Rebecca nodded, but then her bright disposition disappeared like a candle being snuffed out. No doubt worry over Father had brought on her sister's melancholy. Although Verity could have fueled the flame first.

"We've already lost Mother." Rebecca's words choked up in her throat, almost inaudible.

Lillias heard her nonetheless and couldn't agree more. Her own worries had kept her up half the night. But before she could respond, the delicate lace coverlet over their intimate meeting was ripped off.

"What are you two doing?" Verity asked in a voice that dripped with admonition.

Hiding from a monster.

"Talking about how beautiful you both will look tonight," Rebecca said, flashing an innocent smile.

Rebecca's flattery worked. Verity's wind seemed to calm. She glowed, swinging gently back and forth as if she was already on the dance floor.

"If you already have a favor for Nigel, why are you so insistent about attending tonight?" Lillias asked, upsetting Verity's contentment.

"My value to him has yet to be grasped," she said with all seriousness. "When he sees a line of suitors queued to dance with me that rivals no other, my value is sure to increase." Verity puffed out her bosom, raised her chin, and struck an aristocratic pose.

Rebecca burst out laughing. "You look most persuasive."

Verity let out a loud huff and shifted to an offensive stance with her hands on her hips. "You know nothing about wooing a man, missy. When it's your turn for the marriage market, do not expect help from me."

When Rebecca didn't respond, Lillias turned to find her lower lip quivering and eyes downcast.

Turning to Verity, Lillias let out her fury. "You may not talk to your sister like that." Then throwing off her covers, she jumped to her feet. "Apologize at once or you will be banned from the ball tonight."

"You can't—"

"I can, and I will," Lillias threatened.

Her middle sister huffed and turned her back on them, her shoulders scrunching up toward her ears, as if she was puffing herself up to unleash a furious rebuttal.

While Verity was fuming and the two maids were busying themselves drawing a bath for Lillias, she walked over to the other side of her bed, helped Rebecca to her feet and gave her a hug. "When your day comes it will be wonderful," she promised.

"Yes, it will be wonderful," Verity echoed, turning around, her face streaked with tears. "I'm sorry, Becca," she said in a sincere tone. "I want to succeed."

Rebecca rushed over to Verity, squeezing her tight.

Watching the sisters make up, Lillias marveled at Verity's competitiveness. Of the three girls, she had impulses that many would consider aggressive, but she was more feminine than any of them.

Lillias clapped her hands, and all eyes swung her way. "I'll meet you both in the breakfast room. I'm sure Finneas will prepare a platter of food and we can talk more about the ball."

Without waiting for everyone to file out, Lillias stripped out of her chemise and walked to the bath, dipping a tentative finger in to gauge the temperature.

"Where is your modesty?" Verity asked, calling Lillias's attention to her sister's pursed lips and prudent expression, acting as if she were a Puritan.

"I left it at the R.A., remember?" Then she struck a pose.

"You are not setting a good example for me," Rebecca said in a soft voice, but pointed at Verity who she was standing behind.

Lillias clapped her hands again. "Shoo. The show is over."

Responding to her prompt, the ladies hustled out of the room, leaving Lillias to herself.

In no time, she was finally soaking in the warm water the maids had prepared. Stirring her hand around the surface, Lillias created mini whirlpools that mimicked her spinning thoughts.

The Almack's ball was tonight. She slipped a little lower in the copper tub. Would William be there? When she held up her hand, the water dripped down toward her wrist making the *Claddagh* ring shine like a beacon of hope.

Was she still engaged? Even though she'd asked William

to break it, she'd never taken off the ring and secretly, she had been thrilled when her father had refused her offer to cancel the engagement after finding out *she* was not the reason for the duel. It was obvious now that her engagement to William was her aunt's excuse to bring the dueling dukes together to settle an old score.

Yes, she truly hoped to see William tonight. As Verity's sponsor it would be her duty to attend, even though her aunts would be the official chaperones.

Luckily, Madame Pompadour had one of her runners deliver new gowns for Verity and Lillias to wear tonight. The shopkeeper was a skilled businesswoman, as well as a talented seamstress, having had both St. Clair girls pick out the fabrics and styles for their next gowns when they were last in the store.

Every formal engagement required a different gown. The richer the family, the more balls a debutante could attend. But gowns were not her favorite thing to wear. No, Lillias favored the timeless classics. An ivory lace and pale peach satin evening dress with matching satin gloves and a bit of sparkle at her neck. The mix of textures and subtle color along with the graceful silhouette that would be the kind of frock she would be wearing when William undressed her.

The thought would have once shocked her. Once. But being a rebel at heart she wanted to be free to choose when she wanted a man's attention. William had continued to surprise her with his attention and provocative conversations.

First, when she opened her eyes after the R.A. fire to find herself in his arms. What had he said then? Oh yes, she remembered, "I'll never forget those eyes."

Then, at the R.A. studio for her second figure posing assignment, when he asked her, "Can you afford to be an unwilling bride in this line of work?"

And she almost laughed out loud when she remembered him asking, "We have a rivalry going, and we've only just met?" after she punched him in the nose when he'd escorted them home from Crowley Down.

She wouldn't forget the most endearing time when they were dancing at Almack's, and her heart was slamming against her chest when he asked her if she believed in love at first sight.

Of course, he'd deny his ogling if she accused him. But even though she had no experience with men, she had been born with certain sensibilities, like animals had their instincts. She could see him now, in all his glory, naked and virile, all man.

Just then, she had an urge that was pure desire mixed with wonder. Reaching for her own sex between her thighs, Lillias tucked her middle finger into her warmth and began to pleasure herself, dreaming it was William's hand, and he'd found her wet and waiting for him.

The water made the experience feel even more real. After closing her eyes, she could imagine his hard shaft pressing against her thighs, and her begging him to take her.

The release came quickly, and she slid into the water up to her chin, basking in the small contractions that shuddered through her body.

Until she figured out marriage, these indulgences would need to satisfy her. And once she was finished raising her sisters, she might crave a family life with William. At the same time, she could also see herself enjoying a long engagement.

There were moments when she'd considered the possibility of operating as the dowager did, independent of any man, a person of means and influence. Then she could take on a paramour. Or two. She'd no longer risk ruining her reputation, or those of her sisters.

Yet, succession of power and independence was elusive for young women like herself. She was torn between visions of conflicting futures. But before her thoughts drifted off to more obscure scenarios, a soft rapping pulled her from her musings.

"It's Irina, my lady. A message."

"Slide it under the door," Lillias instructed, climbing from the water and reaching for the robe.

"Yes," was the muffled response as an envelope, wax seal side up, slid under her door.

Padding across the plush, Persian rug in her bare feet, Lillias broke open the seal and began to read.

My Betrothed,

I have intercepted a message from your blackmailer.

My hope is to have word of it when I see you tonight at Almack's. You must come, as there is much to discuss.

Your faithful servant,

William

Spinning back toward her freshly made bed, she sank down on it with a feeling of dread. Appetite gone, she licked her lips in an attempt to rid herself of a mouth that was dry as if she'd eaten the note.

She'd wanted to hear from William about his father and the persistence of a duel. But now she had to worry about the blackmailer too. She shouldn't have expected the villain to just stop his harassment. But now she feared it wouldn't be their fathers' possible duel that threatened to tear their budding relationship apart, but William's work of art.

CHAPTER 25

"*I* dare say you've been staring at the entrance for at least an hour," the dowager said too loudly for Lillias's liking. But that was more the norm, as of late. "You are looking for your fiancé, I presume?"

"Should I presume he's still my fiancé?"

"Have you heard otherwise?"

"Have you?"

The dowager snapped open her fan and began her ballroom ritual. The art of the fan instructions had continued from the first time they'd prepared for Almack's and Lillias had to assume they would continue even after the Season ended. Soon Rebecca would need to be schooled.

Her aunt nodded to the fan dangling at Lillias's wrist.

Reluctantly, she twisted the fine silk cord around until she could slip it off, then promptly snapped her rose-colored fan open. The one William had returned. She hoped by bringing it, he'd see from a distance she'd received his missive agreeing to extend his proposal.

"There he is," the dowager said crispy, as if she had spotted a dog. "And there she is." The dowager drew out the sentence and added a "hmm." Her gloved finger landed on her chin.

Lillias turned to find William standing on the raised threshold of the Willis room at Almack's, his head tipped forward as if he were straining to hear the announcer.

Lillias, in fact, couldn't hear the crier over the band. She suspected his missive's promise, to share some information about the missing painting, had sidelined him.

But the bright yellow gown, swishing in an impatient manner next to him, belonged to one woman who would need no introduction, *Lady Sarah.*

The two made their way into the ballroom, arm in arm, heads turning as they walked through the crowd as if in promenade, presumed gossip was on the lips of those they passed. The ripple effect was almost comical, if not for the grand smile on William's face as his gaze lingered over the lady at his elbow, maddening Lillias.

Lady Sarah! How could she have forgotten to ask William about the woman. Once he'd started his pursuit, the pretty parvenu had slipped her mind. But in her lemon yellow ball gown, Lady Sarah came back like a bad memory.

There was no avoiding them now as William made his way toward them, the crowd parting as if allowing royalty to pass.

Responding to the revelers, the couple made small talk as they inched their way closer to where Lillias and the dowager stood.

There was one moment when William turned to Lillias and then did a double take. She expected an expression of embarrassment or shock when their gazes met. William did neither. Instead his slow smile grew into a huge grin. Releasing Lady Sarah's arm, he moved through the crowd toward her.

William walked with purpose, as if they were in an empty

room and he had eyes only for her. The calls from Lady Sarah seem to fall on his deaf ears. When he reached her, he captured her free hand and bent nearly in half to drop a gentle peck on the top of her gloved hand.

Raising only his head from that bowed position, he gazed into her eyes. "You look lovely this evening."

But before Lillias recovered enough to say something in return, Lady Sarah sauntered up.

"You can't possibly mean this one?" Lady Sarah said in an arrogant tone.

"Aren't you the mean one?" Lillias snapped.

"Touché," Aunt Elizabeth cheered before she whispered behind her fan to Lillias, "You can handle this mischief. I have some of my own to attend to." And with a furious flutter, she was off toward Verity and her circle of admirers.

When Lillias turned her attention back to Lady Sarah, she was gone. Poof! The yellow-ball-gowned bully was missing as if she'd vanished.

William began to chuckle but stopped immediately when Lillias's stern look chased the mischievous twinkle from his eyes.

"I need to explain."

Lillias began tapping her foot to the beat of her fluttering fan and the band, a gesture of impatience on her part, but the action also helped release her irritation. As she waited for his explanation, he gently took her elbow and led her to the dance floor. While she acquiesced, slipping her fan back to her wrist, she considered it a handy weapon if she didn't like *his explanation.*

"This is one of my favorites," he said, releasing her and bowing as she stood across from him now with her arms crossed.

"Come." He reached with his right hand for hers. "There's no need to be jealous."

Lillias huffed, refusing to take his hand, but circling around him as the dance required. She planned to glare at him until he delivered *his explanation*.

But he didn't seem contrite, almost appearing as if he was enjoying her confusion.

Finally, he tilted his head and blurted out, "She is my sister."

Sister?

Lillias stepped on his foot, and he let out a howl. She almost did the same in sympathy and shock. She hadn't been introduced to the Cavendish family, although she was familiar with the name. It was never spoken at their family gatherings and now she knew why. It was only because of the R.A. fire she'd met William.

He gave her a sheepish look and shrugged his shoulders as they circled around each other.

"I suppose I should have said something earlier." That silly grin punctuated his statement.

Just then the music swelled, and the dance required them to assemble side by side but facing opposite directions. The immediate closeness startled her, scattering her thoughts.

Circling counterclockwise, arms about each other's waists, William raised a brow. "If you'd known earlier, you may not have accepted my offer."

Lillias snorted. "You have a point," she agreed. "I'd be hard-pressed to find us acting sisterly toward each other."

When the circling slowed to a stop, they turned toward each other and clasped hands.

"She's in a house full of men and acts like one of us most of the time." William pulled Lillias close, then his arms swept hers up and over their heads to form a connecting figure eight around their necks. "I suspect it's a survival instinct."

"Like when a mother bear kills a predator who threatens her cubs?"

"That's overly dramatic," William said, sounding a bit offended. Releasing her hands, he allowed his arm to drift down, then he spun Lillias around.

Once she came to face him again, she said, "And who is overly dramatic?"

William caught her by the waist, and they were side by side again.

"You have a point," she agreed, and her irritation with him began to subside. "We'll have to keep Verity and Sarah from each other at family gatherings."

And at that remark, William's grin faded and his lips formed a frustrated line.

She glanced away from him. *The duel.* No doubt he'd thought of it too.

History had proven their families didn't get along. Drama was a difficult foe and their fathers' animosity toward each other might be insurmountable.

"I know what you're thinking," William said softly. He lifted their arms over their heads again and they spun in the slow counterclockwise motion.

Lillias glanced at the fan on her wrist, knowing William had seen it, but not commented on it. She'd been distracted by Lady Sarah and her agenda had been interrupted. She had so many questions. Could he really know what she was thinking?

William released her hands, and they floated down again, then he clasped one and gave it a gentle tug. "Let's take a walk."

Lillias nodded, and he led her around the couples on the floor, passing Verity with Nigel. The two men nodding at each other with a measure of respect. And before long, they were standing in Lillias's favorite spot, in the doorway to the balcony.

Most of those who attended Almack's for the Season

were dancing. The chaperones and patriarchs were gathered by the far wall, posturing. That left this corner of the ballroom almost deserted except for an elderly nobleman sitting a comfortable distance away.

Lillias started first. "You said you knew what I was thinking."

William's cheeks turned reddish, and he hung his head for a moment. When he looked up and met her eyes, his brows were furrowed, and his gaze clouded with worry. "You made me forget the drama that's been surrounding us," he admitted as if he were embarrassed by it. "When I'm in your company, I feel like it's my birthday, celebrating the gift that is you."

It was Lillias's turn to blush. "Was that William Shakespeare?"

"No, just William Cavendish," he admitted, his eyes brightening from their dull haze. "I am flattered you may have thought it from one of his sonnets."

"Or his comedies," Lillias joked, causing him to smile again.

"Thank you for keeping our engagement," William said with a schoolboy's bashfulness.

"Once I make a commitment it's rare for me to break it. Know that about me, but we are dealing with rare circumstances," she admitted.

William sighed. "We'll never have much privacy, and what we are facing is not normal. I trust what tests us now will serve us well in the future."

"What future do we have, William?" Lillias was always direct and there was too much uncertainty for her to keep a promise unless she had more assurance about the future.

"I can make only the promise to be devoted to you today and every day we are together."

"As in friendship or more?"

"'Words are easy, like the wind; faithful friends are hard to find.'" He took her hand.

"William?"

"Yes?" He gazed into her eyes.

"Shakespeare this time?"

"Yes," he answered, leaning in as if he'd kiss her.

"'Expectation is the root of all heartache,'" she said, taking a step closer to him.

"William Shakespeare?"

"You need to question?"

"I understand his heartache better than his philosophy," he said as if he'd experienced it.

"Perhaps they are one in the same," she said, her lips twitching as if they would take volition on their own.

"Perhaps." His voice trailed off. "But I have been the victim of heartache."

The uncontrollable urge to fling herself into his arms stopped her cold at his confession. "You a victim?"

He claimed her hand and kissed the top of her glove as if he had an energy that needed a conduit.

She put her other hand over her heart.

"Another time. Enough about me. We need to talk about you," he said, gazing into her eyes as if he could charm her.

She stared at him for a few long moments before she shook herself out of her mesmerizing stupor. "The blackmailer? You said in your note—"

"Excuse me, lovebirds."

It was the Baron of Bad Timing.

"Compton, my good man, I've been waiting for you," William quipped, as if greeting his friend at their favorite men's club.

"Perhaps this isn't the best time," Nigel admitted, appearing reluctant to stay as he'd turned toward the ballroom entry.

Rushing to his friend's side, William spun him to face Lillias. "Nonsense, we were just talking about the ransom note."

Her gasp may have betrayed her, but eventually her shocked expression would have. Perhaps she should have expected best friends to share secrets, but this was her secret. Shouldn't she have been consulted? Ready to protest, William pushed Nigel between them.

"Lord Compton is acting as our spy," William said in a hushed, conspiratorial tone. He nodded to his friend. "Hiding in the garden since I arrived. I told you we would need an accomplice."

Again, she should have been consulted. Now Nigel knew about the nude too. Then she almost smacked her forehead over her ignorance. Of course he knew. But had he seen it? Now her cheeks were heating with sufficient embarrassment. She flicked open her fan and began beating it profusely.

"No need to fear, Lillias," William told her with a hint of defensiveness. "Lord Compton is discreet."

"No one has heard about King George's mad man ramblings from me," Nigel volunteered, then clasped his hand over his mouth.

William's eye rolling was not lost on Lillias when he said, "The King's actions are not our concern." Then he stepped closer to his friend, "Did you see the blackmailer?"

Shaking his head like a toddler, Nigel could be so peculiar at times, he appeared defeated. "I did what you told me, William. For the past three hours, I've watched the old oak tree and to no avail, only a few lovers' trysts did I spy."

"Why would you jeopardize our mission and leave your post?"

"I found another recruit to take my place."

Disappointment radiated from William. "'Don't trust the person who has broken faith once.'"

"Cavendish, those are harsh words, even from you."

"Shakespeare had reason to speak them."

"Gentlemen, we are getting away from our purpose." Lillias found the exchanges between the two maddening. Their efforts, childish at best, would not save her reputation.

Nigel swept into a low bow. "Forgive me, my lady, I understand this situation causes you much distress. Be certain there's a plan brewing," he promised with a wink.

Brewing was for tea, not crime solving. Lillias was running out of patience. "With all due respect, it's not your reputation on the line."

But her comment to Nigel appeared not to deter him when he replied with some chagrin, "You may remember Shakespeare has said, 'You have lost no reputation at all, unless you repute yourself such a loser.'"

"Shakespeare was not a woman of the *ton* with a scandal waiting to happen, Lord Compton."

And for the first time since she'd met the man, he was at a loss for words.

CHAPTER 26

The next morning William threw off the covers and rushed to get dressed. Nothing had been accomplished at Almack's. The blackmailer hadn't taken the bait. A pouch of jewels, although fake, had been left in the hollowed oak in Almack's garden, but it was still there at midnight when the party disbanded.

Maybe the brute had no intention of coming. Perhaps the perpetrator was a cruel and jealous competitor who never planned to follow through on the threats or take the artwork public but enjoyed the art of the prank.

Needless to say, William must now prepare for another challenge, a wretched battle of egos. The outcome of the next few hours would settle several scores. His hands shook as he buttoned his shirt. Nothing a good dousing of whiskey couldn't fix when he was ready.

So out of his chamber he went, down to the parlor to calm his nerves. As he was rounding the corner he stopped.

"Under the hatches?"

His brother's greetings were never pleasant. "Good morning to you too," William bit out, making his way to the sideboard. Alex's insinuations were always derogatory. Without giving his brother another thought, he whisked the decanter off the counter and uncorked the top. Swirling the vessel in a counterclockwise direction, he brought the amber liquid into a whirlpool spin, then breathed in the pungent aroma before setting his lips to the opening.

"Save some for the rest of us," his sister Sarah remarked as if he was draining a teapot. To his recollection she hated whiskey.

Finishing his long drink from the heirloom crystal bottle, he made a funny sound when his lips left the opening and his eyes opened. He wiped his mouth. "Good morning to you, Sarah." Extending the almost empty decanter of whiskey to his sister he asked, "Couldn't sleep?"

"How could any of us sleep with Father about to take his life in his own hands?"

"Rather one of us do it?" Alexander said sourly. He had the dueling box open on the desk and appeared to prepare the weapon for firing.

"Anxious for your inheritance money already?" William asked, contemplating finishing the bottle's contents. When Alexander didn't answer he added, "Gambling debts?"

Alexander slowly cocked the gun's hammer, then pointed the weapon at William.

Sarah shrieked when Alexander released the trigger.

William's head jerked back as if he'd been hit in the head with a hard fist. But the hammer had only produced a soft click, barely audible under Sarah's scream. Even now that he knew he was safe, his muscles tingled, ready to flex and fight.

"Good God, you could have killed William," Sarah snapped.

"If I'd only been that lucky. A simple accident, nothing intentional."

"Except you'd have a witness," Sarah said soberly.

"A cooperating witness," Alex said, placing the pistol back in its red, velvet-lined box, then securing the lid with the latch. "Money is a great silencer."

Sarah harrumphed. "I do not care to witness any more of this disgraceful behavior." She started toward the door. "Be careful who you threaten, Alexander."

As their sister sauntered out, the future duke grumbled to himself.

If becoming the heir apparent meant threatening family, becoming black-hearted, and any of the other disgusting habits his brother had adopted, William wanted nothing to do with the title. Being the second son had its challenges, but he'd never trade his ethics for power and prestige.

"What are you staring at?"

William shook his head to clear it.

Alexander held the pistol box and William's eyes moved to it. "Not you," he said in a disgusted tone. "My thoughts were elsewhere."

"On that St. Clair debutante? Poor choice, Brother."

If Alexander hadn't already threatened William with the pistol, he would have chaffed more at the comment. His brother couldn't fathom loving anyone but himself.

But loving Lillias had become a catharsis for William. Visualizing a naked Lillias in his portrait of her right now kept his emotions in check. Somehow, thinking of her snuffed out his rage. This perfect distraction would allow him to approach his brother as he would a lethal opponent, fists ready, defenses up, cool countenance.

"The chit is of no consequence to me," William lied.

"Why the duel then?"

"It's Father's pride. The Duke of Canterbury claimed I wouldn't go through with the wedding and our father took offense. His vendetta against him is no secret."

"Father has a vendetta against most of his acquittances. I cannot possibly keep track of his personal quarrels."

"Why be his second?"

"Would you rather take on the role?"

Shifting the subject from Lillias to the duel was William's intention, but now his brother wanted to transfer the responsibility of the duel? "Are you offering it?"

Alexander's haughty laugh was almost answer enough, but would the eldest son relinquish his role? He waited patiently for his brother's reply.

After a few moments of grandstanding, Alex's said, "I am."

"A coward."

"Protecting my investment."

"In your future."

"In the future of the Cavendish name."

"In your future," William repeated with more emphasis.

"Do you, or don't you?"

"Want to punch your face right now?"

"Take a swing," Alexander dared, jutting out his chin and putting up his fists.

Locking his lips on the decanter opening again, William took another long swig of whiskey with one eye trained on his brother.

After setting the empty bottle in its place, he unbuttoned his shirt with rapid speed, then tossed it aside. Now he was stripped down to his breeches, like any bare knuckles contest he'd fought in the ring. When he was boxing, he was no longer a gentleman. He was a force of nature, and he was ready to unleash that on his brother's arrogant face.

"What's the meaning of this?"

"Father," they both said.

Alexander had stripped down to his breeches too and they were within inches of one of them landing the first punch.

"Boys will be boys," Alexander said, laughing and tossing his shirt back on.

Their father turned to William. "You must have started this."

Hanging his head, he did his best to squelch his rising anger. He wanted to punch Alexander's face and knock a few teeth out. Nothing ever changed in this household. "We were discussing your second."

His father's head swung toward Alexander who had his back to them both. "Of course it's your brother," their father assumed.

Of course, my ass.

But when Alexander hesitated, his father said, "Your brother accepts the responsibility of the first born. It's ingrained in him."

Believe that lie, he wanted to say, but he remained quiet as they both waited for Alexander's response.

"Of course," Alexander finally concurred, turning to face them with an arrogant grin. "I was just telling William how much I appreciate the privilege when he begged to take my place."

"You were going to take to fists, William, to settle it?" his father asked. A vein in his jaw visibly pulsed. "You can afford to lose a tooth or two, but your brother cannot."

"A good round between brothers doesn't have to involve the face, Father," he said, staring at Alex. "We can choose where our punches fall."

"You know I forbid boxing in this household or in public," their father said in an icy tone, then turned to William. "You know how I feel about pugilism."

"You've never made it a secret," he said quietly.

"What did you say?" his father demanded.

"Yes, sir."

The duke narrowed his gaze on him before he turned to Alexander. "Are the weapons ready?"

"Check."

"Are you ready?"

"Check, but I believe William can serve a purpose," Alexander said, looking past their father at him. "We need a witness."

Buttoning his shirt as he walked toward the door with the intention to leave the aggravation behind, William paused when his father cleared his throat in a way that indicated he wasn't yet excused.

"William will join us," his father said decidedly. "Perhaps he'll learn something about his future father-in-law."

Turning back, he caught his father's eye when the duke added, "If he wants to have a future at all with the St. Clair family. This will be telling."

Giving his father a short nod, and with those orders, William left the room before his anger took over. Wishing for a sack to pound, he imagined it be his brother's head. As much as he was vexed about the position he was in, he couldn't blame his father.

It had taken many years to harden the Duke of Devonshire, who'd been a supportive father in William's early years. Around the time Alexander turned twelve, however, William had become invisible, with most of his father's energy going toward the tutelage and grooming of his older brother. Father described it as helping the boy aspire to his rightful place in society.

After walking back to the stables, still stymied over how he could change *his* legacy, it wasn't long before he was saddled on his horse Highflyer and riding hard out the of estate gates.

William dug his heels into the horse's flanks. He wanted to arrive first. Perhaps he'd have a moment to say a few words to Lillias's father. No doubt it would be awkward. He still intended to marry her no matter the duel's outcome. This might be his only chance.

The ride to Putney Heath was peaceful and short. The park was a reclusive spot on the outer skirts of the *ton*. Most Londoners preferred the parks in the central part of the city. This one was considered too rugged and the potential of getting shot by mistake was real, keeping most but the unsavory away.

Riding to the perimeter of his destination without much fanfare, he slowed his horse and pulled out his timepiece.

Half past six. Returning the watch to his breast pocket, he pressed his spurs into Highflyer's flanks, urging the horse forward under some low-lying branches and up the path that led to the summit where the duel would take place.

Reaching the top of Putney Heath, he surveyed the area. A foreboding shiver ran down his back. It appeared he was alone, but this place was notorious for highwaymen. Jeremiah Abershaw was one of those. He'd been hung recently by chain gibbet on the heath as a warning to others of his ilk.

Tying Highflyer's reins tightly to the tree trunk, he secured his horse, then walked the short distance to the crest. Releasing a ragged breath he contemplated what was to take place. Guns were for protection, not for vengeance. Dueling was an archaic method for settling differences and bruised egos.

Turning at the sound of hooves, William watched two riders approach, both wearing top hats and heavy woolen coats. He hadn't dressed for this weather. When he'd left, he'd been warm inside and out. Now the chill in the air began to settle around him and he shivered again. Either from the cold or the ominous gathering about to take place.

"You must be a Cavendish," a gruff voice said when the two men stopped their horses on the crest. "Are you here to tell me the Duke of Devonshire is at Chatsworth House avoiding this business."

Lillias's father was a big man, full in girth and of himself. But she'd spoken highly of him, saying he could do no wrong in her eyes. He envied her devotion to her father and sisters. His family was a collection of self-absorbed aristocrats with dark hearts and small minds.

"Let me introduce myself, I'm Lillias's fiancé."

The duke's face hardened at his words, but Finneas grinned at him. No doubt the male servant was the only available choice to serve as her father's second. The butler appeared unflappable, as he always did. Even at his advanced age, he moved nimbly about his horse, collecting the sword and pistol box.

"You could start a second duel with that claim," the Duke of Canterbury warned.

Swallowing his pride, he remembered the impetus for the original challenge. "Your Grace, I do allow this is the worst time to ask for your daughter's hand in marriage, yet we—"

"Over my dead body," Lillias's father shouted, dismounting swiftly, then stepping within a foot of where William stood.

William wouldn't let it end there. Following the two men as they secured their horses and eager to make a point before it was too late he blurted out, "Know this. I love your daughter and she will be cherished."

The Duke of Canterbury studied him from head to toe. "You are an artist too?" he asked, his demeanor not softening at William's declaration of love.

William nodded.

"She needs a duke, as well as privilege, and peerage acceptance. Those are the qualities in a husband that will support Lillias in a marriage, not art or love, frivolous things." He gave him a second glance. "If you were a duke, I would set aside my bias."

William bowed his head as Lillias's father brushed past him. Finneas followed, giving him a sympathetic look.

Moments later, the Duke of Devonshire and Alexander arrived. Once they'd dismounted, insults were exchanged between both dukes before his brother and father prepared for the duel.

Finneas removed a document from his satchel, and after purposefully unrolling it, began to read its contents.

"His Grace, Thomas Cavendish, the 5th Duke of Devonshire, has called this duel with His Grace, Charles St. Clair, the first Duke of Canterbury, today, May 13, in the year of our Lord 1817. It is customary to open a discussion between both parties to allow for agreement or elicit an apology."

Finneas turned to William's father. "Sir, what say you?"

Steely, gray-green eyes, and an unflinching jaw set in a stubborn jut, William's father shook his head before he uttered, "Never."

Lillias father appeared equally unyielding. "No way in hell," was his adamant response.

Finneas's face fell. Perhaps the servant had seen amends made and apologies offered in the past, but both dukes appeared steadfast in their plans to duel. Nevertheless, the butler accepted the responsibilities of his position and continued with the formalities. "Sword or pistol?"

"Pistol," said both dukes.

"At least you are agreeable on that front," said the butler with a slight bow, his demeanor dry. After a few beats of silence, the servant asked, "To first blood or to the death?"

"To the death," both dukes said simultaneously.

William dropped his head along with all hope that the situation would come to an amiable resolution.

CHAPTER 27

*L*illias sat in her father's chair with her sketchbook in hand, staring at the empty page, waiting in the library for news on the duel. The household had settled back into its normal rhythm after her father left before dawn. She hadn't slept. How could she?

There was a short rap and after she responded, Finneas led William into the room. The long-time servant's face was pale, his hands shaking, as he took off his gloves and William approached her.

"Lillias," William whispered her name and clasped her free hand, paused, then uttered, "He's gone."

She collapsed into his arms and began to sob. Small ones at first, as if they were hiccups. She tried to swallow them by biting down on her lip. She tore herself away from William, wiping the tears frantically from each eye with the back of her glove.

"What happened? You must tell me?"

"My father is dead too."

She stared at William. With a choked gasp, she covered her mouth and buckled at the waist. William caught her shoulders before she tumbled. She wasn't going to faint, but her legs could no longer hold her.

"Sit her down," Finneas fussed, "I'll be back from the kitchen in no time with strong tea and some biscuits."

"When you say strong tea, I suggest you add something stronger than sugar to it," William called over his shoulder. Then he pushed a pillow under her head before he propped her feet up on the chaise. "There," he said, looking shaken and pale, "that's better."

"Better for me, but what about you? This can't be happening." She shook her head. Both fathers dead. It wasn't physically possible, was it? She'd hoped for a miracle, an apology. "I thought matters would be settled. Men would come to reason." She was rambling, but she did that when she was afraid.

William stood and walked to the sideboard as if in a daze. Pouring himself a tumbler full of amber liquid, he downed it in one gulp. He stared at the bottle in his hand for a moment before pouring another and downing it as well.

The simple act of watching him calmed Lillias. She'd rather it be William to share the grave news than anyone else.

He pushed the ottoman next to the chaise with his boot before he stooped low to sit on it. He settled himself with a shudder. "Lillias, I wish there was something I could have done," he said before he dropped his head into his hands.

She touched the top of his head gently. "William, this isn't your fault."

"It all happened so fast."

"Tell me," she whispered, tugging his hands away from his face, encouraging him to look at her.

"Finneas was officiating and no doubt he was shocked as I was when both men unanimously chose to duel to the death after neither offered a retraction or even paltry apology.

Once pistols were chosen, the only option left was to go through with it."

"Or come to their senses and decide they were both idiots," Lillias said with distain.

William nodded. "Oft times, even when pistols are chosen, you can sense a resignation in body movements, a reluctance to go through with the duel. Not so with our fathers. Each appeared determined to kill the other."

"A tragedy they both succeeded," she whispered, still not believing it was true.

"I wish I knew the offense," William mumbled, clearly distraught as she was over the killings, his face deathly pale despite the alcohol.

Alcohol. Where was Finneas with her strong tea?

"Here I am, Your Grace."

"Finally," Lillias blurted out, her proper manners no longer serving her. Then she sat straight up. "What did you call me?"

"Your G-Grace," Finneas stuttered, no doubt more from the emotional strain than his inability to articulate.

"What do you mean, Finneas? This is not time for levity."

"You may claim the title, Your Grace. I was witness to the letters patent."

Lillias's head swung to William for verification, and he nodded solemnly, "If your father's land and title were drawn as fee tail general, that would be true."

Now it was her turn to drop her head into her hands.

"What will become of me?"

William peeled her hands from her face. "You will become my wife, duchess or not," he said.

"Is that legal?" Lillias's head was spinning. She didn't care about a title or position. It was never meant to come to this. She was to be married and become a wife to a second son of a duke. Lady Lillias would be her salutation, not 'Your Grace.'

"Here, drink this." William handed Lillias the tea from the silver platter Finneas held out for her.

She wished it was straight whiskey so she could down it like William had. Blowing across the steaming liquid, she resolved to take dainty sips. Burned lips and tongue would be the penalty if she hurried.

Finneas backed out of the room with a bow. No doubt he was willing to trust Lillias with William under these circumstances. At least Verity and Rebecca were still asleep, and she'd be able to wait a while before sharing the gut-wrenching news with them. The sun was still low in the May morning sky, and that would give her some time with William to sort out the situation.

He watched her set down her cup with sad eyes before she asked, "Where do we go from here?"

"With the details of the duel or with us?" he responded.

That was an unfair question. There was so much to sort out. Their relationship was complicated enough. It would help if she stuck to the events of the morning first.

"The duel. It doesn't seem possible. They're both dead?"

William closed his eyes, perhaps wishing away the memories before he started. "As you know, Finneas was your father's second." She nodded.

"My brother, Alexander was my father's second."

The second? Her aunt had tried to explain, but right now, Lillias was in shock and couldn't remember. "Why are they needed?"

William looked at her with gentle patience. "The seconds handle decorum, make sure the rules are followed. They are also there to finish the job if there's a dispute over the first round. Each gun has only one bullet but depending on the circumstances, pistols can be reloaded. But there should have been no more than three exchanges." He took a deep breath then sighed. "Usually, shots are fired above the head or off to the side. When that happens, both the honor of both partici-pants is restored and the slate wiped clean."

"It doesn't make sense."

"Not unless you are a titled male." William became reflec-tive. "Your father even tried to joke my father out of it with a William Shakespeare quote."

Lillias had stopped crying, but the mention of her father joking had her tearing up again.

Touching her cheek, William caught a few drops on his finger, then he popped them in his mouth. The action threw Lillias's emotions into a spiral. It was sensuous and sweet.

"It was one of my favorite quotes, 'I challenge you to a battle of wits, but I see you are unarmed.'"

"Well, I can see the humor in it. Did he quote the Bard, or just spit it out?"

"He did give credit and that perhaps should have softened the insult," William agreed.

"Well, then, I still don't know how we ended up losing both our fathers." She dropped her hands in her lap. Her father was gone. It would take months to get over her loss. The grief was beginning to overwhelm her.

Grabbing both of her hands, William pulled them to his heart as he leaned in. "You belong to me now. I will take care of you. As long has my heart is beating, I will protect you with my honor and my life."

It was the sweetest thing anyone had ever said to her. His eyes were so dark and ominous, yet there was a light glowing within, as if his heart was strong enough for them both.

"I have only been thinking of myself. You must be grieving too," she said, holding her hands over his heart and sensing the strong pulse beating within him.

"I am still in disbelief," William admitted, shaking his head as if his mind would clear with the action. "Although my father supported me, we never were close, but the loss feels like a kick in the gut." Then he caught a few tears from her cheek again and he put them to his lips. "They are salty," he said after.

She smiled despite it all. William seemed to find good in every bad situation. Her smile deepened as she thought back on how she'd tried to avoid him and had attacked him more than once.

"What made you smile?" he asked, a slow grin appearing too.

"I was thinking about hitting you."

His reflexes kicked in and he dropped her hands and used his own to defend his face.

"Not now," she said and batted his hands down.

"You'll leave me defenseless," he teased.

She gave him a sassy, sideways look. "I meant that I was thinking of the times I'd hit you."

"And—" he said, ducking low and fists up again.

"Well, that I must have seemed quite unrefined and unladylike."

"You were nothing of the sort," he said, defending her. "You are understanding and unselfish," he proclaimed as if he had to convince her to accept such a fine description of herself.

She bowed her head. "Unworthy," she whispered.

"Underappreciated," he said in her defense.

That was true. All she'd handled since her mother had died. Now, she was a duchess? They'd made a game of trying to avoid discussing the real tragedy. Perhaps a little more William Shakespeare was needed.

"'No legacy is as rich as honesty,'" she started, standing. "I begin with Shakespeare, but finish with my own words." She took in a deep breath for courage. "Out with the rest of it. I've gathered by now that you are avoiding it. My sisters will be down soon, and I need to prepare myself."

William's eyes darkened. "They're gone, Lillias."

"One minute you are alive, and the next, you're dead," she said, her heart heavy.

"My father aimed straight over his head and waited, as if he had a change of heart about his vengeance, but yours took careful aim and shot my father in the chest."

Lillias couldn't contain her gasp. As much as she wanted to know what happened, she also wasn't sure she could hear the details without fainting.

William took her hand and kissed it. "I can stop now. You don't need to know the rest."

She shook her head. "No, go on," she said, biting her lip to keep it from trembling.

He gave her a stern assessment, but when she squeezed his hand, he continued. "As my father was falling, his gun fired, striking your father in the heart and killing him instantly. Was it intended? We'll never know."

They were both silent for a few moments. Lillias tried to process all the ramifications.

"Now the fortunes of many have changed," she said soberly.

William stood for a moment and swept into a low bow. "Your Grace."

"Your Grace?" Verity's greeting was laced with sarcasm.

Lillias had some explaining to do. She turned to look up at William. "Would you join us for dinner?"

He took her hand and gave it a quick peck before he said, "I'd be honored." Then he glanced at her sister. "Verity," he said pleasantly, with a bow then turned back to Lillias. "I'll take my leave." And in few short beats he was gone, and Lillias's tears began again.

Verity sat down hard on the chaise, shoving her way next to Lillias instead of taking up the ottoman William had vacated. "What's wrong? You never cry," she said, in disbelief.

"Your Grace, you have visitors," Finneas announced, with a solemn bow.

Verity spun around. "There it is again." She turned back to look at Lillias and scrunched up her face. "Did you and William wed without a formal ceremony? Is that why all the men in this household are giving you a new formal address?" She grabbed one of Lillias's hands. "You must tell me what's happening?"

After a brief moment of silence, Lillias lowered her gaze. "It seems, dear sister, I am going to be a duchess whether I like it or not."

CHAPTER 28

The day had been a blur for Lillias. After William left, she'd resolved her tears and assumed her parental role, doing her best to explain their father's death to Verity and Rebecca.

The news had traveled through the servants quickly. That meant it wasn't long before local dignitaries began to pay their respects. It wasn't just William's brother who received a rejection, although snubbing him gave her some retribution. Frankly, she hadn't the courage to see anyone.

The dining party had now fallen into a somber mood. Verity had her head bowed and appeared to be studying her meal of roasted potatoes and lamb as if expecting to make a scientific discovery. Rebecca was not much better. She was rearranging the items on her plate, but Lillias wasn't surprised the food wasn't being eaten. She had no appetite either.

"The arrangements are underway," the dowager promised, raising her chalice. "Let us toast to your longevity and reign as the Duchess of Canterbury."

Lillias reluctantly raised her glass. The flickering candles cast shadows about the Woodbeck House's opulent dining room, the golden light filtering through the facets of her cut crystal chalice, shooting refracted light everywhere. It was a bittersweet moment.

"Long live the Duchess," William agreed eagerly.

Both aunts sat in their customary places. For the moment, William sat where her father would have, and the table didn't seem as empty without him.

She stole a look at her sisters to her left. They were life-less representations of themselves, a memory she would soon like to forget.

Sighing inwardly, she promised herself to check her emotions for her sisters' sake. But life was out of balance, off kilter, and she didn't expect it to change anytime soon.

"As I was saying," her Aunt Elizabeth broke the awkward silence, "the arrangements have been made."

William turned to her. "For the funeral?"

Her aunt's face soured. She made a tsking sound before she said, "The arrangement for the title transfer."

Lillias shook her head in confusion. She was about ready to object when her aunt pressed on.

"Primogeniture is black and white when there is an offi-cial male heir in the family, but because the Canterbury dukedom was recently created with a fee tail general in the letters patent, your father's directives in his will need to be honored. But Prince Regent needs to sanction your ascen-sion to duchess, my dear. We don't want to risk an amend-ment to the dukedom's patent by sending the vote to parliament."

"What if I don't want to make an ascent?"

The dowager's disposition went from cloudy to stormy in a blink of her eyes. "Didn't your father discuss the responsi-bilities of this household with you?"

Holding her temper in check, Lillias shook her head.

Didn't she already have more responsibilities for *this house-hold* than appropriate for her age? How could she take on anymore?

"Your father lorded over the duchy of Canterbury. We are not about to give that up because you do not want to make an ascent," the dowager said in that aristocratic tone she used when talking down to those she considered inferior.

It took all her control and William squeezing her hand under the table to bite back the words that rose like bile at the back of her throat. She wouldn't win this battle with her aunt. Plus, her sisters looked at her with empty eyes as if they'd be lost if she didn't continue to set the benevolent example they'd become accustomed to.

"What happens next?" she asked, grinding the question between her teeth.

William squeezed her hand again.

She relaxed her clenched jaw. "What's required of me?" she added more softly.

"To become a duchess, of course," her aunt said plainly, like it was time for dessert.

If it had been part of the art of the fan curriculum, Lillias would have taken hers out now and hidden behind it. Fans were the perfect stalling mechanism. When one didn't want to be seen or heard, one could hide politely from public view. She wished she could thrust open her fan and hide from everyone but William.

Turning to him now, she managed a weak smile.

"You'll make the most amazing duchess," he promised.

Thank goodness for William. Although he would not disagree with her aunts now, it didn't mean he wouldn't help her circumvent their intentions. And after the dowager's explanation on primogeniture, Lillias understood her insistence. Lillias must ascend to duchess to keep the property that had come with her father's title.

The table had gone silent after William's professed support of her new role, the sounds of clinking silverware filled the room. Everyone appeared to find the food satisfactory despite her sisters' gloomy dispositions.

Then it struck her, and she let out a little gasp despite herself, bringing the attention of Aunt Elizabeth.

"What is it, dear? Did you bite into a piece of gristle?"

Lillias shook her head. Then the question begged to be asked. "Does this make William a duke if we were to marry?"

"If?" William almost choked on his food when he responded.

The dowager chuckled when Lillias and William turned their heads sharply toward each other.

Lillias gave him a sympathetic glance, and he shrugged.

"Both are fair questions," their aunt replied. "No and yes, would be my answers, but they are not mine to give."

Ignoring the dowager William gave her his answer. "No, Lillias, I do not become a duke if I were to marry you."

"If?" Now it was her turn to rib him.

He smiled at her response. "I was assuming if you were a duchess, not if I would marry you."

"It's clear the two of you have some sorting out to do," the dowager said, breaking into what had become their private discussion. "But there is a hierarchy to nobility, and I would have presumed, my dear, that your family had prepared you for your role in society."

Society could be damned was what Lillias thought, but she'd kept that to herself since her mother had died.

No, her mother hadn't schooled her, because Lillias had rebelled against the norm. Not until she had taken on her mother's role had she assumed any part of what society required. But because she loved her sisters, she was willing to make a sacrifice. To a point. Now, there seemed to be no end to the sacrifices that appeared on the horizon.

But all the while Lillias was rationalizing her reluctance to her new role, Aunt's Elisabeth's expression was souring.

"I don't have a clue," Lillias finally blurted out. "Please provide some clarification."

Her aunt looked pleased at the request. Smoothing back a stray peacock feather on her headpiece from her forehead, the dowager leaned forward after the butler had removed her last dinner plate. "Lillias, the ceremony is quite grand."

Lillias nodded and tilted her head to one side. She would hear the dowager out. No doubt she would need her guidance over the weeks and months to come whether she liked it or not.

"First, you'll meet with Prince Regent for a formal interview."

Lillias's spine went erect. "An interview?" She was thinking a ceremony.

"Now, calm down, my dear. It's not as formal as it sounds. The Prince needs to get to know you on a personal level before he bestows the title on you. Not just anyone can be so anointed."

And they were back to the beginning again. "But what if I am not anointment material?" she asked in a voice that whined despite her efforts.

"You'll have the best coach in the *ton*," her aunt promised, her chest puffing up and her neck stretching to its full height. With her headpiece adorned with brightly colored feathers, the dowager looked as if she'd belonged in a peacock muster.

Lillias pursed her lips, ready with a reason why she would fail, but decided it would serve her purposes better if she gave in. "Go on," she encouraged her aunt.

"Well, the interview will be at Buckingham House and Queen Charlotte will attend."

If she hadn't been already sitting, she would have insisted to do so now. She wasn't feeling faint, but her right leg started to tremble. She took in a deep breath to try to steady herself. "First, an audience with the Prince and now the Queen too? If I didn't know better, you'll be telling me the final approval will come from King George himself."

The dowager offered a smug smile. "My dear, the King is quite mad, so it will be the Prince and his mother."

"Well, that's a relief," Lillias said with some mockery. "I was worried a mad man might have to decide my fate."

Aunt Emma covered her mouth to hide a giggle. She'd been silent the entire time. Although that was clearly in character, Lillias looked at her for further response, but nothing came.

"What say you of all this pomp and circumstance, Aunt Emma?" she asked pointedly.

At first her quiet aunt appeared reluctant to answer, looking at the dowager for approval before she spoke. When Aunt Elizabeth nodded, Aunt Emma looked at her with kind eyes.

"Lillias, if I were you, I'd take Elizabeth's tutelage and this opportunity to heart." The dear woman's eyes teared and she clutched her heart. "You know we all loved your father. Do him the honor of giving this your best."

Aunt Emma's kind words created a lump in Lillias's throat. All she could do was nod. The unwanted ball of emotion was stuck in the way of her words and kept her from saying anything else that might disrespect her father.

One of the servants entered with a platter full of sweet treats and another followed with the tea service. As much as she was ready for this day to end, if she went to bed early, she wouldn't sleep. At least she'd have some time with William.

The prospect of time alone with him and something sweet for her tooth had her out of her seat and in command of her voice. "I'll take my tea in the library with Lord Cavendish." And without another word, she sauntered out of the dining room and into the hallway. If she was to become a duchess, then she better start acting like one.

Assuming William was the owner of the footsteps treading behind her, Lillias made her way quickly to the library without glancing back. But when she spun around just inside the doorway expecting to greet him, it was the dowager she met instead.

"You're not William," she uttered.

"You're not a duchess yet," the dowager replied.

Lillias curtsied with a slight bow of her head.

"That's better," the dowager said. "We have much to discuss that is not for the others to hear," her aunt said as she closed the door.

She peered around the dowager expecting William to knock on the door and step through at any moment.

"I sent him home," was her aunt's response to her anxious look.

Lillias face fell and her shoulders slumped.

"Now, that's the attitude of a twenty-one-year-old debutante, not a duchess."

Let the duchess be damned. She was a woman in love.

CHAPTER 29

*L*illias sat in the vestibule of the Queen's quarters, palms sweaty inside her gloves and stomach doing somersaults, reflecting on the past week full of high emotions. Most of it a blur. Her father's funeral, the daily training sessions on duchess this and duchess that. Formalities that she would prefer to forget. But she was blessed with an exceptional memory, and certain if she remembered what her aunt had taught her, she'd pass the duchess test. For her father, not for herself. A legacy she would endeavor to continue, even though she didn't want to be the one to carry the burden.

Regardless of the motivation, her Aunt Elizabeth had kept Lillias's mind off her grievous loss with excessive tutoring. Reciting the names of all thirty-seven dukes and their wives by memory was the first of her requirements.

After that had been accomplished, her aunt gifted Lillias with her personal copy of *A Guide to Polite British Society*, claiming it was a limited edition and could only be passed from one who knew, to one who needed to know.

Of course she'd learned from her governess the royal

hierarchy of England and Scotland, but she hadn't been tutored on the rules of society and its definition of ducal responsibility.

According to the dowager, Lillias was trailing behind her peers. Any woman who was worth her weight in English shillings should understand that alliances, peerage, financial influence, and strategy would trump love, friendship, charity, and fair play.

This revelation had both surprised and angered her. Perhaps she had always suspected some of it to be true but had ignored it because this concept didn't resonate with her own ideals.

If she could take away one important discovery from this tutelage, it was being privileged had its price.

Now, she had no choice but to become one of them.

Biting her lip to keep it from trembling, Lillias prayed she wouldn't be offered anything but weak tea.

"The Queen is ready for you."

The guard's announcement startled her, and she dropped her reticule on the floor. When she bent to pick it up, she stumbled over her dress. What a bag of nerves she was.

The servant stared straight ahead with a stoic look, not giving any indication he'd witnessed her display of awkwardness.

Filled with dread, she smoothed down her overskirt, then shook her arms as if casting off bad luck. Once she straightened her spine, and squared her shoulders, she remembered the first rule her aunt had taught her. Act the part.

With her head high, trying to breathe and remember everything her aunt had said, Lillias entered the room.

* * *

WILLIAM STUDIED the portrait of his fiancée with a critical eye as it rested on the easel in his student studio. The R.A. competition was just a week away and he was certain the woman staring back at him would help him win the competition if he could just get her for one more sitting. He'd yet to finish her expression on this second portrait of her.

Most of her body was painted. Too much clothing for his liking. But the pose was right, the lighting magical, and her figure, unforgettable.

Leaning in to evaluate the brush strokes with a critical eye, he was satisfied with his technique, but the new portrait of Lillias was lacking her orgasmic expression. Perhaps he could get something close.

It wasn't long ago he'd thought her a harlot, earning money by posing as a figure model. He understood now why she'd taken the risk for his R.A. class.

With their fathers' deaths and subsequent funerals, Lillias had been preparing for the interview with the Queen and Prince Regent, but her dowager aunt had turned William away when he'd come to call. His messages had gone unanswered. Now he was beginning to believe Lillias had taken on the impending duchess role with a renewed vigor.

"Not bad."

He had company?

Wait. Nigel isn't company.

Turning around, William crossed his arms over his chest then doled out one of his favorite Shakespeare quotes.

"'Nothing is either good or bad, but thinking makes it so.'"

"'All that glitters is not gold.'"

"'Nothing will come of nothing.'"

William grinned at his friend. "I didn't expect to see you here."

"You mean, you didn't expect me to track you down to give you news on your missing painting."

"Where? How?"

"A stroke of good luck, I suppose," Nigel said with a satisfied expression. "I found it at Cribs Parlor."

"You won the painting and have it hidden in a secure place?"

"Not exactly," Nigel admitted, somewhat sheepishly, kicking something imaginary on the floor.

"You said you found it." He wanted to punch his friend for all the subterfuge.

"I did."

"Where is it?"

"In the gaming hell."

"Waiting for me to pick it up?"

"It's hanging up."

Nigel ducked before William's knuckles hit his chin.

"Are we fighting?" Nigel asked, putting up his fists. "Ready for a go in the ring?"

"Your answer was fight worthy, but I'm engaged. Keeping Lillias in that state is the only ring I want to focus on now."

"Don't blame me for the painting's location." Nigel took a few large steps backward toward the door. "The messenger is not to be blamed for the news."

Lowering his hands and relaxing his fighting stance, William fought off his urge to lash out. He snatched his tailcoat from the back of the easel and slipped it on, then started toward the door. But Nigel stepped in his path.

"I'll let you pass if you promise we go together."

William wanted to get the portrait back now that it had been found and couldn't hide his intention from his friend.

"We don't have much time."

"Is she a duchess yet?"

"She has her interview today," he told Nigel, concerned the nude painting might ruin her ascension chances only a few farthings away from the R.A. at Buckingham House.

"Interview?" Nigel asked with a mocking tone.

He swatted at Nigel in a friendly manner and his former army mate stepped out of the way. "A formality," William said, his jaw tight.

"What if she fails?"

That was a question William dared not consider.

CHAPTER 30

*L*illias stared at her feet. The question was easy enough, but she had two ways she could answer. One would gain her the title, the other would ruin her.

As in past decisions, her obligations weighed heavy. Her sisters. Her aunts. The Canterbury duchy. Even William. The repercussions of her answer were staggering, but she could delay it no longer.

"No, Your Majesty, I have never done anything that would bring shame to myself or my family," Lillias said, answering what she hoped was the last question of the interview. If the Queen and Prince didn't give her leave soon, her hiccups could diminish all she'd worked for over the last grueling hour of high society small talk.

Never had she had to think so much before she spoke. Although her aunt had given her a crash course in royal protocol, there had been questions the Queen had asked about herself she'd never even considered. Like did she find it difficult to speak her opinions? And would she consider living in Scotland? She'd answered no and yes, respectively, praying they were the answers the Queen wanted to hear.

"Well, my dear, that does conclude our time together," the Queen said with a flourish of her bejeweled hand. Lillias was awestruck at the grandeur, and Her Majesty's required strength to raise it. The analysis made Lillias crack a smile.

"You appear pleased," the Prince observed. No doubt deducing her grin was about the completion of the proceedings and not the opulence before her. She nodded and moved her lips into what she trusted was a demur expression. Demur was a quality the dowager had harped upon.

"Who is this?"

Lillias's head turned sharply to the right and her demur expressions collapsed, her jaw dropping on its hinges.

"Lady Lillias of Canterbury, Your Majesty," said the servant who'd been introduced as the royal secretary.

"Old Charles married himself a young chit," the King said with bemusement, assessing Lillias with great scrutiny.

Lillias wanted to object to his ogling, and in front of the Queen no less. But she guessed the King could not be reproached and did her best to take a bow from her seat while she hid her displeasure.

"This is *Miss* Lillias St. Clair," the Queen said politely, correcting her husband. No doubt the only one who could do such a thing.

With her head down, not sure what to do, Lillias was determined to keep her composure and the hiccups from surfacing. Now that the King had arrived, wasn't he needed for formal, royal proceedings or family business?

"What happened to your father?"

Covering her mouth, Lillias smothered a hiccup with her glove. She'd counted her blessings too soon.

"Your Majesty, he's gone." The Prince Regent spoke for her.

"Where did he go?"

Was the King daft? Yes, she recalled he was, and that's why his son was Regent.

"Deceased," the Queen replied.

"What happened?"

It was time to cry. Perhaps the only way to stop the hiccups she felt coming on. "A duel that ended badly," she said, then burst into tears, burying her head in her hands, shoulders shaking. A peep of a hiccup slid in between the sobs but couldn't have been noticeable.

Lillias didn't dare look up when mumbled whispers reached her ears. Her best hope would be an easy exit. When an arm circled her shoulders gently, she peeked from under her gloved hand.

The Queen handed Lillias a handkerchief. "If you are to be a duchess, you'll need to work on your decorum. We can't have you all weepy at public events."

If? Lillias glanced at the white linen fabric with a capital QC embroidered on the corner in shimmering gold and purple thread. She wanted to hold up her hand and refuse the offering but did not dare offend. She sniffled, dabbing her eyes daintily at the corners and gave the Queen a weak smile.

"There, much better."

"I must admit, Your Majesty, this is only third time I've ever cried."

The Queen made a little gasp. "My dear, that is quite commendable. I'm certain with that kind of restraint you'll fair well. Remember your private quarters are best if you must."

Then the secretary extended his hand to help her up. When she stood and looked about the room, she found the King napping in his throne. Good. Perhaps she'd avoid any further probing questions about her father.

And her lucky streak continued because the crying appeared to have kept the hiccups at bay. Lillias turned to the Queen and curtsied. "What's next, Your Majesty?"

"Dinner."

Lillias cleared her throat. "I beg your pardon," she said, cheeks heating, "In the ascension process."

"Dinner," the Queen said, repeating herself.

A meal with the royals? That had not been in the ascension manifesto her Aunt Elizabeth had drawn up for her. But not wanting to appear dafter than the King, she nodded and asked, "What time?"

"Half past five, tomorrow."

Relief rushed through her. Not that a day would make a huge difference, but it was almost late afternoon already. Surely, the royals dressed for dinner.

The Queen gave Lillias a gentle push toward the door with her adieus, allowing her secretary to take Lillias out of the opulent visiting gallery to the reception area.

The servant gave a short, perfunctory bow and handed her a sealed envelope. Before she could marvel fully at the royal, ruby red seal on the flap, a house steward swept up her right elbow and steered her to the main entrance. With great efficiency, she was guided to her carriage and was off before her heart settled into a normal rhythm that mimicked the horse's hooves cadence on the cobblestones of St. James Street.

With her hiccups less of a threat now that she was alone, she relaxed as the carriage sped along. Perhaps the key to circumventing the hiccups was sobbing. As much as that gave her an option to thwart them in the future, it would be a rare occasion that crying wouldn't be more embarrassing than hiccupping.

Because her curiosity could wait no longer, she slipped her fingernail under the envelope's official seal and popped open the missive. At first the calligraphed text was difficult to discern, as the lettering included so many flourishes and serifs. But as her eyes adjusted to the kerning, she was able to make out most of the words.

After reading and re-reading the four paragraphs, Lillias let her back relax against the leather carriage seat. She'd spent the better part of the day in a rigid posture either practicing at breakfast with the dowager or in the real arena with the royals.

Now, without anyone to judge her stature, either physical or patriarchal, she allowed herself to slump on the seat while the driver led the horses down the familiar streets toward Woodbeck House and she considered what dinner with the royals would entail.

According to the missive, which she pulled into view again, she'd be allowed one guest of either gender, but none younger than herself. She must wear the finest dress she owned. If she had time, she should find one even more splendid. The dinner was to start at half past five, sharp.

While the carriage moved efficiently through the London streets, she was torn between who she would ask to be her guest, Aunt Elizabeth or William.

A few hours later, Lillias was still weighing the pros and cons when she sat down in the Woodbeck library to wait for the dowager's interrogation. From one interview to the next, she braced herself for the dowager's round of questioning.

"There you are." As if on cue, the dowager and her Aunt Emma swept into the library and shut the door. Once they were both settled, the dowager folded her hands in her lap and said, "Well?"

"I didn't do anything to embarrass the family."

The dowager let out a long, slow sigh. "Tell me everything and don't leave anything out."

Now it was Lillias's turn to sigh, but this was the world

her aunt thrived on. Society. The dowager would always be consumed with what was worn, who wore it best, and who everyone talked about.

After being questioned about what the Queen and Prince wore, Lillias glanced longingly at the craft of brandy on the sideboard. Although she didn't drink, a little shot of it in the tea Finneas had set out for them would help settle her nerves.

"You were saying the most difficult question was, 'What type of duchess would you be?'" the dowager asked, repeating what Lillias had just said.

Shaking off the craving for something stronger than the tea in her cup, she thought back upon her answer. Most of the interview was a blur and she'd found herself not remembering much of what she'd said.

But her dowager aunt continued to press her to reveal everything, and she was doing her best not to leave anything out.

"Yes, I remember, the Queen appeared pleased with what I'd said." She paused and bit her lip, staring up at the ceiling as if that would help. Then, like a miracle, a quick flash of reckoning came to her.

"I said I would be an example of strength for all women and a champion of the arts," Lillias said slowly, as if watching herself in a dream. "I promised to do the bidding of my sovereign and pledged my fealty to the crown."

Her aunts burst out laughing.

For a moment, her pride took a hit, until she found the dowager glowing with approval before she said, "You sound more like a knight taking an oath of valor, and you promised much more than necessary, but I'm sure your heartfelt honesty and your pledge of loyalty was what they wanted to hear."

"Yes, but the Queen did say that the R.A. needed another board member."

The dowager clutched her chest.

"Are you all right, Aunt Elizabeth?" Lillias asked, rising quickly to her feet.

Her aunt waved her away. "I didn't mean to frighten you. I was not expecting that kind of acceptance when you haven't been formally trained. And you are a woman."

"You are a woman too, Aunt Elizabeth," she said, then covered her amusement with a cough. She'd meant no disrespect.

"Yes, but I paid for my appointment."

Tilting her head, Lillias raised a brow.

"You see when you are unmarried and rich, you can buy just about anything," her Aunt Elizabeth said smugly, matching Lillias's raised brow.

The three sat for a few moments studying each other. As was the habit of Aunt Emma, she looked upon the conversation with great interest. Until now she'd been silent.

"It's true, Lillias," Aunt Emma piped in. "When you are rich and without a husband, your money will give you entrance into places you'd never dreamed about."

Lillias had her doubts and now she was a bit troubled.

"You mean if I marry, my life would be very different?"

"Assuming you become the Duchess of Canterbury, and with the proper royal degree, you could join me on the R.A. board."

Lillias's mind began to work through several scenarios. Although there was much she didn't like about ascension, if the tradeoff was to live the life she wanted, to take risks, to be independent, then she'd embrace it.

"My dear, speaking of art, we have yet to schedule my portrait. Really, we must do it before your life changes forever."

With both her parents dead, hadn't that happened

already? "Will my life ever be my own?" Lillias asked, exasperated by the daunting possibilities that awaited her.

"That depends on what you chose to become—a duchess, a wife, a mother—all three."

She wanted to be a mother. That was certain. But she had a chance to avoid marriage and become a duchess. The role of an artist was most appealing and uncomplicated. But then there was William. With her father gone, she would have to be a fulltime parent to her sisters, married or no. She buried her face in her hands.

"Now, don't despair, my dear, you do not have to take these roles on all at once," Aunt Elizabeth said in an uncharacteristically soothing tone.

"Yes, we must do your portrait before my life changes forever," Lillias said, raising her face from her hands and forcing a smile. "We shouldn't wait. Let's start tomorrow."

Her dowager aunt clapped her hands together with a satisfied nod. "Splendid. The light in the garden will be best in the late afternoon, around five o'clock perhaps?"

"Five o'clock," Lillias screeched, and both aunts covered their ears. "I, we—"

"Out with it, child," the dowager demanded.

Releasing a loud sigh, she blurted it out, "I'm to dine with the Queen at half past five tomorrow and bring a guest."

"There it is. Your life is already changing."

For good or bad? "I didn't talk about my engagement in the interview because I was interrupted at the end."

With a reproachful look, the dowager said, "Then Her Majesty may already have made a match for you."

"Can she?"

"She's the Queen for God's sake," the dowager said with an escalating tone.

"Let's not forsake the Lord," Aunt Emma replied sharply,

then she turned beet red. She was more religious than most and the dowager was being quite scandalous.

"You said you could bring a guest?" the dowager asked Lillias, ignoring Aunt Emma.

"I did not mention William, nor who I would bring. I didn't want to pick between you two."

"And hurt his feelings, I understand."

The dowager certainly didn't because she wanted to invite William. He was second in line to the duchy of Devonshire, one of the important sovereign strongholds.

"Why didn't you mention your engagement in the interview?" Aunt Elizabeth asked, her gaze resting immediately on Lillias unadorned right ring finger.

"The King."

"His Royal Highness joined the interview?" her dowager aunt asked with her eyebrows arching.

"Rather stumbled in," Lillias admitted. "I believe he slept through most of it."

Aunt Elizabeth tsked. "He is an imbecile."

"Elizabeth." Aunt Emma's voice sounded reprimanding. "That's blasphemous."

It was, but Aunt Elizabeth was right this time.

"Lillias, do you or do you not want to marry Lord William Cavendish?"

Do I or do I not? Her head snapped up from her amusement over her aunts bickering. That was a question that a few days ago would have been easy to answer.

CHAPTER 31

From the gutter to the royal palace, William had been plucked from Cribb's Parlor before he and Nigel had settled on a plan for reclaiming the nude portrait. If only he'd signed it. Then he might have a legitimate claim. But the gaming hell supported nothing but illegitimacy. And now he was being whisked away from the dredges of London by carriage to dine with the most formal of all hosts.

"Your man Finneas is pretty remarkable," William said, shaking his head. How the man found him in the gaming hell to deliver a message from Lillias he'll never know and now Finneas was sitting next to the driver as escort, rather than in the carriage. The man was a saint in his eyes. "The only explanation might be the code of servants," William offered.

Lillias chuckled. At the same time the carriage went over an unruly dip in the road, sending her almost into his lap. When she recovered, cheeks blooming with color, she asked with an embarrassed whisper, "The code of servants?"

He nodded vigorously, as if it were gospel and she'd been skipping sermons. "There's quite a lot I don't know, but I surmise." He gave her a wink. "I suspect information is passed along in a series of codes based on priority."

When Lillias appeared intrigued by his explanation, she leaned forward, exposing more of her breasts than he expected. He blinked rapidly as if a blast of wind had struck his face and rendered him senseless, forgetting what he planned to say.

After a long awkward pause, she said, "You were saying a series of codes," guiding him back to his train of thought.

If he was this distracted alone with her, what would happen in his studio at the portrait sitting? The portrait. So much had happened. But he was talking about codes.

"Codes, yes," he mumbled. "'The chickens are loose,' refers to an urgent matter. 'The pot boiled over,' means a situation needs considerable attention." William scratched his chin. "Another one, 'the milk's gone sour,' suggests the information may not be reliable."

"Well, it sounds like all the problems of a modern household. When would you know whether it was the kitchen staff's problem or the master's?"

"That's the point. We don't always understand what they are talking about and this way they don't get caught gossiping, which most households find punishable."

"Finneas is a gem," Lillias gushed. "Finding reliable servants is an ongoing chore." She sighed heavily as if she'd had a part in it recently.

He reached for her hand and gave it a small peck. "Nothing's changed, has it?"

Lillias blanched slightly. Enough for him to notice the slight pale aurora that clouded her normally rosy cheeks.

"Today will tell," she said ominously. She moistened her lips, as if doing so would sugarcoat the bitter taste of her words. "This is more than a dinner. This is a test."

He'd assumed as much. "If you are wondering, I know

what fork to use for every course. Rest assured I won't let you down."

Thankfully, she covered a twitter with her hand, seemingly to find humor in his words, but she quickly grew serious again. "William, we'll both be tested."

He nodded solemnly. He'd already accepted her ascension and was certain there would be prerequisites involving their plans to marry. "I'll ask you again, nothing's changed, has it?"

This time Lillias's cheeks flushed with color. Even before her lips parted to speak again.

"Not in my feelings for you and my lack of interest in becoming a duchess." She smiled coyly. "My aunt said with an ascension confirmation I might receive a seat on the R.A. board." She beamed.

"You must imagine my concern when my messages went unanswered."

Giving him a blank stare, she contemplated his words. "I must have been so entrenched in the duchess due diligence. I hadn't realized." Her voice trailed off. "I wouldn't want to accuse the dowager of keeping them from me, but she must have had her reasons."

As much as he wanted to feel slighted at her admission, he'd be selfish to expect Lillias to be taking him into consideration when her life had been upended.

While they were both silent for a moment, streaks of late afternoon sunlight filtered through the carriage glass and framed her in gold light as the driver navigated a tight corner and they changed directions.

Changing directions. Both of their lives were about to do the same. With so much riding on the dinner, he decided not to bring up the painting until after. He couldn't say anything that would jeopardize her chances at becoming a duchess. Something neither of them wanted but seemed imminent.

"Where did Finneas find you?" she asked, breaking the silence.

Good old Finneas. Yes, he was the ultimate servant and thankfully had not shared with Lillias where he'd found him. "One of my usual haunts," he responded, stretching the truth a bit as the carriage rocked to a halt. Glancing out the window and back to Lillias as quickly, he stated the obvious, "We've arrived."

The door swept open and a royal footman with white gloves took Lillias's hand as she scooted off the carriage seat.

William followed, giving a nod to the doorman and the line of guards on either side of the carriage door.

Lillias's gown shimmered like the surface of a lake when the late day sun skims across its still waters. She glanced over her shoulder, and he gave her a reassuring smile.

Gawking at the entrance, he trotted up the steps behind his fiancée and into a grand lobby fit for a king. Pillars of marble reached endlessly up to support a ceiling whose canvas was filled with images of angels on gossamer wings. Some of them strummed harps, others reached toward a God who appeared smiling and merciful. If only.

"Sir."

A servant pointed toward a grand archway to the left.

"Right," William said, hiding his embarrassment and hastening after Lillias who'd disappeared. A few long strides had him behind her, however, in no time. She, none the wiser.

The two footmen led them down a never-ending hallway. Even longer than the one leading to the R.A.'s master gallery. A farthing long?

Finally, they entered the dining room. Another masterpiece of architecture. French revival, he presumed. Funny the British palace would pay homage to another country's design influences, but that was one of the reasons he'd chosen to stay in London and study at the Royal Academy of Art. Because cultural resources were easily accessible.

Before taking his seat where the servant had gestured, he reached for Lillias's hand and gave it a gentle squeeze. Their eyes met, hers filled with trepidation.

He squeezed her hand a little harder and gave her a wink and whispered, "You look royal. You'll be perfect."

The corners of her tight smile relaxed a bit and when her eyes narrowed to accommodate a more genuine smile, they crinkled a bit at the corners.

"Her Majesty—Charlotte, Queen of Great Britain."

Lillias nearly bent in half in a curtsy.

Daring not to dawdle, he bent forward too.

Heads bowed, they both genuflected in reverence.

"His Majesty, Prince Regent, George Augustus Fredrick," announced the crier.

The two stayed in their humble and appropriate positions until the Queen said with a regal air, "You may be at ease."

While Queen Charlotte addressed one of the servants, William glanced over at Lillias before he rose. Her eyes were squeezed tightly shut, as if in private prayer. But just as he thought he'd get away with the peep, she opened her eyes and caught him.

He winked, and her eyebrows quirked.

The Queen was still doling out instructions when they both rose, Lillias making the slightest nod toward the Queen at the head of the table to her left. The Prince Regent sat on the other end. A servant drew out a heavy, carved armchair for her and she slid into it like a foot to a slipper.

Making his way efficiently to the other side, and after a reverent nod to both the Prince and Queen, he took his seat across from Lillias.

Two abreast, the servants followed the Queen's directions carrying platters piled high with steaming meats and vegetables. When all were in place behind each guest's chair, the Queen was served first. She made a few remarks he could not discern, but in moments, Her Majesty's plate was full.

The Prince was served next, followed by Lillias. William last.

Then the Queen took her wine chalice and raised it high.

Of course, everyone followed and waited for her message.

"Welcome Lady Lillias of Canterbury and Lord William Cavendish, Earl of Devonshire. The Prince and I are pleased to have you dine with us today. Let's raise our glasses and toast to great possibilities."

"To great possibilities," echoed those at the table.

"Lord Cavendish," the Queen said as she turned his way. "It was fateful that you were available to substitute for the Dowager Countess Lady Elizabeth when she fell ill today."

Was it fateful? Apparently, he wasn't Lillias's first choice? When he stole a glance at her, his fiancée was concentrating on her food. The Queen must not be aware of the engagement.

"Now that I think upon it, this is a most unlikely pairing," the Prince said before William replied.

Determined not to say anything that would put Lillias's ascension at risk, William kept mute as the Queen weighed in with a humming sound of agreement. Then she twisted an enormous emerald ring on her finger before she pointedly asked, "Did not the Duke of Devonshire"—The Queen paused as if searching for the right words—"did he not kill the Duke of Canterbury?"

She could have said Lillias's father, but it would have sounded presumptuous even from the Queen.

"It's true." Lillias's voice rang out shrilly with her confirmation. "We discussed it briefly in my interview."

"Well, I suppose there are stranger liaisons than this," the Queen said casually and shrugged her shoulders. The jewels around her neck sparked in all directions, lit from the cande-labra above.

The Prince chuckled in response and raised his glass. "To strange liaisons."

"To strange liaisons," the room echoed.

"Let us eat," the Queen announced.

Without further pomp, everyone focused on the lavish array of delicacies on their plates. The clanking of silverware filled the room for a few uninterrupted minutes until the Queen set down her fork.

"How is it that the two of you were introduced?"

The bullseye was back on their relationship. William had assumed only questions about Lillias's readiness to become a duchess needed answers.

"We both are lovers of art," he said before the Prince or the Queen could concoct any of their own innuendos.

"Mutual acquaintances of an R.A. instructor," Lillias piped in and gave him a sweet smile as if thanking him for getting them on to a topic she could discuss at ease.

"You are a fan of portraiture?" the Queen asked.

"She is a portraiture artist," he said with pride. Although he'd never rival the dowager in terms of social promotion, he was comfortable tooting a trumpet over Lillias's accomplishments.

"Lord Cavendish is a fan," she said, blushing. "He's undoubtedly biased."

"Would you enter the R.A. competition?" the Queen asked, looking at Lillias.

"Pardon me, Your Majesty, but I thought women were not allowed to enter," Lillias said, appearing taken off guard by the question.

"Any woman, no. But a noble woman like yourself?" The Queen paused, then pointedly gestured to the wall of portraits of the royal family lining the wall around them, the flames from fiery sconces flickering over regal high brows. "Perhaps it's time for a change."

Lillias perked up in her chair and tossed a hopeful glance William's way. Beauchamp had promised he'd help her enter the contest, but she assumed it would be under an alias as she'd originally told her sisters.

"What would it take to make the change?" Lillias asked with a hopeful expression.

The Queen turned and regarded Lillias before she said with the certainty of one who leads a nation, "My decree."

The Prince Regent, who'd been silent for a while, said, "And my blessing." Then he gave his attention to Lillias. "Would you have a worthy entry?"

When Lillias hesitated, William kicked her gently under the table.

"Why yes, Your Highness, I believe I do," she responded, as if she was his ventriloquist doll.

* * *

LILLIAS SET her fork down and stared at it. She had just told the Queen of the British Commonwealth that she had painted a portrait worthy of beating scores of talented male artists at the Royal Academy of Art's International competition. Most with formal training. Was the stress of becoming a duchess altering her common sense?

"Then I will make the decree," the Queen promised.

"And I will sanction it," the Prince said with certainty.

"And you will enter," William said from across the table, bringing her gaze to meet his.

What had she done? She nodded and forced a smile, but her heart raced like a child's who had agreed to a punishment but didn't know how to reverse the deed.

"Your actions will change the way art will be viewed," the

Queen admonished, as if she had a personal interest in being the catalyst for change.

A catalyst for change? If being a confidant of the Queen could bring about opportunities for talented women, then perhaps her disinterest and reluctance in ascension was misplaced. As frightened as she was about these formidable circumstances, she couldn't help but feel an obligation to prove her entry deserving. Now she'd be able to sign her work.

But what about William's entry? She'd be competing against her fiancé. Of course, when she first thought them adversaries, she'd wanted to enter her portrait. Then with the potential ascension, she'd become conflicted. If she became a duchess, she could sell some of the land holdings, but they both needed the money.

"A worthy endeavor," William said, giving her leg another gentle tap under the table, nudging her out of her fog.

"I'm always ready for a challenge," Lillias promised, but her mind spun with worry.

"Then you may be ready for the match we had in mind for you," the Queen pronounced, looking down toward the end of the table at her son.

"The Duke of Norfolk is looking for a wife," the Prince said smugly, as if there was more to tell but he'd rather not.

Lillias breath left her as she glanced down at her ring-less right hand. Her aunt had told her not to wear the *Claddagh*. She avoided William's gaze when she responded.

"Your Highness, I am not looking for a husband," she said with what she meant to be a proper mix of practicality and humility. She clenched her hands tightly to keep them from shaking.

To her dismay and amazement, both the Prince and the Queen laughed heartily, with no attempt to hide how ridiculous they both must have thought her response was.

"No woman ever looks for a husband, my dear," said the Prince in a somewhat patronizing and serious tone. Clearly, he had a stake in this matchmaking scheme.

Lillias kept mum for the moment. If she lied, she'd have to contend with hiccups again. The Queen had already seen her cry and she'd promised that was a rare occasion.

"If I may speak for the lady," William said softly. "She is already promised to me."

"You?" both royals said without hesitation.

When William got angry his jaw tightened, and his hands fisted. Right now, his hands were hidden under the table, but his jaw was twitching. Yet in an unflappable reply he said, "Of course." And after a quick pause, finished with, "Why not?"

Why not indeed? Lillias thought. Would the royal family force her to marry?

"This is quite awkward," the Prince admitted, wiping his mouth with the royal linen napkin.

More than awkward.

The Queen turned to one of the waiting servants. "Would you show Lord Cavendish to the library and bring his dessert." It was an order, not a suggestion.

Lillias's heart sank when he quietly got up, then proceeded silently out of the room. But she was proud of him because he didn't balk and held his head high.

Once the door to the dining hall was closed, the Queen's razor-sharp gaze honed in on Lillias. "My dear, if you want to become a duchess, you must marry at least within your station if you can't rise above it." The Queen was making it clear William's station was not high enough.

"Your Majesty, I completely understand," was all she could muster. Not that she agreed or would comply, but she wouldn't jeopardize all she'd done on behalf of her family so far and Queen Charlotte couldn't be reproached. Whatever

Her Majesty decreed would undoubtedly become doctrine. For now, she needed to be compliant. To a degree.

"The Duke of Norfolk will be a good match," the Prince said dryly, as if he knew he was sentencing her, not engaging her. "You may know the man already."

Lillias nodded her head, not trusting what might leave her lips. Her natural inclination would be to be polite but decline the offer firmly. But under the circumstances, that inclination would only make both her and her family suffer. She had promised her aunt not to do anything that would embarrass the family. That would include, but not be exclusive to, refusing a royal request. At least she hadn't lied. Not yet.

"Phillip is descendent from Edward I," the Prince said. "His land holdings are vast and include Castle Arundel in Sussex. The Duke of Norfolk also holds the tile Earl Marshal, giving him the duty of organizing our state occasions, like the coronation of our King." The Prince steepled his fingers and waited.

Lillias wanted to fill the awkward silence but all she could think to say was, 'I don't bloody care.'

"You are forgetting he's also only one of four men allowed to proceed my husband in any formal ceremony," the Queen added, filling the void.

The weight of obligation had gotten heavier. A proposed yoke was to be placed around Lillias's neck by the royals, strapping her to a match of their liking. As much as she wanted to be compliant, she couldn't stay quiet any longer. She had reached the breaking point. "What about Lord Cavendish?"

The two royals looked at each other and then back at Lillias.

"What about him?" the Prince asked, blinking measuredly.

"For a husband." Did Lillias have to explain herself?

"The subject of Lord Cavendish needs no further discussion," the Queen said, putting her hand on her opulent jeweled necklace. Either a gesture of comfort or to signal her elevated station.

Biting back what she wanted to say, Lillias looked down at her folded hands before she spoke. "We didn't discuss the possibility."

The silence that ensued was detrimental to her sliver of hope. When she couldn't stand it any longer and needed to be assured she wasn't alone in the room after a royal exodus, Lillias lifted her gaze to find the Queen peeling an orange with a look of disdain on her face and the Prince popping grapes into his mouth, staring at the centerpiece.

Lillias swallowed hard. It was now or never to say her piece. "With all due respect, I would like to know the chances of a betrothal to Lord Cavendish." She trained her eyes on the Prince and waited.

"You have two chances," he said, examining his perfectly manicured nails. "If the Duke of Norfolk finds you unacceptable"—he looked up to address her directly—"or if you aren't dubbed a duchess."

When he paused, Lillias's heart skipped a beat.

"Then you may marry the earl," he said and went back to examining his hands.

Nodding like a two-year-old, she fought back tears, and her gaze went back to her folded hands. The knuckles beneath her gloves had to be white from squeezing her hands together so tightly. Her thoughts began to spin, and the words of the Prince echoed in her mind, 'If the Duke of Norfolk finds you unacceptable.' She wanted to be unacceptable, but that wouldn't be an option because it was important to her family's livelihood that she be dubbed a duchess.

"I'll start the proceedings."

The Queen's comment snapped Lillias out of her perplexity, her eyes seeking the sovereign.

"And have your R.A. entry to the officials by the end of the week," the Queen announced.

"Your Highness, it would be my honor," she said, making every effort to keep the fear from her voice. She turned to the Queen for further instructions.

"The Prince will arrange for the meeting with the duke," the Queen told her, then waved to the servant and the man proceeded to help her up. Walking out of the room, Her Majesty turned with her final words, "You are dismissed."

Lillias bowed her head and counted to twenty before she looked up and around the room.

One servant was patiently standing to her right and moved forward with his hand out. "My lady, are you ready to retreat?"

Retreat? Yes, to Woodbeck House with plans to never leave the place because the royal family could force her to marry a man not of her choosing. *Can a person disagree with them and live another day?* Although if she consulted history, it had been many years since King Henry the VIII popularized royal disobedience with beheadings.

As she followed the servant into the hallway, she breathed a sigh of relief to find William standing in the glowing light with a grin on his face. How could he always look ready to defend her and happy to see her no matter the circumstances?

"Ready?" He held his arm out for her.

She grabbed him as if her life depended on it. Ready she was, to leave this place, to start a life with him, to forget about society's expectations.

The servant who'd brought her to the hallway guided them through the corridor and out to their awaiting carriage.

They'd both remained silent along the way until the carriage door closed, then they both started talking at once.

"You first," William said with an apologetic nod.

"You must ruin me."

Her fiancé's eyes went wide, and his face turned ghostly.

Not the reaction Lillias had expected.

"What do you mean?"

"I must be unacceptable to the Duke of Norfolk."

"I don't understand. Can you please explain what you mean by ruining you and why must the duke find you unacceptable?"

Attempting to take a deep breath, she struggled with the effort, her chest heaving as if one of her sisters was sitting on it and she couldn't get any air. Her whole world had evolved around Verity and Rebecca. Even after her mother had passed, her father had protected her from much of the outside world. Now that had changed and all she wanted was to run away and hide in her childhood room. She buried her head in her hands and began to sob.

CHAPTER 32

Ruin her? William sighed. He may have done that already, what with his nude portrait of her hanging in Cribb's Parlor.

Last night, after Lillias had stopped crying, he'd listened to her account of the conversation with the royals and wasn't surprised when she told him Prince Regent had set his sights on a higher prize for her. She was a soon-to-be duchess. Regardless of her demands, William vowed to himself not to ruin her.

For the entire carriage ride, he'd done his best to ease her fears of failing her family before they arrived at Woodbeck House. As much as he wanted to talk to her about the nude painting, her emotional state after the royal dinner was fragile at best, giving him no opportunity to broach the subject. However, she made him a promise to meet him today at the R.A.

While he readied his studio, with the intention of convincing her to pose for the final sitting for his replacement entry, he couldn't ignore the damage his first portrait might cause her. One thing was for certain. If he found a way to get it back, he'd destroy it.

As he studied his new portrait of Lillias, although fully clothed, he believed it had merit. But the work was missing that aura. That expression of ecstasy he'd painted in the nude version.

A light rap on the door had him dropping the cover over his painting.

"It's unlocked," he said.

"Here you are."

Spinning around to greet his muse he offered her a low bow. "Of course, right where I should be."

"You know that I'm not where I should be." Lillias licked her lips nervously. "And without a chaperone," she added, a slight shiver shaking her shoulders. Then she stole a glance at the hallway behind her.

"Sit," he directed. "Your purple wrap is on the settee." When he took her hand, it was cold to the touch. His eyes shot up to find hers. "Don't worry, I'll keep you safe," he promised, first guiding her to the studio settee before shutting and locking the door. "If the door is closed, the staff assumes the room is unoccupied."

"Lucky for me," Lillias whispered through chattering teeth.

He made a path to the settee and squeezed himself next to her on the petite piece of furniture. It was designed as a prop, low to the ground and not a full sofa. His bent legs reached close to his chin. Sitting in the center, he did his best to keep the piece from tipping like a child's teeter totter.

Lillias covered her mouth with a gloved hand and tried her best to stifle one of her girlish giggles, one of her most endearing traits. It was moments like this when her wit and her laughter kept him from his darkest self.

Taking the purple velvet coverlet, the one she'd worn when he'd saved her from the burning classroom, he covered her shoulders with it.

When her eyes softened with gratitude, his heart melted, but his cock hardened. Where was the gentleman who'd greeted her with a respectful bow only moments ago. Now he wanted to rip the purple coverlet off and cover her body with his nakedness to heat them both. But with his luck, the entire settee would split in two in a mighty crash and give away their location locked behind closed doors.

"You look a little overheated," Lillias said with concerned look.

More than overheated, he gulped and tried to cross his legs, which had disastrous results. How could he finish this portrait with her dressed, when all he wanted was to disrobe her one item at a time? A smoldering look from her and he swore his clothes would catch fire.

"Take this," she said softly, offering him a handkerchief that seemed to materialize out of thin air.

Dabbing the few beads of perspiration on his brow, he considered the delicacy of the embroidered linen kerchief as he patted his forehead instead of wiping it as he would with a boxing towel.

"Don't be nervous," Lillias cooed.

Isn't that what he should say?

"We've both been through too much drama in the past two weeks," she said, smiling weakly up at him.

She smelled of roses and linen. Even here, competing with the odor of oil-based paint, her sweet scent permeated the space. He wanted to put his nose between her breasts and take in her essence. Hell, if he had his way, his hands would rove over her nipples and make her rosy tips turn into hard buds.

Leaning forward, and closing his eyes, as if to sniff a delicate rose in his garden, he said in a whisper, "I'm *not* nervous, are you?"

He didn't take her leaning backward as sign to stop his progression. Her curious expression let him know she didn't mind his closeness. She had asked him to ruin her, and although he had not asked for an explanation, he expected to conduct this portrait sitting as a business transaction. Yet, every action he'd taken so far with her was to the contrary, to take risks and handle the consequences later. His resolve was wavering. No, it was failing.

A shift forward in her position woke him from his personal dialog. If he'd been in the ring, he'd been on the floor because he wouldn't have seen her one, two, punch coming. Her lips took command of his mouth and her hand reached for his thigh. Before he gave her credit for a knock-out, he guessed her hand was there for balance and not what he'd first thought.

A gentle groan preceded her parting lips and she asked seductively, "Are you nervous now?"

Not that he was, but he nodded to humor her. What man didn't love a woman who made the first move? She was doing a superb job of taking his breath away, for her lips had sealed themselves tightly against his, moving with the skill of an experienced kisser. He happened to know quite a bit about kissing, even though he wasn't a rake. If he'd been the one to start the— *She bit my lip?*

He chuckled into her smirk.

"Are you paying attention?" she murmured between kisses.

Straining against his breeches, his cock grew even more, as if responding to her question. If she chose to look down right now, she'd find the evidence and he couldn't help but kiss her with a sly smile.

Damning the flimsy nature of the furniture, he drew

Lillias on top of him as he stretched out on his back. Even though the settee was light, at least it was long, long enough for him to lay his head against the heavily padded curved arm and tassel fringed pillow.

When she landed with a little gasp on his chest, he had to give the lady high marks for not letting go of the kiss. If she'd been apprehensive about the new position, she didn't show it.

Winding his arms around her middle, he aimed to move her toward the seam between the back of the settee and the seat cushions. He wasn't in control of his physical reaction, and he didn't want to scare her by positioning her on his expanded manhood.

Frankly, he didn't care if she was acting out in frustration for all the restrictions that had been placed upon her in the past few weeks. Social shackles were hard to break, invisible to the eye, but heavier than their physical counterpart on the soul.

Yet, he cared too much for her and would stop if her intention was to ruin herself with him now. He'd support her through any trial, but he wouldn't allow her to be reckless. Her moral compass, her parents, were gone. And he'd picked up enough from her encounters with her dowager aunt that she wouldn't let the woman rule her life. But rebels always paid a price for their actions.

Despite his mental dribbling, his resistance was unwinding. If Lillias was this good at seduction, and he assumed he was being seduced, he was thrilled for the promise the marriage bed held.

Moving his hands up her back, he began to loosen the strings of her corset, wishing her amorous streak could have started after he'd asked her to remove it for the sitting.

With a petulant huff, she released his lips, admonishing, "Corsets are the evil invention of this century."

"When you are mine, I'll insist you remain corset free whenever possible."

"Fashions are changing. This contraption soon may be out of favor," she said, as if that would suit her, and she didn't reject his possessive assumption.

"Keeping you close to my heart would be my top priority," he said smoothly, drawing her to his chest again where his heart pounded like a boxer taking a beating. The move also allowed him to reach the higher crisscross straps of the corset. With one last aggressive tug, its paneled sides caved.

With a sweet moan, she released his lips. Then giving him a provocative look, she reached behind her back like a talented contortionist, and with a few quick yanks, the female contraption collapsed around her waist. Then, like a magic trick, Lillias wiggled out of the corset and then tossed it to the floor. The sleight of hand diverted his gaze, but when it returned, her breasts dangled before him like forbidden fruit.

Without hesitation, he took one of her supple teats in his palm and gently kneaded it. Gazing into her eyes, he took her nod as an invitation. An invitation to taste her.

Tracking a slow circle around her nipple with his tongue, he enjoyed every bit of this exotic delight.

After another pass of his tongue around her nipple, her groans became deeper and more frequent. Her breathing faster.

She arched her back and murmured, "Ruin me."

He took a pause, his heart almost stopped beating. Gazing up at her, he held his breath. There it was, her ecstasy. The expression he'd painted from his imagination. Now it was real.

His mind whirled. The artist in him wanted to hop off the settee and ask her to stay where she was so he could start painting that face. The scoundrel side of him, although he wasn't miscreant, wanted to take her now and bask in the love he had for her. Ultimately, it was her decision.

A muffled, deep moan settled his debate. He'd take her now.

CHAPTER 33

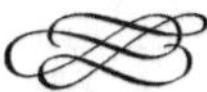

Everything in her rational mind screamed the word stop. But Lillias often ignored that part of herself. It was the artist in her, the risk-taker, who'd agreed to meet William alone in his studio today and allow him to touch her in a way she'd only fantasized about.

She must decide soon. Lose her womanhood here in his creator's space or second guess herself the rest of her life if she'd made the right decision. Because this might be the only choice she'd be able to make for herself.

"Oh," she squeaked. "What are you doing now?" she asked, her voice rising.

William chuckled deep in the back of his throat. He wasn't a reputed rake, but frankly, it appeared he was starting to take off the rest of her clothes.

"Are you afraid of me now?" He growled ever so softly.

She vehemently shook her head, certain if she didn't make it exaggerated, he wouldn't believe her. Nor would she.

"Are you the Big, Bad Wolf?" Lillias asked, close enough to tickle his ear with her breath.

"Grrr, little girl, you should be running home to your granny's right now. I could just eat you up, you're so delicious," he teased, nipping at her neck with little bites, sending her into a fit of giggles.

"I must have forgotten my picnic basket," she said, batting her lashes.

"It's not your picnic basket I'm hungry for," he replied, his eyes going wide, and his tongue taking short swipes between her breasts, all the way to her navel.

When he dipped his tongue into her belly button, a flutter of heat traveled up her spine like a lit fuse, melting her resistance.

Didn't she want to be ruined? *But how far must I go to be ruined?* Conversations with her mother and governess, when she'd been eight and ten, had given her a general guideline and even just being alone with a man would suffice with some of the *ton,* but without specific details, she wasn't sure what ruination entailed. She'd need to trust William would show her.

But his tongue's infatuation with her nipples had her sucking in a sharp breath. If he didn't stop what he was doing for a moment something inside her would give way.

"Have I whetted your appetite?" she asked, purposely wanting to stop his tongue from its glorious torture.

"Have I whetted yours?" And after a long pause he added, "Let me show you the meaning of the expression."

He moved her to straddle his hips, his manhood hard against her thigh. But her eyes flew open when he reached under her skirt, moving his hand up her thigh and beyond her undergarments. Before she had a moment to consider his advancement, he gently pushed two of his fingers into her womanhood. With soft strokes, waves of luxurious warmth began to course through her body, ending in tantalizing pulsations between her thighs.

Where was William taking her? She was certain a secret would soon be shared, one that her mother had been unable to explain. For now she knew words could not describe what she was feeling physically or emotionally.

When did like become love? When did either become lust? Was it unnatural to feel all of those at once?

"Lillias, my love," William murmured into her lips, kissing her with a hunger she too possessed. "Now is the time for you to decide what happens next," he said, moving a third finger inside her.

"Oh, no!" she shrieked.

His lips left hers. "Did I hurt you?" He removed his fingers from her channel as if he'd been slapped.

"What?" she replied, unsure of how to respond. She'd been awake in a wonderful dream.

"You said, no."

"Oh, I didn't mean no." Now she understood what it meant to be in the throes of passion and her confusion had chased away the passion in his eyes.

"You said, 'my love.'"

Tilting his head until his forehead touched hers, he took in a sharp breath. Then after sliding to the settee seam between the sofa's back and hers, he pulled her close and tugged the purple coverlet over them. "Let me take you back to the day we met and finish what you started:

"My mistress's eyes are nothing like the sun;
Coral is far more red than her lips' red;
If snow be white, why then her breasts are dun;
If hairs be white, black wires grown on her head.
I have seen roses damasked, red and white,
But no such roses see I in her cheeks;
And in some perfumes, there is more delight
Than in the breath that from my mistress reeks.
I love to hear her speak, yet well I know

That music hath a far more pleasing sound;
I grant I never saw a goddess go:
My mistress when she walks, treads on the ground.
And yet, by heaven, I think my love as rare
As any she belied with false compare.'"

"Lovely, of course, Sonnet one hundred and thirty." The one she started to quote when she was standing up for herself in Beauchamp's class, wanting to prove she was not a 'chit,' as he'd called her then.

She twisted around and propped her arm under her head, the warmth of his body making her tingle in anticipation of something more. But that sonnet wasn't improving her mood. Was he calling her breath putrid or now claiming she his paramour?

"You are comparing me to a *mistress?*"

William put on a long face. "I'm telling you that I love you."

He loves me? The heat in her body was fading, but a warmth on grander scale began to fill her heart. She had another sonnet in mind.

"'Doubt thou the stars are fire,
Doubt that the sun doth move,
Doubt truth to be a liar,
But never doubt I love.'"

William's dark amber eyes burned with a new glow when he asked, "Is that an example of what I should have said or how you feel?"

"Both," she said without hesitation, surprising herself because she'd never claimed her love until now.

"Then I should have chosen better. Let me try again." He moistened his lips, then his pupils flared as if there was a breeze fanning a fire within. "'I love you with so much of my heart that none is left to protest. And I will live in thy heart, die in thy lap and be buried in thy eyes.'"

Savoring the words, she released a gentle sigh before she awarded her judgement. "Now that's Shakespeare worth quoting. You know the Bard has written hundreds and hundreds of ways to say, I love you."

"And you've memorized them all?" He stared at her with both brows raised in apparent disbelief.

Laughing first, she chuckled through her response. "Not all, but I have tried."

Shaking his head, he gave her a sweet peck on her forehead. Even though the moment of passion had come and gone, there was still a tingling sensation in her belly. It might have been fueled by her desire, but the relationship had moved beyond friendship. Although she'd asked him to ruin her, she didn't want that on his conscious. There had to be another way to be unacceptable to the Duke of Norfolk.

"I can't ruin you," William said with an air of exasperation, as if he'd heard her thoughts. Then after a long pause he added, "It might put me in prison."

"Good Lord, no!" she said, almost knocking him off the settee when she pushed against his chest in utter disbelief. "Surely, there would be consequences, but prison?"

"I told you once I'm a troubled soul, a victim of heartache." William rolled over the top of her and slipped to the floor on bended knee. "That wasn't completely true," he amended. "I am a killer."

She jerked herself to sitting, her mind whirling with the ramifications of his confessions. First he said he loved her, now he says he's a killer? If only he had her malady of hiccupping, she'd know the truth. Even without a test of honesty, she was not about to accept his outburst as fact.

"I don't believe you," she challenged, staring into his eyes that were now a murky brown.

"I killed a man." His gaze veered quickly to the floor, as if he couldn't bare her reaction to his words.

"On purpose?"

"That I don't know," he mumbled, still staring at the floor.

Gathering up her resolve, while she did her best to digest his disturbing statement, Lillias could only defend him.

"If you didn't know then it wasn't on purpose. You can't be a killer if you didn't intend for it to happen."

Her words silenced him. Perhaps they had merit.

Then he stood and his gaze settled on the covered easel before he answered.

"Sometimes my anger gets the best of me, but that time I couldn't remember what I'd done after I took a blow to my head in the boxing ring," he admitted, rubbing his hand slowly through his dusky hair as if there was a wound beneath that needed tending.

"I've never seen you angry."

"I trained myself to control it."

Even though he wasn't looking at her, she was witness to his struggle. Clenching and unclenching his fists. Seesawing his jaw. These were reactions she'd noticed in the past, but not questioned.

"Everyone has flaws. And you deserve to be loved," she finally said breaking the awkward silence.

He turned to her. The torment of his admissions clearly visible in his expression. With a shrug of his shoulders he asked, "Now what do we do?"

"I did come here for a sitting," she reminded him with an impertinent nod toward the covered easel, looming close enough to touch if she reached out. What he'd just told her was unsettling, but there might be a rational explanation for what happened. They needed to focus on their original purpose for meeting today.

His gaze followed hers to the easel. "You had a glow about you moments ago. I'd love to capture it, but I'm uncertain I'd want to share it with the world."

"You didn't paint another nude of me, did you?"

He appeared affronted. "Don't you trust me?"

"I've seen the wolf," she shot back.

"I want to protect you," he said sheepishly, dropping his head and looking up at her with an apologetic expression. "If you'll still have me, faults and all."

"Protect me?"

He drew her up from the settee into his arms, wrapping the purple throw a little tighter around her. She was suddenly back on the R.A. patio when she'd shared the black-mailer's note. He wanted to protect her then.

"If you don't want to be married, I'll still love you. If you want to be married and only a countess, I'll still love you. If you want to be a duchess and remained unmarried, I'll still love you."

Then he kissed her like she'd never been kissed before. Her breath evaporated into the heat of his passion. What she could inhale, came in short supply. Her heart beat as if it wanted to escape. Every fiber of her being thrummed with an energy like harnessed lightning.

When he released her lips, reluctantly on her part, she ushered out a low, rumbling, "Yes."

"Yes, to—"

"Posing, marriage. Damn the royals and ascension. Verity would make a better duchess than I. The dowager has influence, the birth order for girls can't matter as much as the birth order for boys."

He gave her a wide smile. "Primogeniture should be done away with." Then he released her and turned to collect her corset from the floor. "And as much as I'd like to have your clothes done away with, you must put them on, or I'll start a new portrait of you naked."

"The portrait?" Lillias gasped, "The missing one." She

couldn't trust what society had in store for her if the nude surfaced now.

"We need to focus on the new one," William said in an agitated tone. Although he didn't look angry, he sounded that way. Perhaps he did hide his emotions well.

She shook off the notion, considering there was still work to be done and a waiting carriage by noontime.

Slipping out of the warmth of the purple throw, she gathered up her corset, winding it around her middle. "You must be my lady's maid and lace me up," she insisted, turning her back to him while she shoved a few stray pins to secure her loose curls back on top of her head.

He groaned behind her, drawing her into his arms again and kissing her neck. For a moment she gave in with sweet surrender, but after hearing approaching voices in the outer hall, her spine went erect.

"Shh," he whispered, "I'm certain it's a tour of students on their way to the great hall." And instead of following her instructions, he continued to trail kisses up to her ears.

She gave him a gentle elbow to show her concern.

Grumbling, at last he released her, and the corset began to tighten around her middle. She sucked in her breath as she always did, waiting for the laces and the whalebones to pinch, but he stopped too soon. Given the circumstances, she would simply have to make do. She spun to face him. The voices had gotten louder, but he didn't seem concerned.

Taking matters into her own hands, she turned him toward the easel, giving him a gentle shove, trusting he'd take the hint.

Grumbling a bit more, he uncovered the canvas while she quickly put her clothes back in place and took a seat alone on the settee. Just as she'd settled into a comfortable spot, the door's lock clicked, and Professor Beauchamp walked in.

"This is an example of—"

The professor took one look at Lillias and stopped talking. She wasn't sure of her expression, but she had to think quickly.

"It's an example of greatness," Lillias said, finishing the professor's sentence and pointing to William who was standing by an almost completed portrait of her.

Gazing at her, William contemplated his artistic journey as he stood in the R.A. contest gallery the next morning. He was certain this portrait of Lillias was better than his first, which now seemed childish because he'd used the shock value of the naked form to impress.

That vivid image of her face full of passion, when they'd been intimate with each other yesterday, would stay burned in his memory for eternity. But he'd changed his mind about sharing it with the world. It hadn't been easy, but he had modified his entry.

Instead of looking out of the frame, Lillias's gaze was rotated away and up toward an outreached masculine hand that dipped into the portrait from the top of the frame. The inference was left to the observer as to whether she was receiving a blessing from a divine source or seeking celestial guidance from beyond.

As he stood alone in front of his entry before the R.A. opened to the public, he understood now how this finished piece wasn't a solitary endeavor. If not for Lillias, Professor

Beauchamp, and his legendary architect grandfather, he wouldn't be here today.

Plus, Beauchamp had been positive about his work even when William wasn't. The professor had also covered for him when the student tour had barged in on William and Lillias in the student private studio.

No doubt the man's protective nature toward Lillias had smoothed over what could have been a scandalous situation.

If ruination had been her goal, Beauchamp could have made it possible.

But he didn't.

Ruination came with vast consequences. Consequences Lillias hadn't considered because she lived at times with reckless abandon.

Tugging on his pocket watch chain until the cool round piece met his palm, he marked the time before tucking it away. The main door would open soon. He'd promised himself one more walk about the gallery before he met Lillias at the main entrance.

She'd been coy at first, but when pressed, insistent on keeping her entry a secret, even from him.

Glancing around the gallery again, he strained his eyes for a flicker of the familiar.

Color, concept, countryside? She never shared any of her sketches. Even with vision, he experienced blindness. None of the entries were signed, of course. That would happen after the judging. Some would be auctioned, others retained by the R.A., and the rest would be returned to the artist.

William's portrait was not for sale. Not for any price. And he would stick to that plan.

Stopping short at the end of the line of entries, he finally found himself in front of a scene that rang with familiarity. A torso of a man, muscles rippling from the shoulders to knees, hands taped in clean linen strips. A barely visible double rope hung in soft focus in the background. The boxer was at an angle, with much of his back toward the audience, but his middle section was twisted like a wrung-out towel, as if he'd just taken a blow and was spiraling away from the force. With the body tipping backward, it appeared the man was fighting not only an unknown opponent, but also his balance. The creator captured the motion he'd witnessed in the ring.

Even more fascinating, the artist had painted a birthmark on the boxer's left side exactly where he had one. This had to be Lillias's work and it was prize-worthy.

Leaving the gallery with rapid steps, he reached the R.A.'s front entrance in no time. Stopping at one of the stained-glass panels, he peered out. Colorful profiles were manipulated into strange shapes by the thickness and variety of the glass.

The turnout was impressive. The steps leading up to the entrance were beyond full. They formed a cascading parade of the town's most affluent, donned with top hats and plume filled bonnets. The festive scene gave him a moment to reflect on how his life and art had come to a pivotal moment.

"Ready?" A steady hand grasped William's shoulder and he turned to find Professor Beauchamp beside him. "It's going to be a big day."

"Fame and fortune to be had or lost," William countered.

The professor's face clouded for a moment. "No word on the lost R.A. project?"

"Still missing is the best way to describe it." William wanted it to stay stolen. The conversation ended there, for the professor was unlocking the front entrance and appeared to have moved on.

Once the doors were opened, it was as though the flood-gates to a highbrow circus had been breached. Guests rushed past him in a polite, but brisk manner, as if they weren't one of the early spectators, the beauty of the gallery would be less grand.

His height gave him an advantage as the rows of fashionable art lovers of London moved past him. The steps to the R.A. managed a steady stream of visitors as carriages delivered their cargo.

Craning his neck and leaning toward the left, he caught sight of a figure that could only belong to Lillias. No matter how many times she told him she never saw the allure, he'd repeat to her how wrong she was in the assessment of herself. Perhaps he could prove it to her today when they stood in the gallery among the judges and patrons.

"There you are," he greeted her, dipping into a low bow before he brushed his lips over her outreached, gloved hand. Just as he was about to rise, he stopped. The *Claddagh* ring was missing.

When he raised his eyes to seek out hers, she quickly turned away. Perhaps it was Lillias's dowager aunt who'd distracted her as she swept past them, bustling down the hall.

He stood, wanting to sweep Lillias into his arms and tell her that was where she belonged. But that wasn't likely going to happen, especially now after the rumor he'd heard from his brother must be true. That her engagement to the Duke of Norfolk was official. At first he'd assumed it was his brother's morbid sense of humor. Until he could talk with her privately, escorting her through the gallery competition would have to do.

"Ready?" He extended his elbow.

She nodded and hooked her arm in his. They fell into the stream of gentry making their way to the contestants' gallery. Although most of the judges had been named in the *Times*, not many were well known by London, not enough to spot them on the premises. The gallery would be open to visitors and judges until eight o'clock that evening for the first round of judging. Rumor was most visited in the last hour expecting much of the crowd to have thinned by then.

Walking into the gallery behind a few matronly patrons, he slowed to allow them time to begin the tour through the roped pathway toward where his entry hung. But he couldn't see the new portrait of Lillias now because the first visitors were standing in front of it. As much as he relished the eye level position, they wouldn't be able to view it until they were upon it.

Smiling at the museum's volunteer greeter, William handed two tickets to the man, then tipped his hat before he moved into the queue.

Taking a good look about the gallery, he recognized a few of his fellow students. Not all had been invited to enter, but those who came must be curious.

Professor Beauchamp was positioned on a temporary structure that straddled both galleries. The pulpit-like tower had been erected for just this exhibit. It was his job, he'd explained to William earlier that week, to keep the patrons moving through the exhibit and not to let anyone stay too long at one painting.

"You've not mentioned the nude portrait in days," Lillias said in a breathy whisper.

Looking over his shoulder first, he turned back and muttered, "I thought I had a lead on it and that vanished."

"Do you still think it was stolen?"

"Beauchamp refers to it as the lost R.A. project."

"How do you refer to it?" she asked with haunting concern.

He didn't want to call it a lack in judgment, or anything negative, because he did love the painting. But he still couldn't tell her the truth yet. He hoped Nigel had succeeded with their most recent plan, but his friend had yet to contact him.

"My object of obsession, as we agreed the day you confessed to being the figure model," he finally said.

Like a stranger, Lillias sported a strained smile at that. Still cordial, she was holding on to him but in a detached manner.

Needing some small talk to break the tension between them he added, "I've seen nothing about in the papers."

"William." Lillias's voice cracked when she said his name.

He turned toward her now, concerned. That wasn't the most reassuring thing he could have said. He hated small talk.

"I don't know how else to say this." She stopped, tears welling in her eyes. "I must give this back to you." She pulled them out of the line, then took the *Claddagh* ring from her reticule and handed it to him.

Pushing it back, he closed her hand around it. "I don't understand. It's a friendship ring." He tried to ignore the people and paintings around him and focus on Lillias.

She bit her lip and nodded. "The dowager. The Queen. The Prince. The Duke."

He squeezed her hand in a possessive gesture. The action also kept him from clenching his fists. If it was Lillias's love that kept his anger in check, then the lack of it could unleash it again.

Gazing up at him, a pearl-sized tear rolled down her cheek. "I insisted that you escort me today." Lillias nodded toward the bend in the queue where her dowager aunt stood. "She agreed to this one time and told me to say my goodbyes."

He swallowed hard before he put on a false but bright countenance. "No need to say goodbye," he promised, giving the hand another gentle squeeze.

Lillias nodded rapidly and turned away.

They walked awkwardly together now, inspecting the

entries, commenting politely on an artist's use of color, technique, or critical eye. All along his anger toward the royals, the world, even Lillias was building. A smoldering fuse burned inside his heart as he went through the motions of a polite gentlemanly escort, holding back on the familiar.

It must have been his confession that cast doubt on his worthiness and Lillias would have had second thoughts about fighting for him when she could have offered Verity to the Duke of Norfolk rather than herself. Wasn't Lillias's biggest fear failing to have her sister married by the end of the Season?

By the time William had sorted through some of his anger, they were a few paintings away from his entry. Although his emotions were rioting and his heart sinking, he couldn't let her see his confusion. He had to hang on to his only hope, that Lillias would be pleased with his portrait of her.

* * *

THE PAINTING CAME INTO VIEW. It was beyond anything Lillias could have imagined. The beauty of it. Devine and disguise in its duality. With her head turned from the observer, Lillias was incognito. William had protected her identity. If a patron were to claim she was the woman caught between the brush stokes amid the beams of golden light and dazzling shimmer on William's canvas, she could question their certainty without her dreaded hiccups erupting.

While the nude was beautifully painted, the message was dark and subliminal, with undercurrents of obsession.

This portrait hinted at a connection between some higher being and the subject, or perhaps a celestial transformation from beyond. The painting was beyond what she'd expected.

She fought back a sob, her shoulders caving, her heart

wanting to win. But her war with her social obligations was crushing her determined spirit. If she didn't shut William out of her life now, she was sure she'd die a slow emotional death.

"I can't be your friend," she finally said when she wanted to compliment him, thank him for protecting her, and never wanting to leave his side. But instead, she turned and picked up her skirts, and in a frantic dash, she ran from William, from the arts, from love.

CHAPTER 35

A dinner invitation from Prince Regent was unexpected. Dreaded actually. William fidgeted with his pocket watch as his carriage rolled down St. James Place on its way to Buckingham House and that very occasion.

If he'd thought the last few weeks were filled with high drama, he'd been mistaken. For those appeared calm when compared to the last two days. Those were unlike any other. Today, had the potential to make it three in a row.

The worst of it, he and Lillias had been kept apart since she'd seen his new portrait of her earlier that week and run away. He could only imagine she hated it. What else could he think? She'd claimed she couldn't even accept his friendship. That made the situation decidedly bleak.

Poor Finneas. The butler looked pained beyond measure every time he turned William away from his stops at Woodbeck House, stating Lady Lillias was not receiving visitors.

Damn it all. He wasn't a visitor. He was her friend and much more.

The carriage went over an unruly patch in the road,

making William bump his head against the carriage door where the handle grip hung. His luck had turned for the worse and this knock in the head was symbolic of the invisible punch in the gut he'd felt when he'd read in the *Times* about Lillias's official wedding plans to the Duke of Norfolk.

He had failed at ruining her. Tomorrow would be a full week since the show opened, and the winning portrait would be awarded. He planned to be at the R.A. for the announcement and hoped Lillias would too.

At least Finneas had accepted his missives. Whether they reached Lillias or not, he was uncertain, as no communication had been returned from her.

The bumpy carriage ride finally came to an end and William found himself inside the grand vestibule of Buckingham House waiting as he had two weeks ago when he was told he wasn't good enough for Lillias. It appeared to be a theme.

"The Prince will see you now." A butler with a wooden face and similar disposition guided him to the same dining room where he'd sat with Lillias for her review. What perverse requests would the royals make of him? For him to vow to never come face to face with her again? To be banned from London? There were so many wretched possibilities.

"Cavendish."

William spun around to find the Prince behind him. As was custom, he'd waited for his host and was now guided by the same wooden butler to take a seat to the right of the Prince. Once his host was settled in his royal high back chair, William was led to his seat.

"Your Highness," William said reverently, as his own chair was adjusted by the butler, and he was tucked neatly under the massive table burgeoning with the finest linen, china, and crystal.

The Prince nodded and then turned to the butler and the

several footmen who lined the room. After a few instructions, the empty crystal glasses were filled with dark red liquid and in moments the Prince held his glass high.

"A toast."

Raising his glass in unison, William plastered a grin on his face to match that of his host.

"To the Duke of Devonshire," the Prince proclaimed.

"To my father, posthumously, or my brother Alexander?"

The Prince's grin faded, and his arm drooped a bit. "You haven't heard?"

Now it was William's turn to frown. Had his brother been in a duel or an accident? He hated Alexander but wouldn't wish ill upon him. Nor had he ever wished to be the Duke of Devonshire.

"You brother is not a Cavendish," the Prince announced, as if he had made the determination himself.

William was stunned. What did that mean? Not a Cavendish?

"I can see I am the first to break this news to you," the Prince said somewhat apologetically, "but rest assured no harm has come to Alexander."

In a warped sense that didn't relieve him of any of his curiosity. His face must have conveyed a look of total confusion.

"First, drink up," the Prince instructed. "The details will be much more manageable after you've had the best sherry England has to offer."

William didn't hesitate and downed the dark, red liquid as if his life depended on it. Not in a Highlander barbarian sort of way, but as refined, confused earl—now duke? Fueled by hope, his heart picked up speed. *Is there nothing in the way of keeping me from marrying Lillias?* Perhaps this was what this meeting was about.

After the Prince elegantly finished draining his chalice, he set it down and in moments the footmen had refilled both of their glasses.

The Prince gave him a cunning grin before he held up his chalice a second time. "By my decree, you, Lord William Cavendish, are the newly appointed Duke of Devonshire. Let not God take away what the Prince wishes."

Stifling an immodest smile behind his glass, William nodded to the Regent, then took another long drink. Not gulping, but allowing a steady stream of the warm, tantalizing liquid to tickle down his throat as he weighed the possibilities of the Prince's words on his future. If it included Lillias, it would be worth any discomfort for carrying the title. He promised himself he'd have to have that resolution before he left the table.

Once William set down his glass, he tilted his head and peered at the Regent from an angle. He understood decorum. One never gazed directly at a royal. He would do anything to keep his host from deciding he was unworthy of Lillias's hand.

"Now that we've had a celebratory toast, let me give you a few particulars." The Prince waved his heavily jeweled hand in a limp, circular-like motion to the butler with a lazy air, signaling the time to serve the meal.

The staff quickly complied.

"As I was telling you," the Prince continued, spearing a piece of the sliced mutton with a sharp knife, "your brother has not met an untimely demise." After slicing through the meat as if it was butter, the Prince popped a portion in his mouth and began to chew.

"It may not be common knowledge that my brother and I were never close," William admitted, slicing his own piece of mutton, but wanting to wait on the Prince to finish chewing before he took his first bite.

The aristocrat laughed with his mouth full but covered it

with one of those royal napkins embroidered in deep amethyst and gold. After a quick swallow, he held up his third full glass of sherry and said, "Let's drink to that."

William followed suit and was not a bit ashamed of his candor when he set down his chalice and spoke freely. "In truth, I believe he wanted my father dead so he could assume the title as early as possible." He dabbed his mouth with the royal napkin, then offered, "I assume it was gambling debts."

The Prince laughed in a bawdy way this time and did not attempt to hide his sanguine expression. "Rest assured, I did not call you here to settle your brother's gambling debts, nor did he barter the title in a moment of misguided greed," he promised.

He would never accuse the Regent of toying with him, but royals were known to be cruel at times, despite their indifference.

"If not gambling, pray tell, I can't conjure one guess to save my life that would prompt my brother to give up something he's been set on since birth."

The Prince nodded slowly as if William had said something that rang true. "Have faith you won't need to forfeit your life if you can't fathom the possible answer."

A slow grin tugged at the corners of William's mouth. He leaned back to find the comfort of the gilded chair. "Where is he now?" If the Prince planned to make his fate a guessing game, he'd play along.

"Reacquainting himself," the Prince said.

"In new lodgings?"

"Exactly."

"Outside of Devonshire, I presume."

"You presume correctly."

Accepting the silence that followed, William ruminated on what the Prince had told him. If his brother was no longer residing at Chatsworth House, and this was not a cruel royal prank, he was surprised at how at ease he could be about his new circumstances.

"Did I say what province?" the Prince asked, cutting through William's contemplation.

Mindful of his manners, William finished chewing before he said, "Outside of Devonshire."

"Quite right, he's now in West Sussex, where his mother was born. She called him back to take on the title."

Fighting to keep from choking, William grabbed his sherry and quickly washed down the food. "His mother?" he asked, swallowing the rest. "As in not *our* mother?"

The Prince waved his hand over his plate and the butler snatched it up before the Regent's gaze met William's. "The paternity was confirmed by the archbishop. It's not unusual. Your older brother died in childbirth. Your father was so distraught, he took the son of his mistress and pronounced Alexander as his own and the heir to the dukedom."

And his mother had died giving birth to William, so there was no one to provide the truth if his father kept it from him. Why his father hid the truth was a question that would forever remain unanswered. But he had one the Prince could answer. "How did this come to light now?"

"Alexander's mother married beyond her station. To a marquess. He recently passed and she was not about to let the estate be given to her nephew, so she reclaimed her son."

"Here?"

"Here."

"Today?"

"Today," the Prince confirmed, then he steepled his hands. "He wasn't happy about it."

"I assume not."

"Swore vehemently before the Queen and myself that his mother's words were lies."

"That sounds like Alexander," William said.

"It did not bode well and the Queen had his belongings removed from Chatsworth House and they were sent by her staff to his new lodging at Angel House.

Blinking slowly, as if his mind had too much to process, William worked to take in all the Prince had just told him. He was now a duke?

"What happens next?" he blurted out as if his mind had finally reengaged, like a team of horses after a whip had been cracked.

"Before the official celebration?"

"With Lady Lillias St. Clair?"

The Prince frowned. "The reluctant duchess?"

"Reluctant bride perhaps, when she's promised to the wrong man." Although William was only a few minutes into his new title, he would not hesitate to claim what was most important to him. But that argument seemed to make little impact. No doubt the Prince didn't want to lose favor with another loyal duke.

"Now that you are a duke, aren't you being a bit hasty? The Season is hasn't yet reached a crescendo. There are many eligible debutantes, some with even stronger alliance possibilities."

William groaned inwardly. Aristocrats were never satisfied with general alliances. They required strong bonds forged over loyal allegiances.

"The girl is perfect for the Duke of Norfolk. He's been looking for years for a girl who doesn't want the spotlight, is quiet, reserved, and won't bring a scandal to his name."

"Well, I can't argue with you then," William promised, placating the Prince. He smiled to himself. *Now I know what must be done. I can only hope Lillias will forgive me.*

CHAPTER 36

*L*illias was frantic. The Royal Academy of Art's competition would conclude today. Her future hung in the balance. It had been a long morning at Norfolk House in London and the breakfast she'd attended with Lord Phillip's family was one more reason why she was certain she'd never survive a marriage to him.

If she once believed her Aunt Elizabeth to be the *ton's* leading parvenus, she was mistaken. For it was Lord Phillip's sister, Beatrice, who was no doubt London's reigning braggart.

After the dubious meal, she'd spent the better part of the last hour in the parlor staring at her fiancé as he inspected dead bugs pinned to a board, doing her best to hide her disgust.

But a few moments ago, a parcel had been delivered that appeared to be the size and shape of a painting. She now watched with detached curiosity while he unwrapped the package that had been delivered as an engagement gift.

"Is there a note?" Lillias asked, her interest piquing,

because no matter how frustrated she was, a piece of art was always inspiring for her.

He shook his head, and Lillias waited patiently for the reveal.

"Christ. Is this a cruel joke?" her fiancé ground out after taking the last of the packing material from the artwork, then looking up from the framed canvas to Lillias and then back to the gift.

A cold chill climbed up her spine, like a thief scaling a wall, determined and deadly. But unable to wait until more was said, she rushed to his side to see for herself.

When she glided to a stop beside the table where he had the canvas balanced, she covered her mouth in horror.

"Is this you?"

"This is an unusual gift," she said, avoiding his question. "From one of your gentlemen club friends?"

"Pardon me, Your Grace." Lord Phillip's head butler had entered the parlor. Clearing his throat, he went on, "Lord Compton, the Baron of Good Intentions, is in the foyer to see Lady Lillias. He was the one who delivered the engagement gift."

"Explain yourself," her fiancé demanded, his cheeks now colored with blotchy red patches. "I have no doubt this is a portrait of you."

Lillias had learned, when necessary, how to lie with her actions and not her words by keeping her features neutral when her emotions were raging inside. Now, she had to weigh whether an outrageous bout with the hiccups would be helpful if she denied the truth. Was this William's way of trying to rescue her? She needed answers too.

"Your Grace, you must recall my request to attend the R.A.'s event today," she said in a sanguine voice. "Lord Compton will be my escort."

"Clearly, your family did not school you in the proper etiquette for a lady of your standing. If this were to get out to my peers, I could lose my seat in the House of Lords," he charged, the wrinkled skin of his neck shaking with his words.

Turning to the butler she said, "Lester, please let Lord Compton know I will be but a moment and that I'm settling a few affairs before we depart." She now prayed for a miracle. If only she could leave this house free of her engagement and a scandal.

"I clearly made an error in judgment. You have an engagement at the Royal Academy? Well, go then. You no longer have an engagement here."

She responded to his harsh words with an exaggerated gasp, while she put all her effort into a jilted fiancée performance.

"At least there's no guessing where I stand now. You need no explanation from me," she said, yanking off her engagement ring and slamming it down on the table next to the nude portrait of herself, her heart singing with joy while she frowned at him. "And although this was a gift to both of us, I couldn't possibly let you keep it."

Turning to her with a loathsome expression, he countered, "Why would I keep such an abomination in my home that would remind me of a flirtation with dangerous consequences."

"Sir?" Lester's question of impropriety was all over his face.

Then her ex-fiancé did something that shocked even Lillias. He turned the painting to face his butler and declared, "As you can see, Lester, she'll be leaving with the Lord of Bad Judgment and taking this trash with her." His disgust was palpable, and he continued to eye her with suspicion as if she was a witch who'd put a hex on him. Finally, when it was getting uncomfortable, his gaze moved to Lester and he said with an acerbic tone, "Wrap this up and see that it goes with her."

With that announcement, she turned on her heel and sashayed out of the room. Worried if she didn't exit quickly enough, Lord Phillip might reconsider. But she wouldn't leave without the painting now that it was finally in her possession. At least the footsteps of Lester, and his booming affirmation to the duke, assured her the artwork was not far behind.

When she rounded the corner into the vestibule, however, she almost bowled over Nigel in her rush to get out of Norfolk House. After she caught herself on his arm, she managed to avoid a complete collision and exclaimed, "It's my lucky day!" Then untangling herself from his arm she added, "Lord Compton, my Baron of Good Fortune."

With a tentative half-grin, Nigel stepped back and swept into a proper bow. "Luck-y?" he said hesitantly. "That word has not been associated with me lately," he added in an almost apologetic way.

She batted at the air in front of her. "Your visit here is fortuitous at least. I need an escort to the R.A. for the competition announcements."

"Ah, here you are," Lester said, entering the vestibule with the wrapped parcel.

"Oh, my good man, I see you have the painting," Nigel said with a forced smile.

"Lord Compton," Lillias said as if scolding a child, "what is going on? Are you behind this delicious prank?"

"It's an engagement gift from Lord William Cavendish, of course," Nigel said with a bow.

William? And if there was one way to get her out of this

engagement, William knew it had to be scandalous. Would the news of her impropriety stop here at the duke's doorstep, or would it find its way to the gossip mongers and threaten all she'd done to gain the *ton's* acceptance? This potential victory could still lead to scandal and leave her life in ruins.

"Sir, please return this to the sender. There is no longer a need for engagement gifts," Lester said with a twinge of disgust in his tone as if his reputation would be soiled by holding it.

"No longer?" Nigel asked, turning to Lillias and gave a wink only visible to her.

By this time, two other footmen had arrived and after Lester gave instructions, it was a few short moments before she was tucked into Nigel's carriage seated across from him. She began to laugh.

It started as a low rumble in her ribcage, then tickled its way up her spine and finally rose in the back of her throat into a grand chortle. Leaning back into the comfortable seat cushion she said to Nigel, "That was a heist." She smiled. "A duchess heist."

Nigel appeared nervous, but she'd never been alone with him before. Most likely he was apprehensive about the scheme William had concocted and her being unchaperoned.

"It's not often a duchess needs rescuing," he said with a nervous laugh. "But your rescue comes with consequences," Nigel said tonelessly, then he turned his head toward the window as if that's all he would say on the matter.

They fell into silence. Lillias's giddy relief was replaced by a host of wretched possibilities. Would William refuse to take her as a wife now that she was free, but ruined in the eyes of the Duke of Norfolk? Or was her contest entry at the R.A. disqualified because she might no longer be in favor with the Queen? Freedom rarely came without consequences.

The carriage rambled down the familiar streets of London while Lillias stared out her window, uncertain what to say to Nigel. Passing the bronze statue of Charles I at Charring Cross, she calculated it wouldn't be long before the carriage would turn on to the Strand and they'd be moments from Somerset House.

An unexpected sharp turn, however, had Lillias grabbing the safety handle to keep from tumbling over, but Nigel appeared unfazed by the change of direction and continued to ignore her.

Adjusting herself on the seat, Lillias took an anxious glance out the window again. It appeared they'd turned down an alley and the carriage was now making its way now toward the Thames.

About to object to the change of course, she leaned forward to open her mouth to speak, but Nigel held up his hand to protest any comments. After a few awkward moments of them staring at each other, he rapped the top of the carriage with his walking stick.

Lillias finally broke the uncomfortable silence. "I deserve to know where you are taking us," she demanded, thinking the worst. Was he to punish her by leaving her stranded by the docks of the Thames to teach her a lesson? Or had it been Nigel alone who had concocted this scheme? It was no secret he had a penchant for profiteering.

"We are here," Nigel said, as the carriage settled. When the driver opened the door, she tossed Nigel a suspicious look and climbed out.

"I thought I made myself clear," she said with a huff, turning to face him while the driver lifted the wrapped painting from the carriage. "You are to escort me the R.A. for the competition's announcements," she said, doing her best to hide her rising panic.

Ignoring her statement, Nigel pointed to series of fires

burning along the edge of a dock. "You and I are to follow William's instructions implicitly," he told her, offering his free arm.

There was nothing she could do but acquiesce. Now she had an inkling of what was to come.

CHAPTER 37

$\mathcal{W}$illiam imagined it all happening very differently. Standing in the grand gallery of the R.A., he tapped his foot to distract himself from what would happen next.

A lover of architecture and fine art, a champion of the chalk silhouette, and finally an entrant in the R.A.'s international competition and he'd thrown it all away.

Yes, damn it, he'd thrown his goal of winning away for something larger. But now he was doubting himself. Did he do the right thing by sending the nude to the Duke of Norfolk? He believed he acted to save Lillias. Or was he only saving her for himself?

Three weeks ago he was told by the Prince Regent he wasn't good enough to be married to her. Since that raw and uncomfortable realization, he'd been embraced by the very royal who'd disrespected him, anointing him of all things, a dukedom.

Yet, the Prince wouldn't renege on his plan to have Lillias wed the Duke of Norfolk, assuring him a strong alliance would be made by uniting the two. Then the Regent had ensured William he would have an equally powerful match, promising he'd have his pick of any eligible debutante.

Bloody titles and protocol. William had watched his father and Alexander both fall prey to the demon of society's opinion and royal decree. Even Lillias was a victim.

No, he would rise above this. Instead of growing up as the legal heir to a dukedom and the associated expectations, he had learned to put compassion for the underprivileged ahead of personal gain.

He'd also found a friend in Lillias. Although she'd told him repeatedly she'd never wanted to be a cog in the mechanism that was social acceptance, she was shoved into that position because of her kind heart and sense of responsibility.

Shifting his weight back and forth between his feet, he stared at the portrait of the boxer with the birthmark, in awe and frustrated. Her love, it appeared, was the only accolade that could satisfy his future and it kept his anger at bay. If revealing the nude painting to the duke had backfired, and he was the agent of her ruination, he'd never be able to forgive himself.

"Where's your work?"

Spinning on his heel, William turned abruptly, almost knocking down the inquisitor. "Oh, Professor, y—you caught me," he stammered.

"Caught you admiring this work?"

He nodded.

"Are you avoiding my question?"

"I am admiring this work," William said, a bit confused.

"My first question," Beauchamp said, quirking a brow.

"Oh, *my* work?" William hadn't meant to be sidestepping his instructor.

The professor raised his other brow and now they were both arched high above his spectacles. He even pulled his glasses down on his nose and peered over them when William hesitated.

"Where's your work?" This time the question came from behind him, but William recognized the voice.

"Don't feign surprise," Lillias challenged, giving him a grand smile when their eyes met.

She stood next to Nigel, the light from the ringed windows above framed her face, making her appear to be a living portrait. How he longed to take her in his arms and away from here.

Beauchamp loudly cleared his throat, bringing William's attention back to the professor, who continued to stare at him over his spectacles.

Nigel raised a brow.

"It's complicated," was all William could say.

"Now there's an empty place on the wall," Nigel said, pointing to the obvious.

"I removed it."

Directing his comments to Lillias, as if no one else was in the room he said, "I had loftier plans."

Lillias laughed and the professor pushed his glasses back up his nose with a disgruntled snort. No one called him a coward, but that wasn't why he withdrew. At the root of his action was his wanting Lillias to win.

Turning toward the portrait of the boxer, he said to Lillias with a wink, "I've been curious about this one."

Beauchamp snorted again. "Of course you can see the paintings are numbered. The works are only signed on the back to keep favoritism out of judging," he reminded them in his professorial tone. "I do suspect this one will do—"

A loud tapping sound forced the professor to stop talking and they all turned toward the podium.

"Ladies and gentlemen," the crier began, "welcome to the Royal Academy of Art International Competition. You'll see before you"—the man gestured broadly with both arms—"the result of weeks of preparation by students and staff."

The attentive audience—all in their finery—began to twist and turn, looking about the gallery and murmuring words of approval.

"One of the works before you will be crowned the winner. A prestigious prize granted to a very few." He put a hand over his heart as if taking a pledge. "As one of the judges and a former winner, I can attest this privilege is life changing." And after a beat he said, "Art can alter *your* life."

William would agree with that for it already had. If not for art, there would be no Lillias in his life, or the old mansion in Tower Hill.

Also, now that he'd been officially dubbed the Duke of Devonshire, he'd have access to the family's fortune. The prize money wouldn't be needed. His brother had received his due.

Lillias wouldn't need the money either, but the win would bring her great acclaim. The Queen had said she wanted to champion a woman. Lillias had the talent to win this. The prize was Lillias, and now she was here by his side, nothing else mattered.

The crowd was pushing forward toward the podium in anticipation of the announcement and both Lillias and William moved with them.

"And with no further ado," the crier said in a booming voice. "I invite our head judge to join me at the podium to make the announcement."

The room was silent, waiting for the head judge to make his way to the podium. In a group this large, one might hear a mumble, or hushed whisper. But it was so quiet now William could hear his own breathing.

Finally, an elegantly dressed gentleman joined the crier at the podium. It was apparent he enjoyed his grandstanding moment, for he stood erect behind the barrier as if he were sovereign to his loyal followers. The art world did pay homage to its luminaries.

The judge raised his hand and swept it in a wide swath as he began. "The Royal Academy of Art's International Competition has come to a close. The esteemed judges have chosen the winner of the five-thousand-pound prize in this prestigious competition." Then he paused dramatically and you could almost hear a collective intake of air from all in the room as everyone waited. "And the winner is . . . number thirteen."

"Number thirteen," William shouted. He swung around to congratulate Lillias, but she was looking at Nigel, who had rushed forward to the portrait of the boxer.

"I don't understand," he said, cocking his head to the side in confusion. "Isn't that your entry?"

When Lillias denied it with a shake of her head, it didn't seem to matter because her smile lit up the room. In that moment, he decided winning the contest wasn't important to either of them any longer. Whoever had painted number thirteen was worthy of the award.

As the throngs of art lovers moved around them, most pushing toward the winning portrait, Lillias trained her gaze on William and said, "I won the contest, because I've won you back, Lord William."

Getting down on one knee, as he had in the garden weeks ago, William dug for the *Claddagh* ring he'd carried in his pocket since she'd given it back, hoping she'd accept it once more. If not as a promise for marriage, at least a promise for friendship.

"Lillias, Duchess of Canterbury, will you take me, Lord William Cavendish, the Duke of Devonshire, for a husband?"

"Duke of Devonshire?" Lillias asked, shaking her head in confusion first, but then nodding her acceptance.

William slipped the ring on her finger. "I love you, my double duchess."

* * *

LILLIAS'S HEAD WAS SPINNING. William a duke? What did he call her? A double duchess? Laughing, she understood William's meaning. Could she be both the Duchess of Canterbury and the Duchess of Devonshire?

How had she found two times what she wanted to avoid? But somehow, with William at her side, it all seemed possible. How he'd become the Duke of Devonshire was a story she'd need to be told, and no doubt, the royals would have to put up with the union made in such a public way.

The crowd was filing back into the gallery again. For Lillias, the award was anticlimactic to what just transpired.

"That was some engagement gift you sent," Lillias whispered to William as they joined the crowd in the main gallery again. "It ruined me for the Duke of Norfolk." Then she sobered. Her gaze swung over to where his portrait would have hung. "Where *is* your work?"

"That's what I've been asking all along."

Lillias turned to find Professor Beauchamp behind them.

"Call me a coward," William offered as an excuse to the professor.

Lillias couldn't let his explanation go unchallenged and added, "It took courage to withdraw."

William countered with, "'Conscience doth make cowards of us all.'"

"Will, you do know Shakespeare," she said with a disarming smile.

CHAPTER 38

*I*f Lillias believed the last two months had been a whirlwind, it was nothing compared to the last two days. Learning William's brother was a bastard, appeared to be a just end to his reign. The Regent's confirmation of William as Duke of Devonshire would change the Cavendish legacy for the good.

Now Lillias could envision a future beyond what she could have dreamed for herself.

When she was little, she'd imagined herself as a grownup dressed in fine gowns like her mother, with proper manners like her aunts, and talent like the great artists. But she never fancied herself with a husband, a partner, a better half. Least of all, becoming a duchess!

She had sisters, of course, but other than her father, boys had seemed foreign to her. Perhaps it was because little boys were best avoided.

Now that she lay in the arms of a grown-up boy, Lillias marveled at how wrong she'd been.

"Tell me you love me again," she begged. "I will never tire of it."

Sweeping her stray hair from her ear, and it was all stray hair with pins missing, and most of it down her shoulders, William nibbled on her neck first before obeying her command.

"As you wish."

Another peck down to her breastbone.

"Lillias." Kiss. "I." Kiss. "Love." Kiss. "You." Then he flicked his tongue between her breasts and chuckled. "That's for the exclamation mark."

She laughed along with him.

"I thank the Lord you love me," she murmured, tipping his chin up so she could gaze into his eyes, "because now you have officially ruined me."

It was rare for William to blush, but she caught him this time as he collapsed next to her. And like a welcome breeze, he blew a little kiss into her ear.

"I'll remember that when we're old and gray. That the only reason you agreed to marry me was to keep your name from slander."

Sitting up, she cupped her hand around her lips, then cried, "Hear ye, hear ye, read all about it. Duchess does duke, digging for largest dowry in London history."

William sat up and bit her ear before he roared with laughter.

"And we'll move to the country where no one can meddle with the life we want to lead. Being a double duchess requires double the social schedule. I'm certain we can convince the Queen to transfer the Canterbury Duchess title to Verity. That will also take the pressure off finding her a suitable husband this Season and I won't have failed my mother."

"You are worthy of both titles. You are now the Queen's confidante. And your mother would be proud of all you've accomplished."

That was true. Although she hadn't won the R.A. competition, Lillias had earned the Queen's award, and a commission to paint Her Royal Highness's portrait. And she had kept an even bigger promise to her mother, to follow her art and find the love of her life.

"The Queen is much like my Aunt Elizabeth, opinionated, impatient, obsessed with peerage, full of gossip and—"

"Enamored with your talent," William finished.

Laughing, she nipped his lip. "I was going to say a champion of the arts."

William dropped down on an elbow and began stroking her belly, making a circular pattern to the center, bringing heat to all the right places. She sighed with pleasure and stretched out next to him.

"Who knows, you might have beaten me and Nigel in the competition if you'd entered the nude instead of sending it to the Duke of Norfolk as an engagement gift," she proposed, giving him a little nudge in the shoulder. "You've yet to tell me how you *retrieved* it."

Laughing at the memory of how he'd first suggested they work together, he replied, "The painting was my property. I had no qualms about having Nigel reclaim it for me."

"Do you mean steal?"

He ignored her question. "You make it sound as if I am supporting criminal activity. My goal is to save disadvantaged boys from a life of lawlessness with the Tower Hill school, now that the building is officially mine."

She gave him a subtle smile, pleased she was able to support William and his mission in the school for boys by letting her family's lease expire on the property. "I promise not to question your integrity." Then she gave him a ravenous kiss.

Once she released his lips with a sigh, William made another confession. "I thought the portrait of the boxer was yours, but it was Nigel's. I guess if someone had to beat you, it shouldn't have been me."

"It was easy to overlook the portrait of my Aunt Elizabeth, I reimaged her as a young girl and no one but the dowager would have recognized her."

He gave Lillias another smoky look, like he didn't want to talk, but she pulled back when he reached for her. "You can kiss me again after I know the whole story. Why was the painting stolen in the first place? Have you figured that out?"

Mocking a disgruntled expression first, he took in a deep breath as if the full explanation would cause for some angst.

"Blackmail is a terrible price to pay so my brother Alexander could make money to support his gambling," William explained. "The horror of it, my own brother forcing Nigel to blackmail you because he owed Alexander money. Then both of them worked together threatening to take the nude public after Nigel had been forced to steal it from the R.A."

"Nigel?"

"Yes, Alexander coerced him into it. I'm sure at the time my brother made it seem trivial. Alexander is a talented manipulator and gave Nigel a key to the back door of the R.A. That's how he was able to steal it without the guards questioning him. He claimed it as his own. Then Alexander wrote the ransom notes and Nigel hired a boy, a runner, to deliver them to you. I tracked down the runner and had the messages delivered to me as we agreed. But when Nigel found out we left fake jewels as a decoy, he fell short of delivering the goods to Alexander."

"Your friend impressed me from the beginning as a compromising character. But then he charmed me."

"Right, that's Nigel's way. But I didn't know who was blackmailing you then," William admitted. Then he stared off over her shoulder as if contemplating how much she needed to know.

Lillias raised a skeptical brow. She had expected his explanation of the nude's disappearance to be revealing, but this sounded like a mystery novel, and she needed to know how the painting was finally found. She pulled his chin and brought his gaze to meet hers.

He leaned in, moistening his lips, threatening to kiss her.

"Not yet," she said, laughing and when she pushed his chin to the side, William grunted like he'd taken a hit to his jaw. Then she held up a threatening fist. "You know I have a mighty right hook. Tell me, how did the painting return to you?"

Leaning away and giving her a cowering look, he conceded. "Eventually, Nigel *retrieved* the painting for me and offered his apology and the explanation. He even agreed to follow through with my plan to deliver the painting to your fiancé."

When she took in a deep breath, ready to ask another question, he cut her off.

"It had to be done."

Their eyes met, William's full of tenderness.

"I can't believe she's gone. It's like losing an old friend," she said, her heart still aching over the destruction of a perfect piece of art.

"It was difficult to let her go," he agreed, his voice cracking, "but you— I could never let go." His expression told her he understood. Then he kissed her with such tenderness, the sheer fervor of his embrace made her want to forget the loss and the rest of his explanation, but he released her with three quick pecks to her lips as if a promise to return.

Gazing at her lovingly, he spoke in a voice full of emotion, "I decided to take a risk before it was destroyed. You've taught me how to take chances again and fight for what I want, instead of doubting myself." He blinked slowly, as if that had been a raw and difficult confession. Then he flashed her a confident smile before he added, "That's why I asked Nigel to deliver the nude to Norfolk Manor and I prayed it would set you free."

Lillias was filled with admiration and nodded. "We have Nigel to thank, in a crazy roundabout way," she agreed. But that was how the entire courtship had gone, like two contenders circling in a boxing ring, ducking and defending before striking out for what they wanted. "And he deserves the win."

"I suppose neither of us thought Nigel was serious about his art. He was always making Shakespearian jokes and leaving class early. I believe he wanted to test his talents at the R.A. exhibition. At first I thought it was all about winning the money, at least his portrait of the boxer and the grand prize win will go a long way toward settling his debts.

"Plus, he made amends with me before he knew Alexander had been banished. If he hadn't stolen the painting in the first place, I wouldn't have you."

"You *stole* my heart, so apparently thievery can have a positive outcome," she confessed, giving him a peck on the lips, wanting to get back to kissing. She swore she'd never get enough of him. But he was grinning at her and appeared he still had more to say.

"He told me he was going to propose to Lady Agnus."

"The wealthy widow of St. James Place?"

William laughed. "Is that what you call her?"

"Verity and I idolize her. And now that Verity is no longer interested in the Baron of Good Humor, my sister won't be upset about their engagement. We've envied Lady Agnus for her independence and doing what she wants with her money, like my Aunt Elizabeth. Lady Agnus added to the funds we bet on Lord Compton at Crawly Down."

"You bet on Nigel?"

"I didn't know it was Nigel. In the end, I bet on you."

"And you *won* my heart."

She reached for his shoulder and made a circle around it much like he'd done on her belly, with feathering strokes.

"Don't do that, woman, or I'll have to ruin you one more time today."

"No, we can't possibly. I need to return home. It's been two days since I left Norfolk manor and I must check in on my sisters."

"'The lady doth protest too much, me thinks.'"

"'Have you not heard it said full oft, a woman's *nay* doth stand for naught,' Will?"

He pulled her to him. "Shakespeare did have it right when he said, 'Love's not time's fool.' It did take us time to love, but now that we have found each other, I'm certain our love will last for all time."

Then he kissed her with a passion that made her believe it would.

BOOKS BY MARISA DILLON

Also from **Crown & Caste Publishing** and **Marisa Dillon**:
THE LADY OF THE GARTER (The Ladies of Lore Book 1)

When Henry VII takes the throne, not all are loyal to the new king. Garter knight, Sir James, is charged with bringing dissenters to justice. Determined to fulfill his vows, he's unprepared for Lady Elena, a girl from his past.

Lady Elena defies her family and disguises herself as a squire to reunite with the man she's always loved. Determined to thwart the norms of the day, she risks all to learn the secrets of the Garter knights. Although she wields a sword like a man, she must fight with her feminine heart.

Thrust into a world of danger and family rivalry, James and Elena must each choose between personal sacrifice and great consequence as they navigate a second chance at love.

Will Elena find the courage to fight to save James from a dark knight set out for revenge, but loose her chance at knighthood?

Can James avenge his father's death and find passion, or

will his Garter oaths hold him to a life of service without love?

The Lady waits to tell her tale.

Available on Amazon: **THE LADY OF THE GARTER (The Ladies of Lore Book 1)**

THE GOLDEN ROSE OF SCOTLAND (The Ladies of Lore Book 2)

When poisonings are an everyday occurrence, healer Rosalyn Macpherson must be ready with an antidote. Unless it's for the English Lord who means to claim her clan's Highland castle.

What's in a name? Everything, for Lord Lachlan de Leverton, a charismatic English aristocrat. He'll break the law to sever his ties to his notorious family. But first, he must secure the deed to Fyvie Castle before the feisty Scottish lass wins it.

Because of their conflicting claims, Rosalyn and Lachlan are ordered to appear in Edinburgh's royal court, and in an unusual twist of fate, they are assigned as guardians, rather than prisoners, to a caravan carrying the Golden Rose, a papal gift for the King of Scots.

When the royal decree becomes a forced marriage between the two, it's not the remedy Rosalyn had hoped for, but now she doesn't hate this Englishman as much.

Before the knot is tied, the Rose is stolen and Lachlan's suspected of the crime. Rosalyn then faces the hardest decision yet. Must she sacrifice her precious Philosophers Stone or the land she loves, or both, to save him?

Available on Amazon: **THE GOLDEN ROSE OF SCOTLAND**

THE SECRET OF SKYE ISLE (The Ladies of Lore Book 3)

A lifesaving antidote grows as a rare rose on an isle full of faerie lore. Healer Ursula Fraser won't risk delivering her best friend's twins without it, but first she'll need a guide and a miracle.

Both come in the form of battle-scarred laird Alasdair MacLeod, a Highlander who seeks to avenge his father's death and claim the title, Lord of the Isles. He requires an heir, not a wife. But when he offers her his guidance, he also offers her his bed and a bargain.

Insulted, but fearless, Ursula expects she'll convince the laird to do her bidding without sacrificing her morals. Her ability to conjure herbal potions gives her great power until she discovers the Scottish laird is the only one who can save her from the murderous MacDonalds.

Will this Highlander who harbors a family secret keep her from returning to Fyvie Castle in time for the twins' delivery? Or will a faerie prophecy filled with magic and a roll of the dice settle all the scores?

The answers lie in *The Secret of Skye Isle*.

Available on Amazon: **THE SECRET OF SKYE ISLE**

CONNECT WITH THE AUTHOR

With a bachelor's degree in journalism, Marisa has spent many years writing for the television industry. As an award-winning producer/director/marketer, she has worked on commercial production, show creation, product branding and social media.

Marisa has always enjoyed reading romance novels and now fulfills a dream by writing romantic adventures not for the faint of heart. *The Duchess Heist* is her first book in the Art of Love series.

Visit Marisa at: www.marisadillon.com.

Goodreads:https://www.goodreads.com/author/show/10792736.Marisa_Dillon

BookBub:https://www.bookbub.com/profile/marisa-dillon